REPUTATION FOR A SONG

Edward Grierson was born in Bedford in 1914. He was educated at St Paul's and Exeter College, Oxford, where he read Law and was subsequently called to the Bar. He practised until the start of the Second World War when in 1939 he joined the Sapper Territorials. After his demobilization in 1946, he held the post of Senior Legal Adviser (Welfare) in the joint Army-R.A.F. organization in Cairo that had grown up to help troops overseas. From the end of the war until his death in 1975 he devoted himself to lecturing and writing and spent a year in Sydney where he was an announcer with the Australian Broadcasting Commission. *Reputation for a Song*, his first novel, was published in 1952. It was followed by *Far Morning* and *The Lilies and the Bees*.

EDWARD GRIERSON

REPUTATION FOR
A SONG

PENGUIN BOOKS
IN ASSOCIATION WITH
CHATTO & WINDUS

Penguin Books Ltd, Harmondsworth, Middlesex, England
Viking Penguin Inc., 40 West 23rd Street, New York, New York 10010, U.S.A.
Penguin Books Australia Ltd, Ringwood, Victoria, Australia
Penguin Books Canada Limited, 2801 John Street, Markham, Ontario, Canada L3R 1B4
Penguin Books (N.Z.) Ltd, 182–190 Wairau Road, Auckland 10, New Zealand

First published by Chatto and Windus 1952
Published in Penguin Books 1955
Reissued 1986

Printed and bound in Great Britain by
Cox & Wyman Ltd, Reading
Set in Times

QUATRAIN LXIX

Indeed the Idols I have loved so long
Have done my Credit in Men's eye much wrong!
Have drown'd my Honour in a shallow Cup,
And sold my Reputation for a Song.

The Rubaiyat of Omar Khayyam
IN THE TRANSLATION OF
EDWARD FITZGERALD

I

R upert Laurence Anderson, is that your name?'

The clerk of assize looked up over the rim of his spectacles at the prisoner in the dock, cleared his throat, then turned to the indictment and began to read. It was his moment in the trial, a small moment, perhaps, but he relished it, and from long practice performed it well: even the poor acoustics of the courtroom could not defeat him, so that the solemn words rang out, measured, clear, into the recesses behind the well and in the public gallery.

'Rupert Laurence Anderson, you are charged on this indictment with murder.

'The particulars of the offence alleged against you are that you, Rupert Laurence Anderson, on the fifth day of October, 1949, in the county of York, murdered Robert Hemsley Anderson.'

The clerk of assize paused, lowered the indictment, then, with the mannerism so familiar to all the barristers and officials of the circuit, took off his reading glasses and folded back their heavy flanges of tortoise-shell. He was a priest performing at a ritual, and now addressed the sacrifice.

'How say you, Rupert Laurence Anderson, are you Guilty or Not Guilty?'

The attention of everyone in court turned towards the dock. A very slight young man stood there, a youth of eighteen who looked less, untidily dressed, with a shock of hair brushed up into a form of pompadour, an oval face, lean and bloodless, with a snub nose, and ears so small and delicate as to be the envy of every woman in the court. It was an arresting face, provocative and just a little sinister.

Yet the voice in which the charge was answered was agreeably masculine and firm.

'Not Guilty, my lord.'

He had spoken, and immediately the tension in the court was eased. The clerk of assize turned from the prisoner to face the jury, ready with the grave, archaic words:

'Members of the jury, the prisoner, Rupert Laurence Anderson, stands charged under this indictment for murder. Upon the indictment he hath been arraigned, and on his arraignment hath pleaded Not Guilty and hath put himself upon his country – which country ye are. Your charge, therefore, is to say whether he be Guilty or Not Guilty and to hearken to the evidence.'

The clerk sat down at his table, low down in the well of the court, and the excited shuffling and murmuring of the crowd rose around him, reflected even at the table where counsel sat surrounded by piles of briefs and photographs. Even the judge relaxed. There had been the moment of his entry when he had seemed more than mortal, the holder of the powers of life and death, but now a myriad of small touches had dethroned him as he sat, handkerchief in hand, fingering his wig and robes and arranging his own papers on his desk, so that he seemed no more omnipotent than any chairman of a board.

And then as it was seen that one man was on his feet the tension closed in again and silence fell, so deep that the scratching of the judge's pen could be distinctly heard and the crackling of the folio sheets that prosecuting counsel was holding in his hand. The clerk of assize had looked and spoken like an actor, a man of such imposing presence that the uninitiated had believed him to be a person of the greatest legal substance – Sir Evelyn Parks appearing for the Crown, at least, but the real Sir Evelyn, who stood now looking at the judge and waiting for the signal to begin, was at first sight a very unimpressive little man. He wore an old gown, torn and frayed so that it flapped when he moved his arms like a scarecrow's coat flying in the boisterous March wind, his wig was antique and dark and he wore it raffishly pulled down over his left eye; even his voice contrasted unfavourably with the classic tones in which the indictment had been read; it was high-pitched and pedantic, more like an old schoolmaster's than an advocate's, and emerged in jerky syllables that were sometimes lost in the dim recesses of the court. It seemed a disappointing voice, badly matched to the dramatic setting of the trial, and yet as time went on it gained in dignity, so that his hearers, surrendering, saw events in his terms and with his eyes, saw the crime itself raised to greater heights by

8

this contrast between tragic actuality and the dry, unemotional accents of the schoolroom.

All attention was now centred on this figure standing at the table, brief in hand. But it was the judge who spoke. 'Let the prisoner take a chair,' he said.

Sir Evelyn resumed his seat, not well pleased at the interruption, which he should certainly have foreseen. If the truth were known, he was as sensitive to atmosphere as the clerk of assize himself and only appeared to disdain the theatrical byplay inseparable from a murder trial. But when the arrangements were complete and the prisoner and warders seated the effect was to concentrate all attention on the advocate, for the accused could now scarcely be seen by anyone in court; his small face peered over the high facing of the dock like a schoolboy's over the railings of a football ground.

'Yes, Sir Evelyn,' said the judge.

Counsel rose to his feet again, hunched his back against the public eye now fixed unwaveringly on him, and turned towards the jury. There they were, nine men and three women on whom so much incomprehensible legal doctrine, so much eloquence, would be lavished, arbiters of fate, yet herded together like cattle at a fair. Small wonder that they turned quite gloomy eyes on Sir Evelyn and looked prepared to disbelieve everything he had to say. Yet he, for his part, seemed pleased with them and gave them what he believed to be a reassuring smile. They were sullen in appearance, but he knew that they were merely uncomfortable and afraid. Somehow it was never given them to realize how great an honour was being done to them in making them the judges of the guilt or innocence of a man, how greatly the public envied them their seats, that public that filled the small courtroom to capacity and overflowed in frenzied queues into the streets. They were exasperating in their resentful silence, he thought, but it was on them that success or failure would depend, and though justice was the first consideration in his mind, the success of Sir Evelyn Parks was certainly the second. So he smiled at them again, a friendly smile of encouragement to fellow-toilers, and opening his brief, began.

'May it please your lordship, members of the jury, in this case I appear on behalf of the Crown with my learned friends,

Mr Jakeman and Mr Craig, while my learned friends, Sir David Fynes, Mr Massingham, and Mr Grey, appear on behalf of the accused.'

He accompanied these words with a half bow in the direction of his colleagues, commending them to the affections of the court. Then he turned back towards the jurymen.

'It is a painful duty that brings us together. To all of you it has brought inconvenience and discomfort, to some, actual loss. But you are here in the name of justice: you have the rights of British citizens and you have the obligations that go to match, the corollaries of the right to fair trial possessed by the accused. Your presence ensures his right. You will not forget the oath you have taken as jurymen and you will listen to this case, I do not doubt, with a full knowledge of your responsibilities and powers. The life and liberty of this man are in your hands, but so is the welfare of the State. If, after hearing the evidence, you feel that the prosecution has not proved its case it will be your duty, as it will certainly be your pleasure, to acquit the prisoner, but if you come to a contrary conclusion you will not – indeed my lord will tell you that you must not – be guided by mere sentiment to neglect your duty. You must act on the evidence and according to the law – the law of England, not the so-called "Unwritten Law" which, in the words of a great jurist, is only another name for no law at all, for anarchy. Crime must be punished. I am here to see to that; my lord is; you are. But let it be understood from the outset that it is for me to prove the guilt of the accused. If there is any doubt, any reasonable doubt, you will acquit him. But it is the prosecution's case that there is no doubt, not the shadow of a doubt, that the crime as charged was done, and by this boy. He is eighteen years of age. That is very young, and for his youth there must be feelings of compassion.' He paused. 'What feelings are there for his crime?'

Sir Evelyn turned slowly round – and the jury's eyes followed – towards the white face, so absurdly small and out of place in the shadows of the dock.

'Members of the jury, the prosecution's case is that he committed murder; he killed a man. This man was unarmed, and the medical evidence I shall call will show that this unarmed

10

man, past middle age, was struck with a heavy poker, five savage blows on the head so that he died.'

Sir Evelyn dropped his voice, leaned forward on the table and gazed sombrely at the jury.

'That man was his father,' he said.

A hush even deeper than before had settled on the court, broken only by the sobbing of a woman in the public gallery. But in so far as his reactions could be seen, the prisoner seemed quite unmoved by Sir Evelyn's words; for he was looking around him in an interested manner, recognizing relatives and friends as though he were in a box at the theatre.

'Such cases as we have to-day,' continued Sir Evelyn, when the emotional lady had been conducted out, 'are fortunately rare. Of course there is no particular legal distinction in this crime of parricide – it is murder, neither more nor less. It is no part of my duty to dwell on the horror that such a deed creates in normal minds, except in so far as the facts of the case before us must be stated in their simplicity. The prosecution's case is concerned not with who was killed but with the fact that the accused did kill, and the personality of this boy's father, of Robert Hemsley Anderson, though related to the course of our inquiry, is not, at all events as yet, in issue. At this stage I should say no more, except that I may tell you, from the words of a statement made by the accused, that the character of the dead man may be called in question, in which case . . .'

'My lord.'

Counsel broke off resignedly as he heard the deep voice of his rival at his side, and the courtroom hummed with excitement at this first intervention of leading counsel for the defence.

'Yes, Sir David?' said the judge.

'My lord, I submit with the greatest respect to my learned friend, that he should confine himself to his own case and leave me mine.'

Neither in voice nor manner had Sir David shown much noticeable respect towards his learned friend, and the jury, always ready to enjoy a fight, sat up and looked expectantly towards the judge.

'You object to the opening, Sir David?'

'My lord, I do. My learned opponent has already explained,

and most eloquently, how improper it would be to comment at this stage on the virtues or otherwise of the deceased, and having made a precept for himself, he breaks it in the self-same breath. No allegations have yet been made by the defence, and such an opening can have no other object than to prejudice the accused.'

Prosecuting counsel had remained standing throughout these words, and as soon as Sir David had resumed his seat he began in the mildest way to justify himself.

'Prejudice is not for the prosecution,' he said, with a glance at the jury which suggested that it might well be necessary for the defence. 'We may confidently, very confidently, leave the case for the accused in the hands of his most experienced advocate. But the statement made by the prisoner is part of the prosecution's case. I am entitled to open it, and I shall dwell on the features of that statement at some length. That statement contains allegations against the character of Robert Anderson, and in my submission it is relevant, even at this stage, that I should mention them.'

But the judge was shaking his head slowly and reproachfully over this excuse. He looked benevolent but pained.

'I think, Sir Evelyn,' he said, 'that you had best reserve your comments for their proper place.'

'My lord, I was merely proposing to mention them in passing.'

'In their proper place, Sir Evelyn, if you please.'

'As your lordship pleases,' said counsel, bowing his head submissively. It did not do to risk a quarrel over so small a point, but he resented this interference with what he conceived to be a work of art. It was with a trace of the expression of a martyr that he turned back towards the jury to continue his address.

'My lord rightly reminds me of the necessity for relevance and restraint. To quote again, this time from one of the old, respected leaders of the Bar: "The uplifted finger is not for the prosecution." Let me turn to the facts. We are concerned to-day with murder. It is an ugly word. What passions, hates, desires, must be involved in the taking of a life! Is it on account of some dramatic sense that we see this court filled with spectators, people outside clamouring for seats just as though this were a theatre, this trial a play? What words do they expect to hear?

What tragic actions told? And yet, in the case it is now my duty to present there may be – I confess I hope so – much food for disappointing them. For it is of small things that I shall tell, small hatreds, small jealousies, small desires. Small motives, gentlemen, and the sum of them was the killing of a man.'

2

MR AND MRS ANDERSON and their three children lived at 'The Templars', Colbert Row, Turlminster, a Queen Anne house in a quiet street in one of those cathedral cities that have sunk so far from the limelight of the world as to seem as dead as Thebes. Turlminster was a town by-passed in thought by the bustling modern world as it was to be by-passed in fact by the road the County Council was driving through the meadows beside the River Ling, a road of relief to exasperated motorists forced to spoil their averages in crooked streets like Colbert Row. Not a house in it outwardly protested against a dead tradition, least of all 'The Templars', which was so buxomly proportioned with bay windows, so handsomely appointed with brick and paint and plaster, as to resemble nothing so much as a comfortable woman of a certain age and very much more certain fortune. Yet, though the house was built in the architecture of common sense, it could not escape altogether from the atmosphere of make-believe that surrounds survivals from other days: sheltered under the wing of the cathedral belfry, only a stone's throw from the Deanery, it had been so often photographed, so often reproduced, snow-laden, on shilling Christmas cards, that the first thing a man would have expected on entering was the sight of the company in crinolines and periwigs dancing a gavotte; the last, the Andersons at bridge with their wealthy brewer cousins, Mr and Mrs Barry Clarke.

In fact, this combination was unusual, the hidden clash of personalities more pronounced than is normal even around bridge tables, where more than one homicide has probably been hatched, for though Mr Clarke was friends with all the world – he could afford to be – the ladies did not like each other, while Mr Anderson, the most amiable of men, had been compared so often with Barry, and always to his disadvantage, that the very sight of that handsome florid face, the rather prominent blue eyes, the waxy Edwardian look, gave him a definite sense of nausea.

As for Barry's bridge, he found it difficult to endure. Mr Clarke had been lucky in love – and everyone had his word for that; he was lucky at cards as well and could cheat in the friendliest way imaginable. That was the worst of family bridge, reflected Mr Anderson, with all the antipathy of the serious-minded for the Barrys of this world, those men whose native shrewdness, under the bluff and jollity, they are all too liable to miss.

'What am I playing now?' he said.

He had forgotten, for between his final bid and the beginning of the play a monologue of Barry's had been interposed, possibly with the object of amusing Laura Anderson – and possibly not.

'Hearts, old boy. Four hearts.'

'Four hearts, eh,' said Mr Anderson, trying to concentrate and get Barry's remarks out of his head. But he could not; his guest's jokes and anecdotes had that quality peculiar to the products of soiled minds – they stuck. 'Four hearts. Then it's your lead, Rose.'

Mrs Clarke obliged. Having lived in Barry's company more constantly than her host, she was correspondingly more resigned; the sands of a thousand jokes had silted up on her till very little of her original personality showed above the surface, which was monotonous and smooth.

Mr Anderson began to play. He did so in a tentative, nervous kind of way, too conscious, perhaps, of Barry who was trying a surreptitious peep or two, certainly too conscious of Laura sitting behind her dummy hand rather like a lioness who has provided a nice kill for the cubs. It was hardly to be wondered at that he went two down.

'Two light, doubled,' announced Mr Clarke, complacently totting up the score. 'Vulnerable, too. Shouldn't have played that club king, should he, Laura?'

'It wasn't *my* sort of bridge,' replied Laura, and indeed she was right, for those afternoon sessions indulged in by the ladies are things apart, the nearest reminders left to us of the days of tooth and claw.

Knowing this, her husband did not argue but gathered up the pack and began to shuffle it, so slowly, so carefully, that if Barry had been doing it he must have been accused of stacking.

He knew he had done wrong and that his wife would have made the contract: between his fumbling and her decisive handling of the cards lay all the difference of their temperaments – a gulf that in his youth he thought that he had jumped, only to find that he had fallen into it. 'The Templars' was his house; the deeds that lay in his office safe were full of Robert Hemsley Andersons of the first part, proprietors and fee simple owners with livery of seisin and a great deal else besides; but for all that there was precious little now of Robert Hemsley Anderson in the appointments of the house – a chair or two, a few photographs, a study, theoretically his own; all the rest, though purchased with his money, reflected Laura's taste and Laura's personality. The taste was excellent, as even the Dean of Turlminster, that connoisseur of elegance, agreed: carpets, tables, desks and chairs, tallboys, candelabra, sporting prints, all fitted into a picture whose only fault was that it was much too faultless, as though each individual antique had posed itself and was waiting for the photographer's last instructions. In the result the furniture – that sensible Georgian furniture, made for warmth and good fellowship – looked, and for some reason felt, uncomfortable; polished, repolished, dressed up for the party and then put in corners with no chance to fraternize. 'A little like a museum,' said the Dean – privately, of course, and with this judgement Mr Anderson would certainly have agreed, for he had said as much openly in earlier days when he had had more influence and had not himself been one of the exhibits.

Now, while he shuffled, Laura dealt. The cards shot out from her long and bony hands like papers from a press, accurately, very close together, as though there were something that should be hidden in each pile, then, before her husband had completed his easier task, she had swooped down and arranged her hand in a motion so swift and secretive as to defeat even Barry at his best. Dealing such as this, so professional, so terribly like a sharper's on the Brighton train, deserved its own reward: unfortunately all the best cards had found their way into her cousin's hand. She knew this soon enough, for he did not have a poker face – a deficiency that cancelled the fruits of all his peeping.

'No bid,' she said.

Barry sat looking at his cards with a positively gloating expression. There was something satisfying about a good bridge hand, a sense of 'having', a sense of property that was destroyed the moment the honours were put in play.

'Come on, Barry, do make up your mind. I've got coffee coming in at ten.'

That was so like Laura, with whom a hand she could not play was a hand wasted, but Mr Clarke, a practitioner of 'gamesmanship' himself, would not be rushed.

'O.K., wheel it in,' he said.

'I can't, stupid. Where would you put the cups? Oh, come on! It can't be all that good.'

This was not the standard of Laura's ladies' bridge club, but she knew as well as anyone that what is not cricket at Lord's may be good tactics on the village green.

The words had their effect.

'I'll show you how good it is. Two spades.'

The bidding commenced and the Clarkes battled up to little slam, making such heavy weather when nearing port that Laura grew quite exasperated.

'Oh, come on, Barry, please! Everything'll be cold. Six spades? That's right, Rose, get them down. And *that's* a pretty hand.'

But her trained mind, running smoothly ahead, had seen the weakness in the hand as soon as it was on the table. If only her husband would rise to the occasion and make a certain lead! She sat up in her chair with an expression of such unwavering concentration on her face that Barry, who knew her well, could not resist a thrust.

'Come off it, Laura! Stop willing him. And now who's wasting time?'

Mr Anderson led. It was a safe lead, an orthodox lead, quite unobjectionable, but it was not the lead to save the game. And now the play was on and it was interesting to compare the styles. Mr Anderson played carefully, Laura with the precision of someone shelling peas, Barry with immense cunning as though he were manufacturing the answer to each trick. But the result had been inevitable from the first card played.

17

'Six spades, not doubled – pity! Our game and rubber anyway. Well done, Rose.'

'A diamond lead,' said Laura, 'would have put them down.'

Mrs Clarke, a kindly soul, begged that there be no post-mortems, but this was very properly disregarded, for bridge is less a game than a means of recharging personal ascendencies, and Laura was never one to throw a chance away. She might have developed the theme considerably had not Barry, even mellower than usual in the glow of his little triumph, unexpectedly sided with the opposition.

'Thought you were all for coffee: I am, too,' he said.

'Well, yes. But if Rob had had the sense to make a diamond lead ...'

'I'd have made grand slam. Come on with the coffee, there's the girl.'

In such an atmosphere no useful post-mortems could be held, for it takes two at least to cut this kind of body up. She gave in with a sigh and turned her attention to her duties as a hostess. The coffee and sandwiches were brought in, whereupon Mr Clarke turned his attention to his duties as a guest.

'How's the family, Rob?' he said.

'Oh, middling.'

'Margaret not fixed up yet?' then, in order that this might not be taken as an unkind reflexion on a girl who had been rather too long of a marriageable age, he added soothingly: 'I expect she's choosy, like so many of them these days. They know their own minds so well.'

'Too well,' put in Mrs Anderson. 'You can be too choosy in this life.'

Her husband flushed, for Margaret was his favourite. He knew better, however, than to defend her from this sort of talk, for that would only provoke a hotter fire.

'Kay's got a mind of her own, too,' said Mr Clarke.

It could be seen from Laura's face that what was bad in Margaret was very good in Kay, her second daughter, a thinner, paler edition of herself.

'Fine girl, Kay,' continued Barry. But for all that, Kay was not really to his taste: she was too brittle, too finely drawn to appeal to men of experience born in an age whose women had

18

not worn bustles behind and bosoms in front of them just to please a fashion house.

'Where are they all to-night?' he said.

Mr Anderson took it upon himself to answer him.

'Oh, Margaret and Kay are up at Mrs Grey's.'

'And Rupert?'

'He's in bed – or ought to be.'

'In bed! Rupert! My word, times have changed. Thought he was a young fly-by-night, that lad.'

'He *was*,' said Mr Anderson in the discouraging tones of one who wants to change the subject. But Barry, who was fond of the young man, was not prepared to let it rest at that. He had the privileges of a cousin.

'Why, what's the matter? What's he done?'

'Nothing, nothing serious. He's just been disobedient and we've had words.'

It was to be noticed that Laura's face had darkened during this exchange, and finally she burst out: 'It's been a lot of nonsense, Barry. Robert tries to treat him like a child.'

'I scarcely think,' said Mr Anderson, 'that Rose or Barry want to hear of it. So we'll drop the subject, if you please.'

This was a different Mr Anderson from the man who accepted rebukes so mildly at the bridge table; the fact was that where principles were involved he was inflexible – stubborn, as others might have put it, judging from his square, pugnacious jaw, the only strong feature in his face. But Laura was equally inflexible and far more prone to scenes.

'Rupert's nearly eighteen. That's grown up nowadays. And just because he doesn't run to heel . . . '

'Laura, please!'

'Just because he shows a bit of independence, he's put down.'

'If by a bit of independence,' retorted Mr Anderson, unwisely allowing himself to be drawn in, 'you mean staying out till all hours, doing no work and doing the opposite to everything I say, you're right. I got tired of it, that's all; I started insisting for change. There! I'm sorry, Rose; sorry, Barry. Let's forget it, shall we?'

'I've just the same trouble with my own,' said Mrs Clarke, still more unwisely, though she had spoken for the best.

19

Laura, of course, was instantly up in arms.

'Yes, Rose, but yours aren't seventeen. When they are I'm sure that Barry'll have more sense' – she did not credit Barry's wife. 'The result of all this discipline nonsense is the boy's being spoiled.'

'Being spoiled! He *is* spoilt!' cried Mr Anderson, returning to the fray. That was always how it was with Laura's quarrels: she was such an artist at finding the provocative word or phrase that she could lure her husband from his corner even when he had strapped himself in and gagged himself. She did not need to exercise such arts on Mr Clarke, one of those men who can float quite happily on quarrels without seriously offending either side.

'I agree with discipline,' he said.

'Discipline! Oh, Barry, don't talk such nonsense. You can't treat a grown boy the way you would a puppy-dog.'

'Why not?'

'Now you're just provoking. You know as well as I do that times have changed. Children have rights – just the same as adults have. Rupert's got rights and I mean to see he gets them. Don't smile. I'm serious. I mean what I say.'

'So do I,' said Mr Anderson.

Certainly they both looked serious; like a couple of fighting cocks, thought Barry, who had seen some sport in his young days. And though Laura would obviously be the bird to fly in and open the attack, there was no saying whether she would win. An awkward pair of devils, one all fire, the other obstinacy. Odd, when one came to think of it, how two such ill-matched people could have married. Mr Clarke, who had chosen satisfactorily for himself, was sorry for them; his own marriage was a perfect harmony, with Rose chiming dutifully in the minor.

'Oh come on, you two!' he said.

It really was a Christian act, for Barry was at heart what our great-grandmothers called a 'tease' and rather enjoyed seeing Laura's feathers fly.

'Well, Robert shouldn't take up such an attitude. He started it.'

The child – father to the man, thought Mr Clarke, and to the woman too. How like the old Laura of their schooldays, always in the right and prepared to prove it, always provoked and always most provoking! If the truth were told, he had been a bit afraid of her himself. Poor old Andy, what a partner to have taken on!

'I started it,' he said. 'Blame me.'

She would have blamed him if there had been any advantage in it, but it was chilly work trying to score against such a cheerful, unresponsive man. If she had been married to him – more than a possibility at one time – she would certainly have died of discouragement at an early age, whereas she looked very healthy and well set up with Robert Hemsley Anderson, on whom she had been sharpening herself for thirty years.

'All right,' she said. 'Let's think of something else.'

The something else that Barry thought of was another offering on the altar of appeasement. He had not stopped to think whether in the circumstances it was wise.

'If it's right with you I'll drop in to-morrow afternoon,' he said. 'I'm taking the boys and Rose to the circus. You care to join us, Rob? Oh, come on! Surely you can leave the office for one afternoon?'

Mr Anderson, the busy solicitor, shook his head over this manifest impossibility.

'Well, Laura then? Laura'll come. And the family. Just the thing for the girls: get them out of themselves a bit.'

'Very kind of you,' said Mr Anderson, who privately thought the circus was not the entertainment to appeal to Margaret, rather too serious a girl, or to Kay, much too smart a one.

'And of course it'll just be Rupert's cup of tea.'

The mention of that name seemed fated to cause a stir; even Laura made a faint gesture of dissent; as for Mr Anderson, he sat straight up in his chair and said: 'I'm afraid I can't let Rupert go,' then catching sight of Barry's face, honestly surprised, Laura's, as dark as thunder, hurried on: 'He's got work to do, you see.'

'But this is in the afternoon.'

'I know. I'm sorry. You haven't seen the boy's reports. I don't want to go back over that ground again. I've my reasons. He's ... he's misbehaved and he's being punished for it.'

'Hang it all, Rob, you're not locking him in the house! Just one afternoon's enjoyment!'

'No. You don't understand. He's been nothing but idle since

21

he came back from school. The report says he's got to work. I've warned him time and time again and he's taken not a scrap of notice. Well, it's gone too far. He must work. And until he satisfies me he's done enough he's not going to parties, or the pictures – even, I'm sorry to say, Barry, to the circus.'

Mr Anderson's jaw had set in its most pugnacious line. He had not said the half of what he could have done; unfortunately it was too much for present company.

'I'm sorry I mentioned it,' said Mr Clarke, and his voice was so cold and formal that it hardly seemed to belong to him. 'It was just a suggestion.'

'A grand suggestion.'

'Well, Laura, perhaps it was. But since Robert takes that line I'd best forget I spoke.'

'I don't want you to.'

She was standing now, and Mr Clarke saw with the eye of experience that he was dangerously near her line of fire.

'Steady on, Laura,' he said. 'Don't let's make a thing of it.' She swept aside this offer of a truce.

'You meant what you said, I hope?'

'About what?'

'Why about the invitation, of course. You said you'd call for us to-morrow.'

'I said I'd *do* nothing. I asked if I might, that's all.'

'Well then, call for us.'

This was open war and Mr Clarke, out alone in no-man's-land, felt pitifully exposed.

'Hang it all, Laura,' he cried, 'do let up! You're not going to get me interfering in this sort of thing.'

'Oh! So you side with *him*. You think it's fair to come down on the boy! You think he deserves to be shut up like a criminal!'

This, a perfect specimen of Laura's logic, should have been ignored; unfortunately Barry, who was really on her side with all means short of war, felt the slur.

'Nothing of the sort,' he said. 'I wanted to take the boy: I still do. I hope Rob will change his mind.'

But Mr Anderson all too obviously would not. He detested scenes and avoided them when he could, but he would not appease Laura in the matter of his son even to spare his guests.

22

'I'm sorry, Barry. I'm still more sorry we've had this row. But I'm afraid my mind's made up.'

From the look on Laura's face it was very clear that her mind was made up also, but Mr Anderson, intent on his apologies, did not notice this.

'I'm afraid I've been ungracious, that's what worries me. It was such a kind offer and I hate to turn it down. All the same, I know you'll understand.'

'*I* understand,' said Mrs Clarke, making her second disastrous contribution. How much this was a thrust at her hostess, how much the result of mere stupidity, only her husband knew, but it was not to be expected that Laura would be in any doubt.

'Well I don't. I don't understand at all and I don't understand how other people can either.'

She swept the 'other people' with an indignant look, and her husband, noticing the peculiar narrowing of her eyes, the tautness of her mouth, could forecast the violence of the storm that would break on him once his guests had left the house.

Barry was a weather prophet too, though his interest in what happened after he had left 'The Templars' was only academic. He rose to his feet and began that ritual demanded in polite society of the departing guest: that series of hints that precedes a man's outright order to his wife to get her hat. Not that Rose was particularly backward in this case: she hated scenes, she said, though in her mild way she had precipitated quite a few. It was a rearguard action for them both; indeed, on the doorstep the enemy swept right up to the defences.

'Are you coming to-morrow, Barry, like you said?'

His host was standing rather in the background, saying good night to Rose, and this gave Mr Clarke his chance. He said in an undertone: 'You must think I'm a fool.'

'I said, are you coming?'

She was leaning towards him and Barry could see for himself the sort of woman she had become. And he had nearly married her, years ago when she had been warm and young and full of a vitality that had almost swept them both away. Now he could find a word for her – an ugly word that matched the lean and hungry look, the tapering fingers, the mouth that he remembered open to his kisses, now thin and bloodless, shut in a denial of what no one wanted any more.

'You're rather a bitch, you know,' he said, and stepped out into the street before she could say another word.

3

It was the opinion of Mr Anderson's partner, a bustling young Londoner in search of experience and with his way to make in the world, that Turlminster was a faintly comic place. 'It's dead,' he would say – 'dead and doesn't know it,' and he would add not very original comments on Queen Anne that had at least some historical connexion with the architecture of the houses in the Close. The city was not real to him, not as it was to those born to the sound of the cathedral chimes, a reality, pleasurable or otherwise according to personal taste and personal ambition.

Turlminster was, for instance, a pleasurable reality to Mr Anderson, now preparing over breakfast to escape into the practice of a country town solicitor, into the round of wills and probates, death duties and estates, a little world of small complexities in the consideration of which the great complexities of his life and home could be forgotten.

He sat at breakfast in what Laura called the 'little dining-room', the one place in the house, apart from her bedroom and the bathrooms, where she had let the twentieth century in. Here were all the gadgets a housewife could desire: a service hatch and electric lift down to the kitchen, fluorescent lighting, built-in fires, a toaster and a chromium hot-plate, all of which dated Mr Anderson and made him look completely out of place. His two younger children, who were breakfasting with him, helped as well, for they were so unlike him in their different ways: the boy, dressed with that deliberate untidiness that is considered smart in the taboo-ridden adolescent world; the girl of twenty-three, glossy as only the products of the best schools can be. All ate in silence – the one point of etiquette on which all three agreed. But the lady of the house was absent: her chair, flanked by her favourite children, faced Mr Anderson down the length of the mahogany table like some symbol of reproach. The absence was significant and, this morning, so profoundly inconvenient that it called for comment.

'Kay,' he said.

'Yes, father?'

'Is your mother coming down?'

'I imagine so,' said Kay.

Mr Anderson caught the disapproving look: he was being punished for the previous night. Censoriousness can be expected from the young; what was distressing was the sense of plan, of combination, that accompanied his wife's displeasure. 'What do you mean, you imagine so?' he said, never at ease in dealing with this assured young woman. 'Did she say that she was coming down?'

'Yes.'

'When?'

'How can I tell you that! You know what mother's like.'

Mr Anderson did know. Though he had failed to understand his wife in spite of the experience of thirty years, he knew only too well the expressions of her moods. They were becoming increasingly frequent too.

He said, aggrieved: 'I wanted to speak to your mother.'

Kay made no reply. She knew all about the locked door of Laura's room and found even the thought of it distasteful. Parents had no right to quarrel. It was very wrong of her father to give offence, very foolish of her mother to take it, and absurd of them both to behave as though they still had feelings and passions alive enough to matter.

There it was: he had no remedy. There was a business matter that required his wife's attention and he had no access to her. It was irritating that she should not interest herself in such affairs; it was humiliating that he should be forced to eat his breakfast in disgrace; looking up, he thought he saw on the face of his son a small flicker of amusement. He put down his knife and fork.

'Rupert.'

'Father?'

'What are you going to do to-day?'

'Do? Nothing. You mean, what work have you given me, I suppose?' said Rupert, who had discovered in his father a rather amusing kind of butt: it was a game one could play endlessly, subtle, and just dangerous enough to be attractive.

'Then you suppose quite right.'

'Even though I'm on holiday?'

'You are not on holiday,' said Mr Anderson, his voice a trifle sharper as he remembered the events of recent days – the idleness and constant disobedience of his son. 'I set you to read Dicey's *Law of the Constitution* and the *Constitutional History* of Maitland. Have you read them?'

'Yes.'

'And do you understand them?'

Rupert gave his father an ironic look as though to say: 'Do you?' And the shrug of the shoulders with which he disclaimed so great a scholarship was charmingly provocative.

'Then may I recommend you to study them until you do.'

'All day?'

'You find it humorous?' said Mr Anderson, and his voice shook a little. Angry as he was at this impertinence, he was just enough to spare some anger for himself, for he had forced this quarrel on his son and on account of a sensitiveness that might have been deceived.

'I don't find Dicey or Maitland the least bit humorous,' replied Rupert promptly. 'Rather morbid, if you ask me.'

'But I don't ask you. You show a lack of respect that grows every day. This morning you are gratuitously insulting.'

'Scarcely gratuitously,' said Rupert, enticed beyond his depth in the course of this enthralling game. 'I don't know what I've done to call up this. D'you know, Kay?'

'Oh, Rupert, be quiet.'

'What *I* know,' said Mr Anderson, 'is that you'll stay in to-day and work, d'you hear? – work like you've been told.'

'But this afternoon mother's taking me to Ringby to the circus.'

Mr Anderson half rose in face of this ghost of a dead argument and glared down the length of the table at his son.

'Nothing of the sort! On no account! You can go later when you've squared accounts with me, but now, certainly not.'

Rupert looked speculatively at his father. He found something formidable about this large and angry man, the legacy of obscure memories of his childhood dimly understood, the stuff, was it of reality or of dreams? 'There's no need to get so worked up, you know,' he said. 'I didn't mean anything.'

'You were impertinent. I'm sure you meant to be.'

'No, really. It just seemed to me . . . '

'Yes?'

'Well, it seemed you wanted to pick on me somehow. I'm sure I don't know why' – this accompanied by a wide stare of innocence from eyes that the female Andersons were used to calling 'faun-like'.

Mr Anderson subsided in his chair and took up his knife and fork. He made little clearing noises in his throat, the aftermath of his emotions and an indication to the experienced Rupert that the crisis was past its peak.

'I try and work, father, honestly I do. But I'm new to this legal stuff. I bet you didn't use to work the whole day through.'

'That's a thing you can try to-day just for a change,' replied his father, apparently almost mollified. In the circumstances the game might now proceed.

'Yes, but what about the circus?'

'What's that!'

'Well, surely I can go?'

'You can go for a walk, but apart from that you don't leave this house to-day,' said Mr Anderson, with a level glance towards his son.

'Then when mother tells me . . .'

'I don't care what your mother tells you. When I give an order, you obey it.'

'And when mother gives an order I disobey it, is that right?'

'Rupert!' cried his sister.

'Keep your mother out of this!' cried Mr Anderson, pushing his plate away with a furious gesture. It was not pleasant to be presented with this duality of powers that existed in his family. At most times the impasse could be avoided by diplomacy, but this time he had blundered into a collision. 'You keep her out of it,' he repeated.

'Yes, but will *she* keep out of it?' said Rupert.

'You dare say that to me! You dare to speak of your mother in that way!'

'Father, please!'

'Be quiet, Kay! Do you suppose I will sit here and listen to such talk! Withdraw it at once.'

'Withdraw what?'

'You know very well. Withdraw your insolent references to your mother.'

'If,' said Rupert, choosing his words with care, 'I have made any insulting references to mother, I certainly withdraw them.'

Mr Anderson's puffy face had coloured violently and Kay, sensing a storm, rose and left the room.

'And you know that's no apology. You directed your pleasantries at me. If I had said such words to my father I should have been thrashed, yes thrashed. I should have been thrashed.'

The repetition of the words had brought a glitter to his eye, and seeing it, Rupert warily prepared for a retreat.

'I don't know what you want me to say,' he began.

'Say! I don't want words from you but obedience.'

'But I haven't disobeyed you. I haven't done anything. Even if I'd wanted to I wouldn't have had the time.'

Mr Anderson began to feel, as he did in his quarrels with his wife, enmeshed in a cocoon of words in which he was always fated to be outmanoeuvred and misunderstood. The possible injustice of the anger that had launched him on this tirade rankled in his heart and destroyed even righteous indignation, the consolation of injured souls.

'We'll forget it all,' he said. 'But you'll stay in to-day, is that clearly understood?'

'Yes, father,' replied Rupert with the expression of the meeker type of martyr, secretly promising himself an entertaining session later when his mother should be told the diktat.

'And if you don't do as I say I must seriously consider whether it would not be best for you to come into my office till the date of your calling up instead of continuing at school. What you need is work and discipline.'

'And that's forgetting it all! Well, it's nice to know.'

Mr Anderson overlooked the impertinence this time; he felt he had deserved it.

'I'm sorry, Rupert. I don't want to be unfair.'

'That's all right,' replied his son, with the greatest magnanimity.

'But incidents like this morning's aren't that easily forgotten,' said Mr Anderson, looking sadly at the boy. 'We think we can undo them but we can't. I can't forget the words I used to you, or the words you used to me.'

'They weren't all that serious, surely?'

'Not the words themselves but the thoughts behind them. Such thoughts should not come between us. When they do, it is high time we examined the causes, Rupert.'

'Really, I don't understand what you're getting at one bit.'

Mr Anderson looked directly into his son's dissembling face.

'You do understand,' he said. 'You're old enough. Your mother and I do not agree ... about many things. You have seen it for yourself for years. We don't agree except in our feelings for our children.' He added sadly: 'And we differ even there in the way that we express them.'

Rupert made a gesture of disapproval. He disliked the subject.

'But I must explain myself. For unconsciously you are taking sides. It's natural you should love your mother. But for me ... for me you are finding feelings of resentment. God knows I wish you well: your happiness was always my concern. I don't expect you to feel for me as you do for your mother – by the nature of things you can't: I only ask you to try and understand me. You're grown up now. You should know that there's a harsher side of life. The world is a hard world demanding hard preparations: discipline, obedience, industry; love is just something that makes it bearable.'

And still the young man protested:

'I don't resent you. I can't think why you should imagine it.'

'I don't imagine it. I can see and I can feel. You think that I'm hard on you. You see only yourself, a someone you feel you have the measure of, but I see in you your grandfather who inherited a bit of money and never did one worthwhile day's work in his life, your cousins, who're going the same way, as far as I can see – heredity, in other words, working out a bad account.'

'Mother's people,' said Rupert, with a look of great significance.

'Yes, your mother's people. Don't think that I'm attacking her.'

'But it seems to me that all that side are doing pretty well.

30

I should say that Uncle Barry's got the right idea. Mother says so anyway.'

'Your uncle Barry is a fortunate man,' said Mr Anderson, who now regretted very much the line that he had taken. 'I shouldn't have used the words I did about them. They must go their way, but that's not the way I plan for you.'

'I think I'm more cut out for his brewery than a law office,' suggested Rupert, echoing the ambitions of his mother, an ardent devotee of Barry Clarke, his fortune, and the political and social advantages that stemmed from it.

Mr Anderson frowned. His son had touched unerringly on one of the most violent sources of friction in the family, and in his irritation he exclaimed:

'I don't know what you're cut out for, I don't know at all. But I know one thing: the law's the best training for character and mind. I want you in partnership one day, Rupert – it's my dearest wish, but if you never practise for one day the training by itself will have done its part. Application, accuracy, are necessary in a man and the law will teach you them. That's why I'm insisting on your working at it now – you must have a grounding before conscription cuts you out. That's why I'm what you call "unreasonable", why you're to stop in to-day, for instance, and do some work.'

Rupert had been listening with no great display of attention to this harangue, but at the last words he sat up stiffly in his chair. Positions he had believed abandoned were still in the occupation of the enemy.

'Then you mean I'm not to go to the circus with mother after all, even though she wants me to?'

'Oh, devil take it!' cried Mr Anderson. 'Do as you're damn well told.' And he rose from the table and flung out of the room.

4

NOT till he had reached his office did Mr Anderson recover his equanimity. The conflict of emotions roused in the course of the foolish quarrel with his son had so worked as to deprive him of all appreciation of the morning and the scenes by which he was surrounded. To-day he could take no pleasure in the trim perfection of Colbert Row, the plane trees that shaded the promenade beside the River Ling, the old gabled houses in the High Street, and the cathedral towers, rising as background to the Deanery and its gardens, heavy with the profusion of high summer. All these were the setting of a life increasingly bleak and unrewarding.

But in entering the offices of Anderson, Rees & Sinclair-Poole he was escaping into another, quieter world, a world he understood. Though young Mr Sinclair-Poole, his partner – Mr Rees had been in his grave these fourteen years – was his younger daughter's fiancé and suave and keen as only prospective sons-in-law can be, the atmosphere of 'The Templars' had not as yet displaced the cosy, cobwebbed peace that accompanies old leather chairs and legal prints, deed boxes and certificates of competence signed by Lord Chancellors long dead. There was a clerk called Hemmings, as musty as the furniture (his removal was high on the priority list of Mr Sinclair-Poole's 'improvements'), an office boy following in his footsteps, and even the senior secretary, an attractive woman of middle age, was so quiet and ladylike as to give the mechanics of shorthand-typing a flavour of the eighteenth century.

Mr Anderson, crossing the threshold, felt immediately at home. There awaited his attention a troublesome conveyance, several wills, two police court briefs, and the Opinion of a Chancery counsel of Gray's Inn in the matter of a trust that had been getting steadily more incomprehensible with the years, but looking at them as they lay in bundles on his desk, he was aware of a feeling of buoyancy in his heart; there were answers to these problems – even to the trust affair, and that was more than could be said of the problems of his home. Only with his elder daughter was he at ease, and he was too kind and just a man to take pleasure in a divided house. Alliance with Margaret was a comfort to him but a peril to her, for he had few illusions about his wife or the range of her displeasure.

Arrived in the office, he sat down at his desk and rang the bell. It was answered by the secretary, Ruth Hetherington, who stood, though he was unaware of this, as high on Laura's secret list as Hemmings did on that of Mr Sinclair-Poole. She looked too good for her salary of five pounds a week – Mrs Anderson had said so frequently – and continuance in such a situation could only mean one thing – an attachment to the senior partner. It existed – how very right she was! – but this also was unknown to him. Men of over fifty are either determinedly in the arena or as determinedly on the shelf, and Mr Anderson, who had more reason than most men for distrusting the power of sex, had no more guilty feeling for the lady than a Trappist monk. Nevertheless, he was fond of her and grateful, too: she was loyal and gentle and everything about her was subdued. Not for her the elegance of Kay or the brittle looks of Laura, the residue of beauty gone a little sour with the passing years.

With her arrival the morning seemed to be fulfilled. A simple man who took a pleasure in routine, it was comforting to be sitting at his father's desk, pipe in mouth, his secretary at hand to dictate the rhythm of the day, and beyond the door Hemmings and the files and deed boxes, old friends as familiar as the clients themselves, those clients whose fathers and grandfathers had, in their day, sat in this same room with just such problems of the unchanging countryside. Facing him across the room were framed cartoons of legal personalities, relics of his student days: Lord Birkenhead, 'Galloper Smith' that was; Carson of the lean accusing finger and pugnacious jaw; Kekewich J., butt of so many legal jokes still told in the mess-rooms of the Circuits; Mr Justice Avory; Hailsham, gnome-like on the Woolsack. The faces, so varied in their power, all had something in common, the indefinable quality that comes of the practice of the law, and in his humble way Mr Anderson was not devoid of it: a way of life had set its seal on him and labelled him 'Attorney' for everyone to see.

Pencil and notebook in hand, the secretary was standing by the desk.

'Good morning, Miss Hetherington. And a beautiful morning it is, too.' He had only just noticed this: the trees outside his window etched against a sky of purest blue in which floated large fleecy clouds lumbering along like the giant balloons of Mardi-Gras. 'And now what have we to-day?'

Miss Hetherington consulted the engagement book.

'There's Mr Roper coming in at twelve,' she began. 'Something about a Power of Attorney, he said over the phone.'

'Yes, I know all about that.'

'Then you've arranged a conference with Carr and Atkinson about the Prentiss settlement. Mr Prentiss said he'd try and be in by half past two. Oh yes, and a Mrs Grey rang up just before you came in and asked if she could see you this morning at ten.'

'Mrs Grey? Mrs Frances Grey?'

'Of Welby Road.'

'Yes, that's her.'

'We've no record of any business from her before,' said Miss Hetherington. 'I said I thought that ten o'clock would be all right. I hope it will.'

'I'd always spare the time to see Mrs Grey,' said Mr Anderson, with so much warmth that his secretary looked at him in surprise. And catching the expression, he felt he should explain. 'She's a friend, you see, a very old friend. We were neighbours once. Her nephew and Margaret used to play together. What a quaint, serious pair they made!'

'How is Miss Margaret?' enquired Miss Hetherington, who greatly enjoyed these morning exchanges with her employer.

'Very well but rather busy – even though it's holiday time for her. Plenty of go in *her*. Wish she could pass some of it on to that young son of mine.'

'Oh, but he's a live wire, surely?'

'Hum, yes. Perhaps,' said Mr Anderson, and some of the pleasure he had laboriously been building up since his arrival in the office seemed suddenly to vanish.

Miss Hetherington noticed it at once. It was not difficult to deduce from the reticences of her employer a fairly complete picture of life in Colbert Row.

'Is there anything more you want me for?' she said.

'Not now, thank you. I shan't want Mr Hemmings either for a while. I'll ring. You can guess what I'll be on with: this.' He touched the trust opinion and smiled conspiratorially at his secretary, sharing this little legal joke, one of long standing which would not have amused the unfortunate lay client, caught, in spite of Mr Anderson's best efforts, in the octopus coils of Chancery.

When Miss Hetherington had gone he relit his pipe and settled down industriously to his task. People said – and they were right – that he was not a brilliant man, but sound, and that the firm of Anderson, Rees & Sinclair-Poole was a conservative firm, perhaps almost to a fault. But in this it matched its clients very well – a breed of men that distrusted typescript and liked legal documents to be legal-looking and as full of adjectives as possible. Businesses were radical in Turlminster at their peril. At ten o'clock when Hemmings entered to announce the arrival of Mrs Grey he was still hard at work. No sudden flash of insight could be expected to pierce to the heart of the Opinion of Mr Rufus Baring, whose words seemed always to be carefully selected to darken counsel, but Mr Anderson, painfully and clause by clause, had been advancing towards some understanding of the mystery. It was with relief that he put the document aside to greet his friend.

Frances Grey was a widow, a woman seven years younger than the solicitor, with the demure manner that is often termed 'designing' by suspicious wives. An old ally of the husband, it was scarcely to be wondered at that she was detested by Mrs Anderson under the guise of the most confidential feminine attentions. Mrs Grey was not deceived, being fully equipped with that sixth sense that women have. She returned the feeling, and meetings between the two ladies, not frequent now, had all the vibrant quality that precedes the beginning of a cat fight.

'My dear Frances!' said Mr Anderson, advancing towards his visitor with an alacrity considered unprofessional by Hemmings. 'How glad I am to see you! Do sit down.' He moved the armchair up beside the desk. 'It's ages since I saw you. Wherever have you been?'

'Where should I have been? In Turlminster.'

'Then I take it as an unkind act that you haven't been to see us. Laura was mentioning it only the other day.'

Mrs Grey could well imagine the tone of voice in which the 'mention' had been made.

'Well, I'm here now, Robert,' she said.

'It's certainly about time. And how's that favourite nephew of yours? Behaving himself?'

'It's quite unnecessary to ask that. John always behaves. I wish he wouldn't sometimes. He's so much the clergyman these days that it almost bores me.'

'He's a good lad though,' said Mr Anderson, voicing the general opinion held in Turlminster on the young man, only son of Agnes, dead elder sister of Mrs Grey.

'Yes he is, I suppose. How's your brood?'

'Oh, all well. Margaret's very busy – I never see her, and Kay's very engaged and smart, and Rupert's very idle.'

He had not mentioned Laura, and his visitor did not pursue the conversation.

'What I've come for to-day, Robert,' she said, 'isn't social, it's strictly business.' She caught the aggrieved look in his eye and hurried on. 'I know better, you see, than to take up valuable office time. The fact is, I'm in need of your professional advice.'

'Why, whatever's the matter, Frances?'

'The matter? Oh, just a will.'

'A will,' he said, smiling at her in relief. 'I thought for a moment you'd been across the law: keeping a ham in the larder or something.'

'Did you now! Well, there's no knowing what you'd find in odd corners of my house. Still, it's only a will I've come about this morning.'

'You want to remake your will?'

'I want to make one, Robert. It'll be my maiden effort.'

He shook his head at this evidence of the incorrigible foolishness of the layman. He knew from long experience the inconveniences, the tragedies, that such carelessness often causes.

'You should have made one long before,' he said.

'I know. But there's no damage, as it happens.'

'Very well,' said Mr Anderson, taking a sheet of paper and

36

a pencil, anxious to waste no time in putting his friend's affairs in tidy legal order. 'How d'you want to leave it?'

'I have three nephews, as you know,' began Mrs Grey slowly. 'Two are well provided for. I want to leave them a little, all the same.'

'Can be done easily by legacies.'

'And the bulk of my property I want to go to my nephew John.'

'Yes, yes. Is that all?'

'That's all.'

'A very simple will,' said Mr Anderson, writing quickly. 'Wish they were all as simple. Now, executors? Whom d'you want? I think in your case you'd best have two.'

'Then John for one. And would you act as the other, Rob?'

'Certainly.'

'In which case isn't it usual for a small sum to be left to what I'd call the "Disinterested party"?'

'Quite unnecessary,' said Mr Anderson briskly. 'You can leave me something if you like. But you know me well enough to realize that I'd be pleased to act for you in any case.'

'Well, is that really a friendly sentiment? It could be read two ways, you know. Never mind, of course I understand. And, thank you.'

'It'll be ready for your signature this time to-morrow,' said the solicitor, finishing his notes. Then, glancing up, he saw that she was looking at him with such a peculiar half-smile on her face that he added: 'Well, Frances, what is it? Why are you looking at me like Gioconda?'

'Because you're such an extraordinary man, that's why.'

'Extraordinary? What do you mean? Is it so extraordinary to refuse a legacy?'

'But that wasn't what I meant. It's the way that you *accept* a legacy that I find so entertaining.'

He threw up his hands in despair.

'Accept a legacy! I don't understand one word, not one word.'

Before he had recovered she had turned on what seemed to him another tack.

'How much would you say is behind that will?'

He said primly: 'I have never had the impertinence to enquire into your affairs.'

'No, no, you are a man of rectitude, almost as much rectitude as my poor John. It's too ostentatious, Robert. Well, I mustn't tease you. There's eighteen thousand pounds. Take the legacies away and we're left with just fifteen. Not a large amount, but comfortable, wouldn't you say?'

'Clear of duties?'

'Oh, I'd forgotten them. No, you must deduct them, I'm afraid. But even then it's a respectable amount.'

'For these days a very tidy sum,' admitted Mr Anderson.

'And do you mean to tell me,' said Mrs Grey, with another smile, 'that you're not just a little bit intrigued at the way I've left that "tidy sum"?'

'It was a sensible will, as I've said – an admirable will.'

'Well, I give it up. You must be doing wonderfully well, or else you're very callous, if you can remain unmoved at the thought of all that money coming into the family. I know I couldn't have sat by like a sphinx.'

'Into the family! Which family?'

'Why your family, of course,' said Mrs Grey.

She had delivered her bombshell so skilfully that she was forced to laugh at the expression of amazement on his face as he said: 'My family?'

'Yes, your family. Via Margaret, of course.'

'You can't mean . . .'

'I do mean. I have the greatest hopes of John and Margaret. She would be admirably suited to him. She is one of the most charming girls I know.'

'Yes, but . . .'

'You don't disapprove of my nephew, surely, Robert?'

'But I didn't know there was anything between them,' he cried. 'I hadn't the least idea.'

'Then you've been fast asleep.'

'I should have thought Margaret would have told me,' said Mr Anderson in reproachful tones.

'Told you that she was in love with John, you mean?'

'Yes. She always used to confide in me when she was little. I don't see what I've done to lose her confidence.'

38

'She hasn't told you,' said Mrs Grey, 'for the simple reason that she doesn't know.'

Again she could have laughed at the look of astonishment on his face. Men, she reflected, never quite grew up.

'But, Frances, surely she must know. She's over thirty; she's not a young girl.'

'She's an inexperienced one, and that amounts to the same. And she's got the idea – absurd in someone with her looks – that she's on the shelf. She has the feeling right enough, but she won't let herself identify it.'

'It seems to me,' he said, 'that you know more about my children than I do.'

'Fathers never know anything about their children: mothers know too much. The ideal status, Robert, is that of friend or aunt: one sees everything worthwhile in the game.'

Mr Anderson looked at his guest sitting comfortably in her chair, placid hands crossed on her lap, the very picture of knowing, good-humoured ease. A small answering smile now hovered on his lips.

'And you see a romance, do you, Frances?'

'I foresee one. At the moment the chief parties are displaying a gaucherie lamentable in people of their age. Now Kay would go quite another way about it.'

'Kay *went* quite another way about it,' corrected Mr Anderson. 'My poor partner never had a chance.'

'A very suitable young man,' said Mrs Grey, with a marked lack of conviction. 'He will get on, too. Whether John will is quite another matter.'

'John's doing very well. Everyone says so. Everyone likes him.'

'Too many people can like one, Robert, and that is sometimes quite fatal to success. But I suppose one shouldn't talk about such mundane matters in connexion with a clergyman. I can't help it, though. I would like him to do well.'

'He will do well. And I can tell you this: if by any chance your intuition turns out to be right, I for one shall be extremely happy.'

Mrs Grey gave her friend a companionable smile. She recognized in him a truly affectionate spirit, rather a dumb one but capable of being called out of hibernation by any display of warmth. How perverse, but how inevitable, that such a man should be married to a Laura.

'I'm glad you approve,' she said.

'Approval seems a bit premature, from what you say.'

'Oh, very. With a man as proper as John and a girl as sensitive as Margaret one must tread most carefully. Tell them now what it is they're after and they'll run opposite ways like startled rabbits. They've got what our parents called "spiritual natures", and they must be encouraged to think in terms of spiritual affinities till they find themselves in one another's arms. And then . . . well, I have great faith in nature.'

'Really, Frances!'

'Really what?'

'Perhaps I'm not a matchmaker,' said Mr Anderson dryly. 'You women are always down to earth.'

'And a good thing, too. If we waited on men I don't suppose matrimony as an institution would last so very long. Anyway, we've strayed a bit from John. You don't mind my encouraging this friendship?'

'Frances,' said Mr Anderson, with an amused look at his friend, 'you didn't come here on professional business. Come on, be honest! Did you?'

'All this arose out of the details of the will.'

'But that was bait.'

'Then are you going to take it, Robert? Are you going to bless the enterprise?'

'Will I let you scheme for them? Yes, John is a good lad. And Margaret . . . is perilously close to past the marrying age.'

The faces of both wore for a moment a serious air. In his mind was the picture, always afflicting to a father, of his daughter, unsought or rejected, a reflexion on himself; in Mrs Grey's was some understanding of how this fact had come about in Margaret's case. The girl was good-looking, warm-hearted, and gentle. There had been talk of boys. And then Laura . . .

'Would her mother object?' she said.

'Her mother! Good gracious, Frances, why ever should she? She hasn't said anything, has she?'

'No. I just wondered, that was all.'

40

'Naturally Laura wouldn't stand in the way of the girl's happiness. You surely don't suggest it?'

'No, I don't suggest it,' said Mrs Grey, but her face was grave.

'My dear Frances, naturally she'd be delighted. The nephew of her oldest friend' – he saw the brief flicker of an ironic smile shining in the lady's eyes. 'Why, John is just the person she'd want for Margaret.'

In these sentiments Mr Anderson was being less simple than he appeared. He did not believe that his wife had any particular love for Margaret; what he did believe was that she would welcome the chance of getting rid of her, for marriage would mean the loss of his only ally in the house in Colbert Row. He could not explain this to Mrs Grey, for he had an acute sense of loyalties.

'No, take it from me,' he went on, 'there'll be no objections there.'

'Good,' said Mrs Grey, and he saw that she was putting on her gloves. 'Then the matchmaking, as you call it, may proceed?'

'Just as a matter of interest, Frances, what would *you* call it?'

'Oh, matchmaking, of course. And what a way we've got to go! Here we have two people who talk social problems over coffee, play mixed doubles – very badly – and go to the pictures together once a month. That's all. Still, I'm not mistaken: they're in love. But Cupid needs assistance on occasions – the only problem is, just how?'

'That I shall leave to you,' he said.

'You certainly had better, Robert. Your talents lie in other directions: in will making, for instance. And as a reward for a morning's excellent advice, put that "Disinterested executor" in for a legacy of a hundred pounds.'

'Free of legacy duty?' enquired Mr Anderson, the solicitor in him rising uppermost.

'Yes, free of everything. I'll be in at ten to-morrow to sign the will.'

5

In her reading of the characters and inclinations of the two young people whom she loved, Mrs Grey had shown a degree of insight that did her credit, but she had not entirely understood them. It was all too easy for her, a woman of the world, to see in Margaret something of a blue-stocking, in her nephew too much of the prig, and to deduce an unworldliness not to be expected from creatures of flesh and blood. Both John and Margaret were capable of recognizing in the other a focus of physical attraction; what was chiefly keeping them apart was a tendency, bred in both of them by their professions, to recognize the flesh and the devil where the less inhibited would only have seen love. Margaret, in particular, recognized the symptoms, having once, some years before, been in a similar predicament, but it now seemed to her unnatural to associate the unbridled feelings of her heart with so respectable a clergyman. Spiritual her sensations certainly were not, and not being spiritual, it followed that they must be wrong. These fears and passions which they could not share, could not discuss, hung heavily over the radical debates on social and political questions indulged in by these children of a generation that feels that it is free. This comic paradox was concealed from Frances Grey, who would certainly have been amused if she had known. Childless herself, she loved her nephew but she reserved the right to laugh at his absurdities.

The lovers (for so she dubbed them in her thoughts) were together more often than she knew. Perhaps John had shown himself sly in this, for he feared his aunt's sarcastic tongue. They did play mixed doubles – and badly, as she said – they did visit the cinema once a month, but the 'social talks over coffee' were frequent and protracted, so much so that the parishioners of St Andrew's, who demanded a fair field and no favour with their curates, were beginning to say quite spiteful things. What made it all much worse was that Miss Anderson was a Chapel girl, a Nonconformist in a Church of England family in a town with tendencies so High – under the influence of the Dean – as to be considered in some circles as half-way to Rome. Indeed, though Mrs Grey thought of Margaret as the perfect wife for John, this sentiment was not echoed in the parish of St Andrew's: as to who *was* best qualified there were several opinions – as many opinions as there were unmarried girl parishioners.

This hostility had no effect on John and Margaret. They continued together at coffee, at tennis, they met at social functions and they went for evening walks in the countryside. On the evening of the day of Mrs Grey's visit to Anderson, Rees & Sinclair-Poole they were wandering in the footpaths near the River Ling. It was a walk they loved. From the new bridge they could descend the promenade under the trees, cross over a stile into the water meadows, and from the slopes of Farshot Hill look back over the gentle green pastures and woods to the roofs of the old town clustering round the cathedral of St George. In this placid scene the Welby housing estate on the northern outskirts, a sugar-beet factory and the city gasworks, set on a hill and certainly not hid, were left to prove that Turlminster was moving with the times.

They had paid over a dozen visits to Farshot that year. When they had first come there in the early spring it had been an urban view; now that it was high summer and all the trees were out the countryside had advanced like the columns of an army, driving its spearheads along every street and into the very citadel of the Close. And Margaret, looking at it dreamily, said for the third time that evening that it was beautiful.

'It's the best summer,' said John, 'that I remember.' Not till he had spoken the words did he realize the significance at the back of them. He turned towards her to see if she had understood. But her face was averted, and she held a hand over her eyes to shade them against the rays of the westering sun. 'Don't you agree?'

'Yes, John, of course. It's been marvellous.' She added artlessly: 'I suppose it comes of being back in Turlminster. Summer in a big city's so terribly half-hearted.'

'Poor you.'

'Poor me, is right. D'you know it's four years since I last

43

saw a summer out at home? Never mind, I don't regret it. It's been worth waiting for.'

'It has,' said John.

It was not easy this time to mistake his meaning; nevertheless, she remained in the same position, looking away from him, for she was a little too conscious of him there beside her – this agreeable-looking young man with the slight figure and sensitive, intellectual face, this old friend who, each day, seemed to be imbued with new attractions that were not intellectual in the least.

'It has,' he repeated, less pointedly, as he saw how badly she had reacted. 'This *has* been a summer. So much richness and display.'

'Ah, but really, I suppose, that's what we imagine every year,' she said, feeling that they were back on the old familiar ground. 'And why? Because each time we learn to appreciate nature a little more. When I was a child, for instance, summer only meant holidays to me.'

'But what a rationalist you are!' he cried. 'There are other reasons for preferences than advancing age – for my preferences, anyway.'

'Are there, John?'

There was no coquetry in the gaze she had turned on him, none in her tone of voice. But the question opened up a great deal of new ground.

'Yes, there are reasons: you, for one.'

'Me? My company? I talk so much I spoil the view.'

'But not for me, you see. I . . . I enjoy these walks.'

'And so do I. I don't know how I ever had the heart to leave Turlminster. I shan't again. I'd rather teach here at half the salary.'

'You like teaching, don't you?' he said, aware of how he had been moved to safer ground.

'Of course I like it. I have a bossy nature and so it suits me perfectly.'

'Bossy! That's the last thing I should have said of you.'

'Then if you want to prove it, think back on who suggested this walk to-night.'

'I did.'

'You did not. I've organized you on to this hill-top. All you wanted to do – remember? – was to lean over the bridge and watch the fish.'

'And now that you've got me here?' he said.

'We look at the view, of course. What else?'

It is to be feared that the young parishioners of St Andrew's would not have acquitted their sister of a designing purpose had they heard these words, yet she was innocent enough. The fact was that she regarded conversation as an exercise somehow divorced from the heart; love was a silent thing, to be felt rapturously in every fibre of her being but not to be expressed in words.

'Perhaps I also had a hand in arranging we should come,' said John.

'No, you've got too lazy. I don't think you'd walk up here if it wasn't for my urging.'

'True enough. *You're* the reason why I came. There now!' he added, driven by the urge to make his meaning unmistakable. 'It's time you were told how much your company means to me.'

'Yours means a lot to me.'

'How much, Margaret?'

'That's unfair. What are the uses of measurements and definitions? We get on well, we agree. That counts for a great deal.'

'Do *you* think that it's enough?'

She was face to face now with the question that she had often asked herself in waking moments of the night. She was happy with him as she was, and there must be risks in any relationship as violent as the one forecast in her heart.

'I wouldn't want to lose your friendship, John,' she said. 'I should be very lonely if I hadn't you to talk to. You understand me.'

'Not as you are to-day. You're avoiding questions.'

'Because I just can't answer them. How can you expect me to treat friendship like ... like Troy weight? If we're contented we should be grateful for it and make sure we don't lose what we mean to one another.'

'But have you thought that we might gain something instead?'

She did not reply.

'Margaret, answer me. Have you thought of that?'

45

She said in a small voice: 'Yes.'

He did not remember having seen her so silent and submissive. That roused in him emotions that were at most times kept in check by his own bewildered uncertainty of mind. He had already gone dangerously far – far beyond his own intentions on setting out for that evening walk.

'You have! Then you feel as I feel, that we could mean much more to one another.'

'Please, John.'

'But we could. Think of all the time we've known one another, the talks we've had. Half the problem in life is finding someone who speaks one's language, who shares one's ideas. I feel that you and I have the same attitude to life. Don't you?'

'It's just because of that,' she said, looking directly at him for the first time, 'that we should be so very careful not to spoil it.'

'Nothing can stay still for ever, Margaret. We must develop like everything else.'

She shook her head. 'No, I don't see that. You and I stayed good friends for years, and now in answer to your feelings of an evening everything's to change.'

Her resistance had quite wounded him: it was mortifying to be rebuffed in a course of conduct which he believed to be the most generous of his life. And his irritation broke out as he exclaimed: 'How can you judge my feelings? You don't attempt to understand them.' He wronged her, for she understood them perfectly. 'You won't let me explain.'

'As if I didn't know what it is you've got to say! Only I'd rather it wasn't said.'

'But why? Why?'

'Because neither of us is ready for it. And because you won't mean it.'

'You know I won't mean what I haven't said! There's a triumph of female logic!'

But still he did not openly say the simple, obvious words, restrained less by what she had said than by his native caution. For though it had been delightful to linger on this ground, the no-man's-land of their unspoken thoughts, the assault itself was a more questionable matter.

'I don't pretend to be very logical,' she said.

46

'But you have intuition, of course, to make up for that!'

She caught the unkind inflexion in his voice and understood: he was retreating under cover of a sarcasm from the pit he had been digging so enthusiastically for himself. It was the retreat that she had planned for and yet a rather hurt expression crept into her eyes, because alongside her wish for a withdrawal existed another, quite perverse, the longing for the words they had suppressed.

He saw her face turned to his, so bewildered, so unhappy, and some understanding came to him of the weakness of his actions, of the emotions that struggled in her heart.

'I'm sorry, Margaret,' he said. 'You know what I feel for you. I mean it, too.'

As they turned from the hill-side to begin the descent they found that they were walking hand in hand, just as though it were the most natural thing in all the world – as indeed it was.

6

IT was nearly eleven at night before Mr Anderson returned to Colbert Row. For this he had a legitimate excuse – a meeting of the Turlminster Club of which he was the Treasurer – though the last thirty minutes had been spent in the saloon bar of the 'Golden Fleece'. This was the fashionable rendezvous of the business men of the town, presided over by Joy Roberts, a young woman rather too catholic in her affections. Unlike most barmaids, who seem as a class to be suspended like Mahomet's coffin in a vacuum, in their case between the extremes of prudery and licence, Joy was as good as her word and sometimes better, perhaps regarding her position in the licensing profession as a very useful introduction to another. It was freely said that she would not last long at the 'Fleece', even that her presence there was bad for trade, though this seemed to be contradicted by the young men clustered round her bar. Not that Joy unduly favoured youth: it was all too often impecunious, as she knew, and men of substance irrespective of their age were certain to be treated well by her. Few availed themselves. In a small town like Turlminster, where gossip was a living force, the respectable had to give all their attention to remaining so; they had not the advantage of the young, to whom hours spent with a pretty woman in the fields or in the back seats of a car were matters of prestige.

Of Joy's many clients Mr Anderson was among the most respectable; he was not even a frequent visitor, though in deference to his position he was treated as a 'Regular', one of a class of favoured beings possessing a kind of *droit de seigneur* over diminishing whisky stocks. These visits of Mr Anderson's were never of long duration, they could not have been more innocent; nevertheless, as events were to prove, it would have been better for him if he had never seen the 'Golden Fleece'.

On this particular evening, once the inn doors had closed behind him he was struck with a sense of guilt as he remembered how often he had been late back home that week. The prospect ahead was not encouraging, for Laura had much experience as a termagant and after last night's bridge was bound to be in form. But when Mr Anderson, much less confident than his professional air, at last crossed his threshold it was to find that his wife was sitting in the lounge apparently in the sunniest of tempers. Fresh from the rather startling looks of Joy, gleaming like a young sultana behind the counter of the 'Fleece', it was positively restful to see the slim figure reclining by the fireside, grey hair set in an elegant coiffure designed at great expense to flatten out a head a trifle too fine and narrow, to display the ears and beautiful turquoise ear-rings and correct a slight mis-alignment of the mouth.

Laura was undeniably handsome and far smarter than her husband, with the deficient clothes-sense of the male, could ever realize; if she had a fault it was that her appearance, when in-spected closely, revealed a series of corrections: her face was not symmetrical – how that had been dealt with we have seen; she was too tall and wore some artful shoes in consequence, her hands were long and spidery, and here – alas! – her taste for rings and nail-varnish had betrayed her, so that she looked as to this part of her person just a little like a bird of prey. Even her character was corrected, so that it took the most discerning minds to see in her the woman familiar to her husband, a dangerous creature, subtle, unpredictable, sharpened in anger to diamond pitch. He alone had seen her in all the imperfections of her mind and body and even he, when faced with her in gentle mood, could doubt the evidence of the experience of years.

'Hello, Laura!' he said. 'No, don't get up,' for she had un-curled herself from the settee and with a gesture, almost a caricature of wifely devotion, had put the kettle on the fire. Tea-pot and tea-cups were set out on a table: it was to be an amicable evening, and remembering her displeasure of the previous night he could not imagine why.

An idea did soon occur to him: she could have heard of the morning's threats to Rupert and might be trying a little wheed-ling for a change. With this thought in mind Mr Anderson sat down in an armchair opposite his wife and with something of the air of an experienced Trojan waited for the introduction of a wooden horse. None came. In some bewilderment he found himself retailing his experiences of the day: the Prentiss settlement (naturally without the confidential details), the obscurantism of Mr Rufus Baring and his Opinion, the evening's meeting at the Club. Even the direct mention of his son's name brought no response: Rupert, it appeared, had stayed at home and had been surprisingly busy with his work.

'So busy that he's tired out and gone to bed?' said Mr Anderson, not without sarcasm.

Mrs Anderson replied that this was so; that the boy had worked himself out and gone upstairs some time before.

'Worked himself out! Well, wonders will never cease.' Then as though aware that he was taking rather ungenerous advantage of his wife's good temper he added soothingly: 'He only needs to work to become everything we hope for him. All the rest is there. He gets that quickness from you, Laura, for I know that I never had half his natural ability.'

Mrs Anderson looked speculatively at her husband; it was very plain to see that she agreed. 'I hope he doesn't underrate himself the way you do,' she said.

'Oh, there's no fear of that. The boy has an excellent opinion of himself – none better.'

'You disapprove of that?'

'I distrust it. In a way, naturally, it's an asset, Laura, but people with too much self-importance are not very often liked.'

Mrs Anderson shrugged her elegant shoulders. But for the fact that she seemed determined on a peaceful evening it was very clear that she would have expressed some forceful strictures on the advantages of being liked, for the individualist in her, as in Mrs Grey, saw the superior intelligence in the cat that walks alone.

'Oh, you may deny it,' said her husband, seeing her reaction, 'but popularity is an asset to a man in business. He shouldn't court it but he shouldn't turn his back on it. The middle road's the best.' This was an article of faith with Mr Anderson, a man who pursued the middle road with a most determined normality. To him it was a way of life: what it was to his febrile, ambitious wife may readily be imagined.

'I don't think you need worry,' she said. 'Rupert may not be popular with the herd' – injecting a note of venom into this

– 'but he is certain to be liked by the right people, the people who matter. He has the looks and the character for it.'

'But who are the "right people", Laura?'

'Now that's just perverse. You know perfectly well what I mean. Barry is a "right person", so is our sitting member, so is the Lord Lieutenant, so, in a way, are you.'

'My dear, what a compliment!'

'In other words, the people who can push us up the ladder, the people we attach ourselves to so that we get pulled up the ladder after them.'

'People with money, you mean?'

'Yes, or influence.'

'And Rupert, you say, will get on well with them?'

'Yes. You don't mean you don't want him to, surely, Robert?'

The eyes that were now turned on him bore a disturbing resemblance to his son's; with just such an armoury had he been faced – indeed outfaced – at breakfast. It was never profitable to embark on this sort of argument, for he was always worked into the wrong.

'I don't want my boy to be a sycophant,' he said.

'And I don't want *my* boy to be a weak-kneed, popular nincompoop. There now,' with another of her lightning turns of mood, 'don't let's get silly over Rupert. You pull one way and I'll pull the other and between us we'll get him where he ought to be – just dead centre. And that's where you want him – isn't it? – planted on your middle road.'

She was smiling at him in such good humour that he could not be offended. She had been, as usual, far too quick for him, planting her darts and insults and away with the dexterity of a banderillero in the bull-ring. By the time his slower temper could lumber up to hers, she had changed her ground and, elusive quarry, was leading him another way. All their life long it had been like that: they had never truly shared experience because he had never caught her, even in the first rapture of their love.

'All right,' he said. 'We must just agree to differ about the boy.'

'And don't let's differ seriously either, Rob.'

This time he recognized an unmistakable olive branch, for only when in the best of humours did she use the diminutive of

51

his name. He responded immediately. He was a moderate, kind-hearted man without a trace of vindictiveness in his nature, and furthermore, in spite of all the bitterness that had arisen between them, she retained the power to move him still. It was not a happy feeling, for he recognized in himself the trace of appetites that could not be allayed by age, or children, or by the knowledge that she hated him.

'I certainly don't want to differ, Laura,' he said. 'Disagreements are exhausting.'

'And unnecessary.'

'Of course they are. But then we have got into the habit of them. It isn't easy to break habits.'

'We can try,' she said. 'For instance, I wasn't pleased that you were late to-night. Seeing how often it's happened lately I could have become bitter over it. It was certainly a temptation.'

'Which you resisted, I see,' said Mr Anderson, with a glance at the kettle now boiling on the fire.

'Yes, but not without a struggle. You really owe me something, Rob.'

'How can I repay?'

'By telling me about your day: not the humdrum Prentisses, the scandalous part, I mean.'

'It was a dull day.'

'Only because you thought so, I'll be bound. Any woman could have made a dozen really interesting scandals out of it. Who called? Any women?'

'As a matter of fact . . . ' began Mr Anderson cautiously.

'Yes?'

'Well . . . Frances Grey came in.'

'Frances? About what?'

'My dear, you know I can't tell you such things.'

'Oh, I know you've your professional duty, though anyone would think from the closeness of you that you were a priest. But surely Frances had some social chit-chat, and you can pass that on?'

Mr Anderson looked into the fire. A sudden urge had come upon him to confide in Laura, to tell her about Margaret, to treat her as his wife. He knew the imprudence of doing this but he had the confessional urge of the father to talk about his favourite. And the moment seemed opportune as it had not been for months. In the sober light of day Mr Anderson would probably have held his tongue, but the tea-cups now being filled and the aura of domesticity had their effect on him. This was the mother of his daughter, he reassured himself, and as such she ought to know.

'Well, Robert?' said Mrs Anderson impatiently, for her appetite had been whetted by mention of Mrs Grey. 'I can see there was something from the look of you.'

'It was about Margaret,' he said.

'Yes. Yes, go on.'

'Frances thinks that possibly John and Margaret . . . '

'Are going together?'

'Have become very close friends,' said Mr Anderson, with a frown for his wife's suggestive phrase.

'Well you surprise me. Margaret! And John! Just think of that!'

'I think they would suit each other admirably,' said Mr Anderson stiffly.

'Oh yes, admirably. They are very much alike.'

Laura's voice was soft and distant, she seemed to be assimilating facts and weighing their significance; her whole expression was secret and withdrawn, and Mr Anderson, watching her, did not relish what he saw.

'I told you this in confidence,' he said, 'the strictest confidence.'

.'Which I deserve, I hope. I am the girl's mother, after all.'

Mr Anderson was thus presented with the expression of his earlier thoughts. It reassured him somewhat. 'It's a delicate matter, Laura,' he said.

'So it seems. It is so delicate that Frances can gossip about it round the town.'

'Not gossip. How can you call it that? She just told me facts as she saw them.'

'Another case of "strictest confidence", no doubt. And naturally Frances is in favour of the match?'

'As a matter of fact she is.'

'And you favour it. Why then, there is the most perfect

agreement possible. What are we waiting for? Not for the formality of my approval, surely?'

'We are waiting,' said Mr Anderson, the colour rising in his face, 'for the principals themselves.'

'John hasn't spoken?'

'Frances thinks neither really knows what's happening. It sometimes takes a third person – doesn't it? – to tell a man he is in love, or a woman, for that matter.'

'Does it, Robert?'

'But I'm asking you. Do you think Frances can be right?'

'How do I know! I haven't had the privilege of watching them together. Frances has, that's evident, and she's drawn conclusions – and what conclusions! thanks to the extraordinary simplicity of her mind.' Here Mrs Anderson laughed, not altogether pleasantly. 'Wouldn't you think she'd know just a little bit about that thing called instinct – how quick it is and how direct?'

'Laura, you're not suggesting . . . '

'Of course the girl knows,' said Mrs Anderson, so engrossed in her thoughts that she had not heard her husband speak. 'She *has* been different. Now I come to think of it, she *has*. And I was fool enough to have missed it.'

Her husband now had ample opportunity to repent of his foolish impulse, for he saw he had betrayed a secret into unfriendly hands. He would have given a great deal to be able to retract, but since he could not he would attempt to minimize.

'I don't suppose there's anything at all in Frances' story. I haven't seen a thing.'

'You wouldn't, Robert, if it was right under your nose.'

'You saw nothing either. You just pretend to yourself you did.'

'How do you know what I saw?' said Mrs Anderson, showing her teeth in a little mirthless smile. 'The girl's been mooning about the house more drearily than usual: I noticed that.'

He put away his tea-cup and sat up stiffly in his chair.

'Nothing about Margaret is dreary,' he said. 'If she's reserved at home that's because she gets no encouragement. You never bother to take her out, or talk to her, or interest yourself in her.

How could you notice whether she was sad or unhappy – or in love!'

'Thank you for those reflexions on my nature, Robert.'

'Nature! You deny your nature with Margaret. She is your daughter.'

'*Your* daughter, please. Everyone knows where her affections lie – unless, of course, you've had to step aside for John.'

'A nice thing to say!' cried her husband, now on his feet. 'As if I have ever tried to keep her affections from you!'

'But you've done so, whether you wanted it or not. I mean nothing to her, absolutely nothing.'

Mrs Anderson had said these words with a break in her voice, infinitely appealing, but for once her husband had not tried to follow her quicksilver passage along the roads of his emotions; he was too obsessed with her unnatural feelings. 'You have nothing because you gave nothing,' he said. 'You never cared for her.'

He heard his wife's gentle, soft rejoinder: 'Could I say the same of you and Rupert? Of you and Kay?'

'No, you could not;' he cried. 'I have tried to be a good father to them.'

'Oh, no doubt. You have been a paragon. But then it happens that Kay and Rupert care for me. Do you understand that? And what do you think they feel for you?'

He said sharply: 'Don't say it, Laura.'

She would certainly have done so. Instead an expression that he could not interpret flashed into her eyes at the sound of the grating of a key in the lock of the front door.

'Margaret, I expect,' said Mr Anderson, reverting at once to the manner of father of the family. Long practice had made him adept at this camouflage of the relations existing between him and his wife, though the children had never from earliest infancy been deceived. And Laura seconded this change of front so well that the daughter, entering, was surprised at the cosy nature of her parents' tête-à-tête. Late night tea by the fireside! It was a long time since she had last seen that.

Mr Anderson at once reproved her for late hours. He did not mean it seriously, being always tolerant of his elder children, but it gave him something to say at a moment when his mind was in a turmoil with his recent thoughts. And the best thing about Margaret was that she always understood; unlike Kay she was never out of sympathy with this matrimonial charade – was even willing to play a part in it herself.

'I'm sorry,' she said. 'I didn't know it was so late.'

'Not too late for tea,' said her mother, curling herself up again in her corner of the sofa and looking more than ever like a sleek and indolently watchful cat. 'Had a good evening, dear?'

'Yes.'

'How's Bette? Cold better?'

'I don't know,' replied Margaret, who was down on her knees on the hearth-rug, helping herself to tea. 'I haven't seen Bette this week.'

'Oh! I thought you were out with her to-night.'

'I was at Mrs Grey's,' said Margaret. Not for nothing was she Laura's daughter. She had spoken so unconcernedly, with so much skill, that she would have been amazed had she seen the look exchanged by her parents behind her back.

'Yes. And how is Frances?'

'Much as usual, rather busy. I was helping her with the tickets for a bazaar.'

'St Andrew's summer bazaar?'

'An all-denominational one,' said Margaret, smiling at her mother. 'So even I'm allowed in, you see. I know they've got you on the list for at least one stall.'

'Have they now!'

'And they've got father down to run a sort of lottery,' continued Margaret, who believed that she had turned the conversation. 'That's not to mention Kay.'

'And who has planned this general employment of the family Anderson? Not the vicar: he scarcely speaks to us.'

'The committee, I suppose.'

'And *I* suppose that it was John. He always takes such a special interest in us nowadays, though why, I can't imagine.'

'John certainly said he hoped we all would help.'

'Oh, so *he* was there to-night.'

'It's not really so unexpected, mother,' said Margaret, 'seeing that he lives there.'

Her father, hovering like an anxious referee on the outskirts

56

of the fight, shook his head at this. It was always unwise to score off Laura.

'Seeing that you were there,' retorted Mrs Anderson, 'I don't find his presence unexpected in the least.'

'Well, mother, really!'

But Laura had realized that she had gone, if not too far, certainly much too fast. She disapproved of this liaison that her husband's folly had revealed to her as she disapproved of everything not of her own contriving, but she was an excellent judge of character and timing and knew the danger of being premature.

'Oh, I'm not hinting at a romance, my dear,' she cried airily. 'If that had been going to happen it would have happened long ago. No, I meant something else. Pious young men like John who just feed on admiration love nothing better than having witnesses to their good works.'

'I don't think John's a bit like that.'

'But then how could you expect to have the experience to judge? I'm sure you don't know him all that well.'

'I'm sure I do,' said Margaret. Her flushed face as she spoke betrayed her more completely than her words, for there could be no mistaking the feelings of her heart. Indeed Laura, watching with amazement this transformation of the stolid daughter that she knew, must have guessed at more than a shared hand-clasp on a hill.

'You surprise me, Margaret,' she said. 'Before I was married I never allowed myself judgements on a man.'

'But mine aren't judgements, mother. I'm not finding fault.'

And Margaret certainly was not. Under the impact of her mother's criticism a new John Paget was being born.

'My dear, I never thought you were. It's quite obvious that in your eyes John must not be criticized. Now I like John myself, he has many admirable qualities: he is good to his aunt, keen, hard-working, most conscientious and even more respectable.'

'A very good lad all round,' put in Mr Anderson, unasked and certainly unheeded.

'But he is no more perfect than you or me, and you will only deceive yourself and hurt yourself if you think he is. He is conceited, vain: l am sorry to say that he is selfish.'

'I think that's a horrid thing to say,' cried Margaret, quite unable to contain herself. 'How can you say that when only this afternoon he offered you and Rupert a lift home from Ringby from the circus!'

Mrs Anderson drew in her breath sharply. She had forgotten the incident, an unusual lapse in so excellent a general.

'Margaret,' said Mr Anderson, 'please leave the room.'

'But, father, what have I said? I didn't mean . . . '

'It is nothing that concerns you. Just do as I say and leave the room.'

Laura sat bolt upright on the settee. She had walked into a trap of her own devising. But her belief in her ability to extricate herself could be read in every line of her face and figure, the clenched hands, the mouth drawn up at the corners; her friends would have been astounded at the look of her.

'Well?' said Mr Anderson, as soon as his daughter's steps had faded on the stairs. 'Was it to-day? And did you go?'

'Nothing that concerns her, indeed!' said his wife. 'Coming here in that sly, vindictive way and telling tales!'

'That has nothing to do with it. She wasn't in last night or this morning at breakfast. She couldn't know I'd given Rupert orders.'

'She's a trouble maker in the house.'

'You're the trouble maker. Margaret obeys my instructions but you set yourself to undermine them.'

'And who,' said Mrs Anderson, with disdain, 'are you to be giving orders to my son! Stay in like a criminal, indeed!'

'You don't deny, then, that you took him to the circus?'

'You heard what that girl said.'

'And you don't deny that you knew my orders?'

'Orders, orders! Who cares for them! I tell you flatly that I don't.'

'Answer me. Did you go with Barry or did you take the boy alone?'

'I am paying no attention to you,' said Mrs Anderson, her eyes fixed on his with an expression of unwavering scorn.

'Then I think you went alone. Deliberately and against my will.'

'Really, Robert,' said Mrs Anderson, rising to her feet, 'you are the most tedious man I know. Certainly I took him. Now are you satisfied?'

'So you admit it?'

Laura sighed and shrugged her shoulders.

'And you pass for an intelligent man!' she said. 'Do all your clients – or victims, should I call them? – find you so perceptive? Well, now that you have understood the matter and the little comedy is over I think I'll go to bed.'

But he was still standing between her and the door, physically predominant, whatever the condition of his wit.

'You will listen to me,' he said. 'To-day's was not just another quarrel as you seem to think. We have got past that stage with Rupert now. I must tell you – as a lawyer, if you like – that in respect of my family I have rights.'

'Rights, perhaps,' she said, 'but have you power?'

And as she spoke he saw that same strange expression he had noticed earlier pass across her face. He recognized it now. For far off down the kitchen corridor they heard the sound, so surreptitious, of the lifting of a latch, then a stealthy tread upon the stair.

7

Soon after ten that same evening Joy Roberts had left the saloon bar of the 'Golden Fleece', for on most evenings she was relieved just before closing time and was spared the washing-up, some compensation for the rigours of that last hour on Saturdays when even Turlminster descended to a slightly Babylonian level.

Slipping into the service dressing-room she plied her powder and lipstick, put on her smart tweed coat and went out of the back door into the street. At this hour on a Thursday night the town seemed fast asleep; only the famed Turlminster chimes, ringing out at fifteen-minute intervals like the beating of some amorphous heart, proved that there was life in this body, prostrate under the morgue-like lighting of the British Electricity Authority. Some girls might have felt a qualm at walking through those silent streets, in the shade of houses curtained so securely against prying eyes that not a chink of light showed them to be occupied, through back alleyways and along the deserted promenade beside the Ling, but Joy, a creature of assignations, felt no fear; she was as discreet in her own way as the Dean of Turlminster himself, and found an ally in the darkness of the night. A great reader of the Sunday papers, she knew the risks she ran, yet ran them cheerfully, since she believed, and with much reason, that events, commonplace in the London parks, were most unlikely to occur in Turlminster in the shadow of the Close.

She walked briskly along, her heels clicking on the pavement with the regular percussion of a guardsman, so that by the very sound of them one could have guessed at her physical well-being, that harmony of the body that comes of youth, health, high spirits, and determination. And in the semi-darkness between the lamps she would have seemed the embodiment of beauty: the neat compact figure moving to the rhythm of her step, the blonde dyed hair, gold now in that kindly light, the rounded face, the coarseness of complexion veiled, so that it shone with the suffused glow of the old Italian sculpture. This was not the Joy of the bar counter of the 'Fleece'; it was another woman, of whom, it must be said, Joy herself, steeped in the Hollywood tradition, would certainly have disapproved.

Her way back to the small house near the gasworks where she lived with an aunt, a semi-invalid, took her through some of the loneliest quarters of the town. Here the countryside had made a real invasion, as though to cut off, surround, and finally eliminate a sector so offensive to the view; the houses straggled planlessly, forlornly out into the fields, and a wild tangle of scrub and old overgrown slag-heaps lay around the gasometers themselves, relics of a battle of which nature was covering the scars. Here, too, in the by-ways between the roads it was darker than in the town and large patches of shadow lay beneath the trees. She quickened her step, for it was a little lonely and forbidding there on a night so overcast, with a wind that had risen after sunset whipping in the lazy clouds and driving them like sheep across the first quarter of the moon.

She had crossed the stile that led to the gasworks property when she heard a whistle from the shelter of the hedge. This sort of sound was no new thing to her, for the legacy of the American invasion still lingered with the youth of Turlmmster, and Joy, who perfectly represented the spirit of that epoch, had often been the object of this curious form of Transatlantic tribute.

'Who's that?' she said.

A figure detached itself from the shadows and moved across her path, a small figure not very much more substantial than her own, thin, rather feminine, with a shock of tousled hair. 'Oh, it's you,' she said. It was not to be gathered from her manner that she knew of this assignation, that she had arranged it, though grudgingly, the day before.

'Yes, it's me,' said Rupert. He added complainingly: 'You're late.'

'That's my affair.'

'You said you'd get off at half past nine. It's cold waiting out here.'

'So cold that I'm going right on home,' said Joy, always a little contemptuous of small men. And this was only a boy. It was too absurd that she should have committed herself to standing about in the fields with him on a damp and windy night. Nevertheless, there was something about Rupert.

'If you want to go home, you go,' he said. 'Only I always thought you kept your word.'

It was a telling point, for Joy had a fetish for honourable dealing – of a kind. But she would not give in easily and it was quite sharply that she replied: 'I keep my dates with men.'

'And I'm an infant? That's the line?'

'Well, how old are you? Seventeen?'

'And ten months. And you're twenty-one. Almost a teenager, Joy.'

'There's a world of difference,' she said, tossing her head, 'between a woman and a little boy.'

'Not all that much, surely. They seem to like much the same kind of thing.'

That was it: it was his voice. When he used it suggestively, as he had done then, she felt a little creepy, sensuous feeling crawling up her spine. 'Cheeky, aren't you!' she said. 'And just because I once let you kiss me and hold my hand.'

'I'll be a lot more cheeky yet.'

'Not if I know it.' But she had taken a step backwards and was now leaning against the stile. He followed up his advantage at once and placed himself beside her.

'If I'm such a kid, Joy, tell me this: why d'you bother with me?'

'I don't bother with you. I never think of you.'

'You bothered to make a date for to-night. Why d'you pick on me?'

'Because you kept worrying me and fussing round. It gets me talked about.'

'You came just to tell me that?'

'Yes,' she said, still leaning backward against the stile. As an attitude it was provocative.

'So there's not to be another night?'

'There's never been one. D'you think I like kids pawing me around!'

'I think you'll like it a lot,' he said. He was now very close to her, so close that she could feel the slight pressure of his arm against her own. Her voice was by no means so assured as she said again: 'Cheeky! That's all there is to you.'

'And as it's to be our last night, let's make it a good one, shall we, Joy?'

'Oh you!'

'Because it may be my last night too. If father finds I'm out to-night he'll put paid to everything.'

'So Daddy has to be asked when you go out after dark! My! you are grown up.' But the taunt had little sting. She was impressed in spite of herself with the romantic way he ran the gauntlet on her behalf.

'I'm here,' was all he said.

'You don't say! And now what?'

'Well, Joy, how d'you usually start? With a kiss?'

'Usually! You've a nerve!' Then suddenly she put her arm around his neck and kissed him full on the mouth.

He was quite taken aback, so much so that before he could take advantage of the change in her, Proteus-like she had changed again and drawn away. 'There's your kiss. And now you've had your evening, little boy.' For the first time that night he thought that he had lost her, for she had stood up and was moving away from him down the path. There was only one thing to do: he followed and took her arm. She shook herself free. 'Don't put your hands on me,' she said.

'You should have said that before you kissed me.'

'Why?' – with another change: 'Was it nice?'

'You're a devil,' he cried, 'a little devil with soft hands and lips and tongue. Soft.' She stood still, waiting for him to speak again. There was something about him, something that made her weak in all her body and her heart. 'And when you kiss me, Joy . . .'

'Yes?'

'Well you know what you do. I must have more.'

'Must?'

'You want it too.'

'Don't you know all about me!' she cried ironically. 'And don't you talk!'

This time he had summed her up correctly. He pulled her roughly round to him and kissed her as she had kissed him before.

It was a violent, unskilled performance but none the worse in her eyes for that. By the time he had released her she was responding with almost as much passion as his own, so that he cried triumphantly: 'And how nice was that?'

It was a mistake to speak at such a time. Joy was too experienced to give too much away too soon and he had given her a much-needed breathing space.

'Not bad for a little lad,' she said.

He tried to draw her close again but found, much to his surprise, that she could easily hold him off without even appearing to be doing so.

'Why do you treat me like this?' he said.

'Treat you like what?'

'You know.'

'I don't know.'

'First you kiss me, then you don't.'

'Everything's rationed nowadays,' said Joy, with a little vulgar laugh. 'Too much isn't good for babes.'

'Oh, that again! I'm sick of it. Why can't you forget it?'

'Because I have to look at you, that's why. Why can't you look at yourself?' Indeed a note of real contempt had crept into her voice at sight of the small figure scarcely taller than her own. It is only at the beginning of a love affair that women are capable of such observations. 'Why don't you cut your hair?'

'That's my business.'

'And whether I kiss or not's mine.'

'Kissing, "business"! Yes, I suppose it is with you.'

'Now you're rude,' cried Joy, with a great show of being offended, though in reality she never took much account of such remarks, regarding them as compliments if anything.

'Well, you've been rude too,' retorted Rupert. 'So it's quits.'

'It may be for you. Just because I was kind and kissed you once to-night you think you can say anything to me.'

'Twice.'

'Once. The second time *you* kissed *me*.' She was now down on his level – it was where she wanted herself to be.

'We'll try again and see who kisses which,' he said.

'Oh no. Now I'm going home. You'd better be off too or you'll find Daddy waiting with the stick.'

'I don't care a damn for him,' cried Rupert.

'Tut, tut! Fancy saying that of Dad!'

'Well I don't. All I care about is you.'

'Aren't we romantic now!' said Joy, every bit as much enthralled by the relationship as the young man himself. It was not often that she could bring such a mixture of contempt and passion to a love affair. 'My, we are romantic! What a sheikh!'

Rupert was sufficiently perceptive to see where his advantage lay and to appreciate the virtue of the practical. 'Oh, I'm not going to go sloppy over you,' he said. 'Don't worry: I won't moon around.'

'You certainly won't round me.'

'But I meant it all the same. I do care for you: for the certain things about you that a man can reach.'

'What things?' said Joy.

She heard the sharp intake of his breath, felt him move towards her and the almost painful grip of his hand on the fleshy roundness of her arm. It was a dangerous, new, delicious moment with so unusual and so young a man.

He said in a low voice: 'Do you want me to tell you, Joy?'

'No, I don't. I don't want to be talked of like a fat pig in a sty.'

Nevertheless, as she had hoped, he spoke the words, violently, for he was moved and passionate, falteringly, for he was young. She pretended to be horrified by what he said, was indeed surprised how much he knew. She would have to watch him carefully in future and make no more allowances for his age. 'You're too young to know such things,' she said. 'You're much too young. Why, you're a boy.'

'What's that got to do with it?'

'Because it's wrong you should know. And then to say such things to me!'

'You asked for it.'

'I didn't. How was I to guess you were going to insult me!'

He repeated dourly, surprised and hurt at her reaction: 'I still say you wanted it.'

'There you go again! You must think I'm one of those bad women on the streets.'

'But, Joy, I don't.' Indeed he did not, for no thoughts of

comparisons or categories had come to him; there had been no room for any other emotion than the physically overwhelming one of her body in his arms.

'I can't think where you learnt to say such things,' she said, but in much softer tones.

'You taught me when we kissed. Now teach me more.'

'Well, you *are* a cool one!'

'I'm not, you know,' he said, and he put his hand on hers. It was moist and fevered, a woman's hand, long and tapering like his mother's but possessed of a most deceptive strength. 'I'm not cool about you, Joy, not cool at all. I meant those words.' His arm had slid around her underneath her coat and she did not stir. 'You wanted me to mean them too,' he said. 'Didn't you? You wanted them. I know.'

She did not resist as he drew her back towards the stile, she stayed quite still as she felt his lips on hers. Slow in her first reactions, some moments passed before she awoke to the full passionate fervour of his kiss.

It was long past eleven when he unlatched the kitchen door in Colbert Row and began his cautious passage up the stairs.

8

MR ANDERSON was out of the room and on the stairs before his wife could recover herself or say a word. He thought he understood now the meaning of the kettle on the hob, the convivial beginning of the night, and the double deception practised on him had aroused sensations he never remembered having felt before. Rupert, who had got no farther than the landing, was lucky to escape actual injury as he was seized by the coat collar, dragged downstairs and thrust into the sitting-room. The scene was sufficiently humiliating to them all; for Rupert, still in the turmoil of undreamed-of triumph, the heir of recollections tender, fierce, unbelievably sweet and passionate, the shock was by far the most severe. But Mr Anderson, intent only on his anger which he felt as an unbearable burden on the spirit, naturally saw nothing new about his son – only the fulfilment of an old disloyalty. He would have liked, so violent were his emotions, to thrash him there before his mother's eyes, and was restrained only by the belief that this would be unjust, the understanding that the real criminal to be punished was his wife. So it was on her that his rage first fell.

'You knew he was out,' he cried. 'You knew.'

'Did I?' Mrs Anderson was by far the calmest of the three.

'Of course you knew. You tried to trick me.' The memory of the little matrimonial scene so coolly staged returned to him so that in his humiliation he cried: 'Your whole manner this evening was a trick, a mean pretence. You disobeyed me this afternoon and you helped him to disobey again to-night.'

'You seem very certain of your facts.'

'Don't deny it. You knew the boy was out. You knew.'

'Yes, of course I knew,' said Mrs Anderson. Her voice was very quiet. She was too experienced to waste energy on the preliminaries of a quarrel.

'There! You admit it. Could there be anything more dis-loyal!'

'I never told mother I was going out to-night,' said Rupert.

'You hold your tongue.'

'But I didn't,' he said, for in some strange way this assertion, which was true, helped to restore his shattered self-esteem. 'Mother didn't know.'

'Is that so, Laura?'

'Yes.'

'But you found out he had gone?'

'Must I always repeat myself with you!' wondered Mrs Anderson, with the affectation of a yawn.

'That's your idea of loyalty, I suppose!'

She looked from her son to him with great significance as she replied: 'Yes, it is.' There could have been no clearer indication of where her affections lay.

Mr Anderson turned towards his son.

'Perhaps you'll explain where you've been to-night?' he said.

'Out for a walk.'

'With whom?'

'With no one. I looked in at the dance.'

'Which dance?'

'The "Pop" at the Assembly Rooms.'

'And yet you heard my orders at breakfast this morning?'

'Orders again!' cried Laura, less wise at moments when her son was being attacked. 'I've heard enough of them. Leave the boy alone.'

Mr Anderson, his anger reinforced by this ill-timed interruption, turned his back pointedly on his wife. 'You knew I had forbidden you to leave the house to-day?'

'Yes.'

'And yet not once, but twice you disobeyed me. This afternoon you went to Ringby to the circus.'

'When mother says . . . '

Mr Anderson took a step towards his son. His fists were clenched and there was a blank, sleep-walking expression in his eye that the boy had never seen before. In his youth he had been punished by his father, dispassionately, in the way of discipline, now he recognized something else, the desire to inflict punishment for its own sake, the desire to hurt. He moved – it was an involuntary action – towards his mother, but a little gleam of his own hatred shone out in response.

'Get out!' said Mr Anderson, recovering himself with an effort. He was breathing heavily, for the weight of oppression was almost stifling him. 'Get out of here! Go on. Go to bed, do you hear?'

'You'd best go, darling,' said Mrs Anderson.

'Shall I, mother? Are you quite sure you'll be all right?'

She nodded. He went to her and kissed her: it was a familiar action, more significant than ever now in the light of the other kisses that had passed that night. He was aware of emotions in the background of his mind so shadowy that their form could not be grasped, ghosts of sensations half-forgotten, never comprehended, mingling with the more solid remembrances of Joy: the touch of fingers long ago, warmth, security, the yielding lips and tongue of late experience, the sensuous flesh. These were the stuff of life, his life; for their enjoyment he knew he had been born; in their protection he had grown and he must in turn protect them against the threatening alien world. As he passed his father on the way to bed his eyes reflected this inward vision of his mind, and Mr Anderson, even in the darkness of anger, was shocked by the expression there.

'I hope you're satisfied,' he said, as soon as the door had closed behind his son. 'A fine job you've done, putting him against me!'

'*That* you did yourself.'

But he saw now the width of the gulf that had been opened between them. 'No, you've worked for it. Ever since he was born you've petted and spoiled him. You resented it when I touched him. Now see where your pampering has led: to a disobedience so barefaced that it must be broken.'

'Don't put the blame on him.'

'Oh, I know where the blame lies all right. But I care for him, too, and I must hurt him to be kind. Laura, this evening has made up my mind. I am taking him away from school.'

She was alert at once, for the crucial moment had arrived and she must defend her own. 'What do you mean?' she said.

'It's very simple: he is coming into my office where I can keep my eye on him.'

'You can't do it.'

'I can and I will. Only strong action can help him now.

69

Discipline is necessary to him or he'll be a misery to himself and a danger to others all his life.'

'Discipline!' she cried in a voice shrill and vibrant with fury. 'You and your discipline! I have his future planned for him – a better future than you can give him in that dirty, sweaty office.'

'In your cousin's brewery, I suppose?'

'Yes, with Barry. He'll have him. It'll be the making of him. Barry can do everything for him, introduce him to people, to society – yes, don't laugh, to society – not to a few boors and clerks. He can become manager under Barry, yes, and go far beyond those brainless sor.s. Barry knows everyone. And you want him to moulder in an office where no decent fresh air has been for years!'

'I don't care for Barry, or his openings.'

'I know,' she cried, turning from one grievance to another, the original grievance of her life out of which all her antagonisms had grown. 'You never cared to rise. You were born to be a little dingy-town solicitor; you wanted to be; you are.'

'I've done my best,' he said.

'And what a mean little best it is!' she cried, beating her hands together in her distress. 'I could have married other men, real men with blood in them and ambition, and I was forced to come to you. I had to see my first child grow up like you – yes, a cold, spiritless little thing, just like you, only even more spiteful with her nasty, sneering ways, her tales.'

'Stop that about Margaret.'

'I won't. Here I have a son, a real son I can love – and I never loved you, never, never. He's to be sacrificed, and the other, she's to have everything. She spies on me. She watches me and comes here and reports to you.'

'What nonsense!' he said, watching with alarm the rising tide of her hysteria. 'She'd no idea that Rupert was to stay at home. You must see that.'

'It was deliberate. She hates her brother.'

'Laura, really! You don't know what you're saying. I know she's fond of him.'

'No, all she cares about is you – you and a dull, odious clergyman.' A thought struck her. 'She was with him to-night.'

'Yes, at Frances'.'

'How do you know, you fool? She can come creeping home at eleven and that's all right. But Rupert must be victimized.'

Mr Anderson had flushed at these insinuations. 'That was a monstrous suggestion,' he said, 'quite monstrous.'

'How do you know it wasn't true? How do you know she wasn't slinking round the lanes? You don't care to think it. Nothing is too good to be thought of her, nothing too bad about my boy.'

He said sadly, cut to the heart but still trying to reason with her: 'You can't think such things of her, Laura. You can't. As to being out late, you must remember that she's grown up and Rupert's a child of seventeen.'

'A child who's to be sacrificed,' cried Mrs Anderson, who knew the virtue of attacking on every front at once. 'It wouldn't do, would it, that he should do better than his father. It wouldn't do that he should succeed instead of being a failure all his life. Oh no! So he must go into an office and learn to smother common sense. He's not to be allowed to make good because that wouldn't be following in your steps.'

'What I am planning is for the best,' said her husband quietly. His rage had subsided as his wife's had grown; his feeling now was one of profound sadness as he remembered the hopes and passions of the past.

'Best! How can you tell? You've never tried to be anything but second rate. Barry can offer opportunity.'

'What I offer has the advantage of being sound.'

'And my cousin's isn't!' cried Laura, with a bitter laugh. 'You fool! Think of the money behind him, the influence. Ask anyone to compare your business with Barry's. What comparison can there be?'

'None. He is all you say. And I wouldn't trust a pound investment with him, never mind my son.'

Laura had now reached a point at which she would have been unrecognizable by her friends. They would have marvelled at the skill with which she normally disguised that odd misalignment of the mouth, now so obvious that her whole face seemed livid and distorted. 'You dare to say that of my cousin! You dare! You're not fit to be mentioned in the same breath with him.'

'I certainly don't want to be,' said Mr Anderson.

'You're jealous, that's all. He's rich and successful and you've failed.'

'I'm sorry for your sake, Laura: for my own I can tell you that I don't envy Barry anything.'

A little choking sound escaped her. 'How do you know? You don't know anything about him: what he was, what he is, what he's had.'

'I don't understand you,' said her husband slowly.

'He's too far above you, too far beyond your reach. He's everything you're not. And because he's my cousin you think you can insult him, though he's always been kind to you and tried to help you.'

'I could have been spared that, Laura. I've no use for his assistance.'

'That's just like you: you're not only a failure, you're proud and smug as well. You like your horrid cobwebbed offices because they were your father's, this barrack of a house I have to live in, dropping to bits with age.'

'Most people would be glad to live in it,' he said.

'Most people! Most people are up to date. Most people don't have dozens of stairs and landings and attics to keep clean. I know how I should live. And I'd have lived it too if only I'd not been fool enough to tie myself down to you.'

He said gently: 'When you took me you knew I wasn't wealthy, Laura.'

She flung herself back into a corner of the settee. 'I wasn't to know you had so little ambition that you'd be content to slum your way through life. And yet you've money enough to do the things you want. That precious girl could be sent to Oxford for three years. That was all right; it always is for Margaret. I noticed it wasn't done for Kay.'

'You know Kay never wanted it,' cried Mr Anderson, strung by the injustice of all this. 'She could have gone if she'd shown the slightest inclination.'

'You just sent her to the wall. And Rupert's to go too.'

They were back again on the main contentious ground. He was quite calm now – to make him so had been the object of her own ungoverned rage.

'I can only repeat,' he said, 'that I'm acting for the best.'

72

'And am I to be allowed no say?'

'You've had your say – for seventeen years. It's high time we had a change.'

'But, Robert . . .'

'It's no use, my mind's made up. He will come into my office and get a grounding in the law, then, after his military service, he can be articled in London. Alternatively, if he shows sufficient interest and ability he can read law at Oxford and go on to the Bar.'

'So if Barry offers to make his fortune for him, that's to be refused?'

Mr Anderson went over and sat down beside his wife. In spite of all that had been said he was still anxious to be reconciled.

'We've been over this dozens of times,' he said. 'I want what you want, the boy's happiness and success. Barry's is not the way of life for him; I'm sorry, but there it is. Things have come to my knowledge . . .' He paused.

'About the firm?' she said.

'Yes,' he replied uncomfortably.

'What things?'

'I can't tell you. You must forget I said that. I had no right to do so.'

'Nor reason, either.'

'Laura, you must take it from me that we should be doing no kindness to Rupert by putting him with the firm.'

'I don't care for your vile insinuations,' said his wife, drawing away into her corner of the settee. 'I know Barry.'

'I'm afraid you don't. But that's beside the point. I must tell you that I'm determined about Rupert. I'm more than willing to meet you on most points, but this is a matter so serious that I must insist.'

'Have you thought,' said Laura, 'that I might insist as well?'

'Yes.'

'Impasse.'

'There will be no impasse,' said Mr Anderson grimly. 'I reminded you earlier this evening that I have rights, and I shall certainly exercise them.'

'And I shall exercise mine.'

'That's your affair. Believe me, I want nothing better than a friendly settlement. But you have said things to-night . . . such things.' He paused, remembering the sound of them, the expression in her eyes. 'I don't suppose there's much left for you and me. As I'm hateful to you it might be best . . . '

'To separate?'

'I'd say so but for Rupert. Margaret and Kay are very normal persons and grown up anyway, but on Rupert the effects of a broken home would be serious. It's so necessary, Laura, that over him we should agree.'

'I will agree to anything reasonable,' she said.

'My plan is reasonable. The boy will be with us for the time being. He needs us, as this evening showed. In return I'll promise not to impose any more restrictions.'

'You were mad to try to do so in the first place.'

'Let's forget the incidents,' said Mr Anderson. 'If I give you that promise will you agree to my plans for him?'

He was looking at her almost hopefully, for her whole manner had become subdued and reasonable. His was the better case, he knew, and she had always been a realist.

'No,' she said.

'Don't decide hastily.'

'I will never agree. Surely you never thought I would!'

'I hoped,' he said sadly, 'that you'd think of the boy and what was best for him, not of old grievances.'

'And you seriously thought I'd see my son thrown on the scrap heap just to satisfy your jealousy! You must be mad.'

'What jealousy?' he cried. 'You've said so many queer things to-night, there's no understanding you at all.'

'You haven't tried. But you can understand this, I hope: I will not accept your decision.'

'I can enforce it.'

'Try!' she said. 'Try!' She was sitting quite still, but not all that evening had he felt more strongly conscious of her power.

He gave an uneasy laugh.

'Laura, don't be absurd. That almost sounded like a threat.'

'Take it how you like,' she said. 'But you will never have him, never; I won't let you. I don't care what I do but you shall never have him – for he's mine.'

9

RUPERT yawned, stretched out an arm, then rolled over on to his side to find that his mother was sitting in the bedside chair. He had known somehow that she was in the room, a presence linked with the images of his half-conscious waking mind.

'Hello,' he said.

She looked down at him lying there drowsy on the verge of sleep, sleek and graceful like some little animal at the entrance to its burrow in the early sunshine of the spring. His hair was tousled – even more than usual, his eyes misty with the dew of sleep, and there was about him an indefinable air of warmth and secret knowledge.

'Good morning, dear,' she said.

He reached out a hand from the bedclothes and laid it on her own. It was strange to see those three hands linked upon the coverlet, so similar in texture, in size, in shape of nail, a little hydra of the personality they shared. So they remained quite comfortably while minutes passed, and as sleep receded the memory of his father and of Joy returned. He asked the time; she told him it was half past nine. 'It's late,' said Rupert, snuggling down more cosily between the sheets. 'Half past nine. I'd best get up.'

'There's no hurry, dear. Sleep on if you're tired.'

He yawned, drawing back his lips and showing all his regular, sharp-pointed teeth. At such moments he looked like a sleepy, bad-tempered tiger-cub; the narrowed eyes, the ears, small and slightly tufted, all added to the effect, at once charming and a trifle sinister.

'Where were you last night, dear?' she said.

'Where? I told you: at the Pop.'

'But were you really, Rupert?'

His eyes widened in surprise. They were so candid, such reflexions of her own. 'Of course I was,' he said.

She looked at him indulgently. There was something in his manner, a certain repose and satisfaction that told a tale. He had been with a girl – that much was obvious, had taken her home from the dance, perhaps, and had lingered in her doorway for a kiss. Of the existence of Joy, of her extreme complaisance, she never guessed, and like most mothers, in obedience to some deep-seated instinct, she minimized the growth of sexual feeling in her son.

'Did you meet any nice girls at the dance?' she said.

'Girls? Yes, one or two. Why d'you ask?'

'I just thought . . . Oh, never mind. But you were back so late. And you were wrong, really, to have gone at all.' These were the first words of reproach she had found for him and they were spoken in a voice so mild as to rob them of their sting.

'I know. I'm sorry. He had to catch me: that was just my luck.'

'But it was such a foolish risk, particularly after we'd been to Ringby.'

'Ah!' said Rupert, rolling over on to his back. 'And how did he find out that?'

'Margaret told him.'

'Did she, the little cat! I'll pay her back.'

'She made a point of telling him,' said Mrs Anderson. 'That was the start of all the trouble.'

'Poor you!' said Rupert, letting his fingers play along her hands from the knuckles to the wrist. 'It was awful for you.'

'It wasn't what he said, dear: I take no account of that. It's what he threatened to do to you.'

The pleasant visions of the evening had now faded right into the background of the young man's mind. He drew his hand away from his mother and sat up in bed.

'What did he say he'd do?'

'He's taking you away from school.'

'He can't mean it, mother.'

'And he's putting you into his office.'

'I won't go.'

'He can't force you,' said Mrs Anderson, recapturing Rupert's hand. 'He can't. He talks of rights, but that's all nonsense in these times.'

'Well then?'

'But he can refuse to support you unless you fall in with his plans. He can refuse to pay your school bills, dear.'

'Then I'll go to Uncle Barry's.'

Laura looked distractedly at her son. 'We can't be sure he'll have you,' she replied.

'But, mother, you've always said . . . '

'I know, I know. He'll take you on as an apprentice, but he won't pay you or keep you until you've proved yourself. How can I explain it? He's got sons, you see, and your Aunt Rose would be jealous if you were brought into the house.'

All this was news to Rupert, to whom the brewery of Barry Clarke had always seemed a kind of magic castle with the gates wide open for the arrival of the prince. And he was disturbed by the indecision on his mother's face. It was the first time that she had failed him. 'I don't understand,' he said. 'I thought I could always go to Uncle Barry.'

'And you shall,' cried Laura, who had caught the implied reproach. 'You shall.' But the perplexity on her face was all too obvious. She saw in his eyes the knowledge that her promises were valueless. She pulled her chair closer to the bed and gripped his hands tightly, so tightly that it hurt. 'You must believe me, Rupert. You don't think, surely, that I'd let him spoil your life! Anything rather than that. I'll write to Barry, I'll see him; there are ways. But for the present you must do as your father says.'

'Leave school, you mean?'

'And go into his office. We've no choice.' She saw the bewildered, scornful expression on his face and hurried on: 'It'll be only for a little time, darling. I'll find a way. I promise, I promise that I will.'

She would find a way. And not only to defeat her husband's intentions for their son, for she had remembered other incidents from the previous night, incidents which to so neurotic a woman cried out imperiously for revenge.

'Why's he doing this to me?' demanded Rupert.

'How can I explain that, dear? How can I explain jealousy and old resentments? I suppose, really, he's punishing me through you.'

'But for what, mother? That's what I can't understand.'

'For things I've said, perhaps; for not loving Margaret the way he wanted; for loving you.'

'And he hates me for that? Well, then, I hate him.'

A thrill ran through her as she heard these words, the expression of her deepest inward thoughts. But habit and morality find their place in even the most unmoral human souls, and it was not without some genuine feeling that she reproved him. 'Rupert, you mustn't say such things. It's unnatural.'

'But I mean them. What's he ever done for me?'

'He brought you up. He's loved you in his way.'

'In his way! Why do you defend him? You know he's always been against us.'

Laura drew back her hand upon the coverlet. She was uncertain, even in her own mind, how far her defence of her husband was the result of honourable emotions, the recollection of his kindness, his love, their early days of intimacy, how far it depended on the knowledge that by defending him she was increasing the antagonisms of her son. Some vague sense of danger may have reached her, some recognition of the evil seed that she was sowing, some premonition of disaster. 'He's done it for what he thinks is best,' she said.

'Taking me from school? Forcing me into an office?'

'Yes, even that.'

He sat bolt upright against the pillows. 'You're not on his side, too?' he said.

At that all her scruples vanished, for she saw before her the danger always present in her secret thoughts – the possibility of losing him. Besides this her own honour and her husband's were of no account. 'You're everything to me,' she said.

'And yet you talk like father. You say the same things exactly.'

'But you're wrong,' she cried. 'I just didn't want you to misjudge him. How can you think that I'd go against the only person that I love?'

'I'm only going by your words,' he said, secure in his advantage.

'I've told you that I'll find a way. You shan't be sacrificed, no matter what I have to do. Only you must give me time.

'But while you're finding the time, mother,' complained

Rupert pettishly, 'I'll be shut up in his office. And I'll be missing school: that's a thing I won't forgive him.'

'I'm so sorry about it, dear.'

'But he's not sorry, is he? Of course he's not: he's glad. I saw him last night, I saw how he felt for me. If you hadn't been there he would have tried to hit me.' As he spoke he remembered the expression on his father's face, his own feeling of disgust and impotence as he was dragged downstairs. His voice rose. 'He'd best not try,' he said. 'Just let him try to put his hands on me again!'

'Oh, Rupert, he wouldn't.'

'Wouldn't he! I saw. He'd like it if I was a kid again and he could take his stick to me. He did before when I was small. Why did you let him, mother?'

She was now quite on the defensive, unable to meet his accusing eye. 'I tried, Rupert. You must understand that he was stronger. You were a child and he had a father's right to correct you.'

'Correct me! I like that! I remember his corrections. Well, he may have been the stronger then but times have changed. He's still bigger, but just let him try to correct me now!'

'You wouldn't strike him, surely?' said Laura with widely opened eyes. Neither she nor her son seemed to find these threats ridiculous, even in the light of the humiliating experience of the previous night.

'I would. With my fists, with anything to hand. He's a bully and I'll serve him as a bully. He's treated you badly, too, and that's something else I won't forget.'

'I must bear my own load,' said Laura, with a martyr's sigh. This was provocative enough, but she had never hidden from her son her version of her miserable married life, had held him, indeed, on the string of this unhappiness. That such encouragement was dangerous now that the marionette was growing up she only dimly realized; that it was disloyal she never considered for an instant.

'I don't know why you've stood for it,' he said. For you, her eyes replied. 'No, it beats me why. He doesn't belong with us a bit. I've known it, oh for years, but I've never seen it in his face until last night. He hates us because we don't fall in with

79

everything he wants – not like Margaret. Is that why he feels so differently for her?'

'I suppose he loves her,' answered Mrs Anderson, in reluctant tones.

'Well, we're three to two, for it's clear enough he doesn't care for Kay.'

'You shouldn't say such things,' said Laura, in half-hearted reproval, but she did not draw her hand away. 'Such things just aren't spoken of.'

'Why? It's true, isn't it? Of course it is. Well, now that I'm grown up I don't see why I should stand by and let him bully us and make us go his way.'

'You forget that he's the head of the family, dear, and that he pays for us.'

A particularly alert expression had sprung into Rupert's eyes. 'Haven't we other money?' he said.

'None, dear.'

'What about grandfather's trust?'

'It only comes to you when you're twenty-one, and anyway it's very small.'

'Well, what about Uncle Barry, then? He's rich, isn't he?'

'Very rich,' said Laura, seeing in her mind's eye the brewery, the lorries, the great dray-horses, the oast-houses, and the tied hotels, Barry himself, opulent and mellow with his gold hunter and moustaches, the manor house he lived in, a mausoleum of pompous oil paintings and antiques, the cars and horses, the butler – particularly the butler, the living seal of a great success. 'Yes, very, very rich. But he's not your uncle really, as you know.'

'Isn't he? We always call him Uncle Barry.'

'He's your cousin actually – your cousin once removed. My father and his mother were brother and sister, you see.'

'Oh,' said Rupert, who clearly did not think much of this relationship. 'And he got all the money and you didn't?'

'It came from his father, dear, from outside our family.'

'Then why,' said Rupert, 'does he take such an interest in us? Seems to me that from his point of view we can't amount to much.'

'Because he has family feeling, I expect. And he always liked you, right from the time when you were a little baby kicking in your cot. "Jolly little beggar!" he'd say; those were his very words the first time he ever saw you.' A softer expression had taken possession of her face, so that her angular features seemed for a moment quite rounded and composed. 'You were, too,' she said.

'And now I'm not?'

'No, now you're different' – giving his hand a squeeze. 'You're what I want: I always wanted a good-looking, self-reliant son. But when you were a baby you were the chubbiest thing imaginable, quite lovably fat and stupid. Barry said that too.'

'And what did father say?'

'Oh your father thought the same. He was very proud that at last he'd got a son. Yes, you were all the rage. And later, the presents! Uncle Barry bought you a little woolly dog.'

'A live one?'

'Why of course. Don't you remember? It bit Margaret.'

They both smiled at that, in high good humour with one another.

'Seems like Uncle Barry always had the right ideas,' he said.

'He did. The things he gave you! I think your Auntie Rose got quite jealous over them.'

'I don't think she likes me much,' said Rupert.

'She'd no reason to be jealous,' replied his mother, with a frown. 'But then your cousins twice – or is it three times?' – removed, her sons, I mean, were always unattractive little brats.'

'I don't suppose they love me either.'

'That won't hurt. You keep in with your Uncle Barry and you can snap your fingers at them and at Auntie Rose.'

But Rupert seemed perplexed. Small lines had appeared on his forehead and at the corners of the mouth, giving him a petulant appearance. 'If Uncle Barry could afford all those presents when I was young,' he said, 'why can't he step in now and help us when we need it? He could give us money.'

'My dear, one can't do such things. They'd be misunderstood.'

'How, misunderstood?'

'Because, as I've said, he's not an uncle, just a cousin. He's got to think of his sons and Auntie Rose. Even if he did offer, we couldn't accept.'

'But why?'

81

'Because people don't do such things.'

'I think that's silly,' said Rupert, and the petulant lines had deepened on his face. 'I expect our family did something for him once when he was young.'

'It was just kindness,' said Mrs Anderson. 'He was good to all my children.' She gave a wry little smile. 'You and Kay particularly had such fatal charm.'

He ignored the smile.

'So it comes to this,' he said: 'we've got no money and we can't expect any, and Uncle Barry won't take me on a paying basis into his brewery and Auntie Rose won't have me in the house?'

'I'm afraid so for the moment, dear.'

'So father has his way, and I must leave school and go into an office and slave away at work I'll never understand. That's a nice look out.'

She stood up and bent down over the bed. 'It won't be for long,' she said. 'I'll see your uncle. I'm sure things can be arranged.'

'How soon?'

'Darling, just as soon as I'm able.'

'It's a nice look out,' he said again. 'Everything I wanted's taken from me. I've got to suffer: I'm the one.'

She leaned down and kissed him on the forehead though he had tried to turn his head away. 'I've promised,' she said. 'I've promised, darling. No matter what it costs me I'll find a way. Oh, darling, I'll find a way.'

As soon as Margaret had left his aunt's house, John Paget sat down in his study to put his thoughts on paper. The result, posted late that night, was delivered at 'The Templars' about noon, a surprising effusion from the pen of such a cautious, reticent young man.

Dear Margaret [it ran],

I couldn't go to bed without trying to explain to-night. You must have thought me strange on Farshot, but I blame myself less for what I said and did than for what I didn't say and do. I could have explained all this when we were alone together; I should have done so, but I was never good at explanations. It's a fault in me, and has been since my childhood, that I shut my eyes and put off things – even pleasant things – until to-morrow. Then again, I preach too much and put argument for understanding. All these faults of mine have come between us and have complicated our relationship. And that relationship is actually a simple one. Think of it: we stood there on the hill divided by nothing but a gulf of words. I blame myself for this: I advanced and retreated in a foolish way, never finding the words, the simple words I wanted, the words I meant. No wonder that you said you didn't want to hear them spoken, for what words of mine, you must have thought, coming on top of all that rigmarole, could have been worth hearing? And yet, as it happens, you were wrong. The simple truth is that I love you. There now! I have said it at last.

You must think that I'm cowardly because I write the words I couldn't say. I was afraid, perhaps, that if I said them you would laugh at me, argue with me, certainly, from force of habit. Don't think because you find that I have written them that they are less heartfelt: they are more so, for what's lacking in me is courage, not conviction. Will you forgive my cowardice? I think you ought to, Margaret, for in a sense you were cowardly, too.

So far I have spoken only of my own feelings, and I suspect you have known them for some time. I can't judge your feelings, though lately I have felt that we were sharing something that can't be put in words. Perhaps my behaviour this evening disillusioned you. I hope not. I hope that you understand what prompted me on Farshot, or 'unprompted' me, as you might say. You see, I was afraid. I know well enough how much I want your love, but I know also how little worthy I am of winning it.

I don't say things well, Margaret. I suppose I ought to tell you all the things about you that I remember as I write: of the physical *you* that, after all, is the mould of love. But somehow my feelings won't go into the pages of a letter, and I know, as well, that there is more to love, far more, than mere physical attraction.

This letter hasn't been an easy one to write. I wrote it only because I couldn't bear to think that for another day and night you would imagine me weak and indecisive as on Farshot Hill, cold and aloof from you as I was later in the evening when you were talking with my aunt. I felt quite desperate as you left the room. I wanted to say in an impracticable instant all the things I should have said, to take your hand again, to kiss you on the doorstep – to the great scandal of the neighbourhood. And so I sat down right away and wrote you this – a coward's offering, if you like, but a penitent's, as well. Read it in that light and try to understand

your
JOHN.

She put the letter down on the bedside table and lay back among the pillows, her mind in a whirl of emotion. There it lay, the letter that had answered the longings of her heart, a neat letter with well-spaced lines written in his erect and careful script, almost an echo of the personality of the man she loved. She knew that she herself could never have written it; there would have slipped from her own passionate intensity at least some semblance of an error, a blot, an erasure, something to break the accuracy of those measured lines. But the contents were more reassuring. Knowing him, it was impossible not to feel that much emotion had gone to the making of this display; she could not be mistaken, for he had written so carefully, late at night, had inserted alongside his more prosaic utterances true words of love.

She could have wished that he had not mentioned, even jokingly, the 'scandal of the neighbourhood', one more touch that displayed his shyness with the world; she could have wished that he had said how much her hair pleased him, her mouth and eyes, even her body, for she loved him and she was young. Yet he had said he loved her, and judged by that one sentence his letter had succeeded in reaching to her heart. After that all doubts must fall away. He might be diffident and shy; it might well be that she would have to struggle desperately to reach that inner core where physical attraction would mean as much to him as it now meant to her; these were objections to their love affair and only to be answered by the one supreme reason that she wanted him, that he was necessary to her. For like so many intellectual women who do not let intellect past the bedroom door, she had a surprisingly robust sense of sex: she wanted a home and family of her own, she wanted a husband and she wanted love. All these sensations, hitherto held in check by her loyalty to John, by her friendship for him, by shyness and a surface prudery, were now released by the letter he had sent. For a moment there shone in her face the family resemblance to her mother that most friends professed they could not see, a resemblance less of feature than of spirit, some part of that legacy of pride and self-indulgence that Mrs Anderson had passed on to her children, even to that elder daughter who, except in moments of great stress, was so unlike her. If John had seen her he would have been astounded at the transformation – astounded and quite certainly afraid in the presence of a spirit so much more alive than his, so much more violent and barbaric. Far, far away would have seemed that harmless dalliance over tea, the little academic jokes and arguments, the intercourse of two superior minds; indeed so extreme were her sensations that she herself became afraid.

She got up, and went over to the mirror and smoothed her temples with her hands. There in the glass, had she been able to stand apart from her emotions, she would have seen a fascinating study in heredity, the spirit of one parent momentarily peering out from behind the features of the other. But alarmed though she was by the unaccustomed feeling raging in her heart, she had no sooner reached the mirror than she ceased to diagnose herself and began to see herself for John. One arm dropped to her side, with the other hand she patted and smoothed her hair, charmingly disordered by contact with the pillows, touched her forehead and the corners of her mouth, feeling the lines that had gathered there and which now, in the absence of make-up, declared themselves remorselessly. She was thirty-one.

She would write to him. She would write to him at once. But, fresh from the inspection at the mirror, was it for John that she sat down at her desk, took up pen and paper and began feverishly to write? It was not consciously that she remembered other incidents now ten years old, other letters she had received and which lay now, though their exact location was forgotten, in an old trunk in the boxroom of the house. There had been kisses then and open declarations, and at the end of them a parting that had wrung her heart. She would have been hard put to it now to remember him, the tone of his voice, the touch of his hand, the look of him that had once been more real to her than her own existence. But as she wrote the personality of John was not much clearer, blurred in the vague memory of the repetition of once familiar events, the impulses of the flesh and the dread of loneliness.

It was a very different letter from his: the words spilled out unevenly on the lines, the lines on the page; they were dictated from the heart, certainly no grammarian, but their meaning was plain. Yes, she would meet him; yes, she forgave him, though there was nothing to forgive; certainly she understood. How could he have thought otherwise? It was she who had behaved foolishly on the hill, though why she did not know; she had been afraid, she supposed, of the words that she now welcomed; she had at one and the same time provoked him and repulsed him, though all the time she had loved him as she loved him now. It was a candid letter; an expressive letter full of a passionate fervour that she had not attempted to disguise; it was an eager letter, the effect of which would be explosive on any true lover – and having written it she put on her hat and coat and descended hurriedly into the sitting-room for a stamp. There she encountered Mrs Anderson.

This was no accidental meeting, for Laura had been waiting for her daughter. From Kay, an ally of long standing, she had heard of the arrival of the letter and much about the state of her elder daughter's heart; it was valuable information on which to base a campaign of which this meeting in the sitting-room was the necessary preliminary. It nearly miscarried at the outset all the same, as Margaret, with the barest greeting to her mother, made directly for the bureau and began to rummage there.

'What are you looking for, dear?' enquired Mrs Anderson. It was not a very sensible question, seeing that Margaret was holding the envelope quite openly, nevertheless, it suited Laura to be ignorant on a matter so close to the enquiry she had in mind.

'For a stamp, mother. Why does father always hide them?'

'You'll find one in the left-hand second drawer,' said Mrs Anderson. She waited while her daughter verified this, then went on with her attack. 'I wanted to speak to you,' she said. 'About last night, about what I said of John. I'm sorry. I spoke hastily and unjustly.'

'That's all right,' replied Margaret uncomfortably. She was still mystified by what had occurred, the extraordinary reaction to her words, the raised voices, her father's face at breakfast, so worn and sad.

'No, it was wrong of me. I want to explain myself.'

'But just now, mother, I've got to post a letter. I'm rather in a hurry. Do you mind?'

Mrs Anderson shrugged her shoulders. It was a gesture of great elegance, a humorous commentary on a mother's place in the rushing modern world.

'The next post doesn't go till four o'clock,' she said. 'I had wanted to speak to you, dear, but of course if you must get that letter in the box, you must, and I'll just have to wait.'

There was no possible reply to this, and Margaret sat down opposite her mother, right on the edge of her chair so that she seemed to be perched there like a bird.

'Well, it's like this, dear,' continued Laura comfortably. 'You know there was trouble yesterday. Yes, over Rupert. It's regrettable that over him your father and I just don't agree. I'm afraid my whole manner was affected by it and as a result I said things I didn't mean, things that in any case would have been better left unsaid.'

'But, mother, when I came in I remember thinking how good-tempered you both were.'

'Trouble was already brewing,' said Laura darkly. 'Naturally I'm not asking you to take sides, indeed I don't want to mention the disagreement any more and only did so to explain my rudeness about John. I knew, you see, that there was going to be trouble, and, as it happened, some casual words of yours just touched it off.'

'I didn't understand it. I still don't.'

'Never mind. It was all about some misunderstanding of what your father said. Apparently he'd ordered Rupert not to go out with me – what a storm in a tea-cup it all was! But what I'm sorry for is that I said such things of John. They hurt you: I could see that.'

'I thought they were unjust,' said Margaret.

'Yes,' agreed Mrs Anderson, with a covert glance at her daughter's face. 'Yes, they were. But even if they had been true I never would have said them if I'd known.'

'Known?'

'Yes, about you and John.'

'But, mother . . . '

'I think you might have told me, dear,' complained Mrs Anderson in a gently reproachful voice. 'I am interested in you. Have I behaved so badly to you that you've decided that you can't confide in me?'

Margaret looked even more uncomfortable at this and sat even further forward in her chair. She was surprised at her mother's knowledge, uncertain of its extent, and quite undecided how much it would be prudent for her to say.

'You've always known I was a friend of John's,' she said.

'But not how much of a friend, my dear. Ah yes' – the smile was now as reproachful as the voice – 'don't try to tell me that it isn't so. I can see it in your face.' But all she could see really was perplexity. 'And those letters: they're something new.'

'Surely I can write a letter without giving notice to the family!' said Margaret, a trifle sharply.

'My dear, of course. I'm not prying. But it's a new departure, and in my experience new departures in old friendships very often spell romance.' Margaret had half risen from her chair. 'My dear, don't be offended. I only wanted you to know that I'm sorry that I said such things last night. I hope that you accept the apology.'

'Mother, of course.'

'You don't really,' said Mrs Anderson, allowing a hurt and worried frown to appear between her eyes. 'If you did you'd be candid with me. It's a terrible thing when a mother is considered an intruder in her daughter's friendships.'

'But I don't think of you in that way.'

'You say that, but you treat me as an intruder all the same. Put yourself in my place for a moment. What can be of interest to a mother if it isn't the well-being of her children, their hopes and their feelings, their friendships, their love?'

'I'm sorry,' said Margaret, a little touched by this display of maternal feeling which she did not know for certain to be false. 'I don't want you to think that. Only you've Kay and Rupert, and somehow I've never thought you were very interested in me.'

'My dear!'

'I don't mean that brutally. Why should you be? I haven't been very much help to you.'

'Why should I be!' cried Mrs Anderson, metaphorically invoking Heaven for its aid. 'A mother not interested in her daughter! I know we disagree and that you see your father's point of view more easily than mine, as you have every right to do, but surely you and I are not so far divided? What have I done to lose your confidence?'

'Nothing, mother. You haven't lost it.'

'Well then?' enquired Laura, putting the keystone into place. And having said this she sat right back in her chair and waited for the confidences that she knew must be forthcoming. They were quite a time on the way, for Margaret, from long experience, was not devoid of all suspicion, but in the end they came.

'I'm friendly with John. Very friendly.'

'Yes, I know.'

'He is a little more than friendly' – her voice dropped to a whisper – 'and *I* am, too.'

'Margaret, I'm glad. I'm so glad.'

She waited avidly for more. But after a long moment of silence she realized that without urging her daughter would go no further on the road. Nevertheless, what had happened was apparent; it could be read in the girl's face, so rapt and still. 'It is just the thing I would have wished for you,' she said.

'Would you, mother? When you disapprove of him, I mean? When you think him selfish?'

This time the look on Laura's face was really masterly; reproach was mixed with humorous appreciation of the point

89

her daughter had just scored, while the whole effect was so disarming as to ensure against a repetition. 'You see, you haven't forgiven me, dear,' she said.

Margaret was instantly contrite.

'Oh, mother, but I have.'

'Forgive my saying that it doesn't sound like it. I don't blame you, for it's never nice to hear things said against those we love.' Even this word now went unchallenged. 'But I think, all the same, that you might make some allowances for me and for the state everyone was in last night. You don't think, surely, that if I really disapproved of John I could be happy in your marriage? And yet you must see that I welcome it.'

It was a bold advance into the heart of the enemy's defences.

'There's been no mention of marriage,' cried her daughter, rising from her chair. Nor had there been, for that had been another of his letter's failings. 'You're wrong. There's been no mention of it.'

'Well, my dear, I thought ... the way things have gone, I mean. There's more than friendship between you, as you say, and I naturally thought ... '

'No, no, no!'

'I'm sorry,' said Mrs Anderson, watching with scientific detachment the agitation on her daughter's face. 'I thought it was all settled. I would never have spoken if I'd known.'

'Nothing's settled. I knew you were jumping to conclusions.'

'But they were true conclusions,' insisted Laura, who had no further need to indulge the girl now that she knew the truth. 'You'll see. It will come out as I say. And a most desirable match it is in every way, with two people so suited to one another, so steady and sensible, and so ... mature.'

JOHN PAGET'S feelings as he composed his fateful letter had been warmer than Margaret had allowed him credit for; he had felt desolate when she had left the house, had sat down to write a love letter and had not wholly failed; but with the morning his native caution had returned. It was not that he did not want a wife, it was not that he did not care for Margaret; nevertheless, in spite of his sensations of the previous night, the remembrance of her smile and the gentle touch of hands, it was a relief to realize that he had not actually proposed.

The reverse side of yesterday's picture was now for the first time presented to his mind: little thoughts of their religious differences occurred to him, her Nonconformity, his own ambitions; he even found himself contrasting Mr Anderson, small country-town solicitor and father of three children, with Canon Willoughby, a friend, even a patron in a way, who had a daughter too. Miss Willoughby – strange, inconsequential thought for a man so close to matrimony – was twenty-four and was an only child. It was in the train of this that he remembered how he had told Margaret that he loved her, words that had seemed inevitable a few hours before – remembered, and almost saw himself, his cautious, plodding self, as a creature of unreasoned impulse. Though Margaret had felt instinctively that he had said too little, he now felt sure that he had said too much. What had passed between them, after all, in the years that they had known each other? A great deal of conversation, a lot of argument, a handclasp, not one kiss. And now, in obedience to the impulse of a moment, he had pledged himself – well, almost pledged himself – to be a lover. There could not be the slightest doubt of how his overture would be received: she loved him and would respond in the spirit of his words last night, a spirit now modified in the sober light of day. Really, he reflected, there were disadvantages in such a match. It could not be expected that the parish would accept it without a great deal of unkind comment, it could not be expected that his vicar would approve, still less that powerful patron, Canon Willoughby, a stickler for orthodoxy, who looked on Methodism as the fountain-head of heresy. And now, very disconcertingly, Miss Willoughby and her opinion occurred to John. There was no evidence on which he could assess it, for he had said little to the lady and she less to him, nevertheless ladies have opinions and there had been something – he was sure of it – in her eye. Miss Willoughby was orthodox, she would be biddable, an admirable match for a young man looking for preferment; she would be very rich. And that, he had the grace to admit to himself as he came out of church, was an unedifying train of thought. It was disloyal, self-seeking, he reminded himself as he mounted his bicycle and pedalled off towards his home; it was a betrayal of an old friendship that had meant much to him and of new sensations, the breath of which recalled Margaret's charms and the appearance of Miss Willoughby, plain with an irredeemable plainness. If he broke with Margaret he would displease his aunt. That was a consideration, the young man thought, turning into the warren of quiet roads that surrounded the cathedral and cushioned it from even that small stir of life of the High Street and Market Square. There was no denying that Frances would be grieved. But then, a man must choose for himself in life, and where that choice could lead, if made with care, was obvious in the comfortable ivy-covered mansions of the Close, filled with a race of men born to bishops' gaiters and their womenfolk who went to match.

It was at the junction of College Green and Colbert Row, just at the point where he began the uphill section of his ride, that he encountered Mrs Anderson. This was unfortunate. He did not like the lady, distrusting her both as a woman and, in his present state of mind, as Margaret's mother, but so strong are the social conventions in small towns like Turlminster that he realized at once that there could be no escape; there could be no passing this parishioner with a wave and a shouted greeting. He dismounted and put the best face on it he could: a smile as false as Laura's, though rather less convincing.

'Hello!' he cried. 'Good morning. Are you going shopping?'

We are seldom at our best with those who break our dreams.

Laura, basket in hand, agreed she was. It really was extraordinary how tastes could differ. Her daughter was in love with this young man. There was undeniably something about him: his very dark eyes and fair hair made an arresting combination and he was well-proportioned and tall enough: but it could hardly be expected that an intellectual, studious appearance would make much appeal to a woman who preferred the practical and (Rupert apart) liked robustness in a man.

But to-day she needed him.

'You know it's really lucky running into you like this,' she said. 'There was something I wanted to talk to you about.'

He saw the danger signal at once. What was coming now? It was surely not possible that Margaret could have sent Laura to reply!

'Yes, about the stall for the bazaar, you know.' His sigh of relief was almost audible. 'I understand from Margaret that you've got plans for me.'

'Why, yes. That is, my aunt and I both thought . . . '

'That we'd help? Of course we will. You know we're always ready to be useful. You've got a claim on all your parishioners, but now particularly on us.'

He murmured politely, uncertain how to take her words: 'You've always been so kind. No one has done more for the parish.'

'And now you're paying us back,' said Laura sweetly. 'Cast your bread upon the waters! It's all most gratifying.'

'But, Mrs Anderson, I don't see . . . . '

'Never mind, I'm only teasing you, and, after all, I've got good grounds for doing it, haven't I?'

'I'm afraid,' he said stiffly, 'that I don't quite follow you.' But he did: a dreadful conviction was taking possession of his mind.

'Oh, but you do really. Still, you've every right to keep your secrets. Only I thought perhaps you'd like to know that personally I'm delighted and I'm sure her father will be, too.'

'But really . . . '

'My dear John,' interrupted Laura with her most knowing and confidential smile, 'I must tell you that I know.'

'You know!'

'Well, is that so terrible? When I became engaged I wanted the whole world to share my happiness.'

93

He said in a strangled voice: 'I am not engaged.'

'Not formally, perhaps. She hasn't shown me any ring. But I know that you wrote to her and that she's written back. I know – may I say it? – that you love her, and, to betray a confidence, I can tell you she loves you.'

'Has Margaret told you this?'

Laura opened her eyes to their widest extent: they were cornflower blue and as candid as a child's. 'Why, naturally,' she said.

At that he burst out: 'She couldn't have. She'd no right.'

'No right to tell me? Really you're behaving in a most extraordinary manner, John. In a moment you'll make me sorry that I ever spoke.'

'Forgive my saying so, but you should not have spoken.' Mrs Anderson drew herself up with immense dignity, a matriarch at odds with the arrogance and unreason of the male. 'Margaret shouldn't have spoken either. It was wrong of her, very wrong. What I wrote I wrote in confidence and I can't understand how she came to bandy it about.'

'You can say that of confidences given to her mother!' cried Mrs Anderson, who looked more righteously offended with every passing moment.

'I'm sorry to say it, but I can. What passed between us was for us alone.'

'Then you have a very odd conception of a family, Mr Paget. Nothing could have been more innocent or natural.'

He repeated stubbornly: 'It was wrong.'

'Then am I to understand that my daughter has been deceived?' This was turning to the offensive with a vengeance. 'Am I to understand that she has misread your letter – and your sentiments?'

He did not reply. He did not really know himself.

'Then forgive me for assuming that my daughter *has* been deceived. Oh yes, don't shrug your shoulders: this is very much my concern. What confidence is to be put in a man who says he loves his fiancée one minute and denies it the next?'

That could be answered. 'My fiancée! I must regretfully make it clear that Margaret and I are not engaged.' And there had spoken his other self, that legalistic self that delighted in an

94

argument and knew that truth could turn on the shade of meaning of a phrase.

'Is that your answer? Am I to tell her that?'

A renewal of his earlier suspicion came into his mind. 'Did Margaret suggest that you should speak to me?' he said.

'Good gracious, no!' cried Laura in a voice so perfectly tuned to her intentions that it suggested she was telling a diplomatic lie. 'Of course she didn't. Like any girl in her position she wants to explain things for herself. But I must say that we never thought that my approval would be resented.'

'I have never doubted,' he said, 'your approval of our friendship.'

'Friendship! How can you speak so coldly after what you wrote!'

A monstrous suspicion now occurred to him. 'Have you seen my letter, may I ask?'

'Seen it? Why . . . no.'

'You seem very certain of its contents.'

'Oh, John,' cried Laura, looking at the young man with an appearance of deep distress, 'what have I done to make you so antagonistic? I never meant to interfere. I just thought . . . I was just hoping, things were further forward than they are.'

'Perhaps Margaret suggested so?'

'Oh, no, she didn't, really she didn't. I jumped to conclusions, I suppose. I wanted her to be happy. She has had disappointments' – a clever touch – 'and I thought that this time everything had turned out well. I was so happy for her. And for you. You are so suited to one another.'

'Evidently.'

'You're still offended with me, I see,' said Laura with a smile indescribably resigned and sad. 'I don't mind for myself so long as you're not blaming Margaret. I couldn't bear that. She would be so hurt. She loves you, John.'

It may be imagined that this declaration from such a source at such a time noticeably failed to arouse the young man's ardour. Here they were in the open street, discussing his intimate emotions: the whole thing was absurd, it was indecent. For he knew the reputation of the woman he was talking to, and saw in his mind's eye the spreading ripples of her confidences reaching

95

out, primed with dangerous half-truths, into the deanery, the vicarage, into the residences of the canons. If he was not careful he would find himself committed and – this was the most monstrous thought of all – before he himself had had the satisfaction of making up his mind.

'I must ask you, please,' he said, 'not to repeat this matter any further.'

'You don't think, surely, that I would!' protested Laura, and the ring of sincerity in her voice was certainly not feigned. It was no part of any plan of hers to gossip about him to third parties, for she suspected that such talk had taken a lot of people to the altar who might otherwise never have arrived there. No, her work was already done and must not be spoiled by over-emphasis. 'I wouldn't dream of discussing such a thing,' she said. 'If I'd known your feelings in the first place I'd never have breathed a word to you.'

But perhaps, from his point of view, it was as well she had, for now he knew exactly where he stood. He was not the man to misplace his confidence a second time.

'The whole thing was unfortunate,' he said. 'I'm afraid I expressed myself too forcibly. I was upset.'

'That's all right. But you'll forgive her, John?'

It was an appeal to his cloth, to his sense of Christian charity, made by one who had very perfectly assessed the foibles of his heart. She could have made his answer for him:

'I'm very sorry. It's a thing I can't discuss.'

'Then in that case there's no more point in talking, is there? Good morning, Mr Paget.'

In that same spirit he accepted his dismissal, and a moment later, looking back over her shoulder, she saw him pedalling up the hill towards his home, a small black figure in the deserted, sunlit street. She shook her head as an ironic thought occurred to her. She was by no means certain that she had not done a favour to her daughter in scaring off so weak a man.

12

THERE had been a time when invitations to the Andersons to tea at Mrs Grey's had been regular events. In those days before the birth of Rupert the whole family had gone, Mr Anderson in the pride of fatherhood, Laura parading her offspring triumphantly like Niobe, and the little girls in joyous anticipation of a romp in dark attics and cupboards beneath the stairs. These visits, so happy and carefree, had long been discontinued, though no one knew exactly why: the children had kept contact, Mr Anderson had never wavered in his loyalty, even Laura protested her undying attachment to Mrs Grey, but the spell was broken, and such reunions as did take place were generally under the daunting auspices of bridge.

The latest invitation in the series had been sent to Mr Anderson alone. It was an odd departure that it should have been addressed to his office and not his home, an urgent little note, hurriedly, even untidily written, and that was odder still. Mr Anderson, a methodical man, was prepared to see significance in any change, and the letter, unremarkable in itself, filled him with foreboding. Everything seemed to be out of joint these days: he could not understand his wife, his elder daughter had become quite sullen, and now even his oldest friend was behaving unpredictably.

For once even the ordered peace of his office failed to soothe him and it was with a heavy heart that he set out at tea-time along the familiar roads he had trodden so happily in other days. How few anxieties he had suffered then! He had been on good terms with his children and even Laura had been different, another and gentler person, though she had always been possessive and a little jealous of his friendship with Mrs Grey. In those days they had joked of it, companionably, unkindly, as married people will; it would be no joke now if she got to hear of this secretive and unexpected call, for he knew that though she no longer cared for him she cared for appearances more and more with every passing day.

The memories of the past crowded in more thickly on him

once he was inside the house. The furniture was comfortable and old, the same furniture he remembered from thirty years before, and arranged about the room in the self-same order; even the pictures and photographs had survived: a few monumental landscapes in thick Victorian oils and family groups – his own children, John and Frances, Laura and himself. Pride of place, he noticed, was given to something new, a full-length study of his elder daughter, an enlargement of a snapshot, he supposed. It brought him back to the probable underlying reason for his presence there.

Nor had he long to wait. Without preliminary and even before he had had time to settle comfortably in his chair his hostess had burst out: 'Robert, I'm worried about John and Margaret.'

So he had been right. He had been sent for in this conspiratorial way just to indulge her in this fancy of a romance, a romance of which he had seen no signs.

'What's the matter now?' he said.

'There's been a quarrel. Oh yes, don't look so disbelieving. Didn't I say they were in love?'

'You certainly told me so,' said Robert, in a very guarded voice.

'And I was right. On Thursday they were here and even a blind man could have seen it. I tell you the atmosphere was almost unbearable, it was so heavy with unspoken words.'

'Seems to me they've not been spoken yet.'

Mrs Grey made a despairing gesture with her hands. She wondered if he was wilfully blind or only very stupid. 'But they have,' she said. 'I'm as certain as can be that after she left the house that night he sat down and wrote to her. He was in his study till all hours and went out to the post in the middle of the night. Of course it was to her. And next day she replied. I saw that letter in the hall.'

'Perhaps she refused him,' said Mr Anderson. 'Or perhaps he didn't even ask.'

'Oh, why don't you use your eyes!' cried Mrs Grey, quite exasperated with her guest. 'Why don't you use your common sense! Those two children were in love.'

'They don't look like it to me.'

'Because they've quarrelled. Between the time when he wrote

to her and the time when he opened her reply something – or someone – intervened.'

'Now what is this, Frances?' said Mr Anderson. He detested mysteries and was grieved that his old friend and ally, whom he had always found so candid, should be talking in riddles like his wife.

Mrs Grey took a deep breath. 'Well, if you want the truth, Laura intervened.' She saw the amazed, horrified expression in his eyes and hurried on. 'Yes, she did. I know she did. From words John's said I can piece things together very well. He met Laura down in town and something passed between them that's turned him against Margaret.'

'You don't know what you're saying,' said Mr Anderson, pushing his cup away from him.

'I'm afraid I do. Believe me, I don't like saying this; I know it hurts you and I'd spare you if I could. But I happen, you see, to love my nephew just as you love Margaret.' She added appealingly: 'If I tell you what I know will you listen, Robert?'

'I suppose I must,' he said.

'Well then, something was said by Laura, something that I'm afraid was quite deliberate, and the object was to separate these two.'

'Has John said that?'

'Not directly but in effect, yes.'

'That's not knowledge,' said Mr Anderson, in whom the solicitor never wholly slept. 'It's suspicion.'

'It's only part of the story. Do you remember another friend of Margaret's? He was at Cambridge at the time and used to come here in vacation.' Mr Anderson nodded. 'Jeffries was his name, I think. And do you remember how we all thought that he and Margaret would become engaged?'

'I always hoped they would,' he said.

'But nothing came of it. Did you ever wonder why?'

'Young men do sometimes change their minds.'

'And young men's minds are sometimes changed for them.'

'You're not suggesting,' said Mr Anderson, 'that Laura had anything to do with that?'

Mrs Grey looked sadly at her guest. She was truly attached to him and hated hurting him, but where her own interest, her own

99

love, was concerned she was capable of ruthlessness, for there is a little touch of Laura in us all.

'I know she did. You see, she told me so.'

'She told you that she had interfered?' he cried, his face the very picture of horrified amazement.

'Yes.'

'That she set herself to spoil her daughter's happiness?'

Mrs Grey gave a hard and rather unpleasant little laugh. 'Oh, she didn't put it quite like that. She had her reasons. After all, they were very young, and he hadn't much money and wasn't even set on a career. They were convincing reasons and she may even have believed in them herself. I didn't. Somehow after that I was never very much at ease with Laura.'

'I don't believe a word of it,' he said.

'You don't believe she confided in me? Well, it does sound odd. But then in those days we were very, very thick. I think,' said Mrs Grey, with a melancholy smile, 'that Laura must have thought I was a perfect match for her.'

Mr Anderson in his bewilderment and anger may have thought so too, but he could not for the moment find enough conviction to repeat his denial of the charge or even arguments to reassure himself.

'And she succeeded,' went on Mrs Grey. 'They were in love, but Laura didn't want the match and so there wasn't one.'

'She may have spoken to him,' said Mr Anderson, clutching at a straw. 'She had reasons, as you say – for I remember thinking myself that they were far too young – but I don't believe she was malicious and I don't believe anyone is so weak-willed as to be talked out of love.'

'Then you don't know much about young men. For every rash one there are two who keep on looking round to see if they've been caught. John's another, and just the same technique has been used on him.'

'It's a damnable suggestion,' said Mr Anderson, who felt a dull glow of anger rising in his heart. He did not know at whom it was directed, for though he half believed what he had been told, his sense of loyalty had equally been outraged; everything was in keeping with what he had long suspected in his wife, but, a family man to the core of his being, he must defend her to third

100

parties, he must defend her to himself. From the distance beyond his thought he heard the gentle voice of Mrs Grey. 'I'm sorry, Robert.' 'What's the good of that!' he cried. 'You've had your say. How can you expect me to believe such things? That my wife intrigues against her daughter! How could you say it when you have no proof?'

'I have proof.'

'No, no, it's all suspicion, surmise. You have raked up some old story from the past and you had no right.'

But Mrs Grey was growing angry too. She was sorry for him but had nothing but contempt for the way loyalties operated in him to the death of common sense. 'So we must stand aside, I suppose,' she said, 'and see the same thing happen for the second time to Margaret? And all to safeguard your illusions!'

'Your illusions, please.'

'There is nothing illusory about it,' she cried, quite out of patience with him. 'Their love was a fact, Laura's interference was a fact and the quarrel was a fact. And there's another thing: after they parted he wrote again to her. I know the mood he was in: he was sorry for what he'd done and was thinking of being reconciled. He wrote that second letter to her and for three days now he's been expecting a reply. He hasn't had one. Why?'

'My dear Frances, how should I know that?'

'You can find out soon enough,' she said.

'Oh? And how?'

'Ask Margaret if that letter ever got to her,' said Mrs Grey.

13

MR ANDERSON returned home to 'The Templars' in a very
unenviable frame of mind. He had the uneasy conviction that
he had been told the truth, though all his more generous instincts refused to credit it. In his diffidence he could see many
reasons for his wife's dislike, he could even find excuses for her
hatred, remembering her ambitions and his own failure to make
them come to life, but every part of him revolted at the thought
that a similar hatred should be felt for Margaret, for he was a
man of little subtlety who would defend the old ways, the old
conceptions of family life, even against the evidence of common
sense. If what Frances had said was true . . . But it could not be
true; it was unthinkable that Laura should deliberately have set
herself to influence John. As to the last allegation made by Mrs
Grey, that Laura had intercepted and withheld a letter, he knew
what to think of that and had expressed himself most forcibly to
Frances, so forcibly that they had ended in a quarrel. She had
asked for that, interfering maliciously in his affairs; indeed he
had doubted in the end whether perhaps this friendship of so
many years had not been an unworthy one. And yet Mr Anderson, allowing his anger to act against his suspicions like a
purgative, knew in his heart that he was being unjust. Something
else was troubling him as well: a response in the background of
his memory to Mrs Grey's insinuating words, a remembrance –
was it? – or a suspicion. Memory could play such tricks, he
knew, but was it not a fact that he had recently, very recently,
seen a letter in John's handwriting on the table in the hall?

By the time he had reached his home he had decided that
memory was fact, that the letter had been there and that, naturally, his daughter had received it. How she responded was her
business, for she was under no obligation to write forgivingly to
John; he could be left to cool his heels, and no doubt deserved
it since he had behaved so slightingly to her. It was only at this
stage that Mr Anderson saw that he had accepted all the other
allegations made by Mrs Grey: the love affair, the quarrel,

Laura's meeting with the young man in the street. But if all this were true might not the last suggestion be true also? Well, that was a matter that could be proved; even if the rest was surmise he had only to ask a simple question of his daughter to know the truth of that. But it is no easy matter to put the beliefs of a lifetime to the test, and Mr Anderson, who had no reserves beyond illusion, shrank from doing so. If Mrs Grey was right, not only was his marriage a bitter mockery, but parenthood itself and the family, that unity he cherished. It would be easier to think of Mrs Grey's remarks as the outpourings of a frustrated woman and to sacrifice a friendship for the beliefs by which he lived.

But when he reached home one glance at his daughter's face decided him. He saw her for the first time with the eyes of knowledge, an unhappy woman in the toils of love. In that light even his own peace of mind suddenly ceased to matter and he remembered only that she was his child, the person he loved most in the world, and that he had it in his power to help her.

He asked, and received his answer. She had had no second letter and his fears were justified. Mr Anderson, realizing this, was for a moment stunned, incapable of thought or speech. But so strong in him was the instinct of survival, the desire to be deceived and live, that his first returning thought was that he might have been mistaken in supposing he had seen that letter in the hall. Perhaps it had been the earlier one about which there was no dispute, perhaps his memory was at fault and he had imagined the whole incident under the influence of Mrs Grey. With each successive shock, though his conviction weakened his defences grew, sapping his determination to persist and reach the truth, so that if it had not been for Margaret he might have surrendered even then.

But under his questioning she had broken down and told her story from its beginning on Farshot Hill to its miserable end. Even at third hand the activities of Laura wore an ugly look, and Mr Anderson, listening in horror to this tale of treachery and cowardice, felt a violent surge of anger grow within him. These two had hurt and humiliated the one he loved. The young man must be forgiven, if only for his daughter's sake, but he could not find a word for the actions of his wife. Having heard

103

the details of the final quarrel, of John's reproaches at 'gross family interference', he could no longer doubt that her actions had been calculated; every word his daughter uttered seemed only to confirm the accusations he had heard that afternoon, so that even the withholding of the letter was quite credible. He could not even guess what had induced such actions. He had always distrusted modern psychiatric doctrine, and despite long years of legal practice had retained quite an old-fashioned belief in the sanity of human beings. He was not to know that Laura had seen in her elder daughter just a reflexion of himself, the child of a dangerous and painful childbirth who had grown capriciously in the form and personality of the husband she despised. Love and hate were emotions that he could understand, but he believed them to be responses to simple stimuli; the irrational had no meaning for him, brought up in a society that saw life in tones of black and white, an age of reason in contrast with the bewildering new world of reasoning. For a moment in his bitterness Mr Anderson almost wished his wife were mad; that would be the least painful explanation but not the true one, as he knew, for Laura had always been deliberate and this latest work was very much in character. The thought of just how subtly she had played upon the innocence of her daughter and the timidity of John added powerfully to his anger as he went upstairs to find his wife.

Laura was in her bedroom. It was a room decorated in the most astringent modern taste, art not so much concealing art as making comfort look remarkably uncomfortable, and in this setting Mr Anderson was out of place, a solid, absurd relic of another age. She was sitting on a stool in front of the mirror combing out her hair, and turned round in surprise as she saw him standing at the door. He was an intruder and was to be treated like one. But for once Mr Anderson was too angry to be abashed; he came forward till he was standing over her and could see below him in the mirror that petulant, disdainful face, covered with a tracery of small lines quite visible now that she had wiped the make-up from her skin. She avoided his eye and continued to use the comb, drawing it through her hair with sharp jerky movements of the hands that betrayed her rising irritation. So had she sat often in the early days before the children had been born, when he had been no stranger to that room and had taken pleasure, constant physical pleasure, in the details of her toilet. She was still a handsome woman; the flesh of her arms and back shone startlingly white against the dark texture of her négligé, recalling poignantly the memories of the past. Could actions, intimacies so tender, he asked himself, have led to this, to a moment when they must face each other in bitterness and suspicion?

'Well?' demanded Laura, putting down the comb and taking up a pair of ivory brushes, an anniversary gift of his in the year following the birth of Kay. She had not meant to speak but had been driven to it by the sight of him standing there, a silent figure of reproach. Perhaps she too recalled in this sallow, paunchy man someone she had loved when she was young.

'I want to ask some questions,' said Mr Anderson.

She did not reply but continued to ply the brushes, the strands of hair, strong, resilient, springing up in their wake like sheeny blades of wheat behind the passing wind.

'I want to ask you if you met John Paget in the street the other day.'

'Did I? Well yes, I think I did.'

'And what did you say?'

'I gave him my blessing,' replied Laura, and the smile at the corners of her mouth was only just perceptible. 'Margaret had told me that they were in love.'

'Who gave you permission to abuse that confidence?'

She raised her eyebrows; they were carefully plucked, but thin, so that without eye pencil the effect of the gesture was almost lost. 'Permission?' she said. 'I don't know anything about permission. I am the girl's mother, I suppose.'

'Sometimes I doubt it,' said Mr Anderson. Laura treated this remark with the contemptuous silence it deserved, so that he hurried on: 'You had no right to speak of it to John at all. You should have known how foolishly sensitive he is.'

'Very foolish,' agreed Laura. 'Rather an absurd young man, but there! there's no accounting for tastes.'

'Was that the attitude in which you spoke to him?'

'What attitude, Robert, if you please?'

'You know what I mean.' She shook her head. 'Oh yes,

you do. You went down there to him knowing very well that by pretending he'd gone further than he had you'd frighten him off completely. That was your intention.'

But even as he spoke he realized that this sounded thin and it was obvious that it had not dismayed Laura in the least. To accuse was one thing, to prove, another, and this he appreciated very well.

'You succeeded, too,' he said, his anger rising, partly at the thought of her duplicity, partly at his own feeling of impotence when faced with this clever woman who had always been beyond his reach. 'They've quarrelled. And, no doubt, you're pleased.'

Once again he was made to feel a blunderer; the look she turned on him in the mirror was so eloquently reproachful that he should take her for a monster. But she spoilt some of the effect by adding venomously: 'Do you think I hate her, too?'

He ignored the gibe. 'I know it was deliberate.'

'Think what you like,' said Laura, resuming with the brushes. 'I can't stop you. But if you want to know, I hoped they would get married: the girl doesn't like me and has always been the trouble maker of the family.'

This approach came very near to satisfying Mr Anderson, for it was illogical, after all, that in the circumstances she should want to keep Margaret at home.

But then he remembered the evidence of his eyes.

'He wrote a letter to her three days ago,' he said. 'She never got it, and I think that you know why.' He had watched her carefully as he spoke, and saw with an indescribable thrill of horror that the blow had gone right home. For an instant her guard was down and he saw guilt written plainly on her face, saw her involuntary sidelong glance towards the left-hand dressing-table drawer. 'You got that letter,' he said. 'Didn't you? You have it now.'

She swung round on the stool and faced him, the ivory brushes, in normal use no longer, clutched in her hands like weapons with which to threaten him. 'I don't know of any letter,' she said.

'But there was one; I saw it myself in the hall. You didn't think of that, did you, when you made your plans?'

She repeated her denial. But her words no longer had any

106

effect on Mr Anderson. Anger, frustration, love, were working in him towards an explosion of the will; his puffy cheeks were suffused with a rush of colour, little runnels had appeared, red against the putty-coloured skin. His voice when he spoke was scarcely recognizable, it was so harsh and vibrant with emotion.

'You've got that letter. Give it me.'

For the first time in her life she realized that she was afraid of him; in spite of the moral superiority she had built up in the course of years she could not for the life of her prevent herself from half rising from the stool and shrinking back against the cold surface of the glass. But her body was still between him and the private drawer.

He moved towards her, repeating: 'Give it me,' and since she did not reply he took her by the arm. Even at this stage she might have shamed him from his purpose by a calm resistance, but, angry and frightened by his advance, she was ill advised enough to strike out with the weapons in her hand, catching him painfully on the lip. It was almost with pleasure that Mr Anderson felt the blow and the salt taste of blood; it excused him everything, the violence with which he thrust her out of his way, the peculiar mixture of loathing and attraction he experienced for that false white flesh beneath his hand.

But the drawer was locked. A long moment of anti-climax had ensued before he had battered it open, spilling all the aromatic contents of the dressing-table on the floor, and stood with John's letter in his hand.

Immediately his rage subsided. Now that he knew the truth he was faced with something that even anger could not dissipate, the death of an illusion, which is often no less tragic, no less final than the burial of a man. 'So it was true,' he said. 'You did do it. Why?'

'For their good,' replied Laura, in whom the realization of her own worst fears seemed to have worked a cure. She was apparently quite calm, but an angry glitter in her eye showed that she had not forgotten the humiliation he had forced on her and would certainly not forgive it.

'So you were thinking of their good! I suppose that was what moved you in young Jeffries' case? You thought so much of Margaret and him that you broke that match up, too.'

It was seldom that he spoke ironically, and for a moment she quite wondered at him. 'Now where did you get that story?' she said. 'Where? Perhaps from Frances, was that it? Yes, I can see it in your face. We've been down gossiping with her!'

'I heard the truth there anyway,' he said.

'Oh, naturally you believe her in preference to me. That's natural. We've always been such friends with Frances, haven't we! What Frances says must always be believed?' Her voice rose. 'Who could expect a husband to realize that his fancy woman is an intriguing, lying slut!'

He caught the note of rising venom. There was usually a motive behind these hysterical displays, and he saw one now.

'Yes, fancy woman!' she cried, enraged at his passivity. 'She fancies you, you poor fool. Is it any wonder that she spreads lies about me round the town!'

'Lies?' said Mr Anderson, turning the letter in his hand.

'Of course. She'd say anything to harm me and you'd believe it. You'd believe anything of me.'

This so exactly represented his own feelings that he did not reply. It was typical of her courage and of her contempt for him that even at this stage she should abuse him and attempt to justify herself; it was even humorous in a way, if he had had the wit and the detachment to enjoy it. But when she continued in the same vein he brusquely cut her short. 'We'll leave Frances out of it. I'm concerned with Margaret.'

That provided her with another favourite opening. 'You're always concerned with Margaret. You think of no one else. No one would credit that you had two other children and a wife.'

This was unwise of Laura. It was scarcely politic to remind him how much he owed these three and how much they cared for him; it angered him and strengthened that sense of isolation that was leading him to a terrible decision.

'You'll give that letter to Margaret,' he said.

She was aggravated beyond endurance by the words and the tone in which he uttered them. All her married life she had dominated him, and that superiority had become so much a part of her, so necessary to her being, that she could not submit, even though self-interest now required she should. She knew him well and believed him incapable of persistence; it would be so easy to draw his sting by one act of compliance. But she could not yield, and that was a failure from which great consequences were to flow.

'Give it her yourself,' she said.

'You refuse to obey me and give Margaret that letter?'

He could say to her, obey.

'I do.'

'Even though you stole it?'

'I did not steal it,' she cried. 'I told you before: I took it for her good.'

This evasion was the greatest mistake of all. Mr Anderson, who had wanted to be reasonable, who might even have agreed on terms to continue with Laura as before, became furiously angry. All his sense of justice was outraged at the way she could construe her acts into a form of benefit, for he saw the whole pattern of their lives expressed in this one incident – his weakness, his irresolution, the perversion of her mind.

'You took it for her good!' he cried. 'How dare you say such things to me! You hated her and you did your best to break her heart. Don't think I'll let her stay with you another day.'

'And don't think that that way you'll break mine. Let her go and take yourself as well.'

'I will,' said Mr Anderson.

It had been said. For propriety's sake – and they were both worshippers at that shrine in their varying degrees – it was not an action that would commend itself except as a last resort, but, as so often happens when angry people have crossed the Rubicon, both seemed only to be intent on burning every boat and bridge behind them.

'Yes go, and don't come back. I don't want you. You've got that daughter and you can make do with her. She was always a spoilt, petted little thing.'

'Now we're really hearing what you think of her.'

'It's not the half of it,' she cried, and her voice was shrill with the rising tide of hatred and hysteria. 'I'm glad of what I did. Do you hear me? Glad. She doesn't deserve a husband, she isn't fit for one, even for a poor bloodless thing like that.'

'And you did it for her good!'

He was still standing by the dressing-table and she now advanced on him, her hands held out in front of her like a sleep-walker. In her flushed face and staring eyes he thought he saw the gleam of madness.

'Good! I don't care for her good. Take her, take her! I've got Rupert. He's my son. And when you've left this house, as I hope you'll do to-night, don't ever think you'll get another sight of him. He's my son.'

'He's my son too,' said Mr Anderson.

She stopped, not a yard from him, and he saw her smile, an expression intensely sinister and malignant.

'He's not,' she said.

He put his hands up to his throat.

'He's not, you see. Are you surprised?' Her voice rose till it became a scream that echoed through the room. 'He's Barry's son, Barry's. He's Barry's son, you fool!'

He took a step backward, still only half believing, sick with a sudden convulsion that seemed to have drained away his blood. And with a dreadful precision she continued with the proof. 'I was away a week that October, don't you remember? I was with him. You poor fool, do you think I'd have had another child from you? The touch of your hands!' – her eyes had widened, expressing the full horror of her thoughts, a vision of the corruption that can follow on the death of love. 'I had to suffer you just once, just once. For appearances, you know.'

Dazed though he was, he remembered. She was right, she was telling him the truth. In one instant many things that had taxed all his efforts of understanding were explained: her jealousy of Margaret, her hatred for himself, her love for Rupert and the nature of the boy. Characteristically it was not the moment of betrayal that appalled him but the deception she had practised ever since; the one was understandable but the wickedness of the other was beyond his comprehension. In his bewilderment he did not know what to do or say, he only knew that he was sick, that he must leave this room, leave the house, escape from the vile presence of this woman into cleaner air.

He turned from her and moved like an automaton towards the door. She had expected reproaches, anger, possibly even violence, but in the taut state of her nerves this silence unmanned her. She broke into a frenzy of hysterical grief, running after him and clutching at him with her hands as though she had not yet done enough to harm him and must frustrate even this last refuge of escape.

He scarcely heard her voice or felt her touch. There was a sound of rushing waters in his head, and all the mad disorders that had swept over the framework of his life, submerging all its strongholds, all its certainties, seemed to be dissolving in a tide of blood and in the beating of his heart.

If he had not heard, another person had – Rupert in his room far off down the corridor. Mr Anderson had nearly reached the door, had thrust aside his wife's restraining hands, when he saw dimly ahead of him through the mists of sickness the figure of her son.

He made to pass by him. But Rupert barred the way. The prejudices of a lifetime coloured the reality of what he saw: a brutal father staggering from the room, furniture in disorder, and his mother, half dressed, in a state of pitiable grief. All that was needed was an accusation, and Laura supplied this with a gesture: she pointed at her husband like a farmer putting a terrier to a rat.

It was enough. Fists whirling, Rupert flung himself at his enemy; he was striking against what he believed was evil, against oppression, against obscure antagonisms that he resented but had never understood, and felt as every blow went home an elemental satisfaction of the flesh.

But blows from so slight a man were of small account. Mr Anderson used no conscious force; he merely thrust the boy away; and it was bad luck – that and the slippery flooring of the corridor – that resulted in Rupert's fall against the banisters and the thin trickle of blood oozing from a cut above the eye. He did not hear his wife's despairing cry or the threats of the boy he had believed to be his son as he pursued his way, painfully, blindly, down the stairs towards the street.

14

A week had elapsed since Mr Anderson's departure before Barry Clarke visited Laura at her home. He had received more than one anguished summons before he obeyed; he had been busy, he said; there had been an important merger on his hands and he had not been able to leave the brewery.

How glad she was to see him! Though time had robbed her of that infatuation that in early middle age had resulted in the madness of Rupert's birth, she still loved him, only now it was for the sense of security he gave, for his strength and riches. The very sight of him standing foursquare on the hearth-rug warmed her heart, for in this strong male atmosphere she could relax and allow herself the luxury of being overborne. Like so many highly strung women she was abnormally sensitive to the idea of power; she must either exercise it or allow it to be exercised on her, and the principal cause of the failure of her marriage was that Mr Anderson had fitted into neither role, never dominating and never a very biddable form of slave.

All her life since the days of her early childhood she had stood in awe of Barry Clarke, the schoolboy athlete, the rich and brilliant man of business, and it was an irony that neither was able to appreciate that all that time, beneath the veneer of his success, he should have been afraid of her. There was something irrational in her nature that had always daunted him, though his knowledge of the world had helped him to disguise it. They had been lovers before their marriages, and he had returned much later to that relationship more from bravado than from any other cause. From that moment, from the birth of Rupert – an event that had surprised him greatly and shocked him more – he had developed quite a pathological fear of her which had required all his paternal feeling, all his bluster to overcome; indeed, the Barry Clarke of the hunters, the check tweeds, and large cigars, the jovial, boisterous Barry, almost a caricature of the Edwardian gentleman, was in his way a child of that shameful, unexpected birth.

And this afternoon the confident-looking man had business troubles, too. There were already whispers in the county to the effect that his company had achieved the all but impossible in brewery concerns and was beginning to lose money; it had been overstrained, they said, in competition with the London firms. Retrenchment – an ugly word – was in the air and the echoes of it had reached even into the offices of Mr Anderson.

Now on top of this financial crisis he was called in to advise his cousin. Barry Clarke was not a completely selfish man; all things considered and so long as there was no disadvantage to himself involved, he was very ready to assist his neighbour, but he had not built his business on philanthropy, and his usual hearty manner as he stood, hands clenched behind him, warming himself at the fire and showing a prosperous stomach to the world, cloaked a definite sense of grievance. He had known from the beginning that she would involve herself in some scrape. Even his sympathies were not entirely on her side, for he had lived with her just long enough to pity Mr Anderson, a rather likeable though colourless sort of chap and a member of that male freemasonry with which, like all those who are successful in pursuit of women, he had the profoundest sense of comradeship.

Laura, so reliant on this lover, this tower of strength, was quite surprised by the reserved manner in which he expressed his sympathy. 'You needn't sympathize. I'm glad he's gone,' she said.

So, no doubt, reflected Barry, was Mr Anderson himself. Aloud, he said: 'It's not like him, Laura, to go dashing off like that. What did you do to him?'

'What did I do?' cried Laura, more surprised than ever at his way of putting things. 'What did *he* do, you mean. He'd been behaving abominably for weeks.'

Her cousin translated this, reversing subject and object in his mind, and waited for further revelations.

'It was over Rupert,' she said.

This was certainly her surest ground. One of Barry's best characteristics was his affection for his children, particularly for Rupert, who had for him the added appeal that is made by sympathy and the rather pleasurable sense of sin.

'Well, out with it, Laura. What did he do to Rupert?'

113

'He ended by striking him,' said Laura, opening her eyes to their widest extent and looking every inch the stricken mother. Nor was she insincere in this. She loved her son passionately, unwisely, more devotedly than she loved herself.

'He struck him! Did the boy deserve it?'

'Of course not,' she cried. 'He did everything he could for weeks to make things unbearable for Rupert. I told you in my letter how he took him away from school.'

'Yes, that was unreasonable.'

'Unreasonable! That's mild. He deliberately provoked him. He didn't want him to have the career that you'd have given him, so instead he put him in his office.'

'But all that was a week before,' protested Barry, who was acutely aware of the fact that she was holding something back. 'Why the sudden break so long after the event?'

'It just worked up to it, I suppose.'

'And both Robert and Margaret left the house?'

She saw the enquiring expression in his eyes and admitted reluctantly: 'There was some quarrel over Margaret as well.'

'Oh! Was there? Over Margaret?'

But Laura had awoken to his extraordinary lack of sympathy.

'What's the matter, Barry?' she said. 'Why d'you look at me like that? Don't you believe me?'

'Yes, I believe you. Not that you've told me much.'

'It was some quarrel over an affair. She was keen on that young Paget, and she and her father thought that I had interfered. You know Robert. You know how absurdly touchy he was about that girl.'

'Yes, I know Robert,' replied Barry, who would never have referred to any of his own children in such words. 'And I know there must have been a first-class row to have made a man like that pack up and leave his home. The problem is now, how to get him back.'

This time he had really moved her.

'How to get him back!' she cried. 'I don't want him back.'

'But, Laura . . .'

'I tell you I never want him back. He struck Rupert. I never want to see him or hear from him again.'

Barry rocked himself backwards and forwards on his heels.

114

It was a habit of his when he was perturbed, as though he were shifting his position and trying to get a firmer purchase on the ground.

'For Rupert's sake,' he said, 'you've got to send for him. Now, really, Laura, you must look sensibly at this. You must. A boy at his age can't do without a father.'

This was a mistake. Even Barry saw the uncomfortable nature of the ground; as for Laura, she looked paternity at him with her eyes.

'That's why I've sent for you,' she explained.

Well now, he was in the scrape as well.

'He's your child, Barry, just as much as mine.'

Mr Clarke, who knew from other experiences just how such things should be done, saw the indelicacy of this. He looked uneasily round the room as though he expected that some of his fine county friends might be in hiding there.

'He's yours,' she repeated, 'just as much as mine. Now you must keep your promises to him.'

'I tell you, Laura, the best solution is to get Robert back.'

'And send Rupert to his office? Never. I'm glad it's happened the way it has. Now at last we can do what we've planned.'

It is not always pleasant to watch promises coming home to roost, and Barry's face mirrored his anxiety. Seen thus without the usual buoyant smile, it was a sullen, flabby mask, humourless as only the professionally humorous can be once the party is over, the last bar-room story told. 'What is it you want?' he said.

Laura was pained at the words and tone which smacked a little of an auction, but she was ready at once with her suggestions. 'I want you to take him in with you at the brewery. Surely that's always been agreed?'

'Well, yes.'

'Then he'll have a job to look back to when he's in the services; a job to return to. That's what he needs: security, support.'

Barry rocked himself quite violently on his heels, then sat down in an armchair by the fireside. He looked as if he too needed security and support; it was no pleasant thing to be between this devil of a mistress and the deep of his respectability.

115

'It's not all that easy, Laura,' he began.

She bridled instantly. From the outset his manner had been strange and it now seemed all too likely that he was going back on his word.

'It was a promise, Barry,' she reminded him. 'It's always been understood that Rupert could go to the brewery. You know he's got it in him to do well.'

'No doubt of that.'

'Well, what's the matter, then?'

'Rose,' said Mr Clarke, mentioning his wife's name with the respect he reserved for her. 'To put it bluntly, she doesn't want Rupert in the business. She's jealous for her own sons, I suppose. You know how it is?'

Indeed he was speaking to a Leviathan of jealousy and had called it from the deep.

'I do know how it is. But I don't see why what Rose thinks should affect your promised word.'

And that, he reflected, was the devil of it: this woman would not understand. The give-and-take of family life was beyond her; she was incapable of compromise. Well, she might break up her own home life, but he, Barry Clarke, the domestic man whose recent love affairs were almost painfully discreet, had no intention of going travelling.

'It makes things very difficult for me,' he said.

'And how do you think it makes things for me? I've relied on your promises. If you won't help, what's to become of Rupert?'

He seized what he believed to be his chance. 'That's why Robert must come home. With Robert home there's no problem; there's a career mapped out for the boy.'

'In an office,' said Laura, looking in a most unfriendly manner at her guest. 'And you can sit there and say that after all the promises you made! A fine friend! As soon as you're put to the test you back out.'

'Oh, Laura! do try to see my point of view. I'm as anxious for Rupert as you are. I'll make him an allowance. But with Rose as she now is I can't employ the boy.'

'As she now is! What's wrong with her?'

'Well,' replied Mr Clarke, looking round the room again and

unconsciously lowering his voice, 'the truth is that I think she knows.'

Mrs Anderson gave a hard, unpleasant laugh.

'About Rupert?'

'Yes, I'm almost sure of it.'

'Someone else knows, too,' she said.

'Good God, Laura! Who?'

'Robert. I told him before he left, you see.'

It was one of the few solaces of her afternoon to see him leap to his feet, consternation in his puffy, hedonistic face. Much of the admiration she had felt for him all these years was dispelled as she recognized a weakness as contemptible as her husband's.

'Good God! What made you? Suppose he uses it?'

'Well, suppose he does?' said Mrs Anderson, thoroughly enjoying her advantage.

A dreadful vision floated before his mind. He saw the divorce court, heard the rash admissions of this woman, the measured conclusions of the judge, and above them both, the laughter of his friends. How terrible a blow to one who had just received the nomination for his Division of the county! But Barry Clarke, for all his bluster, was a man of the shrewdest common sense, and it was with him the matter of a moment to see the real nature of these fears: he knew men; he knew his Robert Anderson. 'Oh, but of course he won't,' he said.

'Perhaps not,' Laura agreed in her silkiest voice. 'But you've forgotten that Robert's not the only one. I know too.'

This was blackmail, familiar ground to Barry Clarke, and he had never lost a battle on it yet. Laura was quite surprised to see the tension of his face relax, to be followed by one of his most confident and sunny smiles.

'That's not worthy of you,' he replied. 'I'm surprised at you.'

'You don't think that I'd fight to the end for the interests of my son?'

Barry's expression became even more expansive.

'Oh, I'm sure you would. But it would be hardly in his interest – now would it? – to announce things to the world. The world is indulgent, but not all that much, I think. You'd hurt me – I admit that – but you'd ruin him, and I don't somehow see you doing that.'

It was true. She saw that she had made a serious mistake.

'I thought you would act like a gentleman,' she said.

'My dear, I was always sure that you'd be a lady to the last. In the circumstances let us act in character.'

His voice had recovered all its old confidence as he saw his way clearly stretching out before him.

'You see, Laura, you've misjudged me. I don't want to abandon Rupert. I'm fond of him. But you must accept the fact that you have no hold on me except a moral one. If I could, I'd bring him into my office as I always hoped, but that's impossible considering the attitude of Rose. It remains for us to consider what to do.'

This was all in his best board-room manner and she waited, hands tightly clenched, to hear what he would say.

'In the first place I recommend you to make your peace with Robert.' She stirred in her chair and he raised his hand. 'Yes, I know that it's unpleasant for you. My advice is, try. If he won't come back he must make you an allowance. He'll do so of his own free will, and generously, I'm sure. As for the rest, I'll use what influence I have to find the boy a job. I'll make him an allowance so that he shan't be handicapped. He'll be called up soon, and when he comes back, who knows! Perhaps circumstances will have altered and I can keep the promises I made. How's that, Laura? Does it meet the case?'

His manner had already presupposed her answer. Really he had come with unexpected ease through this testing, dangerous interview. He had behaved with generosity, too, and felt the glow of a good action warm his heart. He was genuinely attached to the boy and promised himself that in later years he would do still more for him: find him directorships, even leave him money in his will. It was not every father who exercised such care, who gave so much where there was no legal liability to give at all. Serene, secure in the pleasant aftermath of these good deeds, he would have been quite grieved had he suspected just how ungrateful Laura was for all that had been done – well, promised, anyway.

15

THE night was overcast; there had been rain earlier in the day and more was promised in the heavy bank of cloud drifting from the west; the air was chill with patches of ground mist in the meadows.

Rupert, perched like a raven on the familiar stile, compressed his body in search of warmth and drew his light spring overcoat closer about him. The overcoat was a new addition to these nocturnal outings, a suggestion of Joy's made more for her own comfort than for his, for it had to be confessed that Rupert, too much the realist, showed a complete lack of interest in the trimmings of his love affair. However, no complaint was possible about the central, all-important act itself, and to this and to the element of crude vulgarity in Joy must be attributed her fidelity and her pleasure in these passionate idylls in the grass. There was something elemental about him that was suited to the setting of the open air; perhaps something would be lost in the slattern comfort of her bed. She was not sure. An expert in the art of giving and yet always offering more, she held out for his sensuality – and her own – the prospect of that dangerous passage past her aunt's locked door to her own bedroom on the floor above, the pleasure of light instead of darkness, the undressing, the tumbled sheets, and all the visual accessories of love. It was a prospect that allowed play to an imagination always erotic and now stirred by the recollection of his kisses to a degree that almost frightened her sometimes. She admitted to herself that she loved him; it was her way of comparing the stimulus he brought her with that of the other lovers she had taken in her life.

He looked at his watch. From the luminous dial he could see that it was ten, and in confirmation, a moment later, the chimes rang out from the cathedral belfry. It was closing time and she must be coming soon. For three nights now she had not availed herself of her permission to leave the saloon-bar early and had been late for their meeting by the stile. That being so, it was not surprising that a young man of an imaginative turn of mind should have created rivals for himself, though, as it happened, he was widely off the mark. Capriciousness had been the cause of these delays, that and the little spurt of anger that they struck in him and which was reflected, pleasurably for them both, in a certain roughness of approach. It was surprising, really, considering his age, how adult he was, how quickly he could learn those refinements that came naturally to her with her instinctive knowledge of how love and hate, ecstasy and pain, go hand in hand in an affair.

Ten o'clock. How cold and dark it was! And the ground, though it had been parched by three weeks' drought, had not soaked up the rain that had fallen in the afternoon, so that the long grass in the hedge-bottoms was damp to his touch. This was the latest she had been. Indeed, for a moment, he wondered whether she had gone home another way. Perhaps the bad weather had deterred her and she had gone, not by the footpaths, but by the metalled road, as had happened once before. As usual that night he had been sitting on the stile, looking down towards the town, and had heard suddenly from behind the stealthy tread of her footsteps on the grass. She had nearly surprised him then and might have chosen just such another night to try again, a dark, impenetrable night with just enough wind to mask the sound of her approach.

It was ten past now. And then suddenly he knew that she was coming from the direction of the town. He could hear no footsteps but vague rustling movements in the long pasture of the meadow, the result, as he knew, of the inquisitive interest of the young bullocks grazing there. Any movement on the path attracted them; indeed, earlier that evening they had come to the stile to stare at him, small white shapes, mischievous and a little sinister with their long greasy tongues, and adolescent lumps of horn and cloven hooves. A few moments later and he could see them dimly through the darkness, escorts of a shadow moving in their midst, and he could hear the gentle patter of their hooves as one by one, in answer to some gesture lost to him, they lowered heads and flounced away.

He gave a low whistle, recapturing their attention; stolidly they stood and watched two meaningless shadows merge, and draw apart, and merge again.

'Thought you were never coming, Joy,' he said.

'Did you?'

The tone of her voice expressed the contempt with which she entered on her meetings with this boy; it was most revealing to see how her sensations had altered by the end of them.

'What kept you?'

'Customers,' replied Joy, putting a wealth of meaning into the word. Some day she must let him see that circle of young business men clustered round her bar; it would put him in his place and do him good. Better still, she could accept one of the suggestions made with varying degrees of sportiveness by these gentlemen; they were adult, they had freedom and money, and no one was more appreciative than she of the possibilities of a summer's evening in a car. It would be fun to detail things to him afterwards: the darkness, the ingenuity that defied back-seat discomfort, the cramped intimacy of an embrace. How pleasant, how amusing, how delicious a revenge – if she only dared! But already she knew that she would not. Joy was a woman in whom the realism of her sex remained untempered by too much refinement; she would have expressed it with her usual candour by saying that she liked men to be rough. Coarseness and voluptuousness were very well, but she sometimes felt in the grip of his hands, in his kisses at moments of their most secret intimacies, a little trace of animal ferocity. It was very pleasurable, something quite out of the normal run of her experience, but there were moments when a chill of uneasiness reached her heart as, lying out there in the fields in the deep, sweet-smelling summer grass, she realized how cut off they were from the surrounding world.

The combination of this pleasure and this uneasiness – it was not exactly fear – accounted for the fact that for two months now she had been faithful to him. Rupert himself was among the few who doubted this, he had no notion how powerful was the cord by which he held her, unlike the chagrined patrons of the 'Fleece' who were already whispering that she was settling down, though they could not think with whom. Her recent conduct had aroused his jealousy, so that with little sense of how he was exposing himself to her sarcastic tongue he said complainingly: 'Customers! When you're talking on with them I don't suppose you think of me waiting out here in the cold.'

121

That was typical of how absurdly vulnerable he was in the preliminaries of an affair where other men of her experience were bold. It gave her so many opportunities of displaying her own authority. But the effect was always lost to her, since it was his habit to grow bold himself as time went on, where they would become progressively more timid – in spite of what they imagined later to their friends.

'Customers are interesting, you see,' she said. 'They've been places and seen things.'

'Go on, say it: they're grown up. They're marvellous, so marvellous that I don't know why you waste your time on me.'

Well, she reflected, she certainly had wasted time, though not with him. It must be every bit of half past ten. And since she was not the woman to believe anticipation the equal of experience, she answered in the most telling way she knew, by pressing her body up against him and putting her mouth to his.

'Where?' he said at last, when she had drawn away.

Always practical, she leaned down and felt her shoes; the welts were damp and rough to her touch with loose, sprinkled seeds of grass. Even with his overcoat – which she was glad to see he had remembered – their usual place was quite unfit to-night. It would have to be the shed, the animals' feeding-shed which stood in a corner of the field, musty with the smell of oil-cake and last year's hay.

He protested that it was dark and dirty.

'Well, Mr Particular, you say where.'

He suggested breathlessly: 'What about your bedroom, Joy?'

And why not? Her aunt would be asleep and the thing itself not difficult. It would be warm and cosy there between the sheets. But there was one objection: this was a night that she had been promising herself for weeks; it must differ from these abrupt, scrambled meetings in the fields. It must be prepared for: the clothes she would wear, scanty lace garments to astonish him, must be ready on the bed; there must be no sense of haste, of improvisation, or the effect was gone.

'Not to-night,' she said.

'But that's what you always say. Why not?'

'Because of Auntie, stupid.'

'Oh, her!' said Rupert, who thought of the old lady as a

122

kind of procuress. It was a quaint judgement on one of the most respectable of women, one so innocent of the world that she even believed her niece to be respectable, as well.

Joy, who had all the strong family feeling of those who are only relatives by courtesy, immediately reproved him. 'Don't say, "Oh, her!" like that. If it comes to it, why not your house for a start?'

This was a fanciful suggestion, and his lips parted in a smile as he imagined how his mother and his mistress would figure in it. How pricelessly outraged Laura would be at finding this common, plump young woman in his bed! It would almost be worth trying some time. He was perfectly satisfied that his hold over his mother would survive the shock, for with her, at least, he had no doubt of how greatly he was loved.

Joy had not advanced her suggestion very seriously but only to head him off. 'We can't do that,' she said. 'Isn't it true that you're the boy that gets the stick from Pop if you come in after nine?'

'As a matter of fact,' corrected Rupert coldly, 'my father's not at home.'

For a moment it had slipped her memory, though from her strategic position behind the bar she had heard all the details of how the gentleman had come to leave his home, some of which would greatly have surprised him.

'I quite forgot he'd done a bunk,' she said in the matter-of-fact tones of one interested party to another. Home ructions had been so common in her early life that it never occurred to her that other people might be chary of discussing them. 'Nice chap, too. Often in my bar.'

'One of your customers, I suppose,' said Rupert, and it was really remarkable how bitter his voice could sound and what meaning could be put into the words.

It gave her an ideal chance of teasing him. 'Yes, a customer, and I mean just that. He was in to-night.'

And that's the reason why I'm late, her expression seemed to add. It was not often that he rose so readily to the bait; it was worth persisting in.

'I suppose that like all the others he walks you out?'

'Only once,' said Joy, with the air of one reluctantly making an admission. 'Only once. He went with me to the end of Hunter Street.' This was a dark and narrow lane close to the Ling, a notorious rendezvous for the local youth, its choice an inspiration on the part of Joy, though she had never walked a yard with Mr Anderson or seen him outside the 'Golden Fleece'. 'Why, Rupert!' she continued, as she felt the grip of his fingers on her arm, 'there was nothing wrong.'

And that made it sound very wrong indeed. If he had stopped to think he must have seen that she was teasing him and that his suspicions were absurd, but then, perhaps, there was some urge in him that wanted to believe he had a rival, this particular rival who, through the mists of childhood recollection, had played the same part once before when he was weak and impotent and small.

'You keep away from him,' he said. 'Perhaps you're only joking, but you keep away from him, that's all.'

'Rupert, I believe you're jealous.' She gave a coarse, suggestive laugh. 'You're jealous of your dad.'

It was one of the best jokes she had heard in weeks, and as she remembered the object they had in view that night, the ardour of her companion, and contrasted him with that mild-mannered gentleman who drank an occasional glass of bitter at the 'Fleece', she laughed again, long and heartily, an exasperating sound so inane as to be a perfect match for his suspicions.

'Oh, that's rich, that is, that's rich! Don't you see it's funny? He will, anyway. He's a man that can see a joke.'

She laughed again, sending out a peal of laughter into the surrounding wraiths of river mist, then broke off uneasily. He had taken the bait so eagerly, but now instead of floundering was still.

'Pity you can't see it, too,' she said.

She put her hand out to touch him and felt to her surprise that he was trembling. She had hurt him, then. This absurdity had been a reality for him. At once her manner changed; she had all that softness of heart that so often accompanies a voluptuous, unmoral nature and she sensed unsuspected weaknesses in him. Brought up in a hard tradition, she had seen the tragedies of broken homes in terms of vaudeville, but here was evidence that the thing could be serious enough.

124

'It's all right, Rupe,' she said, and she slid her arm around his neck. 'It's all right, I won't tell. I won't say a word to him.'

He was so far from satisfied that he pushed her away quite roughly, so that she felt some of the reserve of strength in those thin and wiry hands. He was in an unpredictable kind of mood, but if handled right there could be profit in it.

'Don't be silly,' she said, and with a quick movement she slipped between his arms so that he felt the yielding pressure of that body close against him, so warm and strong and richly imbued with the promise of good things, so hateful and so wonderfully desirable.

Instinctively and without another word they moved off, arms locked together, through the long pasture of the field towards the feeding-hut. There in the darkness he spread his coat and repaid her in anger for her words. It was one of the ironies of their relationship that his feelings should have been so transmuted in the course of action. Never in the whole time she had known him had she clung to him so passionately, yielded in such ecstasy, never had she felt he loved her more.

16

IT was natural that Mrs Anderson's first reactions to the advice given by her worldly cousin should have been unfavourable, for though it was easy for Barry to preach forgiveness, it was quite another thing to expect it of so proud a woman. She had been deserted, she had been shamed before the world, and such things are not easily forgiven by characters much meeker than Laura Anderson. Then there was her husband to consider. Like most intriguers she was herself her own easiest victim, not even having the guide strings of an evil conscience, but however innocent she knew herself to be it had to be admitted that her husband had a sense of grievance, too. That being the case, was an approach to him advisable? Might she not expose herself to a rebuff?

As was to be expected her decision was a compromise. Since Barry would not advance her son, her husband must, and he must be led to do so by an appeal to those domestic proprieties that always carry weight with the conventional. Laura's letter to her husband in which this policy was expressed was in its way a masterpiece; it hinted at her rights, at the legal strength of her position – for what had been admitted in confidence could confidently be denied – it expressed a generous desire for reconciliation, and finally it drew an affecting picture of the family, that little nucleus so dear to his heart, at the mercy of all the wagging tongues in town. There was even a suggestion, a nuance of felicitously chosen words, that some design of Frances Grey's was at the bottom of it all. There were scandals and scandals, it seemed to say; some could not be proved, while others could. Desertion was a matrimonial offence, and there were others, too. A word in time could save who-knew-what embarrassments that might react unfavourably on them all, particularly on a daughter with matrimonial aspirations. Not only Caesar's wife needed to be above suspicion; scandal was enough to wreck things when one was dealing with ministers of the Established Church. Already – and here Laura came closest to direct appeal – already people had been gossiping and even reconciliation might not be an excessive price to pay for that daughter's future happiness. As for Rupert, he was not mentioned in the letter, which kept throughout to the highest pitch of tact, though perhaps Mr Anderson might be expected to see some connexion with him at the end, where in a sentence of great magnanimity it was pointed out that in a quarrel in which tempers had been lost, things might have been said that were not strictly related to the truth. There was no denial, for she would not stoop to that, but it was open to him after reading to believe that Rupert was his flesh and blood – provided he was gullible enough.

For three days no reply arrived. She could only wait. She would not call to see him, partly out of pride, partly from the well-founded belief that she could never express herself so ably in the flesh. After such quarrels reconciliation by voice and touch is only to be recommended to the young; Laura had only arguments to offer and these were weapons that were safer at long range. But she was alarmed at the delay, unexpected in so methodical a man, since she had chosen to believe that he would sit down to answer this vital question with the promptitude with which he met his tailor's bills. It was very wrong that she should be kept on tenterhooks, she felt, and a new grievance was ticketed in her brain for future use.

On the fourth morning with the midday delivery his letter came. She had been out for lunch and did not get it till late afternoon, when with admirable restraint she did not open it in front of Kay, who was with her at the time, but took tea quite unconcernedly as though nothing of importance had occurred. But it was with a beating heart that later in the privacy of her bedroom she tore open the envelope and began to read.

Some moments later Rupert was passing by his mother's door on his way downstairs and heard the gentle muffled sound of sobs.

He found her lying on the bed, one cheek along the outstretched arm in which the crumpled letter was still held, her eyelids swollen, her whole body suffused with the warmth that comes to rejuvenate with tears. In an instant he was down on his knees beside her, his hands caressing her face and hair, for in spite of all his faults he loved her truly with an affection that was capable of passing beyond the boundaries of his narrow, self-interested life. It moved him to see her lying there and his expression as he bent down over her was strangely tender, as though some new meaning had been breathed into that sharp and faun-like face.

She seemed a young woman still. She had flung herself down without thought, her skirt had rucked up round her thighs and her well-knit, powerful body lay upon the coverlet, bringing him some faint appreciative memory of Joy.

'Dearest,' he said, 'what's the matter?'

Mrs Anderson buried her face in the pillows and gave way to a fresh spasm of grief. He was wise enough in women's ways to make no attempt to check her or to speak to her again, but sitting on the edge of the bed he began soothingly to caress her arm, administering little gentle pats to that silky flesh, so much whiter, so much finer than the body of his mistress. Lost in this unaccountable train of thought in which his mother's existence as a woman was perhaps for the first time consciously presented to his mind, it was a shock when she struggled up against the pillows and turned her face towards him, it was so old, and puckered and stained with tears. Immediately he withdrew his hand, the executant of perverse and troubled thoughts, but remained looking down at her, moved only by compassion. How ugly she was and how dear to him, so weak and so abandoned!

As though aware of his protective thoughts, she dropped the letter between them on the bed and clutched at him with fevered hands.

He said: 'What's the matter, mother? He's written, I can see.' But for Laura the letter was just the culmination of the series of events begun when her husband had taken Rupert from his school; Barry was a part of it with his rejection of her hopes; the whole world seemed to be in league to thwart her, so that she cried out: 'Oh, it's everything, Rupert. Everyone's against me.'

Yet she knew that he was not. She could see in his face the reflexion of her own self-pity, could feel beneath her fingers that sinewy arm, flesh of her flesh, spirit of her spirit. And of course he replied as she had meant him to: 'You've still got me.'

That expressed it. She loved him – would have died for him – but love with her was rooted in possession. He was hers. She had borne him – very late – and it was right that she should possess him now. Sex was for her a means, procreation not an end but only the title deeds of ownership, love itself at once the prudence of the landlord and the enjoyment of the estate.

She patted his hand, for it was always comforting to know he felt the same.

'I know, darling, I've still got you. But otherwise I'm so alone. There's no one I can turn to for advice.'

Rupert, who had not been kept informed, murmured the name of Barry Clarke. It was enough to set her off again. She flung herself back along the pillows and sobbed dismally, one hand however retaining hold of him with surprising force as though it had become detached from her and were leading an independent existence of its own. In its tenacity it may have represented the real Laura very well, for this time the collapse was quickly over and her manner when she sat up again and faced him was much calmer than before.

'I didn't want to tell you,' she began.

'Tell me what, mother?'

'That Uncle Barry's finally refused to help us, dear.'

This was a shock, and the young man's sympathy momentarily turned inwards on itself as he digested it.

'I don't understand,' he said.

Even the resources of a Laura would have been taxed in making an acceptable story out of this particular truth. Nor did she attempt it. Though in some agony of spirit, she could see the danger and appreciate how much more satisfactory it would be to attribute everything to the selfishness of Barry and the intrigues of Mrs Clarke. It must be admitted that she made out a convincing case. But Rupert, who had believed in Uncle Barry, not having had the privilege of seeing that gentleman in his more slippery moods, was looking elsewhere for the solution of the mystery. 'If father hadn't left,' he said, 'they'd have taken me for sure.'

There was more truth in these words than Rupert could have known, but Laura saw in them a judgement on herself and the tears mounted into her eyes as she asked in her most piteous and appealing voice: 'Darling, is it like that? Do you regret it? Do you want him back?'

He had not been looking at his mother at the time and his

denial was lacking in conviction. But as he turned towards the bed and saw the expression in her eyes all his tenderness for her revived and his hatred acquired a deeper meaning. His father had done this. Her mouth was trembling, her cheeks puffy and soiled with the tracks of half-dried tears, her eyes, usually so alert, were expressionless and glazed, and he, remembering her as she had been when he was young, placed on the shoulders of one absent man the blame for all these things, the result of a lifetime of indulgence and the toll of years.

'I don't want him back,' he said.

They were the words that she had used to Barry and they found an echo in her heart.

And then he saw to his surprise that far from being comforted the storm of anguish was rising in her to a fresh crescendo. He could not know how she had abased herself to write, he had not read that crumpled letter on the sheets with its courteous but inexorable refusal.

He gripped her hand while the wave of tears washed over her, submerging the personality he had known, so that she cried out to him odd snatches of her jealousy and hate, words without a meaning but no less terrible for that, words bewildered, coarse and agonized. He did not understand the sense of them – if he had done so it would have been better for them both – but sat on beside her, appalled by this degradation unveiling itself before his eyes. Something inside him was stirring into life, that response to violence that exists in individuals as in the mob, a community of hatred, active and malignant like all elemental things, the spark of evil that can be struck with such explosive ease within the hearts of men. If he had felt his kinship of the flesh before, this was now converted into a union of the spirit; pity rebounded on itself and emerged in the desire to be revenged. His whole heart and body cried out with hers, but if words were her weapons, what should be his own?

Unconsciously his grip had tightened, so that the woman on the bed, even in the throes of her hysteria, became aware of it and grew calmer under that urgent, painful pressure bearing down on her from the world beyond her dreams. Her cries ceased, her struggles and tears diminished and she rolled over on to her side to look at him, half mesmerized and wholly unprotesting.

130

Very slowly he relaxed his grip, for the spell was still on him. 'What is it?' he said. 'What was in that letter? What's he done?'

The harsh words received as harsh an answer.

'Done!' she cried. 'He's deserted me. For ever, do you see? He's gone for good. He's asked for a divorce.' She paused and laughed – a most unpleasant sound. 'Yes, divorce. Funny, isn't it! In three years I'm to divorce him for desertion.'

She sat bolt upright on the bed and her voice took on a quality at once menacing and pitiable.

'But I'll see to him before three years. He's gone to that woman, Rupert. That's what he'll have done. To Frances Grey. He's left me and he's crept off to that woman's bed.'

17

THE 'Golden Fleece' was the oldest hotel in Turlminster and one of the oldest in the country; it was a four-star hotel on the strength of it, as was only just when one considered the extraordinary number of beams and mullioned windows and inglenooks that were thrown in with the service. No one could fail to be charmed by the elegant exterior of the house, by the cobbled yard overlooked by tiers of galleries that seemed to have anticipated Dickens and his illustrator, Phiz; if the 'Fleece' had a fault it was that it had become more of a coaching print than a live hotel. Even its clients, the country estate agents and solicitors, the rugger players who clustered noisily on Saturdays round its bar, had an old-fashioned flavour, a robust and lively one, let it be said, contrasting with the dead appearance of the decorations, the rows of pewter plates, the coaching lanterns, the fish in their long glass cases – fish of such repellent shape and size that it was plain to see why their captors had stuffed instead of eaten them.

And then to contrast with everything there was Joy, a living proof that times had changed. It was her opinion that they had needed changing too – an opinion natural, perhaps, to employees of the 'Fleece' where service arrangements, the provision of hot water and suchlike, were not considered as among the premier attractions. She would often complain about this. 'It's uncomfortable,' she would say, 'it's behind the times' – an understatement when one considered that in matters of convenience the 'Fleece' was not really in the Christian era. Nor was she reconciled to the place by the attractions that charmed the guests – on first arrival, anyway – for antiquity was just a bore to her, the ornaments almost a form of personal insult, dating from the day when she had been asked to clean the pewter. Naturally she had refused. But still she stayed on at the inn, for though it was dilapidated it was still a shrine, and she was the goddess in attendance.

Her cult was prospering. On Saturdays it was not easy to

approach the bar, for then the gladiators of the Turlminster Rugby Union Football Club would press around it, scrumming as hard as they had done that afternoon, while even on weekdays there was a fairly constant coming and going among the devotees. This was certainly the reason why the management kept her on, but it was not really to Joy's taste; a practical young woman, she preferred one man whispering in her ear to any amount of confused shouting in the distance. On quiet nights – and there were quiet nights, the result of some strange migratory instinct in men's minds – she could enjoy herself to the full; could even forget Rupert for a while and plan to forget him more completely in some new adventure in the country lanes. What was beginning to surprise her, and annoy the customers, was the infrequency with which the plans were executed; she was becoming something of a flirt – a sad regression to respectability that was bound to affect her popularity in the end.

One quiet night in early October Joy found herself with only two 'casuals' in the bar – taproom types, regrettably, for 'casuals' in general were of great interest to her, animated question marks, the chrysalises from which fully fledged admirers might emerge. However, nothing could be made of these particular men, strangers who had blundered into the sacred precincts by mistake, and Joy, who welcomed the occasional period of rest, sat down behind the bar where only her vivid blonde coiffure could be seen and prepared to knit. It was pleasant to see this domesticated Joy, head bent down over the pattern, the needles clicking in her strong, coarse hands, the despair of her fashionable self. She was free to think, and had to think of Rupert: it was an obsession with her now. In three hours – well certainly in four – she would be in his arms again, perhaps for the last time that year in their little hut, a trifle cold now in the damp of an autumn night. They had been happy there; indeed, happiness was too mild a word to express her feelings: the insatiable passion of a woman who has been aroused rather too soon in life and in rather too satisfactory a way. They must find another place. He had no car; that was unfortunate: he had no money, and that was worse. Her aunt's was dangerous. Well, she would find a room, discreetly, somewhere in the poor quarter of the town. That was nothing new. It was only when she reflected that she must pay

133

for it herself that this shrewd young woman realized how much she was a prisoner.

'Two milds, please, miss.'

It was a 'casual', one of the pair over by the window.

She rose haughtily to draw the beer, confirmed in her opinion of these men, for to drink mild at the 'Fleece' was not only a reflexion on a man's palate but also on his social worth. And having served him without a word, she rattled the cash into the register and sat down again to her disturbing, delightful thoughts. To-night in the shed again, and to-morrow – to-morrow her free day – the stolen weekly visit to the sea; the hot darkness of the cinema, the tight clasped hands; the dancing afterwards at the 'Palais', pressed close together when the lights were low, two bodies companionably close, that knew one another, that had no secrets, that knew the ropes.

Her needles clicked faster as her thoughts ran on. They knew where they could go down there by the sea: there was a disused shelter far out beyond the limit of the promenade; the noise of the surf failing on that shingle bed came softly, insistently, like the echo of their movements, the raised, uneven rhythm of their breath.

They could take a room for the night quite easily. It would amuse her to see him take the lead; to see the cheap ring on her finger, his embarrassed, sly approach to the reception desk; to hear the heavy jangle of hotel keys. She would make him. Why not? She would pay. She would pay for the dinner, for the room, for everything. As an adventure it was common form with her. But perhaps he was too young, too suspiciously young. It would not do to expose him to some manager's refusal. Better, perhaps, to put on the brother and sister act. She had played that way before; had laughed delightedly at the simple-mindedness of receptionists, at the masquerade of single rooms.

But the other was the more satisfying way. One bed. With a ring on her finger. As man and wife. Man and wife! Why not? Suppose that were real! It was such a startling thought that she put the needles down and sat staring straight ahead, seeing not the bins, the empty bottles, the disorder underneath the bar, but the lych-gate of a church, the rice, the veils and orange blossom, the livery of respectability. And why not? There were obstacles to such a marriage but, there must be ways around them. They loved one another; that was enough. For unlike so many of the experienced, Joy was never cynical: the ideal of love was very real to her, though she was a little too prompt to recognize it. This time she had no doubts: the mirage had not shifted and she had run up against it at full tilt. This picture of Joy, the settled married woman, would have been certain of a good laugh in the bar-room of the 'Fleece', particularly with those customers - and there were several of them - who had tried to marry her themselves, but it was really an obvious development: characters like hers are made for matrimony, grist to the mill of the Moloch of divorce.

She was getting serious over him. There were disadvantages, of course; his age and the certainty of parental opposition; but how greatly these were outweighed! He was of good family, to begin with, a 'real gentleman', as she would have phrased it - and these words will last be heard on barmaids' lips; he would get on; as the son of Mr Anderson he would some day have money and a position in the world; lastly, and to prove that cupidity cannot hold a candle up to sex, she was madly keen on him - she loved him. In her definition of what this meant she was greatly helped by her experience and by the directness and coarseness of her mind. She could put a word - a whole series of words - to what he meant to her and to the effect that he produced. And consequently love, as she defined it, was a richer thing than some young girl's imagining; its details were filled in with a thousand living touches of remembrance, sordid, tender, gay and lecherous and sad. He loved her, too. How could she doubt it! He wanted her; showed it every day; would show it again to-night. She would choose her time to put the case to him. He loved her, yes, but it was best to choose her time. To-night, early, before he took her to the shed. She looked down at herself and leaning back in her chair stretched her limbs luxuriously, like a cat stirred by some pleasurable sensation as it lies beside the fire. She would give him reason to be grateful afterwards.

And once engaged? Should she wear a ring? She could buy one for herself, a cheap one, something to be going on with till they brought his parents round. A little smile crept into the corners of her mouth as she imagined the mystification of her customers.

They'd be wild – young Ted Sotherby in particular. Wouldn't Ted be wild! Perhaps just once – just once for old times' sake – she'd let him take her driving in his car. A nice boy, Ted, and ever so well off. Wouldn't he be mad! They'd all ask her: Who? Who? Who? Who? And she wouldn't tell.

She was so engrossed in her reflexions that she did not hear the door opening and the steps of a customer coming to the bar. A voice said: 'Good evening, Joy.' At this she started guiltily to her feet, for there had been a little disagreement, even unpleasantness, lately with the management. But it was only Mr Anderson. There he was, his father, almost part of the dream she had been dreaming. It was rather odd.

'Wool gathering, I see,' he said, with a smile at the knitting fallen on the floor, an amorphous bundle in crimson cable-stitch.

'Just thinking,' she replied.

And suppose he knew just what she had been thinking, wouldn't *he* be wild! Or would he? He was a quiet, kind-hearted man, a friend of hers.

Then she remembered. They said he wasn't living with his wife; they said he'd quarrelled with his son; they even said that he was fancying another woman in the town – an unlikely tale to tell to someone in whose eyes the gentleman was rather older than the hills. So was the woman too, a Mrs Grey. She had seen her shopping many times: an old woman, an old stick. With all her bent for scandal Joy thought it was a dirty tale, for they were old and done for and she had all the prejudices of the young.

'A penny for them, then,' he said.

A penny! That was rich; she could laugh at that. If he only knew! Her thoughts, triggers to her actions, were worth a great deal more to him than that.

'I was thinking of my day off to-morrow, if you want to know.'

Mr Anderson was too old a friend to take this as an invitation; he was so little the 'old dog' that he did not even joke with her suggestively about it as most of his cronies would have done. Instead he asked quite seriously:

'What d'you do, Joy? When you're free, I mean.'

That would be a beginning for some men; there would be a

follow-up; it had happened so often in her life. But he was different. He was sensible – and in this phrase she put him in the very last compartment before the grave. Odd to think that for one wild moment Rupert had been jealous of him, jealous of this nice, ineffective man – was perhaps still jealous. It had not been so many weeks ago.

'Do?' she said. 'I stay home and help Auntie mostly.'

Not only 'Auntie' but a considerable percentage of the 'Fleece's' customers could have given the lie to that. But Mr Anderson was one of the few who believed the best of Joy. He said approvingly: 'That's the way. You help her. You'll give pleasure by such unselfishness.'

Well, she gave pleasure right enough: there didn't seem to be much doubt of that. It was really a delightful game to let him talk and use his words as spurs to her own secret thoughts. If he only knew! There he was, praising her, and yet to-morrow in that little shelter by the sea . . . his son.

A new train of thought stirred in her and she began to study him, so artfully that only a young, self-conscious man would have sensed what was going on. Such a quiet, ordinary chap with rather strained grey eyes and thinning hair, a moustache that was still, after thirty years, a raw recruit, a face lined and tired, saved from weakness only by its stubborn jaw. This was the father. Of course she had no suspicions, she accepted it, but on appearances the thing did seem improbable. The man's hands were close to her, one spread out on the counter, the other grasping the pewter tankard; the fingers were short and thick, rather like her own, plodding fingers with wide knuckles enclosed in podgy tucks of flesh; the nails trimmed short, the half-moons only crescents, almost swallowed by the encroaching skin. But Rupert's hands were different: long and spidery, she had so often felt them pressed against her own, lacquered nails, sharp and rather dirty, vibrant hands that caressed and suddenly were strong. Why, they weren't alike one bit.

'I'll have to put down some more money, I can see,' said Mr Anderson.

'Why? Am I away again?'

'You are. Miles away. So far away there's no catching you at all. What *do* you think of there behind the bar?'

137

Joy shrugged her shoulders.

'Oh, I don't know. People, I just think about people, I suppose. I wonder what they are and where they come from, what their businesses are like, what sort of homes they live in – things like that. People are ever so interesting.'

'D'you think so? I shouldn't have thought we amounted to a lot.'

'You'd be surprised,' said Joy, with a knowing laugh. And so he would. The things that had been said about him in that very room! She didn't believe the half of them herself, particularly the bits connecting him with Mrs Grey. But amount to something! She'd say! They'd made it all add up. Someone had seen him slipping in ever so late to Mrs Grey's, or had known someone who'd seen it, anyway, and someone else had caught him very early in the morning walking down the hill not a stone's throw from her house. Only the more disreputable of her customers drew the worst conclusions out of that; his friends were usually content to shake their heads over him and say how greatly they deplored the scandalous stories circulating in the town; they'd like to meet the people who were spreading them, they said. A fine thing if a man couldn't call on an old friend without setting tongues wagging overtime. There was probably some perfectly innocent explanation of the man being out early with the milk. And if these explanations noticeably failed to satisfy, that was no fault of those who sponsored them; it was old Andy's fault, when all was said and done, for giving his defenders such a shaky brief. That was what they said. She wondered if he knew. He must, surely, though he always seemed so unconcerned. It was rather a pathetic pose and Joy, more generous than her betters, truly pitied him; he was such a good sort, so inoffensive, such a poor old fish. It was all nonsense, anyway. What would two old fogies want with one another? Sex! They needn't kid her off with that. Comfort and sympathy, more likely, and she wasn't the one to grudge him that if all the other things they said of him were true.

'Don't you think people are interesting?' she persisted.

He shook his head.

Joy crossed her arms and leaned forward against the bar. When she was thinking her brow was contracted in an effort so violent as to lead to the general belief that she was as stupid a girl as any in Turlminster, the 'dumb blonde' *in excelsis*; it was like watching the mechanism of some ancient clock. But out of this creaking cerebration some shrewd thoughts came.

'That's because you're a solicitor,' she said. 'You only hear the dull side – people's troubles. It's like being a doctor. Doctors only see people when they're ill.'

'And I suppose you see the seamy side of them?'

Well, she heard the seamy side. She knew from hearsay things about her customers that they certainly never even suspected in themselves.

She nodded vigorously. 'Oh yes. You get to know things in a bar. People only tell *you* what they want to, but here they just can't help themselves. It all comes out.'

'You must know quite a bit about us, Joy,' said Mr Anderson, who was amused to see how she had worked the conversation round. A discreet man, trained in a school of secrets, he never ceased to marvel at the things that would interest his fellow-men. There was this case of his separation from his wife, as sordid an event as he could think of, and yet he was well aware of what a tit-bit it had become among his friends, a subject which could be chewed round, and swallowed, and regurgitated, and kept its flavour to the end. He knew most of the gambits now: the shocked surprise and the sympathy offered him in the hopes that he would talk, and to so experienced a hand there was nothing new in Joy's skirmishing up to his defences. He was not a bit annoyed, for he believed, and not without some reason, that she was an ally.

'We all talk too much around closing time,' he said. 'You don't want to believe everything we say.'

'Oh, I don't. I don't reely, Mr Anderson. I know what men are for talk. They say *we* gossip, but I know who's worse.'

On this classic dispute between the sexes Mr Anderson had an open mind. It would certainly have been hard even for a ladies' bridge club to beat the bar-room of the 'Fleece'. It was his opinion that male gossip was the more outspoken, the more colourful, though perhaps the less malicious. If the ladies, as was said, left one without a rag or stitch of reputation, the men made up for it by providing a complete new set of clothes. It was a little hard to recognize oneself in them sometimes.

139

'And I think,' continued Joy, doing less than justice to herself, 'that that's all men come here for – most of 'em. Mind, I don't say you. They just come here to crow about themselves and take each other down.'

He had a smile for this severity.

'Well, Mr Anderson, just you tell me why they come.'

'To see you, to begin with. Ah yes, and a first-rate reason too. And to drink beer and talk; to be friendly. They come for company.'

That was why he had always come: to be companionable – that was one of the nicest words. And since he had left his wife his visits had become more frequent, in spite of the feeling that they were gossiping over him. There was nothing he enjoyed more than a friendly chat over a glass of beer – he didn't care with whom.

She knew it. 'I know that's why *you* come here,' she said. 'It's a break for you when you've got an evening's work ahead. Can't say I'd fancy working on in an office after everyone else has gone. You all that busy, reely?'

She knew the answer to that question, too. He was not so busy, but he had taken to filling in his evenings in this way. It kept his mind from his unpleasant thoughts; it saved him from dwelling on his loneliness, intense whenever Margaret was away.

'Yes, I'm pretty hard at it nowadays,' he said. 'I've work to-night. I must just down this and get along.'

Joy reached out a hand to one of the shelves behind the bar and took down a bottle of Nut-brown.

'Take that along with you,' she said.

It was a kindly gesture. It would help to cheer the evening.

'Thanks, I will. What's it now? Two bob?'

'Two nothing! It's a present on the house.'

'On the house?'

'All right then, on me.'

'Two shillings, Joy,' said Mr Anderson, pushing the money to her across the bar.

But she shook her head. She had a sudden desire to show in some way that she sympathized – an idea so illogical, so absurdly sentimental that it made her feel quite uncomfortable and coy.

'I'll lend you an opener, too,' she said. 'You can drop it back in at closing time.'

Nor would she hear of a refusal. Poor old man, with everyone on at him and taking his character away! He'd been good to her; had bought her a compact only the previous Christmas, a real gift with nothing but kindness at the back of it, not like some other gifts from other men she knew. Now it was her turn. He'd take that beer or she'd know the reason why.

And Mr Anderson, with the best of grace, gave in. With a little more warmth in his heart he put the bottle in the pocket of his overcoat, accepted the opener and went his way. Outside the autumn night had fallen, a damp and foggy night through which the street lamps shone, good deeds in a naughty world with haloes round their glowing heads. There were few lights in the shops and offices; the greater part of Turlminster was home round the fireside; and his evening's work still lay ahead. Even as he paused on the doorstep of the 'Fleece' the chimes rang out from the cathedral belfry, slow and measured, and muffled a little in the surrounding mist. Seven o'clock. Well, there was no point in standing there. The work was waiting for him, and a fire, for Hemmings would have seen to that. It would be quite warm and cheerful once inside, and there was the bottle to provide that other domestic touch of cheer. Alcohol in the office! How shocked his staff would be!

Before the reverberation of the chimes had died away he had stepped out on his last short journey on this earth. Behind him in the bar Joy was reflecting that in three brief hours she would be waiting in the darkness by the stile.

18

RUPERT went quickly down the stairs and out into the street.
He accepted every word he had been told. Indeed, such are
the possibilities of self-deception, it is likely that Laura believed
them too, not on the evidence of her husband's letter, one of the
most cautious and legalistic he ever wrote, but on the strength of
her suspicions and the gossip of her neighbours. If Turlminster
believed it – and the bridge-playing, feminine part of Turlminster
was pleased to think it did – then it was not to be wondered at
that those most personally affected should believe it also. Taking
it all in all, this had been the most satisfactory scandal to break
in the town for years: a husband's marriage, a daughter's
engagement and one lady's chastity all jeopardized – a pleasant
bag.

He was seen by several people as he hurried down Colbert
Row and Redgrave Street towards his father's office. Looking
back, they remembered, with that eye for drama that is so keen
after the event, how pale and harassed he had looked: 'Like a
ghost', had been the opinion of Mrs Fawkes; 'Hatless and with
staring eyes', according to the evidence of Mr Glass; thus and
in similar terms was he described in the statements made to the
police and in the prosecution's brief. Even allowing for the ex-
aggeration of these witnesses brought for the first time into the
intoxicating limelight of the world, a certain strangeness may be
allowed to him. Mr Hemmings, the firm's clerk, a better-trained
observer and a man who was reputed to be incapable of emotion,
remembered that the boy had called at the office just after six
o'clock, and judged him to have been 'Not himself' and 'Just
a bit done in'. 'I told him to be off back home,' this witness
said, 'and then I shut the door.' For Mr Anderson was not at
work; he was in the saloon bar of the 'Golden Fleece'.

Mr Hemmings, a most conscientious man, remained at his
ledgers till half past six, then closed up, locked away the cash and
set off down the stairs for home. There was someone standing in
the doorway of a shop across the street, a position of vantage

from which both the office and the 'Fleece' could conveniently be watched, but with scrupulous fairness, at a later time, he refused to venture on an identification; it was the figure of a man, so much he was prepared to say, a smallish man, but he had paid no particular attention. No, he had not been afraid of burglary, not at that hour, for he knew that soon Mr Anderson would be returning to his desk; it was a habit of some years standing, more regularly adopted, Mr Hemmings had observed, now that his master had no proper home to go to after working hours.

Seven was striking from the cathedral tower as Mr Anderson came out of the hotel and began walking up the road. By that time Hemmings was comfortably at home with a meal in front of him and his slippers on, the affairs of Anderson, Rees, & Sinclaire-Poole not forgotten – for they accompanied Hemmings everywhere, his ghostly and comforting familiars – but at least relegated into the background of his mind; someone else, however, retained a living interest in the firm, a shadow that slipped from its sheltered refuge across the darkened street.

The solicitor ponderously mounted the stairs and unlocked his office door. The fire was still burning in the grate, and having switched on the table lamp and drawn the curtains he went and stood in front of it, warming his hands, for the autumn night was bleak. With the instinct of the householder he tended it, prodding out the embers with the heavy poker, adding more coal and a log of wood till the result satisfied even his exacting taste. Hemmings was a good fellow, an invaluable assistant, he reflected, but a poor hand at a fire, willing but unteachable.

Now that this had been attended to the next task was to select a pipe. A rack containing a dozen of them was hanging beside the mantelpiece, for smoking was his one acknowledged vice, as it had been his father's. There was an old meerschaum there, relic of his student days, a fanciful affair carved in the German style so fashionable in his youth; another was his father's gift in the last year of his life, a briar, solid and severely practical, old and foul now beyond redemption, the mouthpiece stained from constant use. How many happy smokes he had had from them!

He took his most recent acquisition from the rack and leaning one elbow on the mantelpiece began to fill it, seriously, intently, as one who performs a ritual, then lit it, blowing out regular jets of smoke towards the prints and diplomas on the wall above the fire. It was a performance that never failed to comfort him, a sequence of countless repetitions, a pledge of order and normality. Once his whole life had been like that, for no one could have taken more pleasure in the average, but now late in life when his adaptability had deserted him he found himself faced with hateful, bewildering situations. The round of actions had become corrupt: he had fought with his wife for the happiness of Margaret, had been driven from his home in consequence – he who hated scandal more than anything except injustice – and now saw that by that action of deserting, so natural, so necessary, he had completed the destruction of the very thing he had tried his best to save. John had succeeded to the betrayer Laura, a young man also of a conventional turn of mind – conventional in a disgraceful, cowardly way, thought Mr Anderson, seeing with a human weakness his own virtues as vices in another. It was certainly ironical that this man, the pattern of respectability, grieving over his daughter's unhappiness and the break-up of his home, should have been seen at Turlminster bridge tables in the role of an adulterer; it was a tribute to that sense of drama innate in human beings, who can see the light of adventure in the most unlikely places. But even the good ladies of the town, with all their fertility of imagination, had not imagined their story's end – the shadow waiting in the fading light, the footfall on the stairs.

Mr Anderson caught the sound – there was a loose board near the middle of the second flight – and wondered who his visitor could be. Perhaps Hemmings had returned as he sometimes did, around quarter days when the work was heaviest. He would know soon enough, for the methodical clerk, in arrival, in departure, in all his daily round, repeated his actions and his very steps with the regularity of a machine. No sounds of any kind succeeded; it seemed as though the visitor had halted half-way up the stairs, uncertain perhaps whether the offices were open at that hour. The idea of burglary no more entered his head than it had entered Mr Hemmings', for the office was in the centre of the town, a town, moreover, where crime was almost too great a rarity – looking at the matter from the professional point of view.

But there had been someone on the stairs, Mr Anderson was sure of that. When a minute had gone by without a repetition of the sound, he crossed the heavily carpeted room to the private door that gave access to the stairhead and opened it.

He expected to see a figure on the landing just below him; instead, there was Rupert on the threshold not a yard away, his body bent so that he appeared even smaller than he was, his white oval face thrust forward, eerie in the dim light shining out into the landing from the lamp on the office desk.

Mr Anderson took a quick step backwards into the room; he was not a nervous man, but the effect of that sudden snap of vision had been profoundly disconcerting. How silent, how secretive, that passage up the stairs had been; how unnecessary, his common sense reminded him the moment the flash of fear had passed and he was himself again. But a trace of uneasiness remained, and his voice was far from friendly as he demanded: 'What are you doing here?' With any other visitor he would no doubt have added: 'You quite scared me, creeping up like that,' but such an admission in this case somehow seemed unwise – well, undesirable, perhaps. It was a strange time for a call, a very strange time. He looked at the boy again; a puny chap nearly a head shorter than himself; he did not consciously reassure himself by these comparisons. 'Never mind, come in,' he said.

He led the way into the room, pointed out a chair for the visitor by the fire, then seated himself at his desk and swivelled round to face him. His pipe had gone out and he relit it, rather clumsily, being liberal with matches in a way that would have surprised Mr Hemmings very much.

'Well, what is it?' he said at last.

Rupert held out his hands to the fire. It had been cold waiting in the street and he too had been disconcerted by that sudden opening of the door. But he was certainly not afraid. The obvious signs of disquiet in this gross, hateful man delighted him; they lent him the advantage of the hunter, that disparity that gives the fat rabbit to the stoat.

'It's about mother, of course,' he said.

Mr Anderson set down his pipe and his face took on its most stubborn look, 'Old Anderson's pug jaw', as it was known to brother attorneys in the county courts. The chances were that she had put him up to this. It was an impertinence and he was not prepared to suffer it.

'About your mother? May I ask whether she has sent you here?'

Rupert shook his head.

'It would have been most improper if she had. You are not qualified by age or anything else to interfere.' In this Mr Anderson was being a little hard. But the memory of his last experience of this boy had deeply impressed itself on his mind and left him with a feeling of aversion so that he added: 'You and I have nothing whatsoever to discuss.'

Rupert from his chair beside the fire replied very coolly: 'Oh, but haven't we!'

'We have not,' said Mr Anderson, looking at his visitor with distaste. Now that he could see him in the light of Laura's words he marvelled that he had ever been deceived and seen traces of his blood in this effeminate – for even to this extent did he misjudge the boy. Yet his sense of justice did not desert him and prompted him to add: 'I'm sorry things have happened the way they have. You didn't deserve it. But one thing's certain: I won't discuss my wife with you.'

'We'll discuss my mother, if you please.'

'*You* can discuss it,' said Mr Anderson pointedly.

Rupert turned his attention from the fire and looked his enemy directly in the face. 'Are you coming back to her?' he asked.

'I certainly am not.'

'Why?'

There was no answer.

'I said, why? What has she done? Tell me one thing that she's done.'

How much he could have said! But as with her, so with her son: it had always been his fate to be put into the wrong. He did not reply but fumbled with his tobacco pouch.

This silence had all the quality of guilt, and Rupert, observing him, felt the revival of those feelings that had come to him as he had sat beside his mother's bed. This was the author of their misfortunes, this large, smug man who dared to play the role of the respectable solicitor. His anger boiled up and he demanded almost threateningly: 'I'll ask again. Are you coming back?'

'I think you'd better go,' said Mr Anderson.

A dull flush of colour had spread in Rupert's cheeks. 'So that's it! You think you've finished with us. You're very wrong. You think you can write letters to my mother and hurt her and we can't hit back. And then, best of all, you think you can play around with other women too.' His voice rose. 'I know,' he said. 'I know why it is you're always hanging round that bar. And I know how it is between you and Mrs Grey.'

Mr Anderson laughed. He felt that Providence in thus pursuing him was showing a rather low sense of the absurd. It never entered his head to think how close he was to tragedy; indeed, so absent was all sense of danger that he swivelled round towards his desk, reaching for the ashtray near the telephone.

It was the unwisest action of his life. That laugh, which had been his answer to the most ridiculous of charges, had quite another meaning for the boy; to him it could only mean a confession, the blatant confirmation of his mother's words. Almost by chance his eyes lighted on the heavy poker lying against the fender; it was close to him as he sat in the fireside chair, and moved by a sudden diabolic impulse, he leaned forward and put his hand caressingly against the handle. In that instant, as he felt the polished iron, smooth and clinging to his touch, he knew what he would do. His grip tightened and as he drew the implement from the fender, weighing its balance like a man with a new tennis racquet, he rose noiselessly to his feet. From where he stood Mr Anderson's back was presented to him at a range of a few yards; above it the pale waxy tonsure of the skull in its circlet of greying hair. And as he struck there were many conflicting images in his mind: memories of jealousies and small passions, his mother's face and body on the bed, the seductive warmth of Joy, images of a nightmare, sensual, violent, all blotted out in the red tide of hatred sweeping over him as the blow went home.

' Something of these movements seemed to have been divined: the victim had half turned and was rising from the chair; the glancing stroke caught him on the right side of the scalp above the ear. Almost stunned, he still had the strength to stagger towards his enemy and still had the wit to raise his arm as a protection against the blows, till one, more accurately delivered,

147

dropped his guard and three more rained upon him, so that consciousness left him and he dropped on his knees, then rolled on to his left side by the fire. He had not spoken or cried out; his fall made little sound; he seemed dead as he lay there, yet took some time to die. When they found him, late that night, his body was sprawled out on the carpet, his head close against the grate. The fourth in line from the temple had been the lethal blow, the doctors said.

19

JUST before eleven o'clock on that same evening Laura awoke from the sleep of exhaustion that had followed the departure of her son; she had heard a step outside in the corridor – Rupert on his way to bed. Always avid for sympathy and assured of his tender care for her, she sat up against the pillows and patted her hair into place, composing a picture for his entry. But no hand was set on the latch and she could hear the steps grow fainter down the passage in the direction of his room. It was not till she was fully awake that she realized how slight the noise had been, the sound of someone moving cautiously in stockinged feet. Then perhaps it was not Rupert after all. But Laura dismissed the thought, telling herself that it must be he: this silence was just another illustration of his love for her and his anxiety that she should sleep. It was not long before another possible explanation had occurred. This was not the first time he had come in quietly, late at night, returning, as she correctly guessed, from some adventure with a woman. She had even taxed him with it once, tolerantly, with an appearance of good humour that disguised her jealousy, for it was a curiously attractive, curiously wounding thought to imagine a woman in his arms. She would go to him now and speak of it again.

But first she must make up; she must not expose herself to unfavourable comparisons. How hideous she looked! Her eyes were red with weeping, the skin above the cheekbones was puffy and discoloured, the whole face had relapsed into that state from which it was daily rescued at so great a cost of cosmetics and art. She applied herself diligently till the reflexion of her skill gazed back at her from the glass, the mouth and eyes corrected, all possible lines erased – a touch of black pencil smeared in below the eyes, a little reminder of the tragic experience she had undergone, and the picture was complete. Her friends, even her hairdresser, would have applauded the effect.

Thus armed, she went down the corridor to Rupert's room and tapped gently on the door. She heard a scuffling noise beyond, and when, without waiting for his answer, she went in she found him between the washstand and the bed, half dressed and with his shirt – a rather dirty shirt, it seemed – carried in his hand. Unsuspicious as she was, she found his manner odd and furtive, as though he had a secret he did not want to share. And perhaps he had, for she knew something of the habits of young men and the follies of young women; there might be some trophy in the room, or even – amazing thought – the girl herself.

'What's the matter, dear?' she said. She had by now reached the centre of the room and there was no possible mistaking the terrified expression in his eyes. Whatever the cause, the fear was surely overdone: she loved him, she was forgiving, he must know, and even if the girl were there in hiding quite undressed ...

'Why, what is it, Rupert? Why do you look at me like that?' He murmured, 'Nothing,' but in so low a voice she scarcely heard. And now he was sitting on the bed, the shirt still clutched tightly in his hand, absurdly, as though precious to him in some way and not just destined for the laundry basket. How very soiled it looked!

Perhaps at that moment she first had some dim understanding of the truth. Of course her mind rejected it, clinging to the only other explanation that could fit the facts, so that she asked appealingly: 'Is it a girl, Rupert? Is it that?'

He did not reply but remained staring at her from the bed. How ill he looked and how dishevelled! That was no new, surprising thing, for in spite of all her efforts to make him in her image the soul of tidiness, he had always been careless in his dress and in the keeping of his room. But surely even he was not in the habit of throwing his tie and pullover on the floor and bundling his coat up like a sack. There they were, lying in a heap on the patch of linoleum near the washing basin, and with that instinct of fussiness that will reveal itself in mothers at the most unexpected times she went over to pick them up.

Then it was that she saw against the white porcelain surface of the basin the stains of blood.

She bent down towards the coat. And there the blood lay, too, though it was not so immediately apparent against the dark texture of the cloth. Then he must be injured.

She came over to him by the bed. There was blood on the shirt that he was carrying, blood diluted in the washing so that it looked as innocuous as ink; there was blood on his trousers and on his hands. Silently she searched his face, his arms, his body under its thin cotton singlet, hopeful that she would find some explanation there. But there was no wound on him. It sent a shudder through her to see him sitting there so whole, so unblemished, and then to think what he had done. Intuitively she had reached the truth. Yet she remained calm. Her earlier breakdown was an advantage to her now, for it had so drained her of emotion that she had none to spare and could face the new crisis without scruples of conscience and in reliance on her wits. She said very quietly: 'Is he dead?'

And somehow the admission came easily to him, almost as a relief after the intolerable memories of the night. Once the words were spoken they stood between him and his actions, a protective skin, so that what was done seemed almost bearable in the calm light of what was said.

In the same spirit she listened. It was surprising, really, how words could be detached from the ideas dictating them, how one could hear of the weapon without seeing the wound, of death without knowledge of that body writhing in its last agony on the floor.

So though he tried to say what he had done he did not say it, and she, after the first moment of revulsion, was not greatly shocked, for whatever truth may be, it is ephemeral, existing only for the instant and submerged the moment that it enters memory.

She asked him what had made him strike the blow. 'Because you wanted it,' he said.

And had she wanted it? The result, most probably, for she had hated the dead man with all her heart and would have struck him down herself if she had dared. Now she did not hate him any more. With a flash of generous emotion she remembered earlier, happier times, small kindnesses long buried under the accumulation of her bitter thoughts.

But whatever tender feelings for her husband were reviving at this hour were stilled by the sound of a car drawing up outside in Colbert Row. She ran to the window and lifting a

151

corner of the curtain stared down into the street. She saw the compact blue limousine, saw the uniform of the driver as he got out to open the rear door, and turned back into the room, her terror only held in check by her determination to save her son.

'It's the police,' she said.

It was enough to deflate all his new-found confidence; whereas she was vibrant with energy, he sat indecisively on the bed, white of face and very near collapse.

'Rupert, did you hear? They've come to question us.'

Still he could say nothing, while from outside there came the noise of the closing of a door and steps on the pavement of the Row.

'Rupert, listen to me. Did anyone see you there?'

'Hemmings,' he said.

'When?'

'About an hour before.'

'And later no one? Are you sure?'

He hung his head, quite unable to match this tremendous vitality of hers, at its peak now that he was in danger and dependent on her.

'Did you meet anyone on your way back home?'

'I don't remember.'

'You must remember,' she cried. 'There's so little time.'

And as though to prove it there came a loud ringing of the front-door bell. He jumped up from the bed, panic close upon him, till she gripped him fiercely by the arm.

'It's all right. You're safe. Just answer me.'

'I don't think I saw anyone,' he said.

'Good, good! And it happened about eight. You were here then, do you understand?' He looked blankly at her, so that she repeated in a louder voice: 'You were here. Here at home. I saw you. You spoke with Hemmings and then you came back home.'

The bell rang again, insistently, pealing through the house, a terrible stimulus to her wits and to the plan rapidly forming in her mind.

'They've come for me,' he said.

It was not a very helpful contribution to her problem and she shook his arm angrily, contemptuously, as one might shake a stupid, naughty child.

'Listen,' she commanded. 'Listen and you're safe. They'll ask you questions. You know nothing. You called at the office but your father was out, so you came home. Have you got it? You came home.'

His answer was to glance across the room towards the washing-stand. It was another call on her for action.

'Wash your hands,' she said.

His movements were still dazed, lethargic, and she pushed him across the room and turned the tap. And while he slowly began to rinse his hands she seized the bloodstained clothing and ran with it down the passage to her room, thrusting it in a bundle among her underclothes. Her return journey was pursued by the third pealing of the bell, mingled this time with the noise of voices and the heavy clash of the brass knocker on the door.

At last he had been stirred to action of a kind. His hands were washed, but so carelessly that thin rivulets of blood lay in the soap dish and around the waste pipe of the basin. She rinsed them out, then took a quick glance round the room. There was blood on the linoleum at her feet. She used the towel on this, and all the while her active mind was racing on ahead, planning, ordering, encouraging.

'Get your clothes off. Get into bed. You know nothing. You were home. Get into bed and leave the rest to me.'

Gradually under the spell of her energy and courage he was beginning to respond. He slipped off his shoes and socks, his singlet; the trousers too were stained and he handed them to her. She came over to the bed, and though bell and knocker were sounding madly through the house, kissed him gently on the cheek. He was helpless, he relied on her, and the knowledge of these things, the memory of his childhood, brought out all the strength and passion of her nature. She would save him as she had saved him from thrashings in those earlier days, making a virtue of deceit.

And now delay was no longer possible. They were already suspicious and might break down the door. Picking up the towel and trousers she fled down to her room, roughed out her hair, and running down the stairs unlocked the door.

153

She was not afraid when she saw the police inspector and his subordinates standing there. She had retrieved disaster, she had made a plan. In her elation she had not for one moment stopped to think whether that plan was really wise.

20

IN the short time between her father's death and the inquest on his body Margaret had learned the true nature of privacy – a plank over a public abyss. She had learned her lesson painfully in the light of the flares of press photographers, in the columns of the papers, in the faces of her friends, and because she had loved her father and was sensitive for his honour she felt these things and resented them with all her heart. She had led a sheltered life. No one was ever more incapable of profiting by them, as so many in the spotlight of the world have the weakness, or the strength, to do; no one was ever less fitted to take the cynical, disenchanted view and find it strange that one man's suffering and death should have made their small town a Mecca of the nation's thought, where all the efforts of pious ecclesiastical founders and craftsmen and that modern propagandist, the Dean of Turlminster, had only been able to squeeze a small space in Baedeker and an occasional study in *The Times*.

The small house had been besieged; at the inquest she had been exposed. There had been the terrible moment, that afternoon after the adjournment, when they had come from the coroner's court into the street, she and her mother, Kay and Rupert, and the assaulting batteries had been turned on them. They had come down the steps and there, awaiting them, was the heartless inquisition of the world. Their photographs in the evening papers went well with the evidence that had been given in that court, illustrating and underlining by contrast the words that had been spoken from the witness stand: terrible words of violence that had crept their way into the limelight past the doctor's dry, unemotional recitals. In salute to them the papers carried pictures of the chief police surgeon, too, though there was precious little that was dramatic about him or about the impersonal face he had turned towards the cameras. The words that he had used reflected no pity or tragedy on him; they belonged to that poor body on the mortuary slab, and, since that could not be photographed, to these the relatives, the dead man's flesh and blood. That this interest was concentrated on Rupert in particular was no more than proof of the intelligent anticipation of the Press. The boy had given no evidence and had taken no part in the proceedings yet he had earned a photo to himself – a cause of uneasiness to Margaret, who was worldly enough to sense a significance that her mind would not admit. Such things could not be; they were unthinkable, and therefore never far from thought; but there had been such menace in the attitude of the police, a confidence that had impressed itself on every sensitive observer in the Court.

When the bell pealed through the house she did her best to ignore it – it had rung so often in the last few days. Indeed, it was only dimly that she distinguished a second ring, and a third, repeated in a rhythm that recalled the emotions of the past. John! It was the bell signal that they had used in happier days.

She rose rapidly from her chair and almost ran towards the door, slowing to a walk as she reached the passage and the remembrance of reality. They had not met since the quarrel that had followed Laura's interference; months had passed; he would be a stranger to her now. Indeed, it was a stranger's face she saw as she opened to him, the face of the curate, parish visiting, as professional as Laura's, seen on the Court steps that afternoon. What could he know about her sorrow, what could he feel beyond the obligations of routine? There was not even an obligation in her case, some wayward, bitter thought was prompting her, for she was not of his denomination and there was not that shadow of a reason for his call.

Seen now in this moment of detachment, what a Pharisee he looked: his hat, his suit, everything about him, canonical to a degree. All black. He had been careless once, had worn a grey pullover, she remembered, and sometimes, on their country excursions, an open-necked shirt and an old mackintosh of military cut. She was not to see in this new correctness the influence of Canon Willoughby, still less of Mary Willoughby, though she recognized the change and, as one more proof that she had lost him, dimly and instinctively resented it.

For she loved him still. That realization was the bitterest of all. Through the mists of her unhappiness she recognized, with contempt for her own weakness, that he still had the power to move her, to make her tremble so much that she dared not take his hand, and that he could rouse in her heart and body sensations of the most painful, passionate longing.

He looked in better health, a shade heavier and more mature than she remembered, and that was a source of grievance, too. How monstrous that he should come to her door at such a time! How monstrous that it should happen that she wanted him!

She stood still just inside the threshold, and did not move aside to let him in. But clergymen, like door-to-door salesmen, are equipped for such emergencies; they have a technique of visiting and can cope with all but the most intransigent. She was quite surprised to see the easy way in which he insinuated himself into the house, laying his hat – that ostentatiously clerical hat – on the small table in the hall, rubbing his hands together as he manoeuvred her towards the sitting-room, and then sat down, by some unfortunate chance, in her father's easy chair.

'I hoped you'd see me, Margaret,' he began.

Judging from his conduct in the hall he had not relied on hope alone, and remembering this, she looked sourly at him, as he sat with his hands stretched out along his knees, and said: 'I don't see why you had to come.'

'I thought that I could help, you see.'

'Why?' asked Margaret, and as she spoke she had a sudden vision of the role of his sort of comfort in a life – impotent word without a meaning. In one way only could he comfort her, and, to her self-disgust, that knowledge crystallized. Ah, if he were to take her in his arms there would be comfort then. But there seemed small likelihood of that. He remained impassively in the armchair, while with every moment the distance between them seemed to grow, pushing their night on Farshot Hill into that limbo where memory no longer supports reality but has to take its place.

John had not replied to her question. He was uncertain whether words could comfort her and shrank from substituting actions. He did not quite know why he had called: old friendship and the obligation of his cloth would be at the bottom of it, he supposed, for though he could not help softening in the presence of this woman, so much more beautiful than Mary Willoughby, more than an influential canon now stood between him and the

157

old love – there was now a body and a scandal, shortly to be joined, he suspected, by something more scandalous still. But he had his memories, and his office to perform, and he would do it, and do it graciously.

'I was at the inquest,' he said.

At that, he was shocked to see that she was in tears. 'There, there,' he murmured, but he did not rise from his chair, contenting himself with these paternal sounding words which somehow failed to comfort her. The only thing to do was to repeat them, and this he did. 'Margaret, you mustn't really. He'd not have wanted it.'

She raised her eyes to his – beautiful eyes, he noticed with a faint tug of memory; beautiful grey eyes with long dark lashes; honest, candid eyes that he had loved. Without willing it and with the shade of Mary restraining each reluctant move, his gaze travelled down her: past the retroussé nose; to the mouth, trembling now, a wide, generous mouth devoid of make-up; to the pointed chin; down to the neck and breasts, small breasts, delicately formed; to the trim legs in woollen stockings and the feet in their sensible brogue shoes. She had loved him and still loved him. It would be so easy to make up; he had only to rise and go to her and she would be lying in his arms.

It was not Mary Willoughby who held him back, and even the canon, with all his offerings of preferment, was not much more corporeal a shade. No, he was remembering the inquest, recalling the medical evidence as clearly as though it were being repeated in this room. The body had been found sprawled out on the floor, head towards the fireplace, both arms extended, the feet against the office desk. Five blows had been struck at the right side of the skull: three were superficial, glancing blows; two were deep and violent; one of these, penetrating to a branch artery, had been the lethal stroke. There were other bruises: one on the left elbow, caused, no doubt, in falling; others on the right elbow and forearm, raised, perhaps, to ward off the attack. That was the evidence, and hearing it, who could doubt that this was wilful murder, even though the inquest was unfinished and the verdict would have to wait until the morning? Nor was that all. He found himself recalling the evidence of the police, grudgingly given as though everything that mattered were being held back;

the atmosphere in court, heavy with unspoken words and secrets that the police and coroner seemed to share. There were rumours in the town, though naturally one discounted them, persistent rumours on everybody's tongue. They said that an arrest was imminent and that the inquest would be adjourned. They said ... her brother. It wasn't easy to forget these things in spite of loyalties.

Fortunately for his honour and charity the sense of obligation was strong in him. Even while his brain was imagining the reactions of his parishioners – which, if only he had known, were favourable to the family, a very human mixture of generosity, pity and scandalized excitement – the professional half of him, constantly encroached on the man, was determined to do its duty. Nor was he without compassion. He felt truly sorry for this woman in her distress and would have done almost anything for her except the one thing she desired.

'There, there,' he repeated. 'Don't cry, Margaret. It's over now,' but even as he reassured her the gossip of the town redoubled in his brain: her brother, her brother, they'd arrest her brother. It was not all over, but just beginning. She would need to save her tears.

Perhaps the same thought had come to Margaret, for suddenly she sat up against the cushions of the settee and began to dab at her eyes with a handkerchief – not a finicky one, he noted, of the kind that Mary used but large and sensible, already crumpled from earlier use. She was looking far from well, with dark shadows under the eyes and a peaky look, but she had never seemed to him more beautiful. Deaf for the moment to the words of warning ringing in his brain, his gaze returned to her, dwelling on her hair, the delicate skin, the slim figure in the old grey dress. Even on Farshot and at the moment of the writing of the letter he had failed to think of her like this: his for the asking; she was willing; it was written in every line of her.

Miss Willoughby would have been shocked to see the expression kindling in her lover's eyes: sensual, tender, which was bad enough, but matrimonial too, which was far, far worse. Old memories were reviving, an explosive mixture when stirred with new desires; more tears were needed to supply the match, and the train would have been fired to blow these two into each other's arms. So little was required. If Margaret had known she might have stooped to win him; perhaps even without knowledge she would have acted instinctively in her need of him. But at this moment of destiny the door-bell rang.

The Press? Some neighbour? Some Good Samaritan? He rose to his feet and, without the deliberate desire to overhear, stood close to the living-room door while she went to answer. Conflicting emotions were struggling in his heart: pity for her, anger at the interruption, the breathless realization of what they both might do, and, at bottom, an infinite relief. For he was no adventurer, he mistrusted love and feared desire and was still the man of Farshot and of the letter that had followed, never more cautious than at those moments when he was on the verge of an imprudence. Who could it be, this infuriating spell-breaker, this providential interrupter?

The door was opening; there was a rush of steps and he heard a voice he recognized, her sister Kay; then words of a significance he could not miss: 'Rupert . . . The police . . .' What was that? It must have come to an arrest.

He straightened up as the sisters came into the room, feeling almost tempted, in spite of himself, to believe that Providence had intervened and guided him. Pity and friendship he would always feel, but tears would have no object now, neither would Miss Willoughby have further cause for fear.

'Now what the devil were you thinking of!' cried Barry Clarke. He had descended like a thunderbolt on the family in Colbert Row and had heard from Laura a remarkably untruthful outline of events. 'You must have lost your wits,' he said.

She protested but was swept aside.

'Now let's get this thing straight. The boy called at the office and came away. Later Robert was found dead. And a handkerchief with the boy's initials on it was found beside the body. That's the case?'

Laura agreed that it was.

'And all the time that evening while Robert was being killed, Rupert was at home?'

She said defiantly: 'He was.'

Mr Clarke, with a gesture, expressed the profoundest disbelief. 'That's his alibi, I suppose? And you're the witness?'

'Yes, I am.'

'The only witness?'

'Yes.'

'Then God help you both!' said Barry Clarke.

He paid not the smallest attention to her indignant, shocked surprise, but swept on. 'Laura, just for once be reasonable and think. Think of the inquest, the evidence that was given and the atmosphere in court. Wasn't it obvious that the police *knew* and were holding back to get everything neat and tidy? And then think about your story. If you were on a jury would you believe a word of it?'

'Of course. It's true.'

'Then you're very gullible. Other people won't believe. I'll tell you frankly that I don't.'

'You don't believe he's innocent?'

'Of murder, yes. I'm sure he didn't murder Robert; just as certain as I am he killed him.'

'But he wasn't there,' wailed Laura. 'He was at home. Weren't you, Rupert?'

The boy, who had been sitting apart from them in the window seat, echoed his mother's words.

Mr Clarke paid even less attention to him.

'Laura, he *was* there. The handkerchief was his.'

'Yes, but Robert will have taken it. They often mixed theirs up.'

This explanation, more ingenious than convincing, had no effect on Barry Clarke. 'Stuff and nonsense!' he said. 'No jury'll swallow that. Then there's the weapon, a poker, I think you said. I'm sorry, Laura, but I've just got to talk about it. There will have been finger-prints on it, you can be sure.'

'But they'd not take his finger-prints! As though he were a criminal!'

There was a delicious inconsequence in this that would nor-mally have delighted him. But beneath all the callousness and bluster Barry was really moved both by his son's danger and the tragedy of Robert's death; he was in serious mood and, seeing the impression his last words had made, pressed his advantage home.

'They *will* take his prints. They're certain to come down here. They'll probably search the house, and' – with a keen look at Laura that drained all the blood out of her face – 'when they do that, God knows what they'll find, unless you've acted and it's already burnt. Add the boy's calling at the office, the chance that someone saw him going in or out, and you've got the police case to a tee. It's a strong case, and just to make it stronger you get the boy to make a damn fool statement denying everything that wouldn't deceive a child in arms.'

They had nothing to reply to this but stared at him with fascinated horror.

'I don't know how you could have been so stupid. You've tied everything up and handed it to that inspector on gold plate. All he's got to do now is to check up with a bunch of witnesses and then go down for a warrant of arrest.'

Rupert had risen from his seat, and Laura, seeing the stricken expression on his face, cried out: 'Oh, Barry, how could you say it! How could you torture him!'

'To save him, of course,' said Mr Clarke.

'Save him?'

'Naturally. But I can't begin until I get rid of all this rubbish you've piled around the case.' His voice dropped from its casual, brutal tone and became grave. 'Laura, take this from me: if you persist in these denials you risk his life.'

She cried out at that so piteously that he was moved by her distress.

'He'll be all right, I know he will. But not along your lines. No one will accept his alibi in the face of what the police will prove. Come on, you can tell me.' He looked pointedly at the mother and said: 'You know you can. You must tell me if he was there.'

'Yes,' she said.

'Good, good, that's better! And he struck the blow?'

'But he didn't murder him.'

'Of course he didn't murder him,' said Mr Clarke, with enormous confidence. 'I never for a moment thought he did.'

Laura had revived under the spell of her cousin's personality but relapsed into despair as she saw new dangers arising in her path. 'But what can we tell the police?' she cried.

'The truth, of course.'

'The truth?'

'Yes. That Robert was violent, drunk, perhaps; he'd been down to the "Fleece". Rupert pleaded with his father to return to you. There was a violent scene. The boy was threatened, abused, showed spirit, was attacked. He feared for his life and fought back with the only weapon he possessed, the only thing that could make him the equal of that large violent man. And in the struggle he killed him.' He turned to Rupert and looked directly into his eyes. 'Wasn't that the truth?'

There was a long moment of silence while mother and son took in the implication of these words. Then Rupert answered, 'Yes.'

Mr Clarke sighed deeply; it was the measure of his relief.

'Of course it happened just like that,' he said. 'It was never murder, never even manslaughter; it was self-defence.'

'But what about the statement he's already made?'

'He was afraid; you were both afraid. What more natural than that you should both give way to panic when it was realized what he'd done! What more natural than that you should try to cover up! It would have been better, much better, to have told the truth in the first place. But you're a mother, he's young, and the jury will excuse you both.'

'The jury!' cried Laura. 'Must there be a trial?'

Well really, reflected Barry, women were absurd. After this killing, this lying, did she seriously suppose that the whole matter could be forgotten?

'Yes, there'll be a trial. But don't worry, he'll walk out free. The thing now is to see if there's any evidence for our case apart from Rupert's word.'

And here the young man, who had remained quietly in the background, intervened. 'I know the barmaid at the "Fleece",' he said.

Both Laura and Barry looked at him with interest and surprise, the one identifying, not without a sense of shock, the young woman whose trail she had picked up, the other a little enviously, for he too knew Joy, though not with quite the same degree of intimacy. Well, the young dog! And she was a juicy piece – a very juicy piece, thought Mr Clarke, with memories of the favours granted him in other days by ladies just as succulently beddable. Those breasts and buttocks, those lips, those thighs! He sighed, saluting beauty and its thrilling, warm delights from the threshold of his new respectability.

'So you know Miss Roberts?' he said, mistakenly believing that this formal address would mislead his hostess. He did not thereby avoid Laura's sharp, inquisitive and jealous glance. 'Do you know her well?'

Rupert blushed and admitted that he had often spoken with the lady.

And slept with her quite often too, thought Mr Clarke, aided in his detective work less by the young man's manner and expression than by the bias of his own erotic mind. The boy was the right sort to please the ladies. Mere muscle was not the thing desired; personal force of character and technique were more important and he did not doubt that Rupert was equipped with these. After all, this was his son.

'I think,' he said, 'that Rupert or I – dependent on events – must see Miss Roberts very soon.'

'You think she'll help?' enquired Mrs Anderson, not altogether happy on this ground.

'My dear Laura, I'm sure she will. Eh, Rupert?'

'I hope so, Uncle Barry.'

He hoped so, the young devil! Robert *had* been in the bar.
And if a woman who'd been well served wouldn't stretch a point
to help her man then he, Barry Clarke, had no experience of the
sex. She was the sort who would be grateful, a giver, if he'd ever
seen one, and not over-scrupulous in conscience or other things.
And how her evidence would help! It would establish the ground
on which a plea of self-defence could afterwards be raised – very
different sort of evidence from that absurd alibi of Laura's. It
would be independent, disinterested evidence in the jury's eyes,
he thought with an inward chuckle, remembering just how disinterested it would really be.

'Well then,' he continued, the trace of a smile lingering on
his face, 'Miss Roberts is objective number two. But there's
something more important still and that must be attended to
without delay. That, Rupert, is your statement to the police.'

'The one I've made?'

'The new one, the truthful one you'll make to-day.'

'Must he, Barry?' asked Laura, who kept constant watch on
the susceptibilities of her son. 'He's gone through such a lot.'

Her cousin was decisive. 'He most certainly must. He must
go down to the police and tell the truth, the whole truth, and
nothing but the truth. He knows what happened. His father was
the aggressor. He forced Rupert down; there was nothing for it
but to strike. By the way, where were the wounds?'

Laura had given a gasp at the brutal words but Rupert was
now as calm as Clarke. 'On the right side of his head between
his forehead and his ear,' he said.

'On the right side. He had forced you down and was pinning
you to the floor. You must have used your left hand to hit him
there.' This was ingenious and Barry mentally congratulated
himself on the adroit way in which he was turning the case likely
to be put forward by the prosecution. A terrible thing to strike
your man while his back was turned, but introduce the new
explanation and where were you? Half-way to an acquittal. 'Was
it the left hand?' he asked.

165

'Yes, yes, I think so. He was leaning on my right arm so that I couldn't move it. The fender was on my left as I lay there, and I reached out and felt the poker.'

'Good. And you struck wildly, of course. They were random blows, hurriedly given, for you had cause to be afraid.'

'Robert struck him once before,' Laura remembered. 'That was when he left the house. He struck Rupert and left him bleeding. I saw it. He smashed him back against the banisters and cut his eye.'

All three looked in a congratulatory way at one another as the force of this went home. And Laura crowned the triumph by remembering that next day she had taken Rupert to the doctor for the treatment of the wound. Like the pieces of a jig-saw puzzle the evidence was falling into shape, forming a rosy picture for them all.

'It's a clear case,' said Mr Clarke. 'I know a bit about the law.' He did; it had been a useful aid to earlier adventures that had leaned precariously at times towards unwilling matrimonies. 'I tell you that you can use force in self-defence. It was a tragedy but Rupert did no more than his right.'

'Oh, Barry!' cried Laura, voicing her heartfelt relief. 'I'm so glad you came.'

'My dear Laura, that's all right. Naturally I'm here to help.' And truly all his tender paternal feelings were aroused. 'You surely don't think I'd stand by and see the boy' – he nearly added 'hanged', but substituted 'in trouble' just in time. 'We've got the answer now. He must make the statement. Is that agreed?'

They chorused that it was.

'He must make the statement along the lines I've indicated. He must tell the truth. And Miss Roberts will help us with another side of it. We must see the doctor and get his evidence. Can Kay or the housemaid help at all? No? Well, never mind. As for the rest, we play a waiting game.'

It was a masterly summary of their needs, and an atmosphere of sunny optimism now prevailed, not broken when the doorbell rang.

Laura left the room to answer it, leaving her menfolk in a roseate glow. For Rupert a nightmare was at an end, and with a receptiveness that reflected on this sense of memory he already saw the events of that night of horror in the comforting terms of Barry Clarke. He would make a statement, he would clear himself, he would tell the truth. As for Barry, now that the struggle had been won his mind was running pleasurably on thoughts of Joy. So the boy did know a thing or two and did take after him, in spite of appearances to the contrary! Having given much good advice, he nearly felt impelled to give a little more: he wanted to warn this young Lothario of the perils of the chase and to impart a little of that legal knowledge that had stood him in such good stead.

He might have done so if Laura had not reappeared at that moment. She was not alone. With her was a tall, poker-faced police officer whom Barry had seen at the inquest. It had come then. In a moment of emotion he moved over to stand beside his son.

But Rupert had not understood. 'It's all right,' he was saying. 'Inspector, I want to make a statement. Can I make it now?'

The Inspector stood in the middle of the room, woodenly immobile, a monumental incarnation of the law.

'Rupert Laurence Anderson?' he said.

'I want to make a statement. The first one was all wrong.'

But Inspector Carr, his duty to be done, was hardly listening.

'Rupert Laurence Anderson, I have a warrant for your arrest for murder. I must caution you that anything you say may be taken down in writing and may be used in evidence at your trial.'

22

'Remember me?' said Barry Clarke.

Joy, in the process of drawing a glass of beer, looked up at him. She could not altogether place him, but had some vague remembrance; with his check suit and saturnine good looks he seemed just the sort of man who would have made a pass at her.

'No? Pity,' said Mr Clarke cheerfully, quite unabashed by the haughty stare that would have put most men in their place and which had been the only answer to his question. He was not even piqued at her failure to remember him, for he had indulged in the merest preliminaries with her, a little hand squeezing that could hardly have been expected to make much of an impression on a woman's mind. But he remembered her; he always did remember barmaids, their names and dispositions and days off; his mind was a sort of reference library, a guide to what the sexually successful man should know. The information was still there, ticketed, catalogued and up to date but now all too rarely used, for Mr Clarke had reached that morbid age at which a man expects his mistresses to be respectable. It was obvious enough that Joy could not be considered in that category. Casting a professional eye over her, he could see traces of the progress she had made since he had seen her last: bright and tinselled and peroxided, she had set firm in the mould whereas she had been malleable before. He gave a sigh at that, the regret of an artist who has had no hand in fashioning some outstanding work of art. And she certainly was that. She was beautiful, but not more beautiful than thousands of others he had seen; where she scored was in her attitude – a kind of dedication that proclaimed itself in every line of her and in everything she did. Mr Clarke drew in his breath. He had realized with his senses what he had previously only suspected in his mind: that this girl was the mistress of his son. It made him feel extremely old; it gave a very queer turn to his sensations, highly visual, as in so many of his type, and in their suggestiveness great aids to any love affair.

'I remember *you*,' he said.

She tossed her head. They all said that. Cheeky, that's what they were. But when she switched her disapproval on and tried to stare him down she encountered again that smile of experienced middle age, so disarming, so cynical and wise. From his gold watch chain to his flushed cheeks and bulbous eyes she knew the type: a big car, and pink gins, and wine for dinner, and aftermaths that were a little ponderous and rough at first but surprisingly pleasant once one knew the form. One couldn't put down men like that, and that being so, it was as well to keep on friendly terms with them.

'Well, if you know me you've got the better of me there,' she said.

Mr Clarke, who would very much have liked to get the better of her anywhere, doubted the possibility all the same. In his opinion the most that a man could hope for with this lady was a rather dishonourable draw. The look of her was leading him away. And that just wouldn't do, for he had not come to the 'Fleece' to indulge himself this afternoon.

'I'm Barry Clarke,' he said, and then catching the recognition in her eyes: 'Yes, that's right. You've got me now.'

'You're Rupert's uncle?'

Mr Clarke looked avuncular and accepted this. If she had studied him as closely as she had studied Mr Anderson some weeks before, she might have seen a little further than most people did into the relationship. The resemblance was not obvious, but Barry Clarke, who did things well, was not a father for nothing and had left definite traces of his own identity even on Laura's child.

'That's right, Rupert's uncle. And it's because I'm that that I'm here.'

She became immediately attentive, so attentive that Mr Clarke, who had seen nothing in this liaison with his son beyond a cheerful haystack rough-and-tumble, began to be surprised.

'What exactly do you mean?' she said.

They were alone in the bar, for it was barely six o'clock.

'Mean? Just that I've come to see his friend. You *are* his friend?'

'Are *you*?' she said. One couldn't be too careful, for how was

169

she to know that this was really Mr Clarke? He might even be some plain-clothes inspector of police. But it is to be feared that the discreet Joy, who had such praiseworthy control over her tongue, had no means of keeping down the feelings of her heart, and Mr Clarke, catching her expression, found his question fully answered.

'Of course I'm his friend,' he said, 'and I'm going to prove it to you.'

'Oh? And how?'

'By asking you to come out for a run in my car with me to-night.'

This was an invitation in common form. It was natural that Joy, whose confidence in her visitor's good faith was slight, should think of it as such.

'I don't do things like that,' she replied, and though this would have raised a rueful laugh from quite a few of her admirers, oddly enough it did now represent the truth.

'Oh *that*!' said Mr Clarke, shrugging off with a movement of his shoulders all thoughts of back seats, and cars parked in dark secluded lanes beneath the trees, the old, nostalgic, uncomfortable intimacies of other days. 'No, I just want to talk to you, that's all.'

'Then why not here?'

He looked round the room, empty still but with that air of invitation, of expectancy that bar rooms have – hostesses awaiting the arrival of the guests. 'We can't talk here, Joy. Someone might come in at any time.'

'Yes, but how do I know that you . . .?'

She did not complete the sentence but contented herself with looking at him, as though holding a mirror up for him to see the reasons for her doubts in his own clothes and face. That is the worst of reputation: it labels a man with one unchanging label through all the changing circumstances of a life. Mr Clarke was serious; he was consumed with anxiety for his son; but he could not for that reason stop looking like a lecher – though rather an agreeable and friendly one.

'I give you my word of honour, Joy. No funny business, cross my heart!'

To some this might not have sounded very reassuring, but Joy was a splendid judge of men. He meant it: he'd behave. 'Very well,' she said.

'Good girl!' cried Barry, rather offending against the spirit of his pledge by reaching out a hand and slapping her on the shoulder, then withdrawing that hand down the length of her bare arm. He meant it to be comradely and only found when near her wrist how much his touch had changed. He snatched himself away. 'You won't regret it either,' he said, hastily covering up. 'There's something very important I've got to say.'

Joy had run her own hand up her arm in the track of his, though in the opposite direction. Cats act like this sometimes, removing the traces of some contaminating human touch. 'All right, I've said I'll come. What time?'

'Well, what time d'you finish here?'

'At ten. I can be away by ten-fifteen.'

'Splendid! Ten-fifteen. I'll be waiting with the car just this side of the town bridge. It's a Bentley, a Rolls Bentley, a green one. Got it? It'll be the only car.' His voice dropped conspiratorially. 'And don't let anyone see you come.'

He could have saved his breath, for never were instructions less necessary than to this past mistress of the rendezvous, the lady who for the past six months had kept the male population of the town on tenterhooks. He himself was surprised when he heard her tap on the back window of the car; she was five minutes before her time and had come as silently as any poacher along the riverside track beneath the trees. He opened a door for her – the rear near-side door – and no sooner had she slipped inside than he had moved off for the quieter outer lanes, the summer rendezvous of lovers, where the trees and hedges, even in the bare season, looked bent and protective like discreet retainers who could tell a tale.

There, in the shadow of a gigantic beech tree, an old ally of Mr Clarke's from other days, he parked the car. It was almost like old times, he thought, getting out of the driving seat into the road to stretch his legs and breathe the heavy winter air; almost like old times, as he opened the car door – the rear off-side door – and quickly took his seat beside her. It was more comfortable that way, he said; they could talk more cosily and sit more cosily, so his inner self reminded him, in these opulent, roomy seats, free

171

from the entanglements of brakes and gear levers, those banes of his early motoring days.

'Smoke?' he said. It was well not to rush them; not to go too fast. It was some time before the other Mr Clarke, the decorous and respectable one, reminded him that there was no question of going anywhere with Joy at all. He struck a match. 'Go on and take your pick. Churchmans nearest you, then Players, and Turkish and cork tips on the other side.'

It was a resplendent case, large and heavily chased in gold. That was what impressed the women: it was no good putting on an act without all the accessories being to match. In pursuance of this philosophy everything about Mr Clarke was of the best, even to his studs and braces and suspenders. One never knew. One really never knew.

Joy, for one, would not have had a doubt of it. She knew the type if not the man, and accepting a cigarette, settled down defensively in her corner of the car. With his kind a defence was all that was required: what had to be watched was not the enemy but the morale of the garrison within. Hers was excellent, as Mr Clarke would find if he began the siege.

'You brought me here to tell me something,' she began.

That reminded him.

'I did. And to ask you something. To ask you several things, in fact.'

Her voice came out of the corner of the car, cool and suspicious: 'Yes, go on.'

'You said you were a friend of my nephew, didn't you?'

'Of course.'

'Friend is a wide term, isn't it?' He paused, waiting for her to take him up. But as there was no reply he blundered on: 'How much of a friend, my dear?' Still no reply. 'Do you love him, Joy?'

At that he heard the sharp intake of her breath.

'Please answer me. I'm not really being impertinent. You see, I know that he loves you.'

'Loves me?'

She had strained back against the seat and he could imagine her face in the darkness, the expression of the eyes. Mr Clarke, who was not used to making the running for third parties, felt a little

172

piqued and sad. Every moment with this woman increased his certainty that the boy was *homme à bonnes fortunes*, as the French put it in a phrase which, since it cannot be translated, should certainly be anglicized for the use of men like him.

'Yes, he loves you.'

'Has he told you so?'

Mr Clarke, catching the inflection of that voice, so soft and eager, so full of longing, could have no further room for doubt. A quaint little voice, dulled with the burr of a provincial accent, it set off a train of thought alarming in a man who believed himself to be fighting solely for the safety of his son. He said harshly: 'No, he hasn't put it quite like that,' and added almost reluctantly: 'But that's the way he feels.'

'How d'you know?'

Know! How could he know except through his own reactions to the woman by his side! Of course the boy was crazy over her, as anyone would be – anyone who had the least encouragement. And what the encouragement had been in this case was certain: it hung in the air inside the car like something tangible – the certainty of her favours, the memory of her love.

'I tell you I know,' he said. 'I know the boy. I know his feelings. Naturally he wouldn't *tell* anyone the way he felt, but it was far more obvious than words. Now tell me if you love him, too.'

'Yes,' she said.

Mr Clarke sat back and stubbed out his cigarette. Mixed up with the triumph of getting this admission, so necessary to his plans, was an extraordinary feeling of frustration. I'm forgetting myself, he thought. I must take hold. I mustn't feel like this. But his sense of duty was, of course, much the stronger, and aloud he said: 'Good! Then you'll help him, naturally.'

Joy stirred in her corner, and to make things easier for both of them he held out his case again and lit a match. In its glow he saw her face, strained and anxious, turned to his.

'What am I to do?' she said.

He lit a cigarette before replying.

'Look here, Joy, this is how it is: the boy's in serious trouble. The charge is murder. And what's more – and this is what we have to face – there's no certainty that he'll get off.'

It was a hard blow for her, and though he could not have seen

173

her clearly now that the match was out, he looked sideways, away from her, out of the window into the night.

'I don't mean they *will* convict him, Joy, but the danger's there. You see, the court may not take account of his age and sensitiveness, the provocation; they may just think that he took a weapon and struck his father in cold blood.'

And hadn't he? That was the thought that came uncomfortably now. Wasn't that exactly what the boy had done? It was not a very pleasant picture to have presented to one's mind. Joy, whose thoughts may have been similar, said nothing, and he was forced to struggle on.

'If that case reaches the jury then there'll be no question of the verdict; they'll convict him. And after that ... Well, even if the Home Secretary reprieves him it'll mean a clear fifteen years in gaol. I'm sorry, Joy. I don't mean to be brutal, but there it is and we'll not help him by dodging unpleasant facts. Now here's the point: the case I've put so far is not the true case, not by a long chalk. He didn't go to that office to kill his father. He couldn't have. I know him and you know him. He's not that sort of boy. He went there to quarrel with his father, certainly, and he'd every reason to, the way his mother was being treated. You can see what happened: they had a fight; Rupert got the worst of it; and in panic and self-defence reached for the nearest thing to hand.'

'Yes,' said Joy, and Mr Clarke had the uncomfortable feeling that she was seeing the quarrel in the office, the two actors and the falling blows – but not quite in the way he was describing it.

'That's the true story,' he asserted stoutly. 'It's borne out by the way his father treated him at other times. You'd scarcely believe it if I told you the half of what happened between them in the past. If the jury accepts that true story Rupert must be acquitted, certainly of murder; perhaps he'll go scot-free. But we must ask ourselves whether they *will* accept it, Joy.'

'Well?' she asked. 'Will they?'

Mr Clarke turned back towards her and his voice was very grave.

'No. They won't. As it stands they won't accept it.'

Joy, whom the practice of love had made at least as sensitive to words as any barrister or poet, had caught the inflection perfectly.

'As it stands they won't. Then what *would* they accept?'

'They'd accept it if they knew that Anderson was drunk that night.'

If her love had been the foundation, this had been the keystone of Barry's case, towards the laying of which he had been labouring for some time. And having put it into place, he sat back in his corner and waited for the effect.

When it came it was a sufficiently alarming one.

'But he wasn't drunk,' she said.

Mr Clarke turned on her with the eagerness of an advocate.

'He was in your bar, though, wasn't he?'

'Yes' – reluctantly.

'That same evening. He went direct from you to his office?'

'I believe so.'

'And presumably he had a drink?'

'Two half pints of bitter,' replied Joy, with whom the events of the evening were still fresh.

'And who else was in the bar while Anderson was there?'

'Two men – strangers. We were slack that night.'

'Two men, strangers,' echoed Mr Clarke, and there was a little ring of triumph in his voice.

'That's right. But I can't see as how that helps.'

'Can't you, Joy?' he said. And then as though to add to the unmistakable significance of his words he added: 'Remember that you love him and he loves you.'

'What's loving got to do with it?'

He was sure that she was not really stupid. This wilful refusal to understand must be due to other causes, and he put his finger on one of them at once: lover or no, she was too cautious to commit herself, and he must speak the incriminating words.

'Well, you see, except for Rupert you were the last person to see Anderson alive.'

'Mr Anderson,' she said.

Here was a new factor, a new danger, for it looked very much as though she had some sentimental respect for the dead man.

'Yes, Mr Anderson, I should have said. No third party saw him after he left your bar. And you told me that he had had two half-pints.'

175

'That's right.'

'Nothing else?'

She hesitated, then said slowly and in a small voice: 'He took a pint bottle of beer away.'

'Ah, he did! So he may not have been sober at the time when Rupert called.'

'He'd be as sober as a judge,' said Joy, not selecting a very tactful metaphor.

'That's only an opinion, a dangerous opinion – for him.'

'I can't help that.'

'But you can help the boy's death,' said Barry brutally. He could see now that it was his only chance to move her; that her mind was so conditioned by constant fencing with the suggestive that he could only make her see a thing was serious by making headlines of it, and sensational ones at that. 'Yes, I mean that, Joy. Damn it all, you *must* see the way things are! You must see that you're the key to everything and that without you he's quite lost.'

'Lost?'

'Yes, lost,' cried Mr Clarke, repressing an irritated desire to tell her, in terms of flesh that she would understand, just what that loss would mean. 'And the same thing applies the other way: if you want to help him you can save him for sure.'

'By doing what?'

Well, he would have to say it. There was no other way with a woman so determined not to compromise herself.

'By giving evidence that And – that Mr Anderson was drunk, of course. I'm sorry, Joy, but there it is. You were the last to see him, no one can contradict you, and then there's that bottle he took away.'

'But the two men in the bar!' protested Joy.

Barry waved them aside as though they had never existed; he was triumphant. If she could fall back on this sort of prevarication her objections could not possibly be serious.

'Strangers. No one will know they were ever there. They won't come forward, there's no fear of that. And even if they did, what opportunities did they have of seeing whether another customer was drunk or not? Where were they, by the way?'

She told him that they had been sitting in the window alcove.

176

'Well, then, there you are! We don't need to consider them. The only thing we need consider is the safety of the boy.'

'What about considering Mr Anderson?'

This was a ridiculous evasion and Barry treated it as such: he waved the dead man aside even more emphatically than he had done the 'casuals' and was quite surprised to see that his companion was persisting with the point.

'But he's dead. *He* can't mind.'

'He was a nice man,' said Joy.

Barry admitted that he had been. But even so, how did it affect the point they were discussing?

'Because he *was* nice, that's why. He was always kind to me.'

'Yes, but, Joy . . .'

'He'd always got a cheerful word; he was generous. Once, when I had a bit of trouble with a customer, he was the first to try and help. He never tried anything on; I could trust him. He wouldn't have hurt a fly.'

It can be imagined with what feelings Mr Clarke listened to this testimonial. It was supremely ridiculous, he thought; it was worse than ridiculous, for sentimentality can be a very heavy obstacle and one that needs a lot of moving.

'I think we're losing sight of Rupert,' he replied. 'Or isn't he important?'

It was a well-chosen interruption and had its effect on her at once.

'You're suggesting that I should give false evidence,' she said.

'Well, tendentious, that's the word.'

And once spoken, once admitted, the idea ceased to seem so very criminal, for confessions are not only good for the soul, but recharge the conscience too.

'It would mean I should have to go to court?'

'You would.'

'Where I'm on my oath?'

He had got the measure of her now and replied: 'That's right,' with the utmost cheerfulness.

Her voice, when she spoke again, had dropped to that murmurous tone in which we weigh our future actions.

'I'd have to say he was a "regular", that he was often in, that, that night he'd got a night's drinking in in half an hour.'

177

'And took a bottle too,' prompted Mr Clarke, who was not to know that this was a gift of hers and that the action had for her a peculiar poignancy.

'The bottle, yes. I suppose the police would have found it when they came?'

'You bet.'

'And if I said all that, you think they'd let him off?'

'I'm sure of it,' said Barry, in the booming tones natural to him when he was comfortable and satisfied.

'Suppose they found me out?'

He laughed at that. If any counsel – anyone – could trip up this young woman he, for one, would be surprised.

'Find you out! How could they? There's no one to contradict you – not a soul. All you have to do is to stick to your story just like you said it then.'

'*All* I have to do!'

He caught her meaning. It would be as well to refer her back to the more pleasant factors in the case – to the reward.

'Yes, and by doing it you'll be saving Rupert's life. He'll be free. You'll be able to see him again.'

She would see him again. When driven, Mr Clarke could find such satisfying words. Beyond the darkness surrounding them, the stale smell from the cigarettes, the company of this large gross man, she saw their stile, the little bullocks in the pasture, smelt the sweet smell of summer grass.

'All right,' she said.

'You'll do it?'

'Yes.'

So he had won. She would swing the case their way, he had no doubt of it. And in his emotion he put out a hand and fastened on her own with a pressure so friendly, so paternal, so devoid of sex, that he scarcely recognized himself.

23

'SMALL motives, as I told you, members of the jury, small motives and great consequences,' said the prosecuting counsel, returning full circle to his text.

He had spoken for two hours, never faltering for a word, mix-
ing the pedestrian with the tragic in so masterly a way that hardly
a cough or rustle had disturbed the public gallery or jury-box in
all that time, and even the judge had been watching him intently.
To be sure the defender, Sir David Fynes, had punctuated the
speech with yawns, but that was no more than hostile propaganda
for the consumption of the jury; Sir David's frequent glances over
his shoulder at the clock were propaganda gestures of another
kind, directed at the judge, reproachful hints that the luncheon
interval was overdue.

One-fifteen. Most judges would have risen, particularly now
that the opening had reached a logical halting-place; but His
Lordship, who had a bad reputation with epicures on the circuits,
gave no sign and looked prepared to sit for ever. It was no good
looking at Sir Evelyn, for there would be no quarter there, even
after two hours of commentary and rhetoric – a great opening in
a manner that was no longer fashionable at the bar, lucid, persuasive, at times impassioned, a work of art that the advocate,
after the opening moments, had soon ceased to disguise in the
impersonal modern way. It had had a great effect on the jury,
the defender recognized, glancing down the line of intent faces,
all determined to do their duty and bewitched by the discovery
that the process could be pleasant. A brilliant opening. It was a
sobering thought that since he proposed to call witnesses in
addition to the accused, he must allow this rival not only the first
word but the all-important last word too – a long start to give to a
man who already had the better case.

But who had the better witnesses? Stealing a look at his client,
Sir David felt that he might have the advantage there. Of course
one could never tell with witnesses until one saw them leave the
box, but some instinct told him that the small, pale figure hardly

visible above the dock rails was a 'natural', perceptive without being over-clever, frightened enough to avoid the fatal error of cocksureness, courageous, watchful, with an air of candour that Sir David's professional conscience hoped was genuine. Only the slight taint of effeminacy was against him and even this might be turned to advantage in a case of violent crime. Provided the young man kept his head in the witness box he might end by balancing the effect of the prosecution's case, leaving it to Mrs Anderson, obviously a born witness, to the defenders' eloquence and the presumption of innocence to swing the verdict in the desired direction. Such thoughts were reassurances in the midst of the flood of the prosecution's case, still beating up against the jury and threatening to submerge their minds before the trial had properly begun.

Here was the peroration now; it would be a lengthy one, if he knew this man, and might include a recapitulation of the facts. Yet it was impossible to withhold admiration from the gaunt, animated figure in the old silk gown.

'Members of the jury,' Sir Evelyn was saying, 'I will not detain you long. You have heard the story of this crime and it will shortly be my duty to call the witnesses to give it life and texture. Let us be very sure, however, before they come, that we know the framework on which they will be asked to build. To understand what lay behind this melancholy story it would be necessary to examine and dissect the actors' minds – if we could ever be said to understand anything so unnatural, so far removed from reason; but to prove the crime it is mercifully unnecessary to seek so far.

'What in its essence is the prosecution's case? You will long since have seen the answer. A man is killed, and it is admitted in the statement made by the accused that he was the one who struck the blows. He pleads that they were struck in self-defence. Self-defence! The dead man was unarmed. I shall call medical evidence before you and you will hear of the barbaric savagery of that attack. My lord will direct you in his summing up as to the law: he will tell you the exact measure of force permitted to a man in the defence of his own person against attack. It is not for me to anticipate the defence. It may be alleged that this boy went in fear of his life, that he feared for his safety when in his father's

180

company. Well, you will be the judge of that after the defence witnesses have spoken' – he paused significantly – 'and after I have finished cross-examining them. For the rest, we shall look to what he did.

'And what was that? He went to his father's office secretly, at night, and before he had left that room he had destroyed him. What was in his mind when he took the weapon in his hand need not concern us, for motive was never necessary to a prosecution of this kind, as His Lordship will direct. I know that this is not generally believed. But you, who are not concerned with fictions or illusions but with the law of England, will be proof against loose thinking and idle popular beliefs. Crimes are often motiveless – at least regarded from the standpoint of the normal man – and the law in its wisdom takes account of that. If the defence is able to explain how and why this youth could be justified in striking those terrible lethal blows, all well and good, but it is no part of my burden to investigate his mind, even if I could. No, the prosecution will rely on actions that are consistent, in our submission, only with a case of murder.'

Counsel had raised his hand, as though calling those actions which he had recited to testify again.

'Let us remember them: let us concentrate our minds. By doing this we may leave gaps in our story, unexplained matter that might concern the writers of detective tales, but we shall be able to focus the more strongly on the chain of proof. I would ask you to remember the secret visit, the night hour, the blows, the lying evasions that followed, and still follow, in my submission, as evidenced in the second statement of the accused. There the accent of the prosecution lies – on the crime, not on the criminal or on the man who died of it.

'And now I have nearly done. I bring my witnesses before you to speak to fact. They will not explain the secret thoughts of these ill-starred people's minds or shed light on the hidden places of the soul, for in words that come down to us from the ripe experience of the past, "The Devil himself knoweth not the mind of man."

'Well, I will call the witnesses. Judge now of the facts according to the evidence.'

'Sir Evelyn,' said the judge, speaking above the rustle of the courtroom returning to life after the spell.

181

The prosecutor, alert as though his speech were just beginning, was on his feet at once.

'Yes, my lord?'

'It is nearly half past one. I think this will be a convenient moment to adjourn.'

'As your lordship pleases.'

'Yes, I think it will be best. The Court,' said the judge, looking not without a trace of malice at Sir Evelyn, at Sir David Fynes, and at the well-fed gaggle of juniors surrounding them – 'the Court will sit again at ten past two.'

Sir David rose as the judge rose and bowed his head as humbly as the rest, yet it was with indignation that he sought the barristers' robing-room and its frugal meal; luncheon, as a ritual, was dying out even on its last stronghold on the circuits, and he regretted it with more than appetite. To add to his melancholy, the robing-room was a draughty, cheerless place, lined with rows of lockers like coffins standing on their ends, and half warmed by a guttering fire. The one advantage of the place was that it was a haven where one could let off steam about the witnesses and the other irritants of an advocate's life without fear of interruption, since besides the barristers only their clerks – than whom no human beings are more discreet – had a limited form of access.

After a morning spent in listening to his rival Sir David felt the need of self-expression; as soon as he had taken off his wig and gown, and collected a sandwich and a cup of coffee, he made his way towards the prosecutor and took the seat beside him by the fire.

Rotund and genial, tall and bony, what a contrast there was between these two, and yet what a subtle likeness! There was no mistaking them for anything but advocates: there was a dry precision about Sir Evelyn, a weighty good humour about Sir David Fynes, that had clearly been bred in the Inns of Court; years of pleadings and petitions, interrogatories and set-offs, affidavits, answers, defences, particulars, writs and counter-claims, had washed over them, and made of these two widely differing men very much the same sort of sharp-edged legal instrument.

'A most interesting morning,' began Sir David, looking at his sandwich with distaste. 'Most interesting. It would have been more interesting still if you'd kept on the way you started and quarrelled with the judge.'

Sir Evelyn said primly: 'I think that I was in the right.'

'And I'm quite certain you were in the wrong. It was a magnificently illogical opening all the same, and would have had a great effect if I hadn't put my spoke in just in time.'

'Effect! I wasn't striving for effect.'

'Oh, weren't you, though! If I hadn't stopped you you'd have told the jury all about parricides and the Œdipus complex and worked them up till they'd have been ready to bring in Guilty on the spot. The uplifted finger,' said Sir David, raising his hand in parody of the solemn gesture of his friend, 'is not for the prosecution. Ugh! I wonder how you had the nerve.'

'I was well within my rights.'.

'Prejudice, my boy, sheer prejudice. I think you might have been more lenient to that poor child in the dock.'

'Poor child!' exclaimed Sir Evelyn, raising his eyebrows till his whole long and slightly equine face looked like an interrogation mark.

'Yes, a poor bewildered child. A fascinating study, Lynne. Taking him purely as a person I find him curiously attractive.'

Prosecuting counsel gave a sniff of offended rectitude that reproved his friend for such a comment on a murderer. 'I haven't even thought of it,' he said. 'If you want my opinion, I don't admire the boy.'

'Don't you even admire his courage, though?'

But Sir Evelyn refused to be impressed. A man of the highest principles, he did his best to be fair and even tried to be impartial in his mind, but he could not rid himself of a feeling of resentment that so much time would have to be wasted on so clear a case.

'His courage – if he has courage – seems to me quite irrelevant,' he said. 'Crippen had courage, so had Seddon, but I don't somehow feel called on to admire them.'

'Now that's a judicial utterance!' said Sir David, shaking his head. 'The boy's guilty, is he?'

'I didn't say so.'

'But you implied it, Lynne.'

'It's a matter I'd rather not discuss,' replied Sir Evelyn stiffly, every inch the official of the law.

But his opponent was not so easily put down.

'Well, let's discuss the boy *qua* boy and leave his criminality out. Whatever he's done, he's still a human being, so put yourself in his shoes and think how you'd behave' – Sir Evelyn was certainly not proposing this attempt. 'There he is, eighteen years of age, faced with a judge and jury and oh-so-eloquent prosecuting counsel, warders on either side of him and his neck at stake. I know that if I were in that dock I wouldn't be so cool.'

'I think,' suggested Sir Evelyn, 'that we've both met callousness before.'

'But this isn't callousness. A boy with a face like that has sensibility; you've only got to look at him. He's too young for suffering to show but I tell you, Lynne, it's there. You can see the same thing developed in the mother's face. It's fascinating, really, to study the same effect operating on the young and on the old.'

'Remorse in both cases, perhaps,' said his colleague tartly.

'Well, that's another judicial utterance. I suppose you'll suggest next that the mother also should be standing in the dock?'

Sir David, knowing the discretion of his man, could have supposed no such thing; nevertheless similar thoughts were in the prosecutor's mind, for facts that would never be alleged in court were set out in his brief and some people already had an inkling of the truth. 'I suggest nothing against Mrs Anderson; my case is in no way concerned with her,' he said.

'But you don't like her, is that it?'

'I repeat, I am not concerned with her.'

'You will be,' announced Sir David.

'That's your affair.'

'It will soon be everyone's affair. The Press will make it so.'

'The Press!' sniffed Sir Evelyn, elevating his nose.

'Indeed yes, my dear Lynne. The public will want a heroine of some sort and the Press will see it gets one.'

'A heroine! That woman!' and Sir David smiled to himself as he caught the unguarded words and tone of a man who normally talked 'Without Prejudice' like a solicitor's letter, and gave about as much away. Laura must have made a notable impression on his opponent's mind to have drawn such expressions of dislike.

'Yes, that woman, and I appreciate what you mean.' Sir David's eyes had narrowed as he recalled his conferences with the

184

lady. 'I agree with you that not everyone goes for that *femme fatale* act. But if you want to know how she'll come out of this trial, whichever way it goes, I can enlighten you. She'll be lionized. Why, you can feel the atmosphere of sympathy in court already, and just you wait till she's finished in the box. Unhappy woman whose erring husband is slain by her beloved son!' His voice rose. 'Just think of the headlines, my dear chap. "Laura Anderson, A Woman Wronged!"'

24

It was late in the afternoon of the first day of the trial when Sir Evelyn Parks arose and commanded:

'I call Detective Inspector Carr.'

The usher opened a door in the well of the Court and repeated the words in a stentorian bellow for the benefit of those in the corridor outside. A moment later the tall bronzed inspector was seen shouldering his way through the crowd, past counsel's table to the witness box. There he took the oath in the traditional manner of the Force, as though the swearing were part of his police report, and a very dull and formal part at that. A bit of an automaton, thought Sir Evelyn, who always ticketed his witnesses in the formula of a school report; efficient, a good police officer; should give his evidence well.

Everything about Carr's manner bore out this judgement when the examination at last began. By easy stages counsel took him through the events of the fatal night: the routine report of P.C. Burke that had led to the entry through the open street door of the darkened premises, the discovery of the body, the searching of the room. Even a murder in the night, a dead man sprawled out like a broken moth, a spreading pool on the carpet, a stained poker, seemed dull prosaic stuff in such hands as these, and the public, its appetite whetted by the prosecutor's opening, was vastly disappointed in Inspector Carr. The very words he used seemed carefully chosen to dispel all the livelier images: demises, instruments, deceased, issued woodenly from his mouth and it came as quite a shock when he allowed himself to speak of blood. Only a policeman could have robbed drama so remorselessly, but then the witness, a professional faithful to the instruction given in his youth, was concerned solely with the truth; he described what he had seen and done and did it with such clarity that Sir Evelyn was delighted with him and added, 'An excellent witness; as good as I have met' to his other mental tags.

And when the Inspector described what he had found a thrill of interest surged in the crowded court: a blood-stained poker with smeared, undecipherable, marks on its haft; the mark of a hand on the office desk; a handkerchief – and yes, there were initials on it – lying near the body by the fire. At this the eyes of the occupants of the press-box kindled and they scribbled furiously, but the witness remained unmoved; not by a flicker of an eyelid or by any change in the tone of that stilted voice did he betray the Force, but went on to a long discussion of measurements, placing the corpse in relationship to the room with the accuracy of an undertaker. 'I concluded my investigations at the office,' he said, 'at a quarter to eleven.'

That was one chapter closed. Sir Evelyn, with all the self-possession of an advocate whose star witness comes up to scratch, nodded in a congratulatory manner and turned over the pages of his brief.

'Inspector, will you tell the court in your own words what your next actions were?'

In this one sentence counsel displayed his profound faith in Carr. It was his usual custom to keep his witnesses well in leash by a constant succession of short questions; otherwise, as he had learnt from long experience, they were all too likely to run off into pastures of their own, chasing irrelevancies like a dog among a flock of sheep.

The Inspector drew himself up in the box and his manner subtly changed from that of the mere investigator to that of the policeman who sees the goal of an arrest.

'As a result of my investigations,' he began, 'I proceeded by car to the house known as "The Templars", Colbert Row, Turlminster, the home of the accused. It was five past eleven when we rang the bell. We rang several times and knocked, but for five minutes we were left out on the doorstep.' He caught Sir Evelyn's enquiring glance and added: 'I timed it by my watch.

'At last the accused's mother, Mrs Anderson, the wife of the deceased, unlocked the door. We were conducted to a room in which I saw the accused. He was in bed – awake.'

'Hardly surprising, surely, Inspector!' the judge interjected with a smile.

The witness allowed an answering flicker of amusement to cross his face. 'My lord, we *had* made rather a noise.'

187

'Sufficient to wake the neighbourhood, I have no doubt. Continue, please.'

'I asked the accused if he was Rupert Laurence Anderson. He said he was. I told him I was investigating the death of Robert Hemsley Anderson who had been found dead that night on the floor of his office, and that I had reason to believe that he, Rupert Anderson, knew something of the matter. I then cautioned him and asked him if he would care to make a statement. He agreed to do so.'

'Stop there for a moment,' said Sir Evelyn. 'Did the prisoner seem clearly to understand the words of the caution you had administered?'

'Yes, sir.'

'Did he seem to understand that there was no compulsion on him to speak at all?'

'Yes, I explained it carefully. He acted voluntarily. He showed every disposition to be helpful.'

And how helpful he had been! thought Sir Evelyn to himself. How fortunate it was that criminals were so stupid and made smooth the prosecution's way! Aloud he said: 'Very well. Please go on.'

'He made a statement there and then,' continued the Inspector. 'He dictated it and Sergeant Rice took it down in writing. When completed, it was read over to him. I asked the accused if it accurately represented what he meant to say or whether any alterations or additions were required. He said: "The statement is the truth," and signed it.'

'Is this the statement in question?' asked Sir Evelyn, holding up a document to the witness. 'Exhibit 5, my lord.'

'Yes, that's the one.'

'Signed in your presence?'

'Yes.'

The statement was read in open court. If it demonstrated nothing else, it was a tribute to the calmness of the accused and to the literal way he had obeyed his mother's words. He had known nothing of his father's death, which had come as a great shock to him. He had called at the office at half past six, had seen Hemmings and had learnt that the solicitor was not at work. He had called with the intention of asking his father to come back home.

188

He had acted independently of his mother in doing this and had not thought of asking her advice. By seven he had been back at home and had stayed in all that night. He had been in his mother's company till ten, at which hour he had gone to bed. He had been asleep until wakened by the sound of the bell and the knocking at the door.

'And that is the statement?' asked Sir Evelyn, who could not quite keep the note of triumph from his voice. 'That is the statement he made and signed that night?'

'Yes, sir.'

'What happened then?'

The crowd in court realized that something good was coming from the way the prosecutor looked round at the members of the jury as though to reassure himself that at this vital moment none of them was malingering or asleep.

'Well, sir, then I showed him the handkerchief I had found near the body of the deceased.'

'Is this the handkerchief?'

It was of white linen, and even those at the back of the gallery could see that it was soiled with blood.

'It has initials on it, has it not?'

Carr peered at the exhibit as though seeing it for the first time, though he had handled it on a score of occasions and had identified it from the witness box not ten minutes previously when describing its discovery.

'Yes, sir. In one corner there are the intials R.L.A.'

So much for Laura's industrious, tender care.

'Yes, yes. What happened then?'

'I asked the accused,' continued the Inspector, picking his words with scrupulous accuracy, 'whether the handkerchief was his. He denied it. I then cautioned him once more and repeated the question, very slowly, so that there could be no doubt of what I meant. He looked at the handkerchief again and said, "It's mine. I didn't see the initials before." I then told him where it had been found.'

'Did he have anything to say to that?'

The witness, who had watched Sir Evelyn throughout this examination as a dog watches his master, yet sparing half an eye sideways for any intervention by the judge, looked for the first time towards the dock. Perhaps as a man, professional duty apart, he approved the ingenuity of the answer.

'The accused said: "Father's initials are R.H.A. We often mixed up handkerchiefs. I'll bet I've some of his at this moment in that drawer" – pointing to the wardrobe across the room – "and he'll have had some of mine".'

'Yes, go on.'

'I did not press the matter further,' replied the Inspector with massive dignity, and the professional trial-goers in the gallery were whispering among themselves: 'That stumped him. He didn't know how to answer that.'

'Inspector . . .' said the judge.

The witness wheeled round immediately at the summons of that master voice. 'Yes, my lord?'

'The accused is very young.'

'Very young, my lord.'

'And, according to his story, he had just been awakened from sleep. Are you satisfied that he fully understood the cautions and the questions? You will be fair in your evidence, I know.'

The Inspector, who had looked throughout a great deal fairer than the statue of Justice herself, seemed somewhat hurt by this.

'My lord, I am absolutely satisfied. I did not rush him. I spoke slowly. I repeated myself. I cautioned him twice. He was as calm and logical as a man can be. He never hesitated in actions or answers.'

'Thank you, Inspector,' said the judge, retiring once more into the wings. He seemed to obliterate himself, but even his ghost was obviously well qualified to conduct the trial.

Sir Evelyn, who during this interval had been refreshing himself at the water jug, resumed his dominating place.

'And now, Inspector, after the incident of the handkerchief, what happened next?'

'I asked to see the clothes the prisoner had been wearing. I was shown a shirt, a pullover and a suit. These articles were hanging neatly in the wardrobe. The shirt in my opinion –' he broke off and corrected himself – 'the shirt showed no signs of being soiled; it showed no signs of having been worn that day.'

'And then?'

'On the evidence before me at that time I did not feel justified

190

in going further,' replied Carr, greatly to the disappointment of the trial experts in the gallery, who were confidently expecting evidence of arrest. There was always drama to be had from that, and after the evidence they had heard it had seemed indicated as the next item on the inspectorial list.

Sir Evelyn, wiser in his generation, nodded his head in full agreement.

'Quite, quite,' he said. 'At that stage you did not feel justified in further search or in making an arrest?'

'No, sir, I did not. It became necessary that the accused's statement should be checked, though obviously nothing could be done that night. Next morning I instituted a strict enquiry in the town with the object of discovering whether witnesses could speak to any callers at the office about the time of death. Certain witnesses were contacted and statements made.'

'They will be called,' boomed Sir Evelyn, as a sort of accompaniment to this theme.

'It was necessary also to take the finger-prints on the poker and door-handles and to photograph the body and the desk. Part of the veneer of the latter was cut away as an exhibit.'

'But is it necessary,' enquired the judge, suddenly materializing, 'that the witness should explain police process to the court? After all, this is a trial, not a lecture in method, however admirable that may be.'

'As your lordship pleases,' conceded Sir Evelyn, perfectly willing to give way on any point not affecting his own self-esteem.

The Inspector was even humbler. A most conscientious witness, and absolutely wedded to a sense of relevancy, he was shocked by his own misdeeds. 'My lord, I am sorry. I was straying from the point.'

'For the first time,' said the judge graciously, for he liked the wooden official very well. 'Your evidence has been admirably given – admirably.'

Something like a blush of pleasure crept into the Inspector's cheeks.

'Then, my lord, may I pass on to the events of the following day, in so far as they were concerned with the accused?'

'If Sir Evelyn desires it.'

The advocate cleared his throat and gave vent to a display of gown hitching that recaptured the interest of the jury, all too easily stolen by any display of activity from the Bench.

'On the day after the crime you continued your investigation?' he began.

'Yes.'

'Did anything arising out of your enquiries cause you to take fresh steps with regard to the accused?'

'Yes,' answered the Inspector, and one could sense the inward struggle he was having to reply to this question without bringing in irrelevant or hearsay matter that would offend the judge. 'As a result of certain statements made as to the accused's movements on the night in question I paid a second visit to his home in Colbert Row.'

'The date and time, if you please?'

'Five-thirty on the afternoon of 8th October last.'

'After the adjournment of the inquest?'

'Yes.'

'Did you see the accused?'

'There were present the accused, his mother, and a cousin of Mrs Anderson,' replied Carr, in the manner of a secretary reading the minutes of the last meeting.

'Yes. Tell my lord and the jury what happened on this occasion.'

'Yes, sir. As soon as I entered the room accused addressed me, saying that he wished to make a statement.'

'What did you reply?'

'I called the accused by name.'

'And then?'

'He repeated that he wished to make a statement. He said: "The other was all wrong."'

'Referring to his previous *sworn* statement?'

'So I understood it.'

'He said his other *sworn* statement was all wrong, did he?' said Sir Evelyn, looking significantly at the jury and making great play with his comment disguised in question form. 'And what did you do next?'

'I produced the warrant for the accused's arrest and cautioned him.'

'Did he say anything at that?'

'*He* did not,' replied the Inspector, unintentionally accenting

192

the pronoun as he recalled the things that had been said by other persons present at this scene. Words had been used by Laura that he was profoundly relieved not to have to repeat in open court, for he was naturally fastidious and liked to think the best about the female sex.

'Did the accused make a second statement?'

'Yes, later at the police station. He had been cautioned again but insisted on making it.'

'Is this the statement?'

'Yes.'

'I will read it,' announced Sir Evelyn, and he did so, slowly and ponderously, stressing the admissions. 'That is a very different statement from the one dictated to you on the night of the commission of the crime?' he suggested, when this was done.

'It is.'

'This statement alleges that violence was used by the deceased against the prisoner, and in particular the latter states that he was seized violently by the neck. Did you, may I ask, ever notice any marks on the accused's neck or other part of him tending to bear out this claim?'

'Never.'

'Did you have the opportunity?'

'I think so. The prisoner was in pyjamas when I called on the night of the fifth. I could see no mark on him.'

'In any case, he did not draw your attention to anything of that nature?'

'No.'

'Thank you, Inspector,' and Sir Evelyn, with a final smile of benediction for this model witness, sat down in his place, then looked across at his rival as though daring him to do his worst.

Sir David Fynes was immediately on his feet. But the judge was looking at the clock above the gallery, which showed that the time was ten to six.

'Sir David,' he said.

'My lord?'

'You will require some considerable time with this witness, will you not?' ,

'A considerable time,' replied counsel, in his most menacing voice.

193

'Then this will be a convenient moment to end the sitting for the day. To-morrow at ten, then.'

'As your lordship pleases.'

The judge rose and everyone rose with him, advocates, solicitors, officials, onlookers, respectfully at the sight of that bewigged, red-robed figure, the incarnation of the law's majesty; even the prisoner rose, though less ceremoniously, under the sharp prompting of his attendants in the dock.

'What about that evidence?' asked Mr Craig of his leader as they left the court. 'Wasn't Carr first-rate?'

'Yes, very good.'

'And the next witness will be as good. These divisional police surgeons always are.'

'Hum,' mused Sir Evelyn, who had practised too long in courts to be over-confident of anything. 'Trouble is he's unsupported. Pity that that autopsy was so inconclusive and that we couldn't definitely nail the lie of that drunkenness defence.'

'It cuts both ways,' said Mr Craig. 'The report can't help Sir David either.'

'He'll not use it.'

'Which helps us. We're all right. We've other lies to nail. The prisoner's statement's full of them.'

'One witness from a forensic laboratory would be worth the lot of them,' replied Sir Evelyn, tucking his brief beneath his arm.

25

'CALL Henry Matthew Read.'

'Your name is Henry Matthew Read and you are a divisional surgeon of police?'

'That is so.'

'Do you remember the night of 5th October last?'

'I do.'

'1 believe that on that evening you were called in to Number 53 High Street, Turlminster, in your professional capacity?'

'Yes, I was called in, as you say. It would be about half past ten that night.'

'Good. Now will you please tell my lord and the jury what you found?'

The police surgeon, a short stocky man with a bristling moustache, leant forward on the ledge of the witness box and folded his hands together comfortably. He looked thoroughly at home, in marked contrast to Inspector Carr who, in spite of years of experience, had stood as rigidly as a sentry. But whereas to Carr the judge had remained a sort of commanding officer, always present and on the look-out, for Read he was no more than a distinguished partner in the medico-legal firm.

'Certainly, Sir Evelyn,' he replied. 'On entering an upstairs room, I was shown a body. It was the body of Robert Hemsley Anderson. It was lying on its left side, head towards the fireplace, the feet against the desk. I carried out an examination. There was a quantity of blood on the face and skull, but when this had been cleared away I found that there were five scalp wounds on the right side of the head. Three of these wounds (the two nearest the temple and the one farthest from it) were superficial; they had grazed the skin, cutting it and setting up bruising underneath. The other two were serious, and one of these, the fourth nearest to the temple, had cut deep and opened a branch of an artery.'

The advocate had listened, nodding his head to this recital, reflecting that if Carr had made it difficult to see the drama through the screen of words, this man, with his flat unhurried voice, made it next door to impossible.

'Five blows. Were they ruled straight across the head parallel with the brow and eyes?'

'No. Let me make this clear: the wounds were not in any sense regular or part of an orderly pattern; they were set at irregular intervals and angles. There is, I believe, a photograph that has been proved that demonstrates this far better than I can hope to do with words.'

'Exhibit 13,' announced Sir Evelyn, not altogether pleased that the initiative had been taken from him. That was the worst of these expert witnesses: they thought that they were advocates as well. 'Number 13,' he repeated. 'Show it to the witness, if you please. There now, is that the photograph you mean?'

'It is. Here the five wounds are clearly shown. The two deepest are marked A and B. B is the wound that touched the artery.'

'The most serious wound?'

'Yes, the one that killed him.'

Sir Evelyn paused while the exhibit was taken to the jury-box, where the foreman accepted it and brooded over it before passing it along the row. 'Tell me,' he went on, when it was launched on its rounds, 'would you say that these injuries were definitely caused by separate blows?'

'Oh, certainly. Five blows.'

'Did you form any conclusion as to how they came to be inflicted?'

'With what instrument, you mean?'

'Yes.'

'Well, they were such as might have been inflicted with a poker.'

'Of this kind? Exhibit 3.'

Read examined the implement held up to him and nodded. 'Yes.'

'Did you form any conclusion as to the time interval that separated the five blows?'

'I did. I think they must have been inflicted in rapid succession, within seconds of one another.'

196

'A flurry of strokes? Someone striking out, and striking again and again?'

'That is the picture in my mind.'

Sir Evelyn bunched his gown behind him and leaned back against the head-rest of his bench.

'Formally I must ask you this. Is there any possibility that they could have been self-inflicted?'

'None.'

'They must have been struck by some other person?'

'Certainly.'

'Let me ask you this. From the position of the scalp wounds could you judge the relationship in space between that other person and the deceased?'

'How the attacked and the attacker were placed at the moment of the assault, you mean?'

'Yes,' agreed Sir Evelyn, a slight frown forming on his brow.

The police surgeon turned squarely towards the jury. Though they might not know it, this was one of the most vital questions in the case and he was determined to present it clearly for their benefit.

'In these matters it is unsafe to dogmatize,' he said. 'It is only within limits that I can answer such a question. From the nature of the wounds I would say that they were struck while the attacker was slightly above the level of the deceased. The target – if I may be forgiven the phrase – was probably in motion; that is deducible from the three secondary strikes I mentioned. These were glancing blows, the full force of which was lost as the head was moved.'

'Stop there for a moment,' commanded Sir Evelyn. 'Were the wounds consistent with a situation in which the deceased was sitting in a chair and the accused was standing over him?'

A deep silence fell on the court as the witness weighed his answer. At last gently, evenly, it came. 'Yes, it is possible. There is a slight declination in the wounds, a downward angle. We must remember that the deceased was a big man and that the accused is slight. However it would fit the facts better if Mr Anderson were just rising from his chair when struck.'

'That could account for one blow,' said the judge, suddenly

197

intervening. 'But surely he could not have been rising for the others?'

The witness, who had tended to watch the jury even when directly responding to Sir Evelyn, swung round to face the bench.

'My lord, I have thought of that. The same relationship between attacker and attacked would exist if the attacked were staggering and stooping from the effect of the earlier blows.'

'Keeping the right side of the scalp constantly presented to the attacker?'

'Yes, my lord. "Staggering and stooping" was perhaps an unfortunate description. The deceased may have been partially stunned, though still half erect, as a result of the first assault. I am not trying to be dogmatic and your lordship will appreciate that absolute certainty in these matters is not to be expected. There may have been no rising erect at all; the deceased may have been seated, as I said. He may have swung round in his chair and thus presented the right side of the skull to the attacker who had been standing *behind*, but was *now* half facing him. The smallness of the accused could account for the small angle of declination that I found.'

The judge made a non-committal noise at that, which the witness and Sir Evelyn both took as a sign that they might continue. 'It amounts to this then,' said the latter: 'the attacker would be standing; the deceased may have been sitting, or, more probably, was rising from the chair?'

'That is so.'

'Would you say that these were violent blows?'

'Oh yes. Considerable force was used.'

'Was there anything ultra-sensitive about the dead man's skull that enabled an artery to be reached?'

Read looked solemnly down the ranks of the jury and replied: 'I should expect blows of such a kind to kill anyone in court.'

'May I ask you formally if they did in fact kill the deceased?'

'They did.'

'Please tell us your actual diagnosis of the death.'

'Certainly. Death was caused by haemorrhage and shock from violence.'

'Would it have taken long?'

'Probably not many minutes. It is impossible to be sure.'

198

Sir Evelyn paused and glanced back over the pages of his brief; he was closing a chapter and wanted to be sure that nothing had been missed. 'Let me turn from the scalp wounds,' he said at last, after an interval filled with coughing and rustling that broke out in court whenever the guiding hand relaxed its grip. 'Were there any other marks on the deceased?'

'Oh yes.'

'Describe them, please.'

'Well, there was bruising on the right fore-arm and elbow. This could have been caused, like the head wounds, with the poker that I have been shown. The presence of this bruising is consistent with an attempt by the deceased to protect himself from assault.'

'An attempt to ward off blows?'

'That is so. I can account for them in no other way, and they were certainly too extensive to be caused in falling.'

'Quite. Were there other marks?'

'Yes. A small bruise on the left elbow, caused, in my opinion, when the deceased fell on to his left side where he was found.'

'And was that all?'

'Yes, that was all.'

'Thank you. Is there anything that you would care to add to the evidence that you have given in the way of clarification or amendment?'

Almost for the first time the witness looked directly at the advocate, as though assessing him in the way that the prosecutor had assessed Inspector Carr, and his answer, 'No, Sir Evelyn,' carried a similar approval, not unmixed with condescension. It was to be noted that he remained facing the barristers' benches in the well, as defending counsel rose with all the dignity of a whale surfacing from the deep.

In profound silence everyone waited to see the line of approach to be adopted by the defence. In the light of the savage attack that had been described it was not thought that Sir David had an enviable task, though he seemed to be shouldering it buoyantly with all that appearance of good humour that witnesses sometimes found, to their cost, to be deceptive.

'I have listened carefully to your evidence,' he began. 'You have taken care to avoid the dogmatic, have you not?'

'It is a thing to be avoided.'

'Where you have known a fact you have stated it; where you have had to fall back on surmise you have not allowed surmise to masquerade as fact?'

The witness nodded, recognizing a question that was rhetorical.

'Perhaps the word "guess" is better than "surmise",' the advocate continued. 'Would it be right to say that where you have guessed you have been frank about it and admitted it?'

'Scientific deductions are not guesswork, Sir David.'

'Are they not? By deductions, I take it that you mean the inferences you have made from these wounds on the head and body of the deceased?'

'I do.'

'Let us examine these inferences, if you please. You told us that the deceased *may* have been sitting when the first blow was struck at him.'

'It is possible.'

'But then you told us that he *may* have been rising to his feet.'

'That is my view.'

'And then he *may* have been staggering and stooping.'

'As I told his lordship, it was not a happy phrase.'

'He *may* have been stunned then. Is that happier?'

The witness shrugged his shoulders at this pleasantry. He spent a good portion of his life being browbeaten in this way and was almost impervious to the routine.

'He *may* have been doing this,' counsel continued, 'he *may* have been doing that. He *may* have been sitting, rising, stooping, staggering, stunned' – a small ripple of laughter spread through the court at this, a tonic for Sir David, though the judge, with a stern look, put a stop to it at once. 'I have put five mays to you. Five guesses, are they not?'

'They are deductions, Sir David, and in any case the salient matters of the wounds and their declination are facts – unassailable facts.'

'Oh, never fear, when the time comes we will assail them. But for the moment I am concerned with what seem to be quite nebulous matters' – the advocate's voice had taken on the finest shade of irony – 'the prosecution's picture of the crime itself. The prisoner, you say, might have been standing behind the deceased?'

200

'He might.'

'Or in front of him?'

'Unlikely. I have already told the court . . .'

'. . . another version, yes: the version where the deceased rises and swings round in his chair towards the prisoner standing at his back.'

But the prosecutor was on his feet, protesting at the way the witness's answer had been snatched and turned. The judge supported him at once. 'Sir David, you must not interrupt the witness; he must be allowed to finish his sentences and make his meaning clear.'

Defending counsel bowed submissively.

'As your lordship directs. I certainly do not want to take unfair advantage. May I put the matter thus: It is a matter of surmise exactly where the prisoner stood?'

'Half facing deceased and to his right,' the surgeon said.

'Ah! so we have something definite at last. May I ask you how you have arrived at that?'

The witness turned away from the advocate towards the jury-box to make his explanation, doing this in a way that suggested that in this quarter, at least, sweet reason and common sense were to be expected.

'I reached that conclusion from my examination of the wounds. To have caused them, the blows must have come slightly from above and from the right.'

'The striking arm was to the right of the deceased, is that what you are telling us?'

'I am.'

'Suppose the *left* arm was the striking arm. If the antagonists were face to face would not that account for the direction of the blows?'

The witness hesitated.

'Are you suggesting, Sir David, that the prisoner is left-handed, may I ask?'

A comfortable smile spread over defending counsel's face as he chided his opponent gently for this attempted reversal of their roles.

'No, you may not, as I much regret to say. I will repeat my question.'

He was about to do so when he was interrupted by the surgeon with the answer. 'The poker, used in the left hand, could, in the circumstances you have mentioned, have caused the *direction* of the wounds, but I doubt whether there would be sufficient strength in the left hand to cause their *depth*, unless the striker were habitually left-handed.'

'You doubt the strength. Can you be more definite?' Then, as the surgeon paused, 'Come now, I know that you are anxious to be fair.'

'I am trying to be,' the witness said.

'And of course everyone in court knows that. But can you be more definite? Can you swear that these blows could not have come from a *right-handed* man using the *left* hand unaccustomedly?'

'It is unlikely.'

'But is it impossible?'

'No, I cannot go as far as that.'

Sir David rocked back on his heels with a contented sigh.

'So my suggestion is at least a possibility?'

'Yes.'

'Let me press the point. You have already described these blows to the scalp as – let me see – "irregular", "at irregular intervals and angles". They formed "no orderly pattern".'

'That is so.'

'And the blows were inflicted in rapid succession, in a "flurry of strokes", to use the words of my learned friend?'

'Yes, that describes my own impressions.'

'Would you say that they were random blows?'

'Wild ones, certainly.'

'I used the word "random" deliberately. I am suggesting, you see, that these are typical left-handed blows, not accurate, as right-hand blows would have been, but imperfectly directed – wild, to adopt your word as well.'

The witness did not answer.

'At least they were not accurate or regular?'

'No.'

'So they must have been inaccurate and irregular?'

'I suppose so.'

Sir David shook his head reproachfully.

'Please don't let us suppose things; it is so unsatisfactory and uncertain.'

'Panic could upset the aim even of the right hand,' protested the witness, looking around desperately for a reason.

'Of course. These *could* have been panicky right-handed blows. Could they not also have been typical left-handed ones?'

Very reluctantly the witness conceded this.

And that put Sir David in high good humour. With all the ardour of a fisherman who has landed a juicy trout he cast into another pool of fruitful waters.

'Let me turn to the secondary injuries of the deceased. There was a wound on his forearm that you believe *may* have been caused in warding off the assailant's blows?'

'Yes.'

'Although of course you can't be sure. And there was a smaller bruise on the left elbow. Am I right?'

'That was my evidence,' replied the witness coldly.

'That second bruise was caused when the deceased fell down?'

'So I believe.'

'Suppose something for a moment, please. Suppose these two men were face to face; suppose they grappled; suppose Mr Anderson, the heavier, forced his opponent down and fell on him, pinning him to the floor, could not that fall account for the bruising of the left elbow?'

'Put that way, it could.'

'And the more serious bruising on the right forearm and elbow too?'

A sudden stir of excitement in the court had greeted these two questions which lit up the whole nature of the defence, underlining the meaning of the cross-examination; it was hardly damped by the surgeon's answer:

'The bruises on the right forearm and elbow were caused by blows.'

'But there is nothing inherently improbable in the picture as I put it to you?' pressed Sir David. 'The young man was on his back, pinned to the floor; the heavier man above him.'

'No, there is nothing improbable in the picture considered purely by itself.'

'Let me take that further. Suppose again that this youth on the floor feared for his life; suppose he reached out in self-defence for the poker with his only free hand, his *left* hand; and suppose he struck from that position at his rival's head; would not that result in just such wounds as you have described?'

Read slowly digested this. From small movements of his hands it could be seen that he was reconstructing the picture in his mind. After a moment, in the breathlessly silent court, he spoke.

'I cannot agree. Your theory would not account for the depth of the wounds I found.'

'You think the left hand too weak?'

'Of a right-handed person, yes.'

'You are not forgetting the scene I set? You will recall the appearance of the weapon and its formidable weight. Suppose the man underneath were desperate and in imminent fear of death?'

'Even so, I don't think he could have struck so deep.'

'You don't think! Can you *swear* that it is impossible? Can you swear?' and the listeners in court could sense, for the first time to the full, the power and menace of that bulky figure, no longer negligently lounging, but leaning forward like a fencer on the attack.

'It is unlikely, as I said, Sir David, most unlikely but not utterly impossible; the millionth chance,' the answer came. 'Another contrary indication can be found in the slight downward angle of the blows.'

Counsel sniffed loudly and flung out an arm as though sweeping away this jargon into a mental dust-bin.

'May I put it to you that the downward angle was caused by nothing more than the fact of downward blows?'

'Of course.'

'And the youth, lying on the floor in the position I have described, swinging the poker in his left hand, would naturally bring it *down* from above on to the head of the man on top of him?'

'There would be insufficient leverage from that position.'

'That,' said the defender contemptuously, 'is the repetition of an opinion. I am asking you now about the angle.'

'I know and I will answer you. I do not think that a man striking from that inferior position could have caused the wounds either in their depth or angle.'

'That is your opinion?'

'My considered opinion.'

Sir David made a convulsive movement as though shaking himself free from these denials, then resumed:

'Do you appreciate how the proposition I have put to you fits the fact that all the wounds were grouped on one side of the scalp?'

'It provides one possible explanation.'

'The best, I put it to you.'

'I cannot agree.'

'All the blows fell there because the two men, locked together, remained for some time constant to one another; they could not do otherwise.'

'Is that a question, Sir David?' enquired the judge.

'My lord, I am putting my case to the witness. May I be permitted to phrase the matter this way? Can you' – turning towards Read – 'think of any possible position in which these two men could have found themselves (other than the one I have suggested) in which the attacked would constantly present the same side of his face to his assailant?'

'The prisoner may have been standing over his half-erect stunned victim, as I said.'

'May have been! May have been! We are back to that again.'

The voice of prosecuting counsel rose from the well of the court: 'You asked for alternatives; you're getting them,' drawing another burst of that fugitive laughter that lurks below the surface of the tensest trials.

'I am getting his doubts and guesses,' replied Sir David, not in the least put out, with a professional advocate's glance towards the jury to see how the sally was received. Then he swung back towards the police surgeon. 'Will you agree with me that if the men were locked together in a death grapple the blows would naturally tend to fall all to one side?'

'Not necessarily, but possibly they would.'

'So that much is common ground between us. You said in your examination-in-chief that you did not think that the deceased was sitting when first struck.'

'I said so and I have repeated it.'

'If Mr Anderson had been dodging and ducking to avoid the

blows you would not expect them to be concentrated on one side?'

'The concentration is certainly singular.'

'Very singular,' agreed the advocate, looking benevolently at this helpful witness. 'And might not your half-stunned man have crumpled up at the first assault?'

'Perhaps.'

'In which case your "angle of declination" would be too great?'

'Yes.'

'Do you seriously advance any one of these your theories as more reasonable than mine?'

'I do not find your theory, as you call it, reasonable.'

'Don't you?' commented Sir David, raising eloquent eyebrows at this denial of what he was putting forward as manifest common sense. 'Would it not be fairest to say that in this matter of the interpretation of evidence all is surmise?'

'To some extent.'

'Because, of course, you were not present in that office at seven on that fatal night.'

'Does that call for answer?'

'And Mr Anderson is dead.'

This time the witness contented himself with looking scornful and did not reply.

'And one person only knows the truth. The accused, you know,' said Sir David, with artful simplicity, turning towards the jury. 'He was *there*. He *knows*. And shortly he will go into that box and tell us what no one else can tell.'

26

UNDER the guidance of Sir Evelyn the prosecution's case moved on towards its ordered, meticulous conclusion in the testimony of those who had seen the accused in the neighbourhood of his father's office, and when the prosecutor at last sat down it could be seen how well the details had fitted the shape of the opening speech. A good tidy case, was the opinion of the gallery, so impressed with the logical development and with the string of witnesses, whose evidence all dove-tailed into the plan, as to believe that the battle was already won. It was a mistake to which Sir Evelyn did not subscribe; he knew that only formalities had occurred so far and that the real struggle would now begin.

'May it please your lordship and members of the jury.'

Defending counsel was on his feet, a bulky figure radiating confidence and belief in his client's innocence. Things looked black, his manner seemed to say, but now that no more prosecution witnesses were to be called to traduce that maligned figure in the dock, truth would surely triumph. Such was the magnetism of his manner, that even before he had launched out on his case an atmosphere more favourable to the prisoner could be felt in court. And then the case itself! Of course the witnesses to identification had told the truth – and how admirably they had given evidence! said Sir David, gaining the affection of the jury by this magnanimous and wholly irrelevant praise of his opponents. But then, as he blandly added, the defence had not challenged or cross-examined them; the defence agreed with almost everything that they had said. In all this counsel showed how well he understood that nothing disarms the truth so quickly as admissions. Once granted, this part of the prosecution's case seemed suddenly to shrink, and Sir David, turning to the main contentious ground, was at once able to claim the attention and sympathy of the court.

'We come at last,' he said, 'to the heart of the matter that you, members of the jury, must resolve. Was this murder? Was it manslaughter? Or was it an act of self-defence? My lord will direct you at a later stage as to the law. It will be sufficient if I tell you now that a man whose life is threatened is entitled to use any reasonable degree of force to save himself. What is reasonable in each case is a matter to be judged in the light of common sense – your forte, I may say, ladies and gentlemen,' added Sir David, who had that invaluable advocate's knack of making juries feel like shrewd horse dealers and Solomons all rolled into one.

'Normally – and let me make this clear – a man attacked with fists may not use a knife or gun or other such weapon in his own defence; the force would be disproportionate to the violence offered, disproportionate to the provocation. But supposing the attacked is weak, the attacker strong; suppose the victim is a boy who has suffered bodily hurt from the same source before. Suppose the aggressor to be drunk and violent and in that state where hands and fists are weapons dangerous to life. Ask yourselves what force in self-defence would be reasonable then.'

Sir David paused, and his eagle eye swept down the benches of the jury.

'The prosecution brings witnesses here – a plethora of them – to prove what we do not dispute.' He held up his hand as he saw his opponent begin to rise. 'They had to be brought, of course, and I make no reflexion on my learned friend. But these witnesses were – if I may put it so – all on the *outside*; they are witnesses to inference. It is clear enough what inferences you are asked to draw from them: it is a grim and sordid tale of a son who came, full of purpose, to take his father's life, who struck him like a coward when his victim's back was turned. All that – and I cannot stress the point too much – is inference at best. No one saw it, and you are asked to deduce it from a set of facts. But there was a witness *inside* – the accused himself.

'Now he is going into that witness box and you will hear his story. You are his judges. Perhaps when you have heard his evidence there will be other inferences for you to draw – yes, even from these so-called cowardly, wicked blows. There will be other evidence, too, independent evidence to show the power of the physical menace this young man faced that night. When all is said, there may be in your hearts feelings for the boy very different from those aroused in you by the cold recitals of the prosecution –

feelings of pity, maybe; I cannot tell. Of one thing I am certain:
you, as open-minded citizens, conscious of the burden that you
bear, will give a fair hearing to the accused. He is a prisoner
charged with murder, but in spite of that he is a fellow human
being, no less worthy of belief than you or I or any of the witnesses
who have gone before him to that box. He alone *knows* what
happened on that night, and you will listen to him, I do not
doubt, with the knowledge that truth is no monopoly, no preserve
of the prosecution. He will speak now and his evidence will be
tested by the cross-examination of my learned friend – a terrible
and searching test for any man. Yet it is with confidence that I
call him and it is with confidence that I submit him to your care.'

Sir David's voice had risen emotionally throughout his peroration, a trumpet call of faith, and now very slowly, and after
another searching look along the faces of the jury, he turned away
towards the dock. 'I call Rupert Laurence Anderson,' he said.

A stir of tense interest swept the court. It was the moment for
which everyone had been waiting, and pressmen and gallery,
solicitors, the barristers themselves, all eagerly craned forward to
watch the young man's progress to the box. So do the crowds at
a *corrida* eye the first entry of the bull, wild and unpredictable
creature coming for its brief hour into the sunlight from its
prison behind the barricade.

At once defending counsel's words acquired a deeper meaning
as it was seen how slight in build the prisoner was. Many in
court were seeing him properly for the first time, and they could
not fail to be impressed by the contrast between his appearance
and alleged deeds: the boy looked an artist, and it became progressively more difficult to think that he had gone to his father
with premeditated murder in his heart. So while the gallery
whispered and the pressmen used up all their adjectives to describe his pale thin face, the prisoner took his stand midway
between judge and jury. In strange contrast with his predecessors,
the police witnesses, he was so small that he still looked a prisoner
even in the witness box, and a stir of sympathy could be felt in
court for this David ranged against the Goliath of the law. The
jury, a fair cross-section of the community, was sentimentally
impressed. Not so the judge. Capable of anything, from the look
of him, he thought, and then mechanically and almost without

effort suppressed this unjudicial judgement which would scarcely weigh with him at all.

And now an official was standing by the witness box with the Testament in his hand. 'The prisoner took the oath in a voice little louder than a whisper,' the pressmen wrote, then in rounded, well-turned phrases, which only their sub-editors did not admire, reflected on the ordeal before the boy and the efforts he was making to rise to the occasion.

'You must speak up,' said Sir David, with enormous avuncular kindness. 'You know me. Answer the questions I have to put to you and in such a way that those ladies and gentlemen over there' – pointing to the jury – 'can hear you perfectly. Right?'

'Yes, sir.'

'Good, good!' said Sir David, hitching up his gown. Like so many counsel he treated his wigs and robes as very useful tools of trade and by recourse to them could express bewilderment, confidence, disbelief, pity, anger, and a dozen other emotions equally useful and dramatic. Nothing was duller, as he realized, than a voice, however beautiful, however perfectly modulated, booming and droning on, and since counsel were debarred from standing on their heads and indulging in other such methods of keeping the attention of the jury, they must fall back on this wig scratching and gown twisting, the only alternatives remaining to them.

'You are Rupert Laurence Anderson?'

'Yes, sir.'

'Of "The Templars", Colbert Row, Turlminster, is that right?'

'That's so.'

'Rupert Laurence Anderson,' said Sir David, who liked to inject a note of drama right from the start, 'did you murder Robert Hemsley Anderson, your father?'

The answer came, very firm and clear: 'No, sir, I did not.'

Defending counsel shot a quick look at the jury to see how its members had taken this and was greatly reassured by what he saw. There was more than one responsive face, and on these breaches in the prosecution's line he would concentrate his eloquence and canalize the natural pity roused by the youth of the accused.

On this optimistic note he began to take the prisoner through the early stages of the brief, through the relationship existing in what he, following in Sir Evelyn's footsteps, called 'that un-happy, ill-starred family', to the night of the quarrel when Mr Anderson had left his home. Residents of Turlminster would have been greatly surprised by the Mr Anderson that emerged from this recital – a man of unreasonable whims and sudden violence, strange in his manner towards the end, though the witness had never realized the cause of it. Yet the picture was not overdrawn; no monster was presented, but just as certainly not that quiet gentleman known and respected in the town. 'You never can tell,' the gallery was whispering, and perhaps the jury may have echoed this. 'They may *seem* all right, but they're not always quite the same at home.'

'And now we come to the night of 5th October,' said Sir David, lowering his voice. 'You will remember that that was the fatal night?'

'I do.'

'Compose yourself and try to answer me,' continued counsel, adopting the tone of one who has to break bad tidings to the family. It was most effective and removed the jury's mind a thousand miles from the thought that Sir David, on the prose-cution's word, was talking to a murderer. 'Tell the jury, if you please, and in your own words, what happened on that night.'

There was a pause, then the prisoner began to speak, quietly at first, so quietly that the pressmen (placed, as usual in the courts, in positions of the greatest disadvantage) had to invent more than their usual quota of the story, then, as the tale moved on to its unfolding, with ever-increasing clarity, so that at last the words rang out into every corner of the hushed and crowded room.

'I went that night to ask my father to come back. Mother was unhappy' – a felicitous touch that brought a lump into the throats of all but the most hardened. 'I thought that if I talked to him he might come back.'

'Did your mother want him back?' enquired the judge. 'Did she tell you so?'

'Yes, my lord.'

'Even after the events you have described?'

'I think in a way she had forgiven him,' said Rupert, his mother's son and all Christian humility like her. 'Without him

211

my chances in life were handicapped. I suppose the real reason for her forgiveness was her love for me.'

'Hum!' said the judge, less affected by this answer than some members of the public. 'Yes, go on.'

'My lord, that was why I called. The first time my father was not in. I decided to wait, for I knew his habit of working in the office after normal hours. And that evening, sure enough, he came.'

'Did you see from where?' put in Sir David, who had been leaning back against the head-rest of his bench, following the witness in the pages of his brief.

'Yes, sir. It was a foggy night but I was near enough to see. He came out of the bar parlour of an hotel. It was the "Golden Fleece".'

'From the bar parlour, eh!' said counsel, with a quick expressive glance towards the jury. 'And what happened then?'

'He went upstairs to his office and I followed him.'

'Yes, yes. In your own words, if you please.'

'I knocked on the office door. For some time there was no reply, then suddenly it opened and he was standing there. It gave me a fright, really,' said the young man, turning his white face towards the jury as though offering a sort of sample.

There was a pause and Sir David prompted: 'How did he look? Was he normal?'

'No, sir, he was not. His manner was most strange.'

'How do you mean? Was there anything special about him you can describe?'

'His eyes seemed different, somehow – rather red, I thought, and protruding. And his voice was thick.'

The public diagnosed the 'Fleece' without being told. It was more convincing than any direct word.

'Did he ask you in?'

'I went in,' said the witness. 'I was not to be so easily put off.'

'Were you afraid?'

'No, sir, not afraid, not at that time. He was my father and I didn't think that in spite of everything he'd do me harm.'

Admirable! thought Sir David. Quite admirable! The thing could be touched up a bit, perhaps. 'So you remembered your mother's distress and went inside?'

'I did.'

'What did he say to that?'

'He asked me what the devil I meant by coming there.'

'Not a very friendly greeting,' commented Sir David.

'No, sir. It was like him, though – like what he'd become recently, I mean. He seemed to have it in for us somehow.'

'Part and parcel of his changed attitude. We shall hear more of that. But for the moment you are inside the room. Tell the jury what happened next.'

The young man, who had been facing his counsel like a boy answering his catechism, moved his position slightly to confront the jury. He allowed his hands to trail over the woodwork of the witness box. How white and feminine they were!

'I went and stood beside the fire. He came over to me and repeated his question in a louder tone, speaking right into my face.' The witness gave a slight shudder of distaste. 'His breath smelt horribly,' he said.

'Yes,' prompted counsel. 'Yes, go on.'

'He told me to get out. I said that I had come from mother, that mother was distressed and was asking him to return. In reply he used a bad word of her and said that he was finished with her for good.'

'I regret that I must ask you for the actual words,' said Sir David, with the pained air of a man forced to labour on a refuse heap.

The witness supplied them with a becoming sense of shame. 'It was the first time he'd said such things of her,' he said.

'To your knowledge, you mean?'

'Yes.'

'Did he say anything else?'

'He said he'd another woman to look after him and didn't want mother any more.'

'And what did you reply?'

The witness's eyes flashed and he gripped his hands together. 'Must I use the words?'

'I'm afraid so, yes.'

'I said: "It's a filthy, low-down trick. I know the one you're carrying on with, too!"'

'And then?'

213

'And then he came at me,' said the witness, opening his eyes wide as though seeing in terrified recollection the happenings of the night. 'He was shouting, "I'll thrash you" – he'd done it before – "and this time I'll thrash you till you drop. You dare to mention her! I'll break you! I'll finish you!" He used some other words.'

'Yes?' said Sir David, and extracted their full malignant sense with the deftness of a dentist.

'His face was horribly red – just covered with veins – and he was breathing heavily. And as he finished calling me he struck at me with his right hand near the eye, just where the banisters had caught me when he'd smashed me down before. I was half blinded for a minute and then I felt his hands were round my throat. He forced me down on to my knees and I heard his voice – it sounded far away – saying, "I'll finish you, d'you hear! This time I'll settle you!"'

'And then?'

But the witness did not reply. Before the public gaze, now surprisingly compassionate, he slumped back against the walls of the witness stand, his head bowed upon his chest. Sir David, taking advantage of his close proximity, was beside him in an instant, administering first-aid with the melancholy gusto of an expert and by no means unaware of the favourable sensation that was being caused.

'Is he all right?' enquired the judge, something of a connoisseur of judicial – and judicious – fainting fits.

'Yes, my lord, he's come to now.'

'Perhaps you would care for medical assistance? Are the police doctors in the court?'

But they were not, and it was under the aegis of his counsel that he stood forward in his place, palpably weak but sufficiently recovered to continue.

'Let him have a chair,' ordered the judge.

But the accused protested that he would rather stand. Courage now being added to sensibility, his stock stood high in court.

'You were telling us,' said Sir David, returning like a trainer to the touchlines, 'how your father forced you down on to your knees. You heard him say, "This time I'll settle you."'

'Yes, sir. I remember.'

214

'Go on from there, please.'

'He was leaning down over me. I think he must have over-balanced, for suddenly I felt him fall on me. I was pinned help-lessly, only my left hand was free. His grip was at my throat and I could see his face.' Here the witness gave a shudder which found its echo an instant later round the court. 'He meant to kill me. I was sure of it.'

'Didn't you fight back?'

'I tried to but he was too strong. He was twice my weight. I think a blow of mine went home but it only seemed to make him angrier. If I'd fought on with my hands I'd have been done for very soon.'

'Let us get this clear,' said Sir David. 'Is it true to say that at that moment you were in fear of death?'

'I was. I felt that I was losing consciousness.'

'So what action did you take?'

'I told you,' replied the witness, 'that my left arm was free. We were lying with our heads towards the fireplace but at a slight angle from it. In my despair, and looking for some weapon to defend myself, I reached out my left hand and my fingers touched the poker lying in the grate.'

'Yes, go on.'

'Well, sir, he was still pressing, and by this time I was nearly gone. In desperation I raised the poker and brought it down on him with a sweeping motion. I meant to make him release his grip; I meant to hurt him, not to kill him. It was the only thing that I could do.' The young man put his hand up to his head and the ever-vigilant Sir David was preparing to carry out his errand of mercy once again But the witness mastered his emotion. 'It didn't seem to do much good,' he said. 'I think the blow must have glanced off. He was almost lying on me. I struck three more times but even that didn't seem to loosen him. I collected all my strength and struck again. It was horrible. It must have gone in deep. He struggled for a bit and then rolled off me on to his left side. I saw then . . . '

'Yes,' prompted Sir David softly.

'I saw then that the blood was running from the wounds. It was horrible, horrible! I'd killed him.'

In the hushed silence the words had come disjointedly, sharp with agonized remembrance. And even the judge, a man not easily impressed, thought to himself: 'That's true: he's not acting now.'

'Forgive me for asking this. Are you sure that at that moment he was dead?'

'I thought so. After hearing what the doctor said this morning I suppose he wasn't. He seemed dead. I could hear no breath, no movement; he lay so still.'

'Was there nothing you could have done?'

'I see it now. I could have helped him. But I was so certain he was gone. And then, selfishly, I thought of myself and what I'd done. I was afraid. I thought people wouldn't believe me if I told the truth. I acted instinctively and in panic. In that mood I went home, and in that mood I made my first statement to the police.'

'You realize now that you were wrong to do that?' asked Sir David, with a sigh for the fallibility of men.

'Yes, sir, I do. I was very wrong. I can see now what I should have done; it's easy after the event. But I'd been through quite a lot.'

Counsel nodded approvingly at this fresh instance of the witness's excellence, for this understatement was bound to have a wide appeal. Seldom in his experience had a witness risen so superior to proof. It was to be hoped that he would be as effective when confronted with Sir Evelyn.

'Of course you'd been through a lot,' he said. 'But your first statement did not represent the truth?'

'No, sir, it did not. It was a foolish statement. When I made it I was not myself.'

'And later you voluntarily admitted that. You made another statement in its place?'

'I did.'

'You heard that read in court. Is that what you said to the Inspector and does it represent the truth of what occurred?'

'Yes, it does.'

'I want to revert to that first statement for a moment,' said counsel, turning back the pages of his brief. 'Inspector Carr says that when you made it you seemed absolutely logical and calm.'

216

'It was the calmness of despair,' replied the witness, drawing another nod of approbation from the defender. 'Could anyone be calm inside after the things that had happened to me that night?'

'Could they!' repeated Sir David, and noting the favourable reaction caused by the prisoner's words he sat down abruptly in his place.

'Is that all, Sir David?' enquired the judge.

'Yes, my lord.'

'Very well. We will adjourn for lunch in exactly half an hour. Meanwhile, there will be time for you, Sir Evelyn, to begin.'

The court hummed with excitement as the small figure of the advocate rose in his tattered silken gown. How would the prisoner fare against this serpentine, suspicious man?

At first the prisoner seemed to be faring very well. He gave his answers in a clear voice, concisely, confidently, and the prosecutor, for all his wiles, seemed unable to trap him into any damaging admissions. Sir David, sitting watchfully, one eye on his learned friend, one on the jury to point the failure of Sir Evelyn's questions, gradually relaxed. An exceptional witness indeed, armed at all points; extraordinary to remember that he was just eighteen. There could be distinguished careers for such a boy and Sir David was sure that they would hear of him again.

'I come now,' counsel was saying, 'to the events of the 5th October. You called on the deceased that night.'

'Yes.'

'In the evening at half past six?'

'I did.'

'And he wasn't in. Were you surprised?'

'I was.'

'You expected that he would be in?'

'I did.'

'I'm sure you did. You knew that your father seldom left before seven o'clock.'

'Yes, sir, that's so.'

'Finding him out was one surprise. There was another: finding Mr Hemmings in?'

'I don't understand that, I'm afraid.'

'Don't you? Are you telling me that you did not know that

it was Mr Hemmings' normal practice to leave for home at six?'

'I believe he varied, sir.'

'I'm suggesting, you see,' said Sir Evelyn, laying his head on one side like a bird, 'that you deliberately chose a time when you expected to find your father in alone.'

The witness did not reply.

'And eventually at seven-ten you did find him in alone?'

'Yes.'

'Why didn't you call in normal office hours? Why didn't you call in the morning or the afternoon?'

'Because what I had to say was confidential.'

'Or what you had to *do* was secret,' said Sir Evelyn. 'I pass on. You found the manner of the deceased was strange?'

'I did.'

'And you described his symptoms. You are telling us that he was drunk.'

'I suppose he was.'

'Did you consider it reasonable to put your demand that he should return home to a drunken man who had used violence on you some weeks before?'

'Perhaps I wasn't reasonable,' replied the witness. 'Mother was distressed. I wanted an answer, that was all.'

At this there was some nodding among the jurymen and Sir David looked triumphant.

'So you put your questions and got your answer. He struck you – a painful blow and on a place that had been cut before.'

'He did.'

'Did it bleed this second time?'

'No, sir.'

'Was there a bruise?'

'No, no bruise.'

'At that stage he told you that he would thrash you; he used words like "break" and "finish"?'

'Yes, he did.'

'You could have left the room. Why didn't you, since you say you knew that you couldn't match him in a fight?'

'I suppose my blood was up. I didn't think he'd carry out his threats.'

'But he did. He forced you down on to your knees and fell on you. He was choking you. His voice came from far off. You were "going", in your words.'

'I was.'

'How was he holding you? Show the jury, if you please.'

An interlude now occurred in which a court official was prevailed upon to act the part of the accused in a reconstruction of the incidents near the judge's bench. Like most reconstructions it did not suffer from any excess of animation, and there was some tittering in the gallery at the embarrassed expression on the reluctant victim's face.

'He had you round the throat then?' said Sir Evelyn. 'He had you with both hands?'

'Yes.'

'And he was pressing on you?'

'Yes, sir – hard.'

'Not too hard now; let us not be too realistic,' said the prosecutor, supplying the ponderous little joke usual on these occasions, whereat the gallery laughed out openly. But the judge was not amused. 'Continue, Sir Evelyn,' he said.

'Yes, my lord.' He turned to the tableau on the bench. 'Thank you, that will do. Will the witness please resume his place.'

He came through that well, thought Sir David, watching his client go back into the box. Old Eve's got nowhere yet.

But the foundations had been laid.

'That is how your father held you? As you have demonstrated so ably to the jury?'

'Yes.'

'With the force of both hands fully applied around your throat?'

'Yes' – rather impatiently, rather scornfully, for he had answered this before.

'He left some marks on you, no doubt?'

'There were marks on my throat, sir.'

'Oh, there were! I can well believe it after the violence you've described. And they were the proof of the truth of the story you have told, of course?'

The witness did not reply.

'Can you show those marks to-day?'

219

Rupert smiled even more scornfully. What a stupid old buffer this man was! 'Not to-day,' he said.

'Could you show them when arrested, then?'

'No, sir. They'd faded by that time.'

'Three days after the incident! Well then, let us go back three days in time – to the fatal night. The Inspector called on you just before eleven.'

'About that time.'

'Were the marks already fading then?'

'Oh no.'

'Did you show them to the Inspector?'

'I did not.'

'And why?'

'Because at that time I was afraid to tell the truth.'

'And later, when the truth was to the fore, the marks were not.

'They'd faded, as I said.'

'So no one saw them except yourself?'

'Mother did.'

'Oh! your mother did. Didn't your mother also in your presence make a statement to the police backing up your alibi? Didn't she say that you had been home all that night?'

'I think she did.'

'And she will give evidence that she saw the marks! Illuminating testimony!'

Sir David was already on his feet protesting: 'My lord, this is intolerable! My friend is commenting on the evidence of a witness not yet called.'

'Quite,' agreed the judge. 'A most improper comment which I ask the jury to ignore.'

Sir Evelyn in the heat of battle was not disposed even to apologize. 'What colour were those marks?' he said.

'Red, sir, and turning bluish afterwards. They weren't very noticeable, I should say.'

'Not noticeable! I put it to you that they were illusory.'

'No, sir.'

'Bluish, were they?'

'Yes.'

'Bruises, then. Do you agree?'

'Yes, sir. Slight bruises.'

220

'And at the end of three days – three days! – every trace was gone?'

'Yes.'

'Though he'd pressed so hard he'd nearly killed you! Is that what you ask the jury to believe?'

'It's true.'

'When the Inspector called that night you were in bed.'

'I was.'

'You made a statement. Weren't you wearing pyjamas and a dressing gown at that time?'

'I was.'

'And your neck was visible?'

'Perhaps.'

'Would you be surprised to know that the Inspector saw no marks on your bare neck at all?'

'Perhaps he didn't look.'

Another titter ran through the court, speedily suppressed by the judge who said, as judges always do: 'Another such incident and I shall clear the court.'

'And I suppose Sergeant Rice, who was present, also failed to see the marks?'

'Perhaps he didn't look either,' replied the witness.

'It amuses you to be pert,' said Sir Evelyn, in his silkiest voice.

'Well, you're getting at me all the time and twisting all my words.'

'Answer the questions in a proper manner,' directed the judge sternly.

'I'll try, my lord.'

Sir Evelyn turned over the pages of his brief.

'Do you seriously tell the jury that such marks can fade within three days without a trace?'

'They were very slight marks.'

'As slight as the force your father used, perhaps – if he used any force at all?'

The witness remained silent.

'I put it to you that the whole story of force is an invention.'

'Oh no.'

'He gripped you and nearly throttled you and you can show no marks; he struck you on the eye, where you had been hurt

221

before, and you can show no mark. The marks that did show were on him. You struck five blows?'

'I did.'

'One of which penetrated to a branch artery?'

The witness shivered and replied, 'I suppose it did.'

'And you were lying on your back and he on top of you?'

'That's so.'

'Do you ask the jury to believe,' demanded Sir Evelyn, with a fine display of incredulity, 'that from the position you have described you could generate the force to penetrate like that?'

'I did.'

'We know you did. But I put it to you that you did it by striking him with the full force and direction of downward blows, struck while you were standing on a higher elevation.'

'Never, never.'

'You heard the police surgeon? You have heard him say that in his opinion these were downward blows?'

'They were not struck from above. It isn't true.'

'How then, from underneath, did you manage to strike at that downward angle and so powerfully?'

'Because, naturally, as I raised the weapon it came down on him from above; besides, I'm strongish in the wrists,' said Rupert, and there was a little gasp from his supporters in the court.

'Oh, so you're strongish! We won't hear so much now about that disparity of strength between the two of you. Why didn't you hit him in the face?'

'I did.'

'Hard?'

'As hard as I could. It wasn't hard enough.'

Sir Evelyn industriously searched his brief. 'You heard from the medical evidence,' he said at last, 'that there were no marks on the dead man, the wounds on the scalp and arms apart?'

'That's what was said.'

'Do you accept it?'

'I suppose so.'

'And in the light of that are you still telling us that you struck him in the face?'

'Yes, yes, I did. I did.'

'Was he lying right on top of you?'

'Yes.'

'Where was the poker?'

'In the grate.'

'Did you reach out towards it?'

'I did. My fingers touched it.'

'Had you known that it was there?'

'No. I reached out for a weapon, any weapon, something to save me.'

'Would you say that at this moment your father was controlling and dominating you?'

'He was doing more than that: he was killing me.'

'And with this man controlling you, lying on you, almost killing you, are you telling the court that you were able to grope around for a weapon which might or might not be there, find it, seize it, and bring it down on to the head of this dominant assailant?'

'I was desperate,' said the witness. 'You can do extra things when you're like that.'

'And *say* extra things, too, no doubt,' replied Sir Evelyn dryly, with a glance at the jury to draw their attention to the present desperate state of the accused. And with that he fell to searching through his brief again, patiently, and with a methodical industry that brought a qualm even into Sir David's optimistic heart.

Before he could continue the judge had intervened. 'Sir Evelyn, it is nearly half past one.'

'Yes, my lord.'

'Unless you're almost at an end I think this would be a convenient moment to adjourn.'

'Yes, my lord,' agreed Sir Evelyn, and added, not without menace: 'I haven't nearly finished with him yet.'

27

SIR EVELYN had ended the morning with a threat not devoid of strategy. It was his belief that the witness box, though frequently a forum for perjuries and evasions, made for justice in the end; it was a sort of truth machine; he asked the questions, and the bad conscience and exposed position of the witness did the rest. To add to that conscience and that sense of isolation was counsel's duty in the interests of truth, and he had found in his experience that adjournments, in which the subject had time to fear and think, were very useful aids.

As he rose to resume his cross-examination after lunch he studied the witness's face attentively. The lad was very pale, even paler than he had been that morning, and possibly nearer to a real breakdown than at the time of his earlier rather theatrical display. But he must not underestimate this witness whose strength of will might be as deceptive as his strength of arm; he had made some headway with him and had extracted some damaging admissions, but not enough. He must strike more firmly: after the promise, the performance.

'We had reached the point this morning,' he began, 'when you had struck the blows and your father had rolled from off you to the floor?'

'Yes,' the witness said.

'And you thought that he was dead?'

'I was certain of it.'

'How certain? Did you look?'

'Yes, sir. And I listened. I couldn't hear his breath.'

'You looked and listened. Did you touch him?'

Rupert gave a small shudder of aversion and shook his head.

'You didn't feel his heart or anything like that?'

'Oh no.'

'You just assumed it. Your father was lying there; he might be living; he might be dead. And you didn't satisfy yourself for sure?'

'I didn't, I'm afraid.'

'I take it you were sorry for what had happened?'

'Sorry! I was horrified. I never meant to kill him.'

'You mean you hadn't done a crime?'

'Of course I hadn't.'

'And you *knew* you hadn't?'

'Yes, I knew. What I'd done I'd done in self-defence.'

'You *knew*,' Sir Evelyn repeated, brushing away the rest of the answer with a wave of his bony hand. 'And you've told us that you were sorry. Could I put it to you that you pitied him?'

'Naturally I did,' Rupert replied, with an expressive glance towards the jury.

'He was lying there, bleeding, was he not?'

'Yes, yes, he was.'

'Did you attempt to stem the blood?'

'No. What was the use?'

'Did you hold his head or try to make him comfortable?'

'No, I told you. I couldn't touch him.'

'Did you call for help?'

'No, no.'

'He wasn't dead, you see,' said the prosecutor gently.

'Perhaps not. He seemed so to me.'

'Why didn't you call for help?'

'Why? Because I panicked. Haven't I been telling you?' And the witness looked round the court as though seeking allies against unreason.

'What were you afraid of?' continued the level, gentle voice. 'You'd committed no crime. You've told us so.'

'And I hadn't. I hadn't.'

'And you pitied this man. You've told us so.'

'I did.'

'Then, if that were so, why didn't you give the simple Christian help a man would give a dog that lay like that? Why didn't you tend him yourself or call for help?'

'I'd panicked. Oh, I've told you.'

'Why did you panic?' asked Sir Evelyn, raising his head slowly and fixing the witness with a long accusing stare. 'Was it because you knew you'd murdered him?'

The truth machine! he thought, watching his victim's agonized, despairing glance. Strange that it should begin to work on a

225

question not deadly in itself, but that so often was the way. However, this was only a beginning, and he could not be sure that the jury saw what he could see.

'Was that the reason?' he repeated. 'Because you *knew* what you had done?'

'Not murder.'

'You still say that you thought that you had done no crime?'

'I hadn't,' Rupert cried.

Sir Evelyn bent down to the table and turned over a few pages of his brief. A small respite – very small – and then again the sudden spring.

'Did you still think that as you made your way back home?'

'Oh yes.'

'And when the police called, late that night?'

'I've always thought it,' Rupert said. 'It's true.'

'Did you think it when you made your first statement to Inspector Carr?'

The witness looked towards the bench, as though expecting that some help would be forthcoming from that quarter. He glanced back rather quickly, for the judge was looking at him with such a steady, cold expression in his eyes.

'Of course I thought it,' he replied.

'Then why was your statement full of lies?' asked Sir Evelyn, with a lightning dart.

'I don't know. I was afraid.'

'What of? You were innocent? That's what you're telling us. And you *knew* that you were innocent?'

The witness did not reply.

'Your statement was all lies?'

'Yes.'

'Not a word of truth in it? A pack of lies?'

'I suppose so.'

'Why, when you were innocent and when the simple truth would have cleared you, did you tell a pack of lies?'

'I've told you. I'd panicked. I was near collapse.'

Sir Evelyn looked hard at the witness and searched back through his brief. 'Did you hear the Inspector describe your manner at the time as calm and logical? Is *he* lying?'

'I wasn't calm. How could I be?'

'You were asked to describe your movements; you were expected to tell the truth. But did you?'

'At that time, no.'

'At that time!' said Sir Evelyn, in accents of the deepest scorn. 'Sometimes you tell truths and sometimes untruths, is that it?'

Again there was no reply.

'Do you set up as a man whose word is to be relied on?'

'Yes.'

'You do!' – and Sir Evelyn, with a great display of astonishment at this answer, turned towards the jury, whose fixed, unwavering concentration he noted with something approaching triumph. 'When you're not in a panic, I suppose you mean!' he continued, turning back towards the witness and unloosing this sarcasm under him like a fire-cracker. 'At other times you tell the truth?'

'I do.'

'Let us examine this panic, if you please. To what was it due?'

'To what I'd seen, of course.'

'And to what you'd *done*?'

'To what had happened, if you like.'

'Was the panic due to what had happened to *him*?' Sir Evelyn asked, 'or to what *might* happen to you?'

'It was over him, of course.'

'Can you describe this panic to us?'

'I'll try,' the witness said, puckering up his brow. 'I think I lost my powers of reasoning. That's why I didn't call for help. I was in a whirl.'

'Yet you remembered every detail of the struggle and the blows?'

'They came before the shock of finding that I'd killed him.'

'And you were coherent with the Inspector when he called that night?'

'I wasn't calm.'

'Weren't you? But you were certainly logical and coherent according to your lights. Would you care to hear the statement that you made again – the first statement, the lying statement?'

'If you like.'

227

Sir Evelyn obliged, watching the jury's reaction over the top of the document as he read.

'Is that the statement of a man in a whirl, of a man who'd lost his powers of reasoning?'

'I had, I tell you.'

'The jury must judge of that. Had the panic subsided a little by the next day?'

'A bit, perhaps.'

'But still you didn't volunteer the truth?'

'No.'

'Or on the next day?'

'No.'

'And on the day of the inquest,' continued counsel, working up his tone of irony, 'how was the panic then?'

'It was bad.'

'But you went to court. In a whirl and with an inability to reason?'

'It didn't matter. I wasn't called.'

'I know you weren't *called*,' said Sir Evelyn, rapping his hand down violently on the table. 'Why didn't you *ask* to be called? Why didn't you clear things up and tell your version of the truth?'

'I was afraid. It goes on adding up, you see,' explained the witness, turning to the jury. 'In panic I'd lied, and it wasn't easy to put that right.'

The truth machine! Sir Evelyn thought, with a small flicker of satisfaction at a case proved – to himself, at any rate. 'So when you're *afraid*,' he said, stressing the word with all the resources of his voice – 'when you're afraid is another time that you avoid the truth? That is what you tell the court?'

And with a significant glance, as though directing the attention of the jury to the young man's drawn, white face, he sat down heavily in his place.

Defending counsel was on his feet at once, for his opponent's final words were dangerous and he must rub out their impression before they became registered in the jury's mind. 'When you said you were afraid,' he asked the witness, 'did you mean that you were afraid because of the committing of a crime?'

'Oh no.'

'Then tell my lord and the jury what you were afraid of.'

The young man braced himself.

'I was afraid of the remembrance of my father's death, and I was afraid that even if I told the truth they wouldn't believe or understand me.'

Sir David nodded his head in appraisal of this answer. One more question to re-establish the credit of the witness as a truth teller, and he could let him go.

'Are you afraid now?'

'No, sir, I'm not. When a thing happens you know how silly you were to be afraid. I've nothing to fear and I can see now I never had. I'm innocent.'

'Thank you,' Sir David said, doing his own poor best with the jury to second these ringing words. 'Unless my lord has any questions you may leave the box.'

The judge had none, and an instant later the prisoner was making his way back towards the dock. The occupants of the press-box sorrowfully saw him go – the stuff of the human drama on which their readers fed – but fell avidly to their notes again as they heard defending counsel say.

'I call Laura Marion Anderson.'

Mother and son passed one another in the well of the court: it was a poignant moment, of which the reporters made the most – a glance of encouragement and love, the lingering, gentle touch of hands. Nothing that had happened so far had told one half so much in favour of the accused; for the sentimental it was a form of argument.

And Laura was another argument in herself. She was beautifully dressed in a black costume and furs, and wore a little black halo-hat to frame her pallid face, so artfully made up as to appear not to be made up at all, her whole personality dignified and tragic, a mother fighting for her son, as the headlines that evening inevitably said.

'Laura Marion Anderson?'

Sir David's voice and manner matched her perfectly. Here was chivalry of the old school paying its respects to beauty in distress, and the jury was at once beneath the spell.

'And do you live at "The Templars", Colbert Row, Turlminster?'

'I do.'

'You are the mother of the accused?'

'I am,' said Laura, and she turned with an expression of the utmost tenderness towards the dock, where her son's white face could just be seen above the parapet. Even the prosecutor, who knew from long experience how witnesses could be dressed to fit their parts, was considerably impressed: adolescent girls, young "teen-agers", the victims of carnal knowledge cases, always washed off surplus paint and powder and went like little innocents into the box; divorce petitioners wore black and looked more deeply wronged than any human has a right to be; but here the clothes and character of the witness were so perfectly in tone that it was almost impossible to believe she was not honourable and good. He did not relish the idea of cross-examining her.

But for the moment she was the concern of Sir David Fynes.

'You are the widow of Robert Hemsley Anderson?'

'I am,' replied Laura, in so low a voice that defending counsel had to ask her to speak up. He did this solicitously, in such a manner as to suggest it was a miracle that the witness could find the courage to give evidence at all. Frail, tragic woman, he seemed to be saying to the jury, was it not a dreadful thing that she should be confronted with the remorseless machinery of the law! 'I know you'll try your best,' he said.

She gave him a melancholy smile and said: 'I will.'

'Good, good! That's much better. If you'll answer my questions at just that pitch. And first of all: How long were you married to the deceased?'

'For just thirty-four years. We married very young.'

'And you have three children?'

'Yes. Rupert' – with another tender look towards the dock – 'is the youngest of the three.'

'Was your marriage happy?'

'Happy? Yes, at first. We had the usual disagreements.'

'You said, "at first",' pointed out Sir David. 'Are we to infer from that that your relations changed?'

'Yes. They did.'

'When?'

'After the birth of Rupert. Somehow we were never so close together after that. He resented Rupert for some reason, and that resentment grew.'

230

'Let us examine this resentment. How did it show itself?'

'Oh, it was nothing very much at first, except that he was always a bit down on the boy and prompt to punish him.'

'At first,' echoed Sir David, snatching at his cue. 'Did that resentment change in character as well?'

'It did. It became more serious altogether. What at first was just a father's natural control developed into something else.'

'Into what?'

'Into hatred, I think,' replied Laura, wrinkling her forehead into lines of incomprehension at the thought that such things could be.

'Did this hatred display itself in action?' asked Sir David, who knew from the judge's face that he had been manoeuvring on dangerous ground. 'Can you tell us instances of it that you saw?'

'Instances? Yes, several.'

'Tell us, please.'

'One day about six years ago when the boy was twelve he wouldn't, for some reason, eat his food. He was taken upstairs and flogged unmercifully with a strap in spite of my protests. I saw weals on him, and there was blood. The same thing happened three years later over an unsatisfactory school report. I'm afraid my husband was too ready to turn to punishment.' The worried frown appeared on her face again and she said: 'I think he liked using the strap on him; I think he enjoyed punishing the boy. He beat him hard and brutally.'

Sir David shook his head in silent sympathy. 'Were there other instances?'

'Not of beating. He gave that up.'

'And substituted something else?'

'Yes. He took to knocking him about. One day about nine months ago Rupert interfered in a quarrel between me and my husband. Robert struck him in the face. He threatened to do the same a couple of months or so later. On that occasion the boy had come in late from a dance. He was dragged downstairs like a criminal, his shirt was torn, and it was all I could do to prevent another beating before my eyes.'

The witness's voice was becoming increasingly inaudible and she was showing signs of deep distress.

'Please speak up,' urged Sir David. 'We know how you must feel in this ordeal.'

She raised her handkerchief to her lips and said again: 'I'll try.'

'Of course you will. Tell us, now: Were there any other incidents of the kind?'

'Yes, the last. That was on the night my husband left.'

'Tell us about it, please.'

'My husband and I were quarrelling,' said Laura, turning her tragic face towards the jury. 'My husband believed that in some way I had interfered in a matter that concerned our elder daughter and that I had prejudiced her happiness. It was all a misunderstanding, a dreadful mistake on both our parts. My husband became violent – I think he had been drinking – and in the end he struck me and pushed me down on to the bed. He was very angry; he was shouting and abusing me. Rupert heard. He came into the room and tried to protect me from my husband.'

'Just a moment there. When you say he tried to protect you, do you imply that he offered violence to his father?'

The witness's eyes expressed her horror at this suggestion of so unfilial an action.

'Oh, no. He stood between us, that was all.'

'And then?'

'And then my husband went for him and struck him with his fists. He thrust him to the door, opened it and flung him through. I ran to them to protect my boy, and there on the landing I saw the last blow struck. Rupert went down, and as he fell he caught his head against the banisters. He lay still, and I saw there was blood on his forehead from a cut above the eye. It was a deep cut, as I found when I took him down to Doctor Stokes.'

'Having knocked him down,' came the precise voice of defending counsel, 'what did your husband do?'

'He left the house.'

'Was he upset? Did he seem sorry he'd struck his son?'

'Sorry!' cried Laura, with an unpleasant laugh. 'He said that he was glad.'

'Can you remember the words, the exact words, please?'

'I can. They're not easily forgotten. He said: "That's for a beginning. I've been saving that one up for years."'

232

'He did, did he!' said Sir David, complacently surveying the effect of these words on the impressionable jury.

'And then he went straight off down the stairs without so much as a backward glance.'

'Leaving his son lying on the floor?'

'Yes. The boy might have been dead for all he cared.'

'Let me turn now,' said Sir David, congratulating himself on the quality of his witness, 'to your son's reactions to the treatment meted out to him by the deceased. Let us begin from the beginning, from those earliest thrashings with the strap.'

The witness paused for a quick glance towards the dock and then replied: 'Well, naturally he was afraid. He was always small and delicate, you see. And Robert was so big. After the first strapping the boy was so nervous that he wouldn't speak to his father for several days. It was terror, really.' Her eyes grew big. 'You should have seen the marks, a criss-cross of weals quite deep into the flesh. He must have suffered dreadfully.'

'That was the result of what we might call the first occasion? That was the time he wouldn't eat his food?'

'Yes. But the second occasion was worse. He was growing then and was far more sensitive. And at fifteen to be held down and beaten on the bed! I could hear the blows and Rupert's cries quite clearly.'

'You didn't intervene?'

The witness's mouth went taut. 'The door was locked,' she said.

'What was your son's reaction afterwards?'

'Pain and fear; he'd been badly hurt. But humiliation, chiefly. It was a dreadful thing at that age to be made to bend down like a naughty little child. In my opinion he never quite recovered; he could never be easy with his father after that.'

Sir David nodded his head, inviting the jury to acquiesce in this mother's psychological reading of her son. 'May we turn to the later incidents?' he said. 'There was the occasion when he was dragged downstairs and his shirt was torn. Did he seem afraid on that occasion, too?'

'He did. I could see it in his eyes. And next day he told me so. He said he was afraid and didn't know where it would end.'

Sir David turned over the pages of his brief. 'We come now,' he said, 'to the night your husband left your house, the night he struck you. What appeared to be your son's reactions then?'

Laura raised her head and gazed with evident pride towards the small figure in the dock. 'He was terrified. But I was in trouble and he tried to help. When he got between us I could see a look of something like desperation in his face. He was so small,' added the witness, dropping her voice almost to a whisper, but one which by some trick of art or acoustics was heard by everyone in court.

Sir David, a connoisseur of such effects, stood immobile till the impression had gone home, then with admirable timing led the witness to the last pages of her proof.

'I would like to return to one of your earlier answers. You said then – if I remember right,' said counsel, who had noted down the significant answer in the margin of his brief – 'that on that night of the final quarrel the deceased was drunk.'

'I'm afraid he was,' replied Laura, with a show of wifely reluctance not lost upon the jury.

'Forgive me asking this, but did he show visible signs of it? I mean, it wasn't just conjecture?'

'Oh, no. His eyes were red and swollen, his voice thick. Whenever he was gone a bit he always talked in a stilted way, pretending he wasn't really affected, I suppose, and that's how he behaved that night.'

'Ah!' said counsel, pouncing on her words. 'So he had been drunk before?'

'Quite often in his last year. He never used to be like that. He'd always been so moderate in all his habits.'

'But he changed?'

'Yes. It upset me very much. In that year I had trouble with him about a dozen times. Whenever he was like that he seemed to make a set at me; fortunately the children – apart from Rupert on two occasions – were not involved.'

'He made a set at you. Do you mean physically?'

Laura bowed her head as though admitting to the final humiliation of her life. 'Mostly he just got excitable,' she said, 'but he got violent sometimes, too. Once when I'd locked him out he tried to batter in the bedroom door. There were occasions when he put his hands on me, but he never actually struck me with his fists until the very end.'

'With his fists!' cried Sir David, reflecting the indignation of the jury at this sacrilege.

'I'm afraid so. Poor Robert! He was far gone that night. I don't suppose he knew for one moment what he'd done.'

There was a stir in court at this exhibition of Christian charity, and Sir David, always the opportunist, seized the moment to thank the witness for her services and sit down. That's that! he thought, as he saw the slight figure of the prosecutor rise to the attack. Well, Eve, you old devil, I wish you well of her. He would back this witness against all the advocates of the circuits of the Crown.

And in the midst of his elation he felt a slight tug at his gown. It was his professional client, Mr Perks, senior partner of the firm of solicitors that had given him his brief. 'Well?' he said, turning in his seat and cupping his ear with his hand to receive the whispered confidence. He was not well pleased, for he liked the minimum of interference from subordinates during the process of the case. 'Well?' he repeated. 'What's the matter now?'

'It's like this,' said Mr Perks, and there was a rather startled expression on his face. 'The elder daughter, Margaret, is in court. She heard that evidence and she says it isn't true. And if I know what, she'll offer herself in rebuttal for the Crown.'

28

'VERY interesting,' said Sir Evelyn, nodding his head with satisfaction. He was in the robing-room, changing his butterfly collar
for one of fashionable Windsor cut and his white 'bands' for a
pearl-grey tie of exquisite elegance. 'Very interesting indeed, my
boy,' he repeated, patting the shoulder of his junior, Mr Brian
Craig, who had brought him the momentous news. 'This is going
to cook Davie's goose and no mistake.'

Mr Craig looked smugly satisfied, but like most heralds of good
tidings did not openly rejoice. 'He won't appreciate it a bit,' he
said.

'Appreciate it!' cried Sir Evelyn. 'The poor chap'll have a fit.
And serve him right too, fluttering round that Borgia woman like
a great blind moth. D'you know, Craig, he was so wrapped up
in her that I honestly believe he swallowed everything she said.'

'So did the jury,' said Mr Craig.

'Oh, the jury! They'll come round. Just wait till they hear the
daughter, and then they'll see our Laura in another light.'

'She made an impressive witness, though.'

Sir Evelyn's flippant manner fell from him and his face grew
stern. 'She was a vile witness,' he said, 'absolutely unprincipled
and vile. That poor man, such an ordinary, pleasant sort of chap!
I don't suppose he ever did a mean action in his life. And she
held him up as a sort of monster.'

'You don't think it could possibly be true?'

The leader looked at his junior as his shipmates looked at
Ulysses off the coast of the Sirens long ago. 'True? You think so?
It was lies from start to finish – such clever lies. She took away the
reputation of a lifetime and even looked sorry she was doing it.
It was degrading. I tell you frankly, Craig, I could hardly bear
to listen to her.'

'The judge was listening,' said Mr Craig. 'He was listening
attentively, almost sympathetically, I thought.'

'It's his business and our business, more's the pity. If that
woman's believed it'll be the triumph of evil – a small triumph,

perhaps, but that's how evil works, termite-like, in driblets of specimens like her.'

Mr Craig, who was at that middle age that believes itself beyond enthusiasms, looked at his leader in surprise. He had not expected to find the moralist behind that forensic, smooth exterior. 'We can probably scotch her now,' he said.

'Yes, if the girl comes up to scratch. By the way, what exactly did she say?'

'Not a great deal, nothing specific, I'm afraid. She just said that the evidence was false, but she wouldn't make a statement – not to-night. She wanted to sleep on it, she said.'

'Pity!' said Sir Evelyn, brooding over the tactical opportunity they had missed. 'Why did she leave it all so late? Why didn't she put it down in writing?'

'She was overwrought, poor girl, she was in tears. It would have been cruel to press her as she was.'

The prosecutor shrugged this sensibility to one side. 'She should have spoken up,' he said.

'She will to-morrow. She promised to make a statement, and I thought it best to let it stay at that. She was in that mood,' said Mr Craig, who believed he understood young women and that his leader certainly did not, 'when driving might have ruined everything.'

'And lack of bridling might still ruin everything,' said Sir Evelyn, hanging up his gown. 'You should have sent for me.'

He would have been even more perturbed if he had guessed what was to take place that night fifteen miles away in Turlminster, in the small house where Margaret now lived alone. Knowledge would certainly have fortified his belief in the dark talents of Mrs Anderson.

Margaret herself was surprised and shocked to see Laura at the door. At the conclusion of her mother's evidence she had seen Mr Craig and hurried from the court, her mind in a ferment of bewilderment, fired by her loyalties to the living and the dead, and here now before her was the author of her wretchedness, the person she regarded as the betrayer of her father's memory.

She might have refused her visitor admittance had not Laura, with an exact appreciation of her daughter's mind, taken the

237

precaution of stepping quickly across the threshold with the evident intention of remaining there even at the price of scandal. And since she knew her mind she had her way and was able to confront Margaret in the sitting-room – a poor, shabby little room, she noted, with few ornaments except a cabinet portrait of Robert Anderson on the mantelpiece. It took more than that to disconcert so practical a woman, and she opened her campaign at once.

'I've come about your evidence,' she said.

'My evidence! I should have thought you would want to justify your own.'

A quick girl, noted Laura, an angry girl with collapse not far away. Well, she had been hardly tried: first the breakdown of her engagement – how cowardly, how afraid of scandal that odious young man had been! – then the death of her father and the stresses of the trial. She felt a little sorry for the child, might even have felt some affection for her, perhaps, if she had not represented a threat to Rupert's life. But, since she did, she was prepared to manoeuvre her with just the same cold disregard for truth she had shown in the witness box disguised with just the same display of human, generous emotion.

'I don't think I need justify my evidence to you,' she said.

'It was horrible. Lies! Dreadful lies!'

Laura remained quite unmoved. 'But necessary lies,' she said. 'It is sometimes necessary to invent things in order to clear the way for truth.'

'Truth! What truth? What truth was there in anything you said?'

'None in my evidence, perhaps,' admitted Laura, with the utmost candour. 'But there was a truth beyond. The plain fact is that Rupert killed your father accidentally, but without a bit of gilding the jury won't believe it.'

'Gilding! How horrible! How could you say it!'

'Margaret, is it as horrible as the thought that your own brother went there with the intent to kill?'

There! That had had a good effect. The girl had her hands up to her face.

'Or as horrible as the thought of Rupert out there on the trap-door one morning very early? What do you say to that?'

238

And what could the girl say, when all was said and done? She was not without sisterly feeling, one must hope.

'Of course you know what happened,' she went on. 'They quarrelled as they did before, that other night, and Rupert lost his head. It was just as dreadful as you say, but is that any reason why we should make things worse?'

'You said he was brutal. You said he was a drunkard.'

Mrs Anderson shrugged her shoulders comfortingly, like a parent who has told too vivid and frightening a story to her child.

'And we know that he was not. Do outsiders matter? He was always a man who cared for his family and not much else beyond. But it was necessary that the jury should believe.' She turned her melancholy face, that careful artist's preparation that had served her well in court, towards the girl and said: 'D'you think that I enjoyed it? D'you think I liked saying such things about him?'

It was an appeal to reason well calculated to impress a trusting nature such as Margaret's. There was even an element of truth in it, for though Laura, like a good artist, had enjoyed her mastery in the box, she was well aware that brutal, drunken husbands do reflect a certain measure of discredit on their wives.

'No,' replied Margaret, 'I don't suppose you did. You must have had some feeling for him.'

Mrs Anderson bowed her head in acknowledgement of this tribute to her finer feelings. From the moment the police had knocked at the door she had put her dead husband entirely out of her mind. Odd to think now that that shadow of the portrait had once had life, had once lain beside her with the power to move her senses and touch her heart. 'Stone dead hath no fellow.' And precious little remembrance, thought Laura, who had elevated selfishness into the likeness of a philosophy. It was not an attitude that would find a welcome here.

'Of course I felt for him,' she said. 'We'd been together so long.' She looked her daughter full in the face, and encouraged by what she saw turned suddenly to the attack. 'But in spite of that, what I did was natural and necessary. As a woman you must see that. In my circumstances you'd have done the same yourself.'

'Said such things of him! I never would.'

Her mother, with all the weight of long experience, shook her head. 'But yes, Margaret. You'd have seen it as I did.' And greatly daring she went further, adding: 'You *must* see it as I did.'

'How do you mean? How could I do that?'

Well, really! what a stupid girl! The thing was so obvious that even a child should see.

'I mean you mustn't give evidence in court,' she said.

There was a moment of silence during which Margaret weighed this sinister suggestion. She thought that it had emanated from Sir David, having, like most women, small notion of the extreme standard of probity demanded at the English Bar.

'Of course I take no account of you,' she said at last.

'You'll persist in giving evidence?'

'Certainly I shall.'

'And help to convict your brother?'

Put like that, her decision did sound less heroic. But she had a romantic sense of loyalty and would uphold it if she could. 'I shall defend my father's name,' she said.

'Your father's name!' cried Laura, with a brutal laugh. 'You'll defend it by labelling his son a murderer! That would give him the greatest satisfaction!'

'My evidence won't do that. I shall only deny the rotten lies you've told.'

'Now listen to me,' said Laura, suddenly very grim. 'My boy's life depends on those "rotten lies", for if I'm not believed they're bound to find against him. Everything depends on them. We've reached a stage when we must forget the dead and think only of the living.' She was about to follow with a threat, thought better of it at the sight of her daughter's determined face, and said instead: 'That's what he'd have wanted. You know that.'

Margaret did not reply, for the thought had occurred to her that perhaps what Laura said was true. The memory of her father returned to her: he had always been so magnanimous and just, never revengeful, never mean. Its effect, so easily read in that unguarded, candid face, was clear encouragement to Laura and she hurried on:

'Of course he'd not have wanted harm to come to Rupert. He was always so full of common sense. Let bygones be bygones, don't you remember how he'd say it? It's done. He's dead. And do you think he'd want to take his son as well? It wouldn't bring him back,' said Mrs Anderson, allowing a break to fall into her voice.

'But what you said! His reputation!'

'Reputation! What's that? What other people, who don't matter and don't care for us, choose to think of us. Your father was a realist. Did he care for reputation when he left me? No, he tried to do what he believed was best in situations as he found them. You knew him. He wasn't one for vindictiveness or revenge.'

It was an eloquent appeal – too eloquent, for it invited dangerous comparisons.

Margaret had stiffened suddenly. 'But *you* were,' she said.

'What's that?'

'*You* revenged yourself. First of all on me. Oh, I know that wasn't important. I didn't matter much, neither did John. But the second time . . .'

'What nonsense!' Laura cried, catching the light of unmentionable suspicions in her daughter's eyes.

'You did. You killed him. You killed him just as if you'd struck him. He'd left you and you were ashamed.'

Every trace of colour had left Laura's face, and there was a ring of true emotion in her voice as she protested: 'You don't know what you're saying.'

'But I do know what you said. To Rupert. Not the words, perhaps, but the meaning, the wheedling, the suggestions. I can see it' – and indeed, such is the power of words on guilty minds that it seemed to Laura that her daughter had suddenly been gifted with the vision to see into the past. It was not a pleasant thought for one who could remember all too vividly her own violent words and wondered still how much had been instinctive, how much she had intended.

But conscience, no matter how bad, could not destroy Mrs Anderson's undoubted courage. She replied promptly: 'That's an accusation.'

'Yes.'

'That I drove Rupert to it.'

'You know you did.'

'Then you must think that I'm a fool. D'you imagine that if I'd wanted to get rid of your father I'd have chosen to use my son?'

There was a good deal of Laura visible in Margaret's face as she replied: 'I do. Why not?'

'Risk the one person that I love!'

'But you don't love him,' Margaret said. 'You've never loved anyone except yourself.' And, filled with sudden understanding, she added: 'All that you love about Rupert is yourself in him.'

'Now we're hearing home truths! Now we're hearing what you really think of us!'

'I've always thought it.'

'I know you have,' Laura cried, goaded beyond endurance by this answer. 'You always hated us. You were always a trouble maker in the home. You always sided with him against me. The two of you!'

'Yes, the two of us.'

That calm repetition had its effect. A spot of colour burned suddenly in Laura's cheeks and she cried out: 'I can't think what you saw in one another. A pretty pair!'

'Now we're hearing what you thought of *us*. Not that I needed to be told. I heard you in the court.'

That one word 'court' brought home to Laura the measure of the failure of her diplomacy: she had been tempted, as had happened on another terrible occasion, to forget aims in the indulgence of surrendering to feelings. She pulled herself up and said in a much quieter tone: 'It doesn't matter what *I* think; it doesn't matter what I said.'

'Don't expect me to forget it.'

'I'm not expecting it. You can think what you like of me. As it happens, I've told you the truth: Rupert killed his father accidentally.'

Margaret had moved pointedly towards the door. 'Accidentally!' she cried.

'Believe the worst, then; believe that I was the criminal. Take your choice, it doesn't matter. For whichever way you look at it, Rupert's not to blame.'

This exercise in logic had no apparent effect on Margaret, now standing with her hand on the latch of the open door. She replied abruptly: 'You did it between you. He was to blame, too, and he must take his chance.'

'You'll be taking *your* chance to-morrow,' Laura said, snatching something from the wreck in the very moment of ignominious defeat. 'Your chance to revenge yourself, I mean. But I wonder whether Robert would approve.'

29

'CALL Joyce Roberts.'

Joy went into the box and took the oath in a loud, clear voice. There was nothing nervous about *her*; she didn't mind being on view; she was used to it and would give the customers their money's worth. Like Laura, she had dressed carefully to impress, though from the amount of her that was exposed it might have been inferred that she had too sanguine ideas about the susceptibilities of jurymen. She would have liked to have been more generous still, but the witness box, provokingly and to her hurt surprise, was not of the kind she had envisaged – one of those raised stands that seem specially designed to encourage jury-service in the United States – but a small dark-panelled pulpit in which much of the best of Joy was so much waste.

The top half was certainly engaging: the mask of a face, red splashed on white, a ripe inviting mouth, so large, so succulent that it triumphed from sheer humour, long blonde hair falling to her shoulders and crowned with a hat of such pert, ridiculous shape she ought to have been slapped for it – bringing into the old dark court of tragedies the flavour of a bawdy world of taprooms and casual amorous embraces.

My word! thought Sir David, who was seeing the witness for the first time. Look what I've drawn now! But even his professional manner was affected: he pulled his wig on straight, hitched up his gown, and by a score of other gestures that would certainly have called down wifely thunder on his head showed that a man still lurked beneath that pontifical exterior.

'You are Joyce Roberts?'

'Miss Eileen Joyce Roberts,' replied Joy, who was something of a stickler for the proprieties.

'Of Tews Cottage, Corporation Road, Turlminster?'

'That's right.'

'And you are employed as a barmaid at the "Golden Fleece" in that same town?'

'I look after the saloon bar,' said Joy, insisting on her status.

Barmaid indeed! Who did he think she was! He should see her customers: respectful, every one of them. No one took liberties with her – not publicly.

Sir David saw that he had been rebuked. 'In the saloon bar, yes. That is the bar patronized by the professional and business men of the community?'

That was better. He would learn.

'And how long have you been employed there, may I ask?'

'About a year.'

And she had doubled the custom in that time. Those business men he talked about, they knew what they wanted right enough: a bright, smart girl who knew the answers, someone good for a laugh and a story so long as they didn't overstep the mark. And Joy, who had the soundest commercial instincts, knew another reason why she had succeeded at the 'Fleece', for beneath the orderly conduct of her bar there was always present the possibility of 'fun and games'; the favoured knew, and even the most respectable suspected.

'During that period of a year were you regularly employed in the bar?'

'Yes, quite regular. Morning and evening hours and one day off a week.'

'Did you know the deceased, Robert Hemsley Anderson?'

'Oh yes.'

'Was he a customer?'

'He was a "regular",' said Joy, saluting the dead man's memory with almost the highest praise she knew.

'A "regular", eh! How often would he come into the bar?'

'Oh, sometimes five nights a week, sometimes less, sometimes more. He'd come in lunch-times some days, too.'

'How long would he stay?'

'Depends,' said Joy, puckering up her forehead into a frown of concentration that contrasted charmingly with the doll-like accessories of her face. As one pressman put it, 'She can even think' – a great injustice to a very smart young woman.

'Yes? You said that it depends.'

'Well, every night is different. Sometimes he'd chat and sometimes not. Sometimes he'd meet pals. Sometimes he'd walk in and have a glass, and off.'

'Must we go drink by drink?' enquired His Lordship in a resigned voice. 'I hope the phrase will be excused.'

Sir David turned his most benevolent expression on the judge and reasoned with him like a father with an erring child.

'My lord, the evidence is relevant. The sobriety or otherwise of the deceased . . .'

'On the night in question, Sir David; on the night of death.'

'My lord, yes. But previous habits are surely relevant too. The evidence of this witness may support the evidence of Mrs Anderson; it may support other periods of insobriety and account for some of the fear of his father expressed by the accused.'

'Very well,' said the judge. 'It is my practice to give the greatest latitude to the defence. Continue, please.'

Just like that! Men! They could argue and carry on and keep her standing around in this uncomfortable little box, and then, when it suited them, they could just tell her to get on. She tossed her head, expressing her own feelings for these precious dried-up legal gentry.

'Miss Roberts, can you tell us on the average how much the accused would drink?'

'That depends as well.'

'On what?'

'On what he felt like, I suppose. He was a beer drinker to begin with. He wouldn't have much in my early days: say two pints or so.'

'And later?'

'Well, he took to whisky at the end. He'd mix his drinks sometimes, and that,' said Joy, with professional seriousness, 'is a mug's game and no mistake.'

'So he'd mix it. Let me ask you this: Did you ever see him drunk?'

'Depends on what you mean by drunk,' said Joy, who had seen her customers run the whole gamut of intoxication from saloon bar tipsy to taproom paralytic.

Extracting definitions from this witness was a job for experts in her trade, and Sir David, perhaps for the first time in his career, was conscious of his inadequacy.

'Was his speech ever slurred?'

'Sometimes it wasn't; sometimes it was. And I've seen him

246

walking queer. Naturally,' said the witness, who had the hotel's reputation and her job to think of, 'I've never seen him carried out or anything like that.'

'How often have you seen him affected in that way?'

'Well, really affected, as you might say, about three times.'

'Can you remember dates?'

'Not of the first two times I can't. But they were all late on. After he'd left his wife, you know.'

'You think that had affected him?'

'Sir David,' said the judge, 'don't strain my indulgence unreasonably, please.'

'I beg your lordship's pardon. The question was ill conceived and I withdraw it. I pass on' – turning to the witness – 'to the third occasion, the date that you inferred that you remember.'

'That last night, you mean? Oh yes.'

'How do you remember it?'

Joy opened her eyes to their widest possible extent. Really these lawyers were too silly; they didn't seem to know a thing! 'Because next day it was in all the papers,' she explained.

'What was?'

'The murder, of course.'

'So the day before it was in all the papers the deceased was in your bar?'

'Oh yes.'

'What time did he arrive?'

'Soon after six, it was.'

'Was that the time he usually came?'

'No. It was earlier. We don't have much custom in so soon, and I was real surprised.'

'What did he drink that night?'

Joy screwed up her forehead again and began to compute the score. 'About four doubles, I should say,' she replied at last. 'About four doubles in an hour.'

'Doubles of what?'

That fat man again! Why couldn't he attend!

'Of Scotch, of course,' she said.

'Eight measures of whisky in all?'

'Yes, and a pint of mild.'

Sir David shot a quick look at the jury to see how these

Bacchanalian details were being received. He saw that though all were shocked, some looked incredulous as well.

'All that in an hour?'

'Oh yes. He'd be gone by seven when my next regular came in.'

Sir Evelyn could be seen noting this answer down with a flourish, and Sir David thought it wise to pursue the point.

'You were alone with him all that time?' he asked.

'Yes,' replied Joy stiffly, for it almost looked as though some reflexion on her propriety was being made. 'I was alone with him except for two casuals over at a table near the window.'

'How far away from you were they?'

'Oh, yards and yards. It's a big bar.' And it had to be, with her public. 'They were miles away.'

'Out of earshot, perhaps?'

'Oh yes.'

'Was it usual for the bar to be so empty at that hour?'

'Depends,' said Joy, falling back on her defences. 'Sometimes ...'

'... it is, sometimes it isn't,' whispered the pressmen to one another.

'And this night, casuals apart, you were alone?'

'That's right.'

'Did anyone speak to Mr Anderson except yourself?'

'Oh no.'

'Or approach him?'

'No.'

'And what was his condition when he left?'

'Quiet, but otherwise pretty bad,' said Joy, to whom the various similes for inebriation were taboo.

'Drunk?'

'It dep ... Well, yes, he was.'

'How did he behave that night while in your bar?'

It was a shot in the dark. But if Sir David had any hopes of the question he was speedily disappointed. Joy drew herself up with offended dignity and said: 'He knew how to behave himself with me.'

There! it had miscarried; it was a point in favour of the other side. Not for the first time in his career, defending counsel reminded himself of that legal saw that bids practitioners never to ask a question of a witness unless they know the answer in advance. He must immediately correct any misapprehension of the jurymen. 'I wasn't suggesting that he pestered you,' he said. 'I was only asking about his behaviour generally. You have already told us that he had been affected by the drinks.'

'Affected!' exclaimed Joy, and her eyebrows shot up as though she were hoisting some signal of astonishment. Had they any idea – any idea at all – of what four doubles and a pint could do even to the most regular of 'regulars'? 'Course he was affected. He was rolling a bit and none too certain of his words. What's more he broke a glass. And paid for it,' she added, supplying a decisive, homely touch which drew a titter from the gallery and a smile from the judge himself.

'We must remember he'd taken these four doubles and the pint,' put in Sir David. 'I take it that was the accurate sum total for the night?'

The witness, who had visibly enjoyed her small triumph of humour, was seen to hang her head. 'Except for the bottle he took away with him,' she said.

'Oh! He took a bottle away, did he! What sort of a bottle, may I ask?'

'A beer bottle. A pint of Nut Brown, actually.'

'And he took it away with him! Thank you, Miss Roberts,' said Sir David, and confident that his fortunes had been retrieved, he sat down in his place.

Joy was left in possession of the field. She knew they hadn't finished with her yet: someone else would be up asking questions any moment now – and just as stupid ones, most probably. Yes, there he was: a little one this time, a proper little bantam of a man with his feathers already ruffled, from the look of him. She would ruffle them some more. Really in this court, in this witness box, it was very much like being behind her bar: a place to lean on; cheeky customers, just one or two, types who'd get inquisitive and answer back; a large circle of admirers ready to applaud; and a judge, a sort of landlord, hovering in the background to see fair play.

'Miss Roberts, may I have your attention, please?'

Sarcastic! He'd kept her waiting and hadn't she the right to take a good look around her if she wanted to? She turned back towards the prosecutor and said, 'Certainly,' in so offended and pert a voice as to delight Sir David, sitting maliciously at his rival's side.

'Miss Roberts,' said Sir Evelyn, who knew when to ignore impertinences, 'your bar at the "Golden Fleece" is very popular, I think?'

She agreed it was.

He bowed with affected gallantry. 'That is easy to understand. Let me see now: on an average week-day night how many customers would you have in all? Yes, I know that it depends,' said Sir Evelyn, anticipating the witness, 'but it is surely possible to agree an average. Now then, would sixty be too high?'

Joy, always the propagandist, was only too willing to agree that the figure was not unduly so.

'So it might be even higher, might it not? And most of these customers were business men, I think you said?'

'Oh yes.'

'Restoring the tissues at the end of the day's work?' suggested Sir Evelyn, with an encouraging and friendly smile.

'That's right.'

'What time do the offices shut in Turlminster, would you say?'

'Sixish. Six-fifteen or so.'

'I see. So they'd be in for their refreshers (if I may term them so) soon after the half-hour?'

'It was late custom mostly in my bar,' said Joy, who saw the way she had been manoeuvred towards the precipice.

'How late?'

'It was densest between nine and ten.'

'You see, I put it to you, Miss Roberts,' said counsel, the smile now faded from his face, 'that there was a dense concentration between half past six and seven o'clock.'

'No, at nine.'

'Do I understand you to deny that there was that concentration earlier? It is a matter on which we could consult your employer, I suppose.'

The threat sufficed. 'Well, yes, sometimes there was,' she said.

'Often, I put it to you.'

'No, not often.'

'Almost every night.'

'Oh no.'

'And at this time, between half past six and seven, there was always, if not a concentration, at least some representation in the bar? I mean, there was always someone there?'

'Perhaps a casual or two.'

'You admitted to two. How far were they from the bar?'

'Oh, miles.'

'How many *yards*, Miss Roberts?' said the advocate, dropping his voice menacingly.

'Fifteen or so.'

'And there were just four of you in the bar. If anyone had been listening he'd have heard what the couple in the other group were saying?'

'I don't think so.'

'It's what the jury thinks that matters. The deceased was drunk. In your words he was behaving "pretty bad". He even broke a glass?'

'That's right.'

'And one must assume, Miss Roberts, that your casuals had eyes to see, even if they hadn't ears to hear?'

'Being casuals,' said Joy, 'I don't suppose they'd be even interested.'

'But your regulars would?'

'Yes, if they'd been there.'

'You see I'm suggesting that your regulars were there. I'm suggesting that your business men came, as business men will, for a "quick one" before going back to their dinners and their wives.'

'Some did sometimes,' admitted Joy. 'But my regulars, as a rule, they come in nineish – *after* their dinners and their wives.'

There was a short burst of laughter from the gallery at this thrust, but no answering echo from the jury-box where everyone, being in an exposed position, looked extremely shocked.

'And I suggest again,' said Sir Evelyn, 'that if for a moment you can put your flippancy aside and remember where you are, you will remember also that some of these business men were there at the time the deceased took his last drinks at the bar.'

'Not that I remember.'

Counsel gave a sharp look at the jury and started to play with

his heavy horn-rimmed spectacles. These were for display pur-
poses only, for if the truth were known his sight was excellent,
but for some reason myopia is expected – even demanded – of
professional men, and Sir Evelyn, whose place in the hierarchy
was eminent, could look terrifyingly myopic when necessity
arose. 'Come, that's better,' he said. 'It may be only your memory that's at fault. Let us assume for a moment that there were
regulars in that bar that night, customers known to the deceased.'

But he can't produce them, thought Sir David, who had been
watching his opponent narrowly throughout the duel. He can
talk at her and bully her, but he's got no one to go into that box
and contradict one word she says.

And Joy handled the question with the utmost assurance. 'If
there were five pals of his,' she said, 'and all in the same school
with him, they wouldn't remember what he drank as well as
me.'

It was a good answer, a comprehensive answer, appealing to
the common sense of everyone, and it swept away the ground
from under Sir Evelyn's feet; it was so good an answer that the
witness could not resist a quick significant look towards the dock.
This was a mistake, for though it went unobserved by nearly
everyone, it was seen by the prosecutor and gave him the clue
he had been seeking from the moment the witness had stepped
into the box.

He bent down to Mr Craig and whispered in his ear: 'She
knows him; she knows him well.' Then very slowly he straightened himself up, and holding his hand out in a gesture designedly
theatrical, demanded: 'Roberts, how long have you been a friend
of the accused?'

Poor Joy! Poor Miss Eileen Joyce Roberts, how grievously
had her status fallen now! But however much shaken as a witness, as a woman she retained her wits. 'I knew him, certainly,'
she said.

'Ah! You knew him! It is remarkable the way the picture gets
filled in if one persists.'

'Is it so remarkable,' came Sir David's voice, 'when one re-
members that they are fellow-townsmen and that the town is
small?'

'I am always obliged by the comments of my learned friend,'

said Sir Evelyn, making formidable play with his spectacles, 'even when, as it happens, it is not his turn to speak. Perhaps I may now be permitted to proceed. May I repeat my question to the witness? How long were you his friend?'

'We weren't exactly friends,' replied Joy, picking her way carefully between the dangerous truth and lies which might, if anyone had talked, be still more dangerous. 'We'd spoken together several times. I thought of myself as his father's friend, you see.'

'You walked with the accused, perhaps?'

'Maybe down the street.'

'Or in the fields? Or in the fields on summer nights?'

Joy drew herself up. She saw that if this continued the effect of all that she had said would be destroyed; he would pursue her. step by step, till even those hot, secret evenings in the grass would be dragged like the sordid aftermaths of an adultery into the law's unfeeling sight. It was a time for bold decisions, and she did not hesitate. 'I never went with him,' she said. 'There's not one person in Turlminster can say I ever did.'

'But you were friendly with him all the same?'

'Yes, I suppose so. In a normal sort of way.'

'It is a matter of definitions,' said the advocate in a suggestive voice. 'Parents on the one hand and cynics on the other might have different views on the subject of what "normal" relations amount to between young persons of opposite sex. I suggest that in your case "normal" meant friendly in a sense certainly not platonic.'

'Oh, but it was platonic, really.'

'Did you volunteer to give evidence on the prisoner's behalf?'

'I was approached.'

'By whom?'

'By his family, I suppose.'

'You suppose! Don't trifle with me. Answer the question you are asked.'

'Is it suggested,' said Sir David, this time rising to his feet, 'that this witness was in any sense improperly approached by the defence?'

'Well, Sir Evelyn?' echoed the judge.

'My lord, far be it from me to impute improprieties to my

253

learned friend. It was merely my intention to establish a connexion between the witness and the accused and the family of the accused.'

'In order to impeach her testimony?'

'Yes.'

'It is for you to judge, Sir Evelyn,' said His Lordship in a tone of voice that indicated clearly enough what he thought of this attack, 'how much such a connexion, if established, would assist you.'

Now thoroughly aroused, Sir Evelyn persisted. But he had no success whatever with the witness who, with sharp feminine intuition, had seen the nakedness of her tormentor's case. That horrid little man, he didn't know; he could shout the truth from the housetops and no one would believe him! She was born under a lucky star, she reflected comfortably: there had been only two untraceable casuals in the bar that night, and no one, no chance walker or Peeping Tom, had seen them in the shadows near the stile.

For his part, the advocate knew the danger of pursuing an impregnable witness for too long. Better to let her go rather than to double the importance of her testimony in the jury's eye by the persistence with which he unsuccessfully assailed it. But something in the manner of the witness struck him at the very moment he was about to resume his seat: she looked so absurdly confident, so pleased with her victory in what must have seemed to her a game, and – this was the oddest thought – in spite of all her lies, so fundamentally honest and good at heart. For all his thirty chastening years of court experience, Sir Evelyn was touched.

'Miss Roberts,' he said, 'is that all you have to say?'

'Yes, I suppose so. Don't you want to ask me questions any more?'

That was like her: pert to the end! Well, he would see.

'No more questions,' he said slowly. 'I just want to remind you . . . of something you forgot.'

Had she slipped up then? Had she let him in? A small feeling of panic ran through her and she began to go over her evidence in her mind. She had been so careful, so discreet.

'Yes, I think you've forgotten the dead man, you know. You

said he was your friend. And I don't think you've quite realized what your evidence has done to him.'

'Done to him!' cried Joy, who had the most uncomplicated attitude towards the dead. What could they care, once they were nailed up under the ground!

'Yes. His name is at stake, and you know very well how much that meant to him.'

She turned towards the dock; saw the triumphant face of Rupert as he realized that even this last assault of the prosecution had no sting; caught the glance that he exchanged with his mother down below him in the well. They would win. In a flash of intense vision she remembered the iron grip of his hands on hers, heard his stealthy tread on the carpet of the office, saw the lowered head and the falling blows. They would win because of her. And from the faces of that smiling pair her mind went back to Mr Anderson, to that gentle, quiet man who had never said one wrong word to her in all the time that she had known him, who had been always so cheerful, and generous, and kind.

She was so far away that she could only just hear the whisper of the prosecutor's words.

'He never did you harm. And yet you hold him up as a drunkard. You told us that he went out to his death quite unprepared and like a drunken beast.'

She looked stupidly at him for a moment, and he said: 'It's not too late. I appeal to you to be just and honourable and tell the court the truth.'

'Yes,' she said.

For an instant of time the balance wavered. She looked towards the dock. There was no smile now on the prisoner's face: it peered back at her, white against the dark oak panelling. When would she see him next? In the small prison visiting-room with a warder close at hand, the day before he took that walk – such a short walk, they said – from cell to execution shed? Or to-morrow in the fields? It could be to-morrow. He would have reason to be grateful. And so would she. Perhaps now that the grass was sodden, the hut walls damp with winter rain, they would do as they had planned – creep up that stairway in her home towards the warm delights awaiting them in her bed. It could be to-morrow night – the sheets, the yielding, springy mattress, his lips and youthful skin, the clinging pressure of his hands.

'Miss Roberts. Please will you answer me?'

She turned back towards Sir Evelyn.

'I told the truth,' she said. 'I told you everything.'

And, rather theatrically, she laid her hand upon her heart.

30

'WHAT did I tell you!' complained Sir Evelyn, moving up the court towards his table in a flurry of robes, with his juniors at either side.

Mr Craig did not precisely hang his head, which would have been unthinkable in so self-assured a man, but the truth was that from the moment, that morning, when he had arrived in the robing-room to hear from his clerk that Margaret Anderson had not appeared, he had not dared to look his leader in the eye. Now, after luncheon, he knew for certain of her refusal to give evidence.

'I can't think how it happened,' he murmured miserably.

'Can't you? That woman got at her, of course,' announced Sir Evelyn, taking his seat at counsel's table. From this position he looked round the crowded court-room, taking very little time in finding Laura in her usual place below the dock. The sight was a spur to his irritation, and rustling his papers open, he repeated: 'She got at her. We should have known. I could even guess the arguments she used.'

'If we could only prove it!'

'Prove it! How?' snorted Sir Evelyn, still staring round in his challenging, irritable way. 'We should have held the girl and got her statement, as I said. There's no doing anything about it now.'

Mr Craig had followed his leader's glance towards the door. There was a stir and bustle there among the policemen and officials, and a large confident figure could soon be seen pushing past them into court – Sir David Fynes in high good humour with a smile for everyone. Not much perception was required to know the cause of it, and Craig turned towards Sir Evelyn. 'We could shake him. We could force that evidence, still,' he said.

It was true enough; they could. But if defending counsel was relieved by Margaret's absence, his rival, in his secret heart, may have been relieved as well. Unwilling witnesses were the very devil, and Sir Evelyn had suffered too much at Laura's hands in cross-examination to make him relish any part or parcel of the female Andersons.

He shook his head.

'No, it's done with. We'll do without her. We've had Hemmings and the secretary to speak to character. They must do, and here's His Lordship now,' he said.

So that afternoon they came to final speeches. It fell to Sir David Fynes to address the jury first, for by calling witnesses for the defence other than the prisoner he had forfeited the right to the coveted last word. Sir David was persuasive, he was eloquent, he could make even an appeal to sentiment sound like a call to duty; in his hands the very failings of his witnesses were changed into arguments in favour of the accused, so that in the end there seemed cause for wonder that the boy had been put on trial at all.

What reason was there, demanded Sir David passionately, for disbelieving the story of the actual killing as told by his client in the witness box? Did the jury really think, after seeing him, that this was an infamous, cowardly creature that had struck a man behind his back? To believe such a thing was to credit this young man – this normal young man – with the instincts of a monster. Sir David had intended a literary allusion here but had been quite unable to think of one simple and telling enough to fit the bill. Was it necessary to strain credulity in seeking for such an explanation for the death? It certainly was not. There was evidence that the tragedy had happened, not deliberately, but in the course of an unsought quarrel – in self-defence. Even the wounds, of which the prosecution had made such play, had been explained by the accused: they fitted like every other piece of evidence into the patchwork picture, the picture of the innocence of the accused.

There was the condition of Robert Anderson. It was distasteful, said Sir David, to speak ill about the dead, but better that than falsely to condemn the living. On the evidence there could be little doubt, in his submission, that the deceased had been drunk at the time of death; here was a case where the evidence of the accused could be checked, and the jury would note that it was corroborated not only by his mother, but also by quite independent testimony. On the attempts made by poor Sir Evelyn to suggest an association between the prisoner and Miss Roberts Sir David was at his most scathing and tremendous. The prosecution was alleging a conspiracy; it was a suggestion as monstrous as he had ever heard mooted in a court. The jury had seen Miss Roberts and had seen the boy. They were men and women of the world and would know what to think of a suggested liaison so absurd. And at this stage Sir David's face, mobile ally of that grand triumphant voice, was wreathed in a smile of scorn that anyone – even the prosecutor – could imagine that such a girl would find her pleasure in a place so immature.

Nor was that all. Not satisfied with its attack on the witness, the prosecution had even suggested some corrupt bargain between her and the family of the accused – a suggestion that had been speedily withdrawn, he was glad to say. Well, the jury had seen her; its members would be judges of her good faith; they knew that she had come unscathed through her ordeal by prejudice.

The advocate was at his best in this. He clothed the witness in robes of spotless white, put a halo round her head, and having canonized her in terms that would greatly have surprised the patrons of the 'Fleece', proceeded to point the moral of her morality: if she had spoken truth, so had the prisoner; the more reason to believe his story of what had happened in the office on the fatal night. And he alone knew the truth of it. Not one prosecution witness had been near the crime. 'They came,' said Sir David, in a happy phrase, 'afterwards: to pry, to surmise, to reconstruct, to *guess*. They did not *know*.' And what was the evidence they had laboriously raked up? Evidence of wounds: explicable on the hypothesis of the prosecution's doctors, but explicable also by the story of that last desperate struggle, as told by the accused.

A tremendous onslaught against the evidence of the police surgeon was now developed.

'You listened to that evidence, members of the jury. Did you ever hear such a confession of doubt before? The prosecution must assume the burden of proof and it is their duty to provide and prove a coherent picture of the scene that they allege to have been a crime. What has that witness, the key witness of the prosecution, proved? Absolutely nothing except a train of conjecture without end. You can search his evidence in vain for one solid fact to support my friend's persistent charge of murder; you can search in vain for a sentence unqualified by a "may" or a "might", or by some other expression of this man's honest, abysmal ignorance. Think, members of the jury, of the suggestion that finally emerged from the welter of this guesswork: that picture of the deceased rising from his chair at the moment of the strike and then remaining, semi-stunned, obligingly holding the right side of his head towards his enemy, while the latter swings at him four more times. Can you take that picture seriously? Does it not seem to you one of the wildest propositions ever put before a jury by a prosecution that must, of its very nature, be clear, logical, and convincing if it is to succeed at all? Would you, may I ask, drown a kitten on such evidence where they are asking you to hang a man?

'Murder, they say. How can the prosecution persist with murder when they cannot even place the parties to the blows? They are asking you to infer malice from a set of incidents they are unable to describe. As to the lesser charge of manslaughter, the evidence before the court is fourfold.' Sir David held up four fingers of his left hand and struck each down in turn as he made his point. 'Firstly, the deceased bore a grudge against the prisoner; secondly, he was in the habit of using violence with him; thirdly, the deceased was drunk; fourthly, the deceased, without provocation other than verbal reproaches and appeals, attacked the prisoner, forced him down, and tried to kill him. The evidence for these propositions ranges from the disinterested evidence of the barmaid, through that of the widow of the deceased, to the bruised elbows and the grouped scalp wounds, mute testimonies from beyond the grave, all of which are consistent only with my client's story. If that is believed I submit, subject to His Lordship, that manslaughter is as remote as murder from this case and that there is no just verdict but acquittal.'

What other evidence was there against his client? counsel asked. There were the statements made to the police. Here Sir David was on uncertain ground, but no one could have guessed it from the confident, contemptuous expression on his face. The jury – men and women of the world again – would understand perfectly what had occurred. The boy had panicked. 'And who wouldn't in such circumstances?' cried counsel, drawing a poignant picture of the blows, the blood and horror, the corpse lying on the floor. It was better than the movies, really: the dialogue was so extraordinarily suggestive and one could make up one's own pictures as one went along. Fear and panic! What follies were committed under their spur! Was it surprising that this boy should have lost his head and told untruths – anything, anything, so long as it led away from his share in his father's death? 'Think of it, members of the jury, he had destroyed his father. The wonder isn't that he lied, but that he ever steeled himself to admit the dreadful truth.' And that led counsel on to firmer ground. Under the stimulus of his enthusiasm the second statement could appear as an act of courage very nearly sublime. The boy had told the truth. From that moment his courage had returned and he had held consistently to the truth in the face of public disgrace and rigorous cross-examination. Consistency, that was the acid test.

In this elevated mood Sir David passed on to his peroration, an appeal of great emotional quality, beautifully phrased, in which Justice itself was invoked as the major deity of the defence. The onus of proof was on the prosecution. Were the members of the jury satisfied that this burden had been shouldered, that this guilt was proved? Would they say that it was murder? Would they even say that it was manslaughter? Were they not satisfied that the only evidence directly on the point was conclusive and that self-defence was established beyond all reasonable doubt? He would ask for that: for a verdict of Not Guilty at their hands. 'I demand it at the bar of justice,' cried Sir David, who knew that no gestures, no words, were ridiculous in their proper context. 'I challenge you to send that young man to an ignoble death.'

Spontaneous applause broke out in court. Indeed, it was already clear how opinion among the public had swung round in favour of the accused.

But Sir Evelyn, rising against the background of this excitement, did not seem in the least perturbed. He was concerned not with the public but with the jury, not with sentiment but with fact. Unemotionally and without raising his voice he took his listeners back over the prosecution's case: the secret visit, the savage blows, the evasive, lying conduct of the accused.

'My learned friend has seen fit to attack the evidence of the distinguished police surgeon; he has found most unflattering words – may I suggest that they were unfair ones? All was guesswork, it appears. And yet you may remember that a clear picture was presented for your consideration: the deceased rising from his chair; the first blow; the half-stunned reaction; the succeeding blows all struck at that half-crouching target till it collapsed and fell. You were asked to dismiss this from your minds. What were you asked to substitute? A young man pinned to the floor, who, with his weak left hand, inflicts these fearful wounds, and who, though half throttled and on the verge of death, can show no bruise. I leave it to you to judge which of us, my friend or I, has been fanciful in our submissions.' Here Sir Evelyn looked at the jury in a way that suggested that he had no doubts of the verdict on this point, then turned from his study of the crime to comment on the dead man's character.

Up to this point nothing could have exceeded the calm decorum of Sir Evelyn's manner. But now, as he approached what he had called 'The most bitterly contested issue in the case,' his manner changed; a ring of absolute conviction crept into his voice, his eyes flashed with generous indignation, so that for the first time the advocate merged in the man.

'We have listened to an attack upon the dead. You may think that it was an infamous attack. These people, the wife he married, the son he brought into the world, the girl that he befriended, have seen fit to vilify his character, to label him a drunkard, a brute and a degenerate. It has been one of the severest trials of my experience to sit in this court and listen to this mean, disgraceful testimony; they have spared nothing to insult and degrade his corpse. It was not enough that that young man should strike his father down; he must cut off his reputation, too; twist it, mutilate it, hold it up to contempt and ridicule. Was there ever a meaner, viler attack on a man who cannot answer back, whose body is beyond their malice but whose name is not?'

Sir David, protesting, was on his feet. 'My lord, I must

262

object. Such expressions! ... My friend's personal opinions!
The evidence was given and not contradicted. It was before the
court.'

'And what disgraceful evidence it was!' cried Sir Evelyn,
abating not a jot of his disgust and gazing at the interrupter with
undisguised hostility.

'Sir Evelyn!'

'Yes, my lord?'

'What the jury thinks of the evidence is a matter for themselves.'

'Yes, my lord. And what do they think of it?' He wheeled
round on the fascinated jurymen. 'What do you think of a wife
who gives such evidence of the man she took thirty years ago
for better or for worse? What do you think of the evidence of
the son who dishonours his own father, even in the cause of
saving his own selfish, worthless life?'

'My lord, my friend's words! I must appeal to your lordship
for protection for my client. Selfish! Worthless! This is not a
speech; it is an appeal to blind, unreasoning prejudice.'

'I think, Sir Evelyn,' said the judge, 'that you exceed by a
wide margin the legitimate bounds of advocacy. You may feel
strongly in this matter ...'

'Strongly! My lord, I do. I have sat for days and heard a dead
man slandered – viciously, wickedly.'

'You have heard evidence, Sir Evelyn. It is for the jury to
decide whether that evidence has broken down. You may comment, but you may not label testimony.'

'He has been most scandalously improper!' boomed Sir David
from his seat, a kind of unofficial chorus to the strictures of the
judge.

Sir Evelyn ignored his rival but bowed towards the bench. 'If
I have offended ...' he began.

'You have offended – seriously.'

'Then I did so in the heat of indignation, my lord – in the
heat of just indignation.'

His Lordship sat up erect on the bench for the first time since
the beginning of the trial; his scarlet-robed figure, his umpire's
coat, was suddenly filled out with the power of the man within.
'There is nothing just about an impropriety,' he said. 'You

will obey the rules of advocacy or you will no longer be permitted to address the court.'

'As your lordship pleases,' said Sir Evelyn, overborne, but conscious of the fact that words spoken cannot be revoked. The jury had heard him and had appreciated the violence of his indignation. 'Members of the jury, you have heard the evidence and seen the demeanour of the witnesses. Did you believe this wife? You have heard the rebutting evidence I have called: the evidence of the dead man's clerk and secretary. Was he the man to strike and abuse his wife? Was he the unreasonable tyrant of the home? Was he a drunkard with a homicidal hatred for his son? Or was he, rather, a much wronged man?

'I come now to the witness Roberts, the barmaid, we saw yesterday.' The tone of the prosecutor was now disrespectful in the extreme. Not thus did those business clients at the 'Fleece' refer to her, those keen young men who knew their place – and very often found it after hours. Poor Joy! Alas for her pretensions! The young lady who presided with such benevolent decorum in the bar, the recipient of, and donor of, so many favours, the heroine of a lustful amorous tradition, had never been disposed of in quite such harsh, uncompromising terms even by the disappointed – or the satisfied. It was not so much what counsel said, for he had to restrain his imagery in the presence of the judge, but the tone of voice expressed his meaning perfectly.

'You have heard the dead man's employees assess his character: a sober man. What do you think of this convenient witness on the other side? Do you believe that this man went out through the door of that saloon with a drunkard's load on him? She says so; she comes here to tell us so – after being approached, to use her words, by the family of the accused.'

The advocate's voice had taken on a fine shade of irony; one could almost hear the sound of money passing, the rustle of pound notes. It was a pity, really, that Barry Clarke's existence had escaped Sir Evelyn; it would have opened out other tantalizing vistas; but of course the words brought defending counsel to his feet.

'I have never,' he said, 'had to interrupt a prosecution final speech before. But my friend is so perverse to-day.'

'You object to the word "approached", Sir David?' asked the judge.

'My lord, with respect I do. The only possible reason for its use is prejudice: it is to impute corruption and undue influence to the defence.'

'Sir Evelyn?'

'No, my lord. I have merely repeated the very words the witness used. What the jury sees in them is, as your lordship has already pointed out, purely a jury matter.'

'Hum!' said the judge, digesting this impertinence. 'Very well, go on.' And I shall watch you closely too, his kindling expression seemed to say.

'I have no desire to foster prejudice,' said the prosecutor, turning back towards the jury. 'I am here to dispel prejudice, not to create it. The Crown made no issue of the sobriety of Robert Hemsley Anderson, but the defence made an issue of his drunkenness. Yet we are wicked; we defend ourselves when attacked; in my friend's view we are perverse. For why? Because we uphold the honour of a man who is on trial and yet who cannot, like this accused, go into the box. There is a trial within a trial, and the defence, turned accuser, sheds its privilege and steps down into the ring. Well, I shall fight it there – in spite of the interruptions of my learned friend; I shall continue to put before the jury the dead man's character as attested by disinterested parties – as good and quiet a man as lived. You are free to believe that he changed all on the sudden into the person described by Roberts as a "regular"; you are free to credit him with a Jekyll and Hyde existence if you can. Do you believe it? It is for you to say, drawing on your knowledge of human nature and your experience of men.

'The hour of your decision is approaching. When, after my lord's direction, you retire you will consider the deceased's character as one of the most important facets of the case. Do not for that reason ignore the other things that you have heard: the evidence of the wounds, deep, down-struck wounds, delivered with terrifying force; the choice of time, late and secret; the choice of place; that heavy weapon convenient to the young man's hand; the denials; the false alibi; the reluctant admissions after the truth was out.

'The case is put; my task is done. It may be thought that in my last words to you I have exceeded the normal prosecution's bounds. Perhaps I have. But this was no normal prosecution because this was no ordinary defence. If my friend's interest was to blacken the reputation of the deceased, it was certainly my duty to defend him. I have done so to the best of my ability, and if I have offended, then let the blame for the procedure rest with me.'

On this note of challenging humility Sir Evelyn sat down – not in his usual place, it was observed, but at a corner of counsel's table far removed from his opponent.

All eyes now turned towards the judge. His Lordship seemed in no hurry; he nodded to Sir Evelyn, turned over the pages of his notes, and adjusted his chair so that for the first time he was inclined towards the jury-box. Then leaning forward, handkerchief in hand, he began to speak, slowly, evenly, almost without inflection in a soft voice that contrasted agreeably with the rhetorical methods of the prosecutor.

The members of the jury were all attention. In their eagerness they gave the impression, so chastening to counsel, that only now at the last, when the tumult and the shouting had died down, was some sense to be expounded, some reason heard; they leaned back receptively, arms crossed, fellow-toilers with the judge, fellow-sufferers under the lash of special pleading, ready at last to get things done.

His Lordship began with some words of commiseration with them for the long course of the trial, passing on to some comments on the function of justice in general and the law as applied to murder in particular; only when he began to comment on the facts and witnesses could it be seen how the mass of verbiage had affected him. But soon an expression of some complacency could be noted on prosecuting counsel's face.

'It is for you to say,' the judge's voice ran on, 'whether you think the whole truth has been told about the departure of Mr Anderson from his home . . .

'Do you believe that the accused had grounds for fearing for his life at the dead man's hands? . . .

'Much depends on the credibility of Miss Roberts. Were you impressed with her sincerity? . . .

'Do you believe that it was possible for the accused, from that inferior position underneath his father, to strike such lethal blows? ...

'He's against him,' the pressmen whispered among themselves, and behind the quiet phrases of the judge a little stir of angry comment could be heard – it was scarcely a disturbance – from a gallery now solidly in favour of the prisoner.

But the judge, even if he were aware of this emotion, continued calmly on his way.

'It is relevant to consider the actions of the accused after the striking of the blows. According to the testimony of Inspector Carr the boy was completely self-possessed when he made his first statement to the police ...

'Was ever a prisoner's statement more grossly inconsistent with the truth than that? ...

'When an alibi fails it is a serious matter for its maker ...

'What caused the retraction of the lying statement? Remorse? Or policy? ...

'What do you think of Mrs Anderson's part in all this and how does it affect your opinion of the value of her evidence?'

'He's dead against him,' said the pressmen. And the public was on the other side. There might be – beautiful, ecstatic thought! – an incident. Suppose the jury brought in Guilty in face of popular hostility. Scenes in court! Scenes in the street! There was endless promise in the case.

But still the judge went on. As for the members of the jury, even Sir David, who gazed at them with an expression that plainly told of his horror and contempt for this prosecutor on the bench, could not guess their thoughts. Sphinx-like, attentive, they sat on, unmoved by the shuffling and the barely repressed indignation of the gallery, but seemingly equally unmoved by the steady judicial indictment that was piling up.

'Do you think the accused was open with the police? Do you think that he has been open with this court? ...

'Do you accept his explanation of the fatal struggle? If you do there is an end of the prosecution's case.'

'He's damning him,' the pressmen said. 'He's being unfair;' but there they erred. The judgement was unexceptionable from every point of view; it just so happened that it was tinged throughout by the knowledge of a man less gullible than most.

'And now I must direct you on the law,' the judge was saying. 'You have three possible verdicts. If you think that the accused behaved as the prosecution alleges, then you may find a charge of murder proved. Irrespective of what may have brought the accused into that office, if he took a weapon like that poker and, without sufficient provocation, struck at his father's head with it, causing death, then, no matter what his intention might have been, it is murder, no less. People use such weapons at their peril. In this context I must tell you that words of abuse, even directed at the mother of the accused, could not amount in law to sufficient provocation.

'If, on the other hand, you believe that what really happened was that there was a violent quarrel in the course of which great violence was used on both sides, and that Mr Anderson met his death from violence inflicted by the prisoner in these circumstances, then this is a case of manslaughter.

'There remains the third possibility. If you accept the story advanced by Sir David Fynes, if you believe that this young man was savagely attacked without being guilty of the least violence, if you believe that he had cause to fear for his life and could find no other way to save himself ,than by the infliction of these blows, then you are accepting the plea of self-defence and you must acquit the prisoner. It is for you to say, and, no doubt, you will pay particular attention to the wounds and bruises found on the deceased as aids to your decision.

'There is only one thing further I must say. You have heard from counsel on both sides that the burden of proof is on the prosecution, which must prove its case beyond all reasonable doubt. Fanciful doubts and speculations you may dismiss, but, if there are substantial doubts in your minds after listening to the evidence, you will remember that for centuries courts in this country have acted on the principle that the acquittal of ten guilty men is preferable to the conviction of one innocent – remember, and act in accordance with this usage which expresses a great principle of justice. You must be *certain*.

'Members of the jury, that is all. Please retire now and consider your verdict, being assured that if you are in any doubt about the law, as opposed to fact, you may return here and I will assist you.'

The clerk was sworn to guard the jury, the judge rose, the prisoner went below, the jury filed out of the box. In spite of what counsel and His Lordship had suggested, its members did not look like arbiters of fate; they wore the sad gregarious look of trippers at the seaside on a wet Sunday afternoon. It seemed absurd to think that a man's life depended on them and that their word could spell liberty or the ritual of sentence – the solemn invocation, the square of black cloth on the judge's head.

Intense speculation at once broke out among the public in the court. It was of a nature that made the police officers in attendance glance uneasily around them, for they knew that crowds were already forming in the streets outside and feared a demonstration. Sympathy for the prisoner was everywhere intense – at its most intense among those who knew the least and whose picture of the trial was the most hopelessly incoherent. The boy had become a symbol, a rallying-point for the sentimental and the muddle-headed who seem to predominate in every mob, and who have destroyed more good causes and sanctified more evil ones than all the tyrants and sinners who have lived in history.

This feeling had ample time to grow in the two hours of the jury's absence; a hum of chatter filled the court, expectant, hostile, sibilant – and suddenly was stilled. The door leading to the judge's private room was seen to open and the bulk of the judge appeared, a vision of white and scarlet framed like some portrait in the Inns of Court. Next moment, as though in counter, the prisoner came back into the dock, greeted by a low murmur of sympathy from those of his admirers who were in a position to catch a glimpse of him. A louder murmur of excitement was reserved for the jurymen, who now filed in through a side door behind their box as enigmatically as they had gone, heavy and solemn with their secret but still incorrigibly ordinary, like players in a pageant, out of their dramatic depth. How had they decided? One could guess one's choice from those studiously careful faces, from their foreman, the most solemn of them all, sitting at the right of the line with a sheet of white paper in his hand.

'Members of the jury, are you agreed upon your verdict?'

It was the clerk of assize again, his resonant actor's voice rounding on these final lines, this scene reserved to him that never failed, and he nodded with qualified approval as the faint chorus came back. 'We are,' a moderate response, adequate – just adequate to the occasion.

One person, one may be sure, was not conscious of any failings in this regard. Absolutely white of face, the prisoner gazed towards the jury; his hands had gripped the front ledge of the dock and by this means he held himself erect, more rigidly than the soldierly figures of his attendants who had closed in behind him, watchfully, prepared to restrain or to support.

'Will the foreman stand up?'

He did so. Boy and man looked at one another, strangers, drawn by such a web of circumstance into this intimate, terrible relationship.

'Do you find Rupert Laurence Anderson Guilty or Not Guilty of murder?'

There was a brief instant of silence, so profound that the rustle of the paper in the foreman's hand could be distinctly heard as he raised it up to read.

'Not Guilty, my lord. We find that he killed the deceased in self-defence' – but the last words were drowned in the roar of excitement of the crowd.

Of course Laura was there beside the dock; her arms reached up and lovingly enfolded that head bowed down to hers; tears of joy, quite ruining her mask of powder and mascara, acquitted her of acting her emotions: triumphant in her strategy, triumphant in her maternity, what a moment it was for her!

Soon the remaining formalities were completed and her son could join her in the corridor outside the court. Together they approached Sir David Fynes and thanked him for his vindication of the truth. How the public applauded that! And outside in the streets the enthusiasm was greater still. There was applause for the judge – a contemptuous witness, certainly, of so emotional a scene; cheers for counsel and the witnesses indiscriminately; an ovation for that gallant mother and her son driving in triumph from the scene of calumny.

They sat well forward in the car. From the narrow lane of bodies between which they drove hands reached out to them,

270

excited faces pressed against the glass, hundreds of faces, white, anonymous, peering in – and one they recognized. But he could forget Mr Hemmings soon enough; he was too young to know that though a man may sometimes escape the public consequences of his acts, he cannot escape his own character. Meanwhile the illusory prospect of life and liberty stretched intoxicatingly out ahead of him, food and comfort, and the body of his mistress. If he thought of his father at this moment it was with the same feeling as the crowd: as something of an ogre, but, being dead and done with, now of very small account.